BY THE SAME AUTHOR:

The Stark Truth

Hollywood Requiem

Peter Freeborn

SIMON & SCHUSTER
New York London Toronto Sydney Tokyo Singapore

Simon & Schuster
Simon & Schuster Building
Rockefeller Center
1230 Avenue of the Americas
New York, New York 10020

Copyright © 1991 by Peter Freeborn

Designed by Irving Perkins Associates, Inc.
Manufactured in the United States of America

1 3 5 7 9 10 8 6 4 2

Library of Congress Cataloging-in-Publication Data
Freeborn, Peter.
Hollywood requiem / Peter Freeborn.
p.   cm.
I. Title.
PS3556.R38287H65   1991
813'.54—dc20   90-25940
CIP
ISBN 0-671-72749-4

For J, again and again

Part One

Chapter One

I WAS IN the barn, between assignments. Ice on the pathways, the bare branches of the trees ice-coated and bending, time on my hands. I'd turned the telephone off, but the blinking lights on my desk console would let me answer, if I wanted to, before the answering machine cut in.

No lights flashed that afternoon. And then one did—the house line, not mine. And then stopped: someone was talking. Idly—it must have been idly—I pressed a button and brought on their voices, without a click.

She was saying something about how strange it was to hear his voice after such a long time. It didn't seem strange at all to him. More like yesterday, he said. But then he had the requisite props: a bowl of red caviar on a bed of ice, wedges of rye bread and pumpernickel, capers, chopped onion, lemon halves. Also a bottle of Beaujolais Nouveau, slightly chilled.

Did she remember?

She laughed. And with whom was he eating this feast, she wanted to know, at 4:30 in the afternoon?

With nobody, he said. He was alone, and three thousand miles away, where it was only 1:30. He mentioned the name of some Russian restaurant, in Beverly Hills.

Alone? She found that hard to believe. Unless somebody had stood him up?

No one had stood him up, he said. He often lunched alone when he was in California. He found the film people, especially his brother,

9

hard to take on an empty stomach. Besides, didn't she really know what day it was?

No, she said. Honestly she didn't.

This disappointed him no end. Deeply, irrevocably. If he wasn't such a sentimentalist—more sentimental, apparently, than she—he'd even be offended.

"Faith, fickle Faith," he chided her. "Don't you really remember where you were ten years ago today?"

"Oh," she said. Actually it was more "Ah" than "Oh."

And laughed.

And fell silent.

It annoyed me that I couldn't immediately place his voice. It was deep, had a liquid quality. Eastern, educated, and the persistent manner of somebody used to getting what he wanted.

"I miss you, Faith," he said. "I'd like to see you again."

"You're not serious, are you?" she asked.

"Yes. Very."

No laughter this time. I felt her hesitate, and even a building away from her, I could imagine her expression: mouth slightly ajar, the doelike eyes wide and startled. But make no mistake, underneath, her mind would be rapidly calculating the pros and cons.

"I don't think that's a good idea," she said finally.

"Why? Tell me. Is it because of Dan?"

(That was me, Dan, the husband.)

"Not at all," she answered forthrightly. "It's because of you."

In the solitude of the barn, I laughed out loud. That was quintessential Fawn: the direct response, all the more cutting because it came out of such apparent innocence. Once, those tawny eyes, larger in their wide white pools and swept away by the lines of her cheekbones, must have expressed a genuine innocence, and a young girl's genuine surprise at the devastating effect her remarks had on others.

"Now that you mention it," he said, recovering, "how *is* Dan? He must have finished the Castagni book by now."

"Yes, he just sent back the proofs. It's coming out this spring."

"And it's going to be a winner. I wish it were ours."

Ours? And then—right then—I had him. After all, how many publishers are there who have brothers in Hollywood?

"Who's he doing next?" he asked.

"I don't know. If he has anybody yet, he hasn't told me."

"Really?" he said. "That doesn't sound like Dan, not to know where his next million's coming from." (Mind you, I'd never met the man.) "Well," with a brief chuckle, "maybe he's working on that novel of his."

"What novel?" the Fawn asked.

"Don't you remember? You once told me you hoped the day would come when he'd be writing his own fiction instead of other people's."

"God, Lew," she exclaimed, laughing, "you have the memory of an elephant!"

"Only where you're concerned," he said.

Not only, it seemed, had I stumbled on one of my wife's former lovers, who had both predated and maybe—surprise, surprise—post-dated me, but I got to listen to the Fawn's prescription for what I ought to be doing for a living.

In addition, that is, to paying her bills.

But there was more to come, because Lew—Lew Rhinelander—went on talking about me. He reminded her that he'd given me my start, back in my freelancing days. (This was only technically true. Yes, I'd once written for Rhinelander magazines—including some he didn't like to acknowledge owning—and my first two ghosted books had been published by his company. But he, at the time, wouldn't have known me if he'd tripped over me.) He'd always admired my work enormously, he told the Fawn. It was no accident, he said, in a day when celebrity memoirs were shoveled into the marketplace by the pitchfork, that the ones I'd written not only made the best-seller lists but stayed there. That was talent, craft. That was hard work and the magic touch.

I wondered, in passing, what he was really after. And why he felt compelled to sell me to my own wife.

Lew and the Fawn, though. Jesus Christ, I thought, ten years ago she'd still been in her twenties. And he'd have been what? Pushing fifty anyway. Wasn't that a little long in the tooth for the Fawn?

"Come to think of it," he was saying, "I've stumbled onto something that could be interesting for Dan. Do you think he'd be open to a new project?"

"I don't know," the Fawn answered. "It's not Hollywood, is it?"

"It might be."

"Then I don't know. He says he's sworn off Hollywood."

"Really? Why?"

"I think it wore him down."

"Understandable," said Rhinelander. "After the Farran fiasco."

"Yes."

"Well, but she's a terrible bitch. This would be different. And worth a great deal of money, potentially."

"Then why don't you ask him yourself?" the Fawn said. "Or his agent?"

"Well, it's a rather delicate situation. I can't quite explain it over the phone. And then, I've never met Dan."

The Fawn, direct as ever, said, "Is that why you called, Lew? To get me to intercede for you?"

"Of course not," he answered smoothly. "I don't want you to do anything for me, other than to indulge a lonely and sentimental man and allow him to take you to lunch. For Auld Lang Syne, if nothing else."

What can I tell you? We live in perfidious times. To my surprise, I heard the Fawn accept. For Lutèce, no less, though whether it was Lutèce that changed her mind, or Auld Lang Syne, or "a great deal of money potentially," I couldn't say.

Moments later, the light on my console went out.

I SAT IN the gathering gloom of the barn, listening to the intermittent plipping of the icicles which overhung the windows we'd had cut into the old timbers. Time was, I realized, I'd have been in the Fawn's bedroom, or studio, or wherever the hell she was, before she even hung up.

Times change.

A while later, she came in.

She did this now and then, when she worked at home. The clay— a recent phenomenon—was still visible under her fingernails, and she wore her hooded fake-fur greatcoat over a smock and high after-ski boots. Even though she watched herself like a hawk for the telltale signs, she still held her beauty, which people found breathtaking, and that ability, presumably God-given, of endowing whatever she put on her body with an artless, careless elegance.

Inside my doorway, the fake fur glistening from tiny droplets of melting ice, her angular cheeks aglow from the cold air, she said:

"Dan, did you ever think of writing a novel? Your own fiction, I mean?"

"No," I said. "I never did."

But I was never one to waste a punchline.

"And where did he put the red caviar?" I asked, watching her eyes. "In your belly button?"

She did a quick double-clutch. Then:

"You eavesdropping son of a bitch."

The net was cast.

Chapter Two

S HE WAS BRED, as they say of horses, in the purple. The money
went back to the nineteenth century, which made it old money
by American standards, the best, the least destructible kind. Whatever
chicaneries had produced the original stake were lost in the mists of
family history—something to do with railroads on her mother's side,
pharmaceuticals on her father's. Now they owned land, houses, islands,
precious metals and gems, art, antiques, not to mention shareholdings
in Big Board companies which had been bought generations ago and
left to germinate. They also possessed that greatest luxury of accumulated wealth, which is the right to affect a large indifference to it.

The Fawn, though, was a little different. The Fawn was high style,
even the first time I saw her, when her red mane was dark and matted
by rain. I'd just delivered a manuscript to the Rhinelander Group,
cause normally for a small celebration, but when I came out of the
building in the east fifties, I'd gotten a ticket. There went the celebration. And there came the Fawn. She was standing in the gutter by
my front bumper, a black model's bag in one hand, a large, black
leather portfolio in the other, flailing the two clumsily at taxis and
shouting into the downpour, cursing, gorgeous and bedraggled.

The redhead in black, I thought. She had on an ankle-length, black
leather coat, black boots. Out of sheer altruism, I offered her a ride.
With some annoyance, her tawny eyes still scanning the street, she
accepted. I lived at the time in a hole on the upper West Side. She
already had the SoHo loft. I drove her to the loft, and ended up

15

spending the night, and the next time we went to bed, a few nights later, she told me she was going to marry me.

In those days she was always in a rush—mostly, it seemed, to escape from the old-money family who'd bred her, she said, for breeding only. By the time I met her she'd long since dropped out of college, dropped out of the Art Students League, had worked as a secretary, a barmaid, a UN receptionist, most recently as a model which, much to her family's horror, was beginning to produce results. She had bought the SoHo loft using her grandmother's trust fund for the down payment. And even though still in her twenties, she had already had two abortions, and a third to come.

In a rush, as I say.

Her family, when I met them, seemed afraid of her. Afraid, I guess, of what she might do next. And relieved, clearly, that the extent of what she might do next was marrying me. I may have represented the bottom limit of what they'd expected for her, with my middle-class, middle-west, middle-everything background; still, it could have been worse. And from their point of view—call it the breeder's perspective—the Fawn was getting on. She was twenty-seven when we met.

I also worked for a living, though I couldn't say whether that was good or bad in their eyes. The big-bucks magazines for men in those days were *Penthouse* and *Playboy*, but below them came a whole array of low-budget, newsstand imitations which needed "editorial content" to accompany all the high-gloss, airbrush skin shots. This was where I came in. I could type like the wind. Once, over a sleepless four-day period, I even churned out a whole issue under a variety of pseudonyms, containing a "debate" on the use of sexual accessories, a retrospective on Muhammad Ali, a rating of personal computers, and a "think piece" on sex scandals in the nation's capital. And all for Lew Rhinelander, because the magazines, though you'd never have known it from their dummy corporate names, or the dingy offices on the wrong side of town, belonged to the Rhinelander Group.

In time, I graduated to the big building in the east fifties where, for flat fees, I ghostwrote first one, then a second, baseball autobiography, and it was while doing the second—the diary of a season on the L.A. Dodgers—that I was introduced to somebody who had a real book to write. And then the money started to get exciting.

"You're such a hustler," the Fawn would say. "I love the way you hustle for a buck. You're also a genius."

"At what?"

"Everything—and you know it too."

"Know what?"

"Know that you can . . . that you can write anything. You're going to be a great writer."

"A rich writer," I would correct.

"Rich . . . Oh, God . . . and great."

"And what else?" I would say, leaning on her.

"What else?"

"What else makes you want to marry me?"

"Because you're such a . . . such a brute. Because of . . . Oh God, Dan, you're hurting me. . . ."

"What else makes you want to marry me?"

"Because you want . . . want to own me."

Of course, she had it backward. I wasn't such a brute until she made me one, and I didn't want to own her until I discovered that ownership, the sense of being possessed in every detail, was what turned her on.

The day I moved into the loft, with two suitcases and my typewriter, she banished her independence. The same energy which had gone into cultivating it now went into becoming my possession. She even insisted on my going with her to buy her clothes. Not only did she want me to pay for them, I had to pass judgment. Sometimes she asked me to dress her, as well as undress her. "Here," she would say, striking a nude pose before me, "pretend I'm your mannequin," twining the long red locks of her hair across her breasts.

I set up my small office in a sunny corner of the loft. The Fawn brought me little things while I worked: food, coffee, good-luck charms, a single rose in a glass vase. When I worked late, as I often did, she brought dinner on trays and sat cross-legged on the floor. Sometimes she read what I wrote, thumbing through manuscript but making few suggestions. And when I returned from being on an assignment, I'd find her waiting anxiously, barefooted on the bare polished floorboards, when the old jaws of her groaning freight elevator parted.

"Did you really think I wasn't coming back?" I'd say.

"That's what I always think," she'd answer, face buried in my shoulder.

The one exception to her abdication was the wedding.

"I want it to be perfect," she said, "perfect in every way." She put her mind to making it that, and I guess, from her point of view, that's what it was.

We were married in June, in the white steepled Episcopal church of the Fawn's hometown in Connecticut. The bride, at twenty-nine, wore white, complete with veil and train and bridal bouquet. The groom, who had just turned thirty-three, wore a morning suit, with boutonniere and lapel handkerchief. His best man was a burly writer from his skin-magazine days named Frank Falcone, a ham-handed Italian, sweating profusely from a hangover, who, having just had his first novel accepted for publication, was out to take the literary world by storm. The ushers were the bride's two brothers, both Princeton and Wall Street, and the groom's half-brother, Iowa State and Procter & Gamble.

The reception was held on the grounds of the bride's birthplace, a majestic Connecticut mansion surrounded by tall trees and blooming beds of rosebushes and rhododendrons. A dance floor had been set up on the rear lawn under a striped canopy, not far from the tennis court. A five-piece orchestra played. There were bars scattered around, and waiters circulating with champagne bottles, and waitresses in black uniforms with white aprons passing trays of canapés. The bride, it seemed, had even ordered the weather. It was a gorgeous day, if a little warm for the groom. A few white clouds advanced like slow ships across an otherwise azure sky and, when they crossed the sun, pulled large swatches of shade across the assembly.

My God, she was beautiful. More than beautiful. I remember, when she said the words at the church altar, the repeat-after-me words, all in that clear and confident voice, how her eyes never left mine. And how, when I saw them go moist with emotion, I could feel the answering ache in my throat.

I remember her whispering to me on the dance floor, while we did the traditional first dance and the Badger waited for the second, "I know you hate this, darling. Go get drunk, or stoned. Anything. I'll make up for it later, I promise."

I remember Falcone, one massive arm around my shoulders, saying, "I can't believe all this is happening to you, babe. I can't fucking believe it. I hope you know what you're doing."

I remember her father, a.k.a. the Badger, shaking my hand a little reluctantly, as though I'd just won out over him, although we'd never exchanged more than two words alone, saying, "I'm supposed to wish you luck, Springer. Or maybe," with a creased grin, "it's commiseration."

It was her family's custom, I should point out, to give each other animal names, whence the Fawn, whence the Badger. The Badger was a beefy figure, good-looking in a ruddy, blue-eyed way, with bristling gray hair. He called himself an investment banker, but I think he spent more time sailing the Sound. We ran into each other later in the house.

"It won't last, Springer," he said conversationally. "Sorry about that."

"What won't last?" I must have asked.

"You and the Fawn, this marriage thing."

"Why?" I asked. "Do you think I'm not good enough for her?"

The Badger shrugged. "She's one of those women, you know, who, when they want something, that's all they want in the world and they're all hell out to get it. Then, when they've got it, they want something else. She's not a finisher."

"So what do you advise me to do about it?" I said, becoming irritated.

"Advise you?" His eyebrows went up and down, as though he wasn't used to being asked for advice on family matters. "Hell, nothing. Nothing you *can* do. Except enjoy it while it lasts."

After that, I did get drunk.

The Fawn threw her bouquet at people. People threw rice at us. We drove off in a festooned limo and woke up, late the next afternoon, a married couple, in the George V Hotel in Paris, France.

The years passed. I made money; she spent it. She had, I assumed, her little affairs; I had one or two of my own. Every so often we collided. We fought, subsided. A couple of times we moved, trading up, but the Fawn hung on to her loft.

At the time, she was everything I'd ever wanted. Better put, she was everything I'd ever dreamed of, and knew I could never have.

Chapter Three

LEW RHINELANDER CALLED a couple of days after his long-distance tête-à-tête with the Fawn. No secretary to serve as intermediary, I noticed, just his deep and liquid voice.

"Dan? This is Lewis Rhinelander."

"If it's Faith you want," I said, "you'll have to call back on the other line."

"Faith?" Momentary confusion. "No, not at all. It's you. . . ." Then, with a chuckle, "I guess she told you about our conversation."

"Yes."

"Ahhh," as though that explained everything. "Well, you can't blame a man for inviting a beautiful woman to lunch. I've got to tell you, Dan, I think she's splendid. Thoroughly splendid. I've always been a little bit in love with her, and I'm the first to admit it."

"That's nice," I said, impressed by his enthusiasm.

Actually, according to what the Fawn had said that night in the barn, once she'd gotten over her outrage at my eavesdropping, "a little bit in love with her" pretty much summed it up. According to the Fawn, they'd had an affair; it had predated me; it hadn't lasted long; he'd helped her in her career; done and good-by.

Well, not quite good-by, I'd pointed out.

What did I mean, not quite good-by?

I meant that, sometime or other, she'd told him she wanted me to become a novelist. I doubted she'd said it before she met me.

So? Probably she had said that, but so what?

So where had she said it, in bed?

21

She didn't have any idea where she'd said it (tossing her hair). It wasn't as though she hadn't seen him since.

Oh?

Yes. She ran into him now and then. Lew Rhinelander was the kind of person you ran into, places.

Oh?

That's right.

And so, when she'd run into him, places, she'd said, Gee, Lew, I want my husband to become the new F. Scott Fitzgerald? And what had Lew said?

No answer.

Had he said, Gee, Faith, I think that's a great idea, but is he going to be able to keep you in the style to which you're accustomed?

No answer.

Well, I bet Lew would remember where they'd been when she'd said it.

What did I mean by that?

Just that he had the memory of an elephant where she was concerned.

So it had gone, that same night in the barn, when, in this latter-day, broken-down version of our catechism, the eavesdropping son of a bitch she was still married to ended up calling her a two-bit slut, which led her to retort, eyes flashing, that if that's what she was, it was his doing and nobody else's. Which had led, in turn, to a shouting match of major decibels, and her shrieking at him, "You bastard! Where was I supposed to be when you were fucking Gloria Farran and all your other Hollywood whores? In the kitchen, keeping your dinner warm?"

Not, altogether, one of our nobler moments. And though it ended predictably—i.e., horizontally—and with, as the Fawn put it, each of us "taking back the bad," there was a sense, I guess, in which we could no longer take back all of the bad.

Not after eight years of marriage, ten living together.

At the same time, how could I hold that against Rhinelander? After all, you can't blame a man for trying, can you?

"I think it's time we met, Dan," he said over the phone. "As I told Faith, I admire your work enormously. Clearly you're the best at what you do, but so are we, and I think it's a shame we're not publishing you now. I want a chance to change that. I may even have a project that will appeal to you." Pause. Then, his voice modulating, "It's a situation that requires a certain delicacy. Why don't you come to the flat for lunch, and we'll talk about it?"

Lunch again. But not Lutèce.

The "flat" to boot.

He mentioned a date some ten days off.

"Why don't we pencil it in," he said, "and I'll call you the day before to confirm?"

Pencil it in is commonplace publishing lingo, but it always seems to me to imply an affront, suggesting that, if anything better came along, you could always erase it. Well, that sword cut both ways, although Tinker, when I reported the conversation, said I'd be crazy not to go. Tinker McConnell was my literary agent. "You don't turn Lew Rhinelander down," Tinker said. "That's where the money grows. You'd better go find out what he's got in mind."

The Fawn, herself, could shed no light on it when she came back from Lutèce. Lew had said nothing about his "delicate" project other than that he was looking forward to meeting me.

But then something else came up—out of the blue, or so I thought—another phone call followed by an impromptu, thirty-six-hour visit to California, and by the time Lew Rhinelander called to confirm, I had already changed the penciled-in lunch to carved-in-stone.

In other words, I wouldn't have missed it for the world.

THE SECOND CALL was from Jilly Rogers—at night, inevitably, for Jilly slept days. I hadn't talked to her in quite a while. Her book (our book) was still in print, but the money from royalties had long since slowed to a trickle.

"You'll never guess who wants to talk to you, Sweetie," Jilly said.

"Not in the middle of the night, I won't."

"The middle of . . . ? But it's not even midnight, I'm waiting for the show to start. Oh Lord, but you're in *New York!* How could I be so stupid? Are you asleep, Sweetie?"

"I was."

"Alone?"

"You know I'm a married man."

"That's not what I asked," she said with that familiar, throaty giggle.

As it happened, the Fawn was asleep, next to me, one arm thrown over her face in a protective gesture. I told Jilly I'd call her back, took her number at the studio and went downstairs, trying to think of a graceful way to say "no" again. I imagined she'd run into yet another somebody who had a fabulous story to tell and only needed a writer to make it happen, because savvy as she was about life and business, Jilly still believed that the success of her book had been magic, my magic mostly, and that having waved the wand once, I could do it all over again any time I wanted.

In fact, I owed her. I also admired her. A onetime starlet, her career over as she'd neared forty, she'd nonetheless balled enough people along the way, from the bottom to the top of the film industry, to make *Friends, Lovers and Other Members* as juicy and explicit a memoir of bedtime Hollywood as had been published, but done with enough wit and good humor that nobody had dared sue. Besides, everybody liked Jilly, even after the book. A surprise best seller, it had also launched her on a second career as a live, late-night talk-show hostess, and it had made me as a ghostwriter.

"Okay," I said when she picked up, "who wants to talk to me?"

"Are you sitting down?"

"Yes."

"Sonny does."

"Sonny who?"

She burst out laughing, that full rumble that had become her trademark.

"*Sonny who!* Listen to him. There's only one Sonny, Buster."

"Sonny Corral?"

"Sonny Corral."

She'd just been with him, she said suggestively, but he'd spent the whole time pumping her about me. Well, not the whole time, but practically. If it hadn't been about me, she'd have been monumentally insulted.

Sonny Corral, I remembered, had ranked near the bottom of the Life List in Jilly's book. I was surprised, given this published opinion, that he'd come back for more. According to Jilly, though, they'd stayed good friends.

"Why me?" I said.

"Because you're a writer, Sweetie."

"And he wants to do his autobiography?"

He says he's been thinking about it. He asked all sorts of questions about you."

"Like what?"

"Like your background. What you're like to work with. How long it took. Whether you're straight—I don't mean hetero, but stand-up. Whether you can be trusted. And what the deal was between us, how much you got, how much we'd made."

"And what did you tell him?"

"Everything except the stand-up part," she said, giggling. "I told him I didn't know about that part, which is the truth, you handsome Irish bastard."

"Only on my mother's side," I reminded her.

"I also told him you were the most demanding and professional s.o.b. I'd ever run into, including the so-called tough directors. And that, for my money, you were the best damn writer around."

"Thank you, Jilly. And what did he say?"

"Not much. He did say fifty percent for the writer sounded like a hell of a lot. I told him fifty percent of something was better than a hundred percent of nothing, that if anybody had gotten a free ride on my book, it was me."

I thanked her for that too. Of all the stars I'd worked with, she was the only one who felt that way, and the one for whom it was least true.

"So what do you think?" Jilly said.

A complicated question.

"I don't know. He's got an interesting story, but—"

"*Interesting?*" she interrupted. "Are you kidding? Sonny Corral? It's a *dynamite* story! He's the last of a breed, wait till you meet him. You do want to meet him, don't you?"

"Sure."

"Well, look, Sweetie, you make of it what you want to. I've given him your number. Meanwhile, this ole gal has got to run." Then, more sweetly, "I miss you, honey. Go back to bed. Talk to you." At which she hung up.

If anybody actually called, I thought, it would be Corral's agent or lawyer, whom I would pass on to Tinker McConnell, and that would be the end of it. We got a lot of feelers; few amounted to anything. As for his story, yes, it was interesting. You couldn't pick up a book about Hollywood in the postwar period without running into Sonny

Corral, né Timothy Matthew Corrales, and the same anecdotes every-body repeated about him—the hobo years, the brawling in and out of Hollywood, the prison term, the time he'd allegedly told a certain studio head to stuff his contract up his ass (and, some claimed, then proceeded to show him how), which had led to Sonny's dropping out for a couple of years while he sailed around the world. But all that was a long time ago, another era, and the contemporary audience, except for insomniacs hooked on late-night movies, knew him mostly from supporting roles in prime-time mini-series.

I had another problem with it too. Call it my Chinatown syndrome. If you remember Polanski's movie, you'll remember how Jake Gittes, the private eye with the ripped-up nose, felt about Chinatown. It was the place he had to get away from, the place where bad things happened to people he cared about. Including himself. Well, in a way, even though that's where I'd struck it rich, Hollywood had become my Chinatown.

Corral himself called the next day. He was coming to New York. Could we meet for breakfast, at some joint he liked off Eighth Avenue in the forties?

I agreed, with misgivings. Breakfast meetings were bad enough, and, based on his reputation, I expected Corral to show up with a monstrous hangover and a disposition to match.

Jilly had called him the last of a breed. Fair enough. Most of them were dead, and those who'd survived, at least the ones I'd run into, had been dried out and face-lifted so many times that they'd become living parodies of their own screen legends. But Sonny, even though heavier, and rheumy-eyed, gray-bearded, beer-bellied, still resembled Sonny: the same slow-moving nonchalance, the deep American drawl, the heavy-lidded, world-weary eyes. When we shook hands, he seemed to hulk over me.

"So you're the Shakespeare of the ghostwriters," he said after we sat down. "What makes you so good, Danny Boy?"

He gave me the famous ruined grin, one corner of his mouth lifting sardonically. I wondered who, if anyone, had told him that the quickest way to antagonize me was to call me Danny Boy.

"I'm only as good as my subject," I said.

"Now there's a crock if I ever heard one," he replied. "You forget, I know them all."

He then named the stars—all women—whose books I'd written. Apparently he'd talked to all of them about me.

"Now you take Boylan," he said. "I doubt she can write an English sentence, even when she's sober. But people bought her book—it was Numero Uno, wasn't it?—and that had to be your doing. Unless all they were buying was her picture on the cover?"

What he said had some truth in it. To a greater extent than I'd thought anybody realized, I'd had to invent Betty Boylan's story for her. But I resented his saying it.

He grinned at me. "And then there was Gloria. What in hell went wrong?"

Gloria Farran was a subject I didn't much like talking about.

"She just decided she didn't want the book published," I answered noncommittally.

"Really?" He raised his eyebrows. "How come?"

"I guess there wasn't enough money in it."

"But you got three mil for it, didn't you?"

"Is that what she told you?"

He nodded.

"Well, then, it's true."

"And half of it yours," he said. "Not bad. Plus you got to fuck her in the bargain."

For a second, I thought I'd heard him wrong.

"Come on, Danny Boy," he said, his head hunched into his shoulders. "I told you, I *know* them. Farran fucks us all at the beginning of a picture just to get the juices running. It doesn't mean anything. But Sweet Jesus, you're a *writer!* And a pretty one. You'd have made her come just looking at her. So I don't get it."

I didn't say anything. It occurred to me that I hadn't asked for the meeting, also that I had better things to do than suffer his put-downs over a meal I didn't ordinarily eat anyway.

"Look, Sonny," I said finally, "maybe you ought to write your own book."

"Hell," he said, laughing, "maybe I should. But if I could do that, why do you think I'd be wasting my time talking to you?"

"Amen," I answered, at which I stood up, scraping back my chair.

At the same time, though, the great hams of his hands went up in the air, and he lifted his head, his expression rueful, his eyes watery.

"Hey, wait a minute," he said. "Hold on, Danny. Jilly said you were a touchy bastard, but if we've gotten off on the wrong foot, that's my doing. I apologize for it. Most humbly do I apologize. Come on, now," with a large gesture toward the waiter, "sit down, and calm down, and, Sweet Jesus, have something to eat. It'll take the meanness right out of you."

He did most of the eating—a throwback, he told me, to a time when he'd never know where lunch and dinner were coming from— and while he ate, he questioned me closely. He wanted to know all about my working methods: Did I tape and then write from tapes? Did I write on the spot, or go away and show up later with a manuscript? Did any of my subjects write any of the books themselves? Did they get to see it as it went, and did I rewrite if they wanted me to? How much did the publisher have to do with the process?

Few people had ever asked me questions like this. In fact, my "methods" varied from book to book. The most recent, Leo Castagni's, had evolved almost entirely from written questions (mine) and taped answers (his), but the stockbroker was by far the most articulate partner I'd ever had. Mostly I taped, in face-to-face interviews, but at least in the Hollywood books I'd also done a lot of "sub-interviewing" of people who knew the star, and this not only to check facts and versions but, on occasion, to stimulate otherwise empty memories. Jilly Rogers, for instance, had a memory like an overstuffed quilt, but to hear a Gloria Farran talk about her past, even with all those husbands and assorted lovers, you'd have thought she'd been born that very morning, a fifty-six-year-old virgin.

"You know," Sonny said, "I've always been in awe of you guys. The rest of it I get—camera angles, makeup, costumes, lighting, actors learning their lines, editors splicing—but it's all so much bullcock if you don't have some guy first with a typewriter and a ream of blank paper. The script is where it all begins, believe me. It's fucking amazing. And you, Danny Boy . . . you write *books!* Whole books!"

To each, I thought, his own legend.

"All right," he said finally, putting down his coffee cup and wiping his mouth, "what's the bottom line? Suppose I do decide to do a book, how much could I get for it?"

Normally that's a question I try to avoid, but the opportunity was too good to be missed.

"Don't shit me now," Sonny said. "How much?"

"Two, three hundred thousand," I replied, watching for his reaction. "Half a million, tops, but you'd have to be very lucky. Of course, that's only one man's opinion."

I saw his face droop, and his lower lip protruded.

"That's all? With all I've got to tell? Shit," he said, "I know where all the bodies are buried."

"I'm sure you do," I said. "And maybe if you wrote the book first, it would be different."

"Half a mil," he repeated. "Well, tell me this, Danny Boy. Would you work on it for two hundred and fifty grand?"

"No," I answered truthfully.

"Well, fuck me," he said, leaning forward. "Between us, pretty boy, neither would I."

He glanced at his wristwatch, and before I could so much as react, "One last question, Danny. What are you doing the rest of today?"

"I'm going home," I lied. "I've got work to do."

"Well, maybe that can wait," he said. "I'll tell you what. I've got a one o'clock flight to catch. Why don't you just come along for the ride?"

I started to laugh. "Where're you going?" I asked.

"L.A. We'd be there by three, California time. All expenses paid. Plenty of time to talk along the way, and you'll get put up for the night. What do you say?"

It would make a better story if I could say I simply got up with him from the table, out the door and on our way to Kennedy, flying blind, and let myself be delivered, in time for champagne, to the massive hacienda in the Pasadena hills. But it didn't work that way. Instead, I stared back at him, trying to figure out the joke.

He grinned.

"Let me reassure you, ole buddy," he said. "I've got no intention of writing The Sonny Corral Story. I could care less, and if it's worth as much as half a mil, I'll piss in my hat. But I'm in New York on a scouting expedition for somebody else. Actually, I'm here to size you up. What's more, I think you'll do."

"Who sent you?"

"A friend of mine."

"Who?"

"Come on," he said, enjoying the moment. "You mean if I promise you you wouldn't be wasting your time, that wouldn't be good enough?"

"No," I said.

"Well, I can't say I blame you."

And then, fixing me with his lidded eyes, he told me who his friend was.

To say that I'd have been better off if I'd stayed in New York is like saying I should never have started going to the movies at five. Sure, and the world would have been a happier place if Hitler's mother had had her tubes tied. As it was, such must be the power of the silver screen on our imaginations when we're young that it was only after we'd taken off from JFK that I began to worry about the mundane details, like the Fawn not knowing where I was, or that I was dressed for New York winter, not California sun, or that I didn't have so much as a toothbrush with me, much less my tape recorder.

None of which, as Sonny pointed out to me, was worth worrying about. All would be provided.

A little after five, California time, we stood in Nina Hardy's doorway. Ms. Hardy, in the cool, red-tiled entrance hall, in some light-colored dress, rose on tiptoes to kiss Sonny on the cheek. Then she turned, reaching a long arm toward me, and took my hand as Sonny introduced us, saying:

"Please call me Jeannine. All my friends do."

Chapter Four

I IMAGINE, FOR just one instant, I saw her age—fifty-four at the time—but it was gone the moment she spoke, the moment I heard the accent and felt the soft prickle at the back of my neck.

A question of timbre, probably. Her voice set off vibrations that lit on the back of my neck in something less than an itch, more than a caress. It was low in pitch and cool like water, and though she spoke English flawlessly, the cadence of her sentences sounded foreign, indefinably European.

She looked European too. I don't even know what I mean by that exactly, but her body, her clothes, the way she moved. The way she wore her hair. She had a dancer's build, tall, long-limbed, long-necked, small-breasted, and a dancer's gestures: graceful, frequent use of arms, hands. She wore her dark hair short, almost like a boy's, brushed straight back off the forehead and cut severely at the nape. She had on a yellow dress, cotton, full and long in the skirt, gathered tightly at the waist, with buttons, open from the breastbone up, running into a high collar.

Wide mouth, impossibly wide when she broke into a smile. The prominent nose. Hollows in her cheeks under high cheekbones. Dark brows. The famous, expressive eyes shaped like almonds, dark with large whites. Heavier makeup than most American women wear, more visible, the lips vermilion, the eyes accentuated in dark black, the hair brown, almost black but shifting into russet hints and tones. Impossibly white, even teeth. A dazzling, totally disarming smile.

Impossibly. I see I've used the word twice. But almost forty years

31

have passed since she'd made her debut on the London stage, and wasn't it impossible that she look the same, sound the same, move with the same artless grace? Where were the scars and wrinkles?

Of course, they were there. You would see them if you witnessed the pains of her toilette, or when, after a full day's work before the camera, she couldn't move until her back had been massaged and her feet, one after the other, had been worked back into the ankle and kneaded. And, yes, she carried stretch marks on her belly, and there were other signs, small, inobtrusive, which not even the high art of a Beverly Hills surgeon had quite concealed.

But then—that first time? No, nothing was impossible.

I should be able to describe those first thirty-six hours in sequence with beginning, middle, end. But I can't. They were a blur to me, then as now, like pictures taken out of focus or through gauzy screens, broken now and then by clear images of flowers, or paintings, vines, fruit in a bowl, candles, sunlight suddenly bursting onto red-tiled floors, or her eyes inches from mine. And always the silent buzz at my nape when she spoke, somewhere between an itch and a caress.

I remember a tour of the house—this must have been soon after we arrived because Sonny was still there, or Tim, as she called him— and how she showed it off, her haven, she said, far from the dragons of Bel Air and Brentwood. Who had ever heard of a movie star living in the hills above Pasadena? I remember the three of us sitting at nightfall, sipping champagne, her teasing Sonny into telling the famous story of his contract fight, and the studio head with the pants around his ankles who was none other than Claude Rhinelander (Lew's brother), because it was through Claude, a long time ago, that she and Sonny had first met. And now, a little later, she dismissed Sonny in the nicest of ways, that is, without seeming to, thanking him profusely for having brought me there and for all his kindness.

They were standing; so was I. She was kissing him, a seemingly spur-of-the-moment gesture, holding his cheeks in her hands while Sonny beamed down at her, heavier-lidded than ever yet somehow uncomfortable with it. Then Sonny looked at me over her head, tipping two fingers from an eyebrow in a mock salute. I remember her coming back from seeing him to her front door, twining my arm into hers, saying in a mock-deep voice, "And now, Daniel, my new friend, we will have dinner together. And then we will talk about our great book."

Talk we did. I know I was there, that first time, for some thirty-six hours. It could as well have been thirty-six days. Once started, she talked about her own life with a seemingly endless fascination, at least those parts that came easily: the childhood in Europe, her Moroccan-Jewish mother who had been a great beauty and had died when her only daughter was twelve, her father, Belgian-born, who was a Harley Street surgeon, the summers they'd spent in Provence when she was very little, just before the war, the year of the buzz bombs when she and her mother, already ill, had been shipped out of London to a small town in Dorset, her stage debut at fifteen, playing a girl who'd been impregnated by a G.I., at which time she'd also said good-by to her own virginity. She'd been the darling of the British film industry in its golden age, had known all the great figures—the Kordas, Carol Reed, once she'd even been introduced to J. Arthur Rank, who'd made his money in flour. All of them, she said, had wanted to preempt her, protect her, as though she was some asset of the Empire, but she'd been too wild, too young, and London too claustrophobic to hold her. So, at nineteen, she'd conquered Hollywood. (When I, I remember thinking, was six.) She never, she admitted with a rueful smile, had even graduated from high school.

Talk, talk. Countless times, in those thirty-six hours, I kicked myself for not having a tape recorder. Not so much for the stories she told, which I could always recapture, but turns of phrase, little nuances, pauses, and the wonderful, delicious melodies of her voice.

"Why do you want to do a book?" I asked her, an old basic question.

"Well, because everyone is advising me against it. Tim, Claude, everyone. They say I'm such a private person, why do I want to expose myself in that way?"

"Why do you?"

"Well," thoughtfully, "it's a great story, don't you see? Tim says the only true love affair of my life has been with the camera. I think Tim exaggerates, but if that is true, then you have the boy-girl story, don't you? Girl meets boy, girl loses boy, girl gets boy?" She was referring, I assumed, to her comeback, after all the years away from Hollywood. "It is the classic plot. Or is that too banal, do you think?"

"Not at all," I said. "Not as a theme, certainly. But that's not all people are going to want from you, your love affair with the camera."

"Oh, I know that. They'll want the dirt too. Well, I have the dirt to give them, things nobody knows. But I want them to have fun with it. We can be nasty as long as we're funny, can't we? Isn't that the trick?"

"Nasty but funny," I agreed.

"I will hold nothing back, Daniel. I promise. I want to tell everything."

Talk, talk.

And, inevitably, not just talk.

It was late, probably very late, and my internal clock was three hours ahead of hers, and nobody, including the Fawn, still had any idea where I was. We'd been talking in deep, comfortable chairs, drinking brandy out of oversized crystal snifters in what she called the library, a room filled with books, yes, but also curios, mementos, photographs, and her collection of antique dolls in glass-fronted cabinets. Somewhere a stereo was playing. I had begun to think the what-happens-next thoughts, when she, in a characteristic pose, legs crossed beneath her, chin resting on her hands which were linked together on the arm of her chair, said softly:

"Well, Daniel, it is very late. I think you have three choices before you. Either you can leave now, go somewhere, and come back tomorrow, when we can talk some more. But it is very late. Or you can stay here. I have any number of rooms, and too many of them are empty. Or you can come stay with me . . . which I think I would like best of all."

The prickling sensation again, warm, insistent.

"Would you like me to choose for you?"

"I think I would like that best of all," I answered, at which, sliding her legs out from under her, she stood, stretched, and, smiling broadly, reached out her arms to me.

In the darkness upstairs, she told me what she wanted, regulating me with her voice, her arms, her legs. She whispered, purred, breathed in short little gasps. She twisted, slithered, rolled onto her face and, reaching back between her legs, pulled me into her from behind. I rode her, hands on her buttocks, sweat breaking out on my back. I smelled the sweet aromatic musk at the back of her neck where the hair was cut short, and bit into the flesh of her shoulders until, with a gasp, she pulled free of me, unaccountably sliding from my grasp and reversing the position. I heard her laughter in the darkness. Then close, whispering, her small breasts in my face. She wanted to slather me with kisses, she whispered. And she did, then rose to a sitting position, pulling me stiff inside her, and off abruptly, leaving me hanging in midair, a bellow in my lungs as I reached for her.

What did I say? Somewhere between an itch and a caress? Making love with her drove me through itch and into a heaving, unassuaged craving. Always she slipped, slid, slithered in our mingled sweat. I could never have my fill of her. It was as though sex itself was some intricate and prolonged foreplay without resolution, and it wracked me with desire and the need for release. At some point—was it still that first night when, asleep, I smelled her, heard her murmuring, felt her licking me awake with her tongue?—the need drove me, heedless, into the forbidden, and she sat bolt upright in the darkness, then, before I knew it, left our rumpled bed and disappeared into the bathroom.

I followed her there, found her seated in a lacy robe at the long, delicate-legged table, holding a hand mirror and studying the cheek where I'd slapped her. Her skin looked extraordinarily pale in the sudden light, almost ashen. There was no mark that I could see. She rose when she noticed me, clicking off the light. She stood against me, robe parting, arms around my neck, face close to mine.

"No more of that, Daniel," she said softly. "Do whatever else you want with me, but nothing rough, and never my face. It is my one irreplaceable possession."

I started to apologize but, laughing, she pushed me back into the shadows of the bedroom.

There were other people during the day, around the heart-shaped pool, but I'd be hard-pressed to say who they were, other than Sonny Corral, in faithful attendance, and Jeannine's daughter. Christine Hardy, thirty-two and unmarried, was draped over somebody as we approached. She bore a striking resemblance to her mother, or would have but for an almost perpetual frown, more of a scowl, and a cynical jut to her mouth. She appraised me briefly, sunglasses tilted into her hair, as Jeannine introduced me around, and when we went on, I heard her say something like: ". . . never last. Much too old for her." Loud enough for me to hear, more important for Jeannine to hear.

"My ever-gracious daughter," Jeannine said, squeezing my hand.

Otherwise it was as though there was no one, just us. We swam in the pool. We toured Jeannine's rose garden, set into terraces which traversed the hillside beyond the pool. We must have eaten. And always, when we returned to her bed, it had been—miraculously—

freshly made. This was one of the luxuries, she said, that she would never again live without—that there always be fresh linens, freshly ironed, on her bed and in her bathroom, once a day and more often (with the broad smile) when necessary.

She told me about Claude Rhinelander. At first he had been against her doing the book, and that had worried her. He was a very powerful man in Hollywood, probably the most powerful, even now. Also she'd known him a long time, a very long time. He was against publicity of any kind, but how could she do a book without him being in it?

"Is that why you've talked to him about it?" I asked.

"Yes," she said. "And no." Pause. Then, "Daniel, if I tell you something only a few people know, can I trust you?"

"I think you're going to have to do that sooner or later," I answered.

"Yes, you're right. Of course you're right. And this will have to be in the book, won't it? You see, I once slept with Claude. Well, more than once. It was a long time ago, I was very young, you see, and he was . . . well, he was . . ."

"Very powerful?" I suggested.

She smiled, pushing dimples into her cheeks.

"Yes. But also charming. Ugly men can be charming in a special way. And persistent. Very persistent. I used to like that in a man. He once told me he'd never sent anyone so many flowers as when he was trying to get into my pants. That's the way he talks, you know, but it's just Claude being Claude. People say the worst things about him, you know. I think that's his own fault. It's this business about shunning publicity. It means he never defends himself, and people tell these awful, paranoid stories about him—you must have heard them, too, about the Mafia connections from years ago, and how ruthless he is, ruining people's careers, firing people when they're too old to get other jobs, and so on. Tim insists he's been on some blacklist of Claude's, and how Claude once tried to get the other studios to go along, but I asked Claude outright if it were true, and he said absolutely not. Now where was I?"

"You were explaining why he was against your doing the book. But it wasn't just because you'd once had an affair with him, was it?"

She looked at me thoughtfully.

"Who knows?" She shrugged. "He was married at the time. So was I, technically at least. But then Claude called me back. He said he'd talked to his brother—you must know him, don't you? Lew?" She hesitated. Then, smiling: "I met him, but it was such a long time ago. Is he still so handsome?"

"So I've heard people say."

"Anyway, Claude said his brother was very excited about a book by Nina Hardy, that he insisted on publishing it. In that case, Claude said, if it would help his brother, and since it was for me, he would withdraw his objections."

I told her about my own phone conversation with Lew Rhinelander and asked her how my name had come into the picture.

That had been Tim's doing, she said. She had asked him to find her someone to work with, and he had chosen me.

"Aren't you glad he did?"

"Yes," I said. "Very glad."

"Do we want him to be our publisher?" she asked. "Claude's brother?"

"That depends."

"Depends on what?"

I gave her Springer's Theory on how to go about choosing a publisher. All you had to do, I said, was count the number of zeros after the dollar sign. The rest, in my experience, was all window dressing.

"Well," Jeannine said, "in that case, I'd like lots of zeros. But I leave all that to you."

"And who'll represent you?"

"You, Daniel," she said, smiling at me. "I want you to represent me. You and no one else."

But that, flattered as I was, would mean Tinker McConnell. I explained that Tinker would undoubtedly want to hold an auction for Nina Hardy's memoirs.

"An auction?" she exclaimed. "Where, in New York? How exciting! But what shall I wear?"

I started to laugh, the more so since, at the moment in question, she was kneeling above me on the bed, wearing nothing at all. Then I explained to her how publishing auctions worked.

The idea of setting a record was Jeannine's, not mine, and what prompted it, she admitted, was beating out "that dreadful bitch" whose book I'd written. The one who'd gotten three million dollars.

"You mean Gloria Farran?" I said. "But the book was never published."

"I can't bring myself to utter her name," Jeannine said. "And if you told me you slept with her too, Daniel, I think I should absolutely die." She watched me for my reaction. I said nothing. Then, "Well? You didn't, did you?"

I guess each of us has his own piece of forbidden territory. I'd crossed into Jeannine's when I'd hit her, and now she was trespassing into mine.

"That's something I think I'd rather not talk about," I said.

"Well, I think you have to," she persisted.

I shook my head. Put it that this particular stretch of territory had a signpost where you came into it, and that the signpost read "Chinatown."

"My dear Daniel," Jeannine said, studying me, "you've said to me that if we are going to work together, it has to be a spirit of honesty, of mutual confidence, and holding nothing back. And I have accepted this. But if I accept, then don't you have to as well?"

I hesitated. Then, reluctantly, I told her the story.

Some six months in, the work about three-quarters finished, Gloria Farran had announced that she didn't want to go ahead with her book. She'd decided that she didn't like the manuscript. It bored her; the whole thing bored her. This change of heart was communicated not by Gloria to me, but by her attorney to the publisher, who'd called Tinker McConnell, who'd called me. The truth was that I could easily have finished the book without her, but she threatened, through her attorney, to disavow it and to sue the publisher if we proceeded. Panic in New York, and—worse for me—whereas Farran was offering to pay the money back, I had already spent my share.

I knew, though, what the trouble was, or so I thought. It wasn't that she was bored with the book. I doubted she'd even read it. Rather, she was bored with me. After six months of arm's-length coquetry, I still hadn't delivered. Besides, she was about to go into production on a new picture, and her male lead, another younger man, had already started courting her, plus she'd been approached about launching a new line of cosmetics with, as I recall, an eight-figure guarantee. What did she need with—her words—a lousy book?

Money, I guess, can be a powerful persuader. Also reputation. To cut an ugly story short, I got on a plane to L.A., ostensibly to plead the publisher's case and mine but actually to seduce her. This I did, shamelessly. Only, apparently, to fail. Some ten days later, she delivered her final pronouncement via her attorney: the book would not be published.

Jeannine didn't speak when I finished. I remember that she poured both of us more brandy.

"Perhaps one gets what one deserves," she said finally. "But you will have to pay me back for this, Daniel."

"What does that mean?"

"I can think of only one way. You will have to pay me more money than she got. Otherwise—and I will tell you this now, not at the end—I won't do the book."

"But that's absurd, Jeannine. *I'm* not the one who pays you. Besides, I can't promise anything. These things—"

"Never mind," she interrupted, shaking her head. "Don't promise me anything. But you and your Tinkerbell, you will find a way. Now let's not talk about it anymore."

I said before that I wished I could tell it, those thirty-six hours, with a beginning, middle, and end. I do know there was an end. It began with the way she made love that second night. I remember how she held onto me, gone the pretense and the play and the tantalizing odalisque, and clamped me in the shadows, not only with her arms and legs but inside her, until I came in throbbing, heaving spasms, gasping out her name, words, sounds, I don't even know what. And even then, when I was spent, no, she wouldn't let me go, she clamped me still.

"Don't say anything," I remember her telling me, holding her hand over my mouth. She was leaning over me in the darkness, her breasts grazing my chest. "I know you have to go. I know you have your wife to go to. That's good. I understand she's a very beautiful woman." This was the first time the Fawn had been mentioned. Again Jeannine pressed her hand to my mouth, stifling the obvious question. "Shhh," she said. "I've found out all about you, Daniel, more than you know about yourself. I made Tim be very thorough. I'm going to let you go, and you'll hold your silly auction, and we will make all the money, and then you will have to come back, won't you?"

"Of course," I managed finally.

"And how long will that be?"

"I don't know. A few weeks. Maybe a little longer."

"I don't think I can bear it, Daniel." There was a tremor in her voice.

The truth was that I was feeling my own version of the lover's anxiety: once I left her, reality would set in, it would be as though it hadn't happened.

"There's a way of making it sooner," I said.

"What is that?"

"You can make me write a sample."

"A sample?"

"That's right. It's pretty foolish actually—a waste of time as far as selling the book is concerned—but suppose you say to yourself: 'He says he's a writer, but how do I know how good he is? How do I know if I'll like what he writes for me?' "

"So that you would write . . . what? How much?"

"I don't know. A chapter."

"Before you have your auction?"

"Exactly."

"And how long would that take?"

"A few days. Possibly a week. And then I'd have to come show it to you, wouldn't I? For your approval?"

She started to laugh even before I finished, and the sound of her pleasure set my skin alive.

We hardly slept the rest of that night. We talked, and we planned, and sketched out the chapter I would write. I remember having vague misgivings about it. If Claude Rhinelander was going to make trouble over the book, weren't we asking for it if we put their romance on display in the first chapter everybody would read? Jeannine, though, thought I was wrong. And even if I were right, she said, wouldn't it be better to find out early?

She had arranged for a car and driver to pick me up at six in the morning so that I could catch an early flight to New York. I must finally have drifted off, but only, it seemed, for a few minutes before she was kissing me awake in the darkness, stroking my hair, whispering that it was time to get up.

"I think I will stay here till you are gone," she said. "I won't even say good-by. That way I will know that you are coming back, my Daniel. Just kiss me now, once. And then go."

It is only now, a long time later, that I understand why it was that she didn't want to see me to her door—at six in the morning, with the house lights on and no makeup.

Chapter Five

I N AN IMMENSE living room, half-circled by a continuous picture window and terrace forty floors above the East River, Lew Rhine-lander held the weekly meetings of his top executives. That is also where I had lunch with him.

The crasser aspects of his business, it was said, he left to others, and there was even a joke among the working stiffs in the offices, where Lew seldom went, that he didn't in fact exist but had been invented by Jenny—Genevieve Bergler—the book division's publisher, to give the place some tone, also as a means of ducking immediate answers. "I'll have to talk to Lew," Jenny Bergler was prone to tell people. On the other hand, Rhinelander was known to use the same ploy—"I'll have to talk to Jenny"—so it could have been that they'd invented each other.

He was tall, taller even than in photographs I'd seen, with several inches on me, and dressed in navy blazer and gray flannels, white shirt open at the neck, a figured silk ascot on a yellow background, matching suspenders and pocket handkerchief. Gold cufflinks, tasseled loafers. Elegant, casually elegant. And expensive. His head descended in a long triangle, broad at the prominent forehead and tapering, past a slightly aquiline nose, to a pointed chin. Olive complexion, deep-set brown eyes, an immaculately groomed silver mane. In repose, his face might have seemed bland, but when he smiled, or frowned, or advocated or argued, it broke into networks of furrows and crevices, a topographic map, suggestive of intelligence, energy, and, most of all, his total concentration on you.

He talked straight through lunch. Although I doubt he'd actually read my books, he knew exactly how many copies had been sold of the Jilly Rogers, which he called the best book he'd ever read about Hollywood, but he thought my real genius had been Betty Boylan, since his brother, Claude, had always called her the dumbest broad in the film industry. He knew Lerner, of course, the pollster whose scenario of the twenty-first century I'd written, and he believed that Leo Castagni was the most brilliant operator Wall Street had seen since Bernard Baruch.

And so on and so forth, even to the point of asking if I'd ever thought about writing fiction.

Gee, I thought, where had I heard that before?

I shook my head.

"I'm not that kind of writer," I said.

"I think you are, Dan, though maybe you don't know it. After all, what does a novelist do that a good ghostwriter doesn't?"

"He invents his own stories, for one thing."

"And you don't?" Eyebrows raised. "You're making books out of other people's lives. What more does a novelist do? The great writers—Balzac, Flaubert, Proust, Joyce—didn't they take ninety percent of their material from real life and call it fiction? Besides, isn't it time you took home a hundred percent of the royalties and had your name alone on the jacket?"

"It's an interesting idea," I said, irritated again at the Fawn's prescription. "But I assume you didn't invite me up here to offer me a contract for a novel."

"You're right," he said, laughing. "But we would, gladly. And when the day comes when you decide you're ready, I hope you'll remember this conversation."

The Rhinelander treatment.

He was sitting, legs crossed, relaxed, on a cushioned window seat with the river, Queens and the downtown skyline as a backdrop. He made a steepling gesture with his long fingers.

"Let me ask you a hypothetical question, Dan," he said. "Who, in your judgment, has the best untold story in the entertainment field?"

The game, I realized, was on. I'd played it before with publishers. First you soften up the writer with kind words and warm praise, then, out of your own overflowing goodness, you offer him the plum. On your own terms.

"Well," I pretended to think about it, "I guess most people would still say Sinatra, but my hunch is he never will do it. Or Elizabeth Taylor, but I'm not sure how much people care about her anymore."

"I didn't ask what most people would say," Rhinelander said. "I'm interested in what Dan Springer thinks."

In that case, I decided on the spur, let me turn over my hole card. "Hardy," I said. "Nina Hardy."

"Either you're remarkably prescient," he started to say, "or—"

But then the telephone intervened and, visibly annoyed, he excused himself and picked up the receiver.

It was, I gathered, Jenny Bergler. Rhinelander listened, distracted, and while I waited, I gazed comfortably past his shoulder, glimpsed other towers soaring into the gray and wintry sky above the city. Towers of power, I thought, but for once—thanks to Sonny Corral, thanks to the thirty-six hours—power was shared. After the Farran affair, I'd virtually had to start over again. I'd done Lerner's book on the cheap, and though few people knew about it, one of the reasons I'd gotten the Castagni job was that, at the time, I was willing to work for less than half the take.

No more, I thought. Jeannine and I had already agreed to be partners. Lew Rhinelander was presumably about to tell me that he'd put me at the top of the list of eligible writers for Nina Hardy—pending, of course, my financial "needs." But the list, Lew, was already down to one, and Ms. Hardy wanted lots of zeros behind the dollar sign. And so, for that matter, did I.

A sudden irritation in Rhinelander's voice drew me back.

"But why can't this wait till later, Jen?" he said. "I told you I have somebody with me."

Then: "Dan Springer. That thing I mentioned to you."

Then, tersely: "Later, Jenny, it'll have to wait . . . yes, this afternoon."

He hung up and, turning back to me with a sigh, said, "I know this is a people business, Dan, and Jenny's a star in it. Believe me, I wouldn't trade her for anybody. But there are times . . ." He caught himself. "Where was I? Oh yes, Nina Hardy."

He fixed me with his dark eyes. He was trying to figure out, I imagined, if it could be just a coincidence or if I knew something he didn't. I said nothing, and apparently he opted for coincidence.

"What's the expression?" he said. "Great minds think in like ways? Well, it so happens there are people who agree with you. She's a remarkable creature, I have to admit. Or rather: a remarkable *creation*."

He paused. ·

"I met her," he said, musing. "It was a long time ago. Incredibly vivacious. My brother, Claude—I don't think this is any great secret— he was absolutely, desperately, in love with her. He'd discovered her, brought her over here. I think he thought he'd created her."

Here he chuckled, stirred by some memory.

"It's quite a story," he said. "She's a countess, did you know that? That fellow she married when she quit Hollywood—my brother almost had a nervous breakdown!—but what was his name, the diplomat who shot himself? And there are all the European years, the great directors—she was friends with Fellini, Antonioni—the love affairs, then the comeback in Hollywood long after everybody had forgotten her? It *was* remarkable, when you think about it. I mean, when she was young, she invented a whole new style—the gamine look, they called it. Sex appeal in a new and, for its time, totally unexpected package. And she had the charm, the wit, the youth, to carry it off. She was linked with all sorts of people in those days, even the Kennedys—yes, she too, though I understand that was mostly publicity. And then she married her count and simply dropped off the face of the earth. So that when—it was a good two decades later, mind you— she reappeared in *Eva's Story* . . . well, it was as though she—or we— had been in a time warp for twenty years and nothing had changed. A remarkable tour de force. Of course she worked like a dog to do it. And she became a star all over again."

He leaned forward, uncoiling his long legs, his hands extended in an opening gesture.

"You're right, Dan," he said. "It's quite a story. We want to publish it. What's more . . ." Here he paused for effect. "All things being equal, we want you to write it."

The little phrase—*all things being equal*—didn't escape my attention, but again I said nothing, letting him savor the drama of the moment. Of course, there were complications, he went on. Weren't there always? Ms. Hardy might need some convincing. She was, he understood, a very private person, and there were things she might not want to talk about, wouldn't talk about. Nothing wrong with that, but that was why they wanted me, someone experienced in dealing with a great actress's natural reticence and still able to give the public what it wanted.

And, of course, there was, as always, the question of money.

I felt—not for the first time—this terrific urge to jolt him. If he hadn't played his elaborate games, beginning with the phone call to the Fawn, if he'd simply said, ten days before: We think we can get Nina Hardy to do her autobiography, are you interested in writing it?, then he could easily have kept control of the situation.

But that, it seemed, wasn't Lew's style. I'd already been there—beyond the rainbow, so to speak, to a place where there were always flowers, and fresh sheets on the bed, freshly ironed towels. Lew's style was going to cost him now.

"There's something I'd better tell you before you go any farther," I said.

"What's that?" he asked sharply. "You don't have anything else on your table, do you?"

From his conversation with the Fawn, he already knew I didn't.

"No, it's not that. It's just that I've already been approached to write Ms. Hardy's book. In fact, I've already talked to her about it."

To my disappointment, there was no jolt. Only a slight, puzzled frown that set off vertical creases between his eyebrows. He reached for a cigarette from a silver box on the glass table, offering me one first. I declined. It was the first time he'd smoked since I arrived.

"Who approached you?" he asked, exhaling through his nostrils. "Not another publisher, I hope."

"No."

"Who, then? Not my brother, was it? Was it Claude?"

"No. I've never met your brother."

"Then how did you get to her?"

"I didn't," I said mildly. "She got to me."

"You've met her?"

"Yes."

"Ah," he said, smiling, but for just a split-second I thought I could read his mind: *How did this mere mortal, this hack-for-hire, beat me to it?*

Then he recovered, saying, "And here I've wasted your time selling you on a project you clearly know more about than I do! Well? What do you think?"

"I think she's a remarkable woman," I said, smiling back at him. Then, after a pause of my own: "And I think it will be a great book."

Something about the situation amused him, I couldn't tell what. Presumably, in his scenario of the luncheon, we would at this point have reached that rose-tinted moment when he would lead me up on the proverbial mountaintop, far removed from the grubbier details of writing and publishing, the dollars and cents, to admire the view below. The promised land of Nina Hardy, so to speak, with Dan Springer at the keyboard.

But his scenario hadn't played.

"Well, that's wonderful, Dan," he said, stubbing out his cigarette and standing, "just wonderful. I haven't even thought about the terms, but if you can deliver Nina Hardy, I'm ready to make a handshake deal. Right here and now."

Tinker McConnell had warned me this might happen, that Lew was capable of throwing dollars at me on the spot. In which case, per Tinker's advice, I was to duck in a hurry.

"It's not quite that simple," I said.

"Why not? You *can* deliver her, can't you?"

"Yes, I think so."

"Well? We have a great star's untold story; we have the best writer for the job to do it; we have the best publisher in New York. What, for once, could be more simple?"

"For one thing, we've decided to write some of it first. A sample chapter."

His nose wrinkled in distaste.

"Why would you, a professional writer, bother with that? I don't have to read anything."

"Because that's the way Ms. Hardy wants it," I answered.

"But why? Surely you don't have to prove yourself to her, do you? Oh yes, I'd almost forgotten. It's that Farran business, isn't it?"

I was pretty sure he hadn't forgotten, that it had been on his mind all along: how to get Springer cheap.

"No," I said. "In addition, Tinker plans to hold an auction when we're ready."

"Of course Tinker does. What else do literary agents do these days? They hold auctions. But what does Tinker McConnell have to do with it? I know she's your agent, but she doesn't represent Nina Hardy."

"I'm afraid she does."

"Oh? Since when?"

"Since I came back from California."

That Tinker, a high-powered agent, now represented both Jeannine and me meant that Lew had lost control. Every other publisher in town, we figured, would want Nina Hardy's book, and Lew clearly understood that. But I guess one reason the Lew Rhinelanders of this world are so successful is that they bounce back quickly from bad news.

"Well," he said blithely, "you can tell Tinker this for me: I want the book, I'm going to publish it, but I don't expect to be held up and mugged in broad daylight for the privilege. Publishing Hollywood memoirs isn't exactly my métier, you know. They're always expensive, always troublesome, and what are you adding to the culture? This isn't personal, Dan, obviously. I really do think you're the best man for the job—and Nina Hardy, I admit, is a little different. And . . . well, I probably shouldn't be telling you this, but there are people around here," with a cufflinked wave, "who think it's going to be a once-in-a-decade success. I only hope they're right. Make no mistake: we're going to publish it. But please don't ask me to bankrupt the company in the process."

"That, Lew," I said, grinning, "is exactly why we're going to do the sample. So that we can prove ahead of time how much money the project's worth."

He laughed at this.

"Touché," he said. "Probably you're looking at the only publisher in New York who can laugh when there's a gun in his ribs. You're two jumps ahead of me, Dan, and more power to you! But tell me this: What do you suppose would happen if I said to you, as persuasively as I know how: 'Let's forget about your sample chapter and your auction?' Supposing we made you an offer, right now, with deal memo to follow this afternoon?"

There it came again—the money.

"I'd say you'd have to talk to Tinker."

"Yes, of course, we'll do just that. But what would your own inclination be?"

"I'd say let's wait for the sample."

By this time, the phone was ringing again, and Lew was standing;

so was I. Without his having said anything, the interview was clearly over, and for some reason, it occurred to me just then that the Fawn's name hadn't once been mentioned.

He escorted me slowly toward the front door, and the phone kept ringing behind us.

"That's what I thought you'd say," he concluded with that creviced smile as he helped me with my overcoat. "We'll get along. Go do your chapter. I want to be the first to read it. And don't let what happened with Farran get you down. My brother says she's the worst bitch in Hollywood." His hand was now on the doorknob, his other hand ushering me out. Still smiling broadly. "Apropos, Dan, if you really want to convince us—about the money, I mean—just make sure you put my brother in it."

Chapter Six

I MISSED THE point. That's easy enough to say now. At the time, I simply didn't know any better, and the idea that the only role Lew Rhinelander was playing, that lunchtime, was messenger would have struck me as totally off-the-wall.

It doesn't really matter, though, any more than it mattered that I didn't like him. I don't think this was because of the Fawn, either. It was more a question of instinct. On the other hand, I had Springer's Theory to think about. Whoever said you have to love the man who signs the checks?

Lew, it turned out, wasn't easily thwarted. In the week after the lunch, I don't think a day went by without his calling me, or Tinker McConnell, or both of us. Or leaving a message that he'd called. Or leaving a message that he would call back at such-and-such an hour.

In between, Genevieve Bergler, the publisher of the Rhinelander Group's book division, became a telephone pal too, all agush over Nina Hardy's book, and I had calls as well from other editors and publishers. Most of these I deflected to Tinker, but one I couldn't came from an Allen Fryberg, vice president of Rhinelander Films and, I learned, Claude Rhinelander's number-one gofer. Laughing, Fryberg confessed that he didn't really know why he was calling me any more than I did. But Mr. Rhinelander (Claude) was taking a special interest in Nina Hardy's book and had asked him to keep track of how it was coming. Fryberg was ever persistent about it, to the point that, when

I tried to duck having lunch with him in New York, he intimated that his job would be on the line if I didn't.

In his hip rapid-fire style of speech, Fryberg was very forthcoming about the Rhinelanders. Other than Allen Fryberg they were, he said, his favorite subject—The Claude and Lew Show—and the weirdest love-hate relationship he'd ever run into. A New Yorker himself (and an unmistakably gay one), he had once worked for Lew. Something in magazine distribution, I gathered. Then, wanting a change of scene, he'd gone west, and Claude had offered him a job. Lew, he thought, had never forgiven either one of them.

According to Fryberg, there was nothing unusual about Claude disapproving of Nina Hardy's book and Lew insisting on publishing it, if that's what had happened. "When one says black," he said, "the other says white. Not that I think Claude really disapproves. Why wouldn't he want people to know that he used to *shtup* her? But maybe that's what you get when one brother's natural and the other's adopted: one disapproves, the other approves. Don't make the same mistake other people have, though. When it comes to the really important things—like money—they're deep in each other's pockets."

"I didn't know that about them," I said. "Which one was adopted?"

"I'll give you one guess," Fryberg said, relishing the moment. "You've never met Claude, have you? He's probably one of the ugliest men in the world. Maybe *the*. Self-made. Not a nickel from the family when he walked out on Nat and went to L.A. to make movies. His wife died years ago, no children, lives alone. His only hobby is his work, hasn't had a vacation in years. Believe me," laughing, "I should know."

The Nat he'd referred to, I assumed, was Nathaniel Rhinelander, long since dead, Claude and Lew's father and founder of Rhinelander Distributors, out of which the Rhinelander Publishing Group had evolved.

"And Lew?" Fryberg said, grinning at me. "Well, you know Lew. Horace Mann, Harvard, the Sorbonne, the family business laid in his lap. Married umpteen times. Claude used to call him The Playboy of the Western World—well, he used to call him a lot worse than that— and I hear they're *still* lined up outside his door, each one younger and more luscious than the next."

"So you're telling me Lew was adopted?" I said.

"Congratulations," Fryberg answered, "you've just won the gold pumpkin. Apparently Momma Rhinelander couldn't bear any more children after Claude. Or maybe wouldn't. Maybe they threw away the mold after Claude. Claude used to say that Lew was her revenge on him. But as I say, don't be misled by what they call each other. Rhinelander finances are a closely kept secret. But it's no accident that Lew is a director of Rhinelander Films and Claude of Rhinelander Publishing."

"Who owns what of what?" I asked him.

"Aha," he replied. "If you and I knew the answer to that one, we'd make the front page of the *Wall Street Journal*."

For the moment, then, I had Fryberg looking over my shoulder, as well as Lew, Jenny Bergler, and Jeannine and Sonny Corral from long range, and even Tinker McConnell, who, from the reaction she'd been getting from other publishers, clearly scented the perfume of money.

And then there was the Fawn.

The Fawn was excited that I was working again. I was unbearable, she always said, when I wasn't. Impossible to live with. When I'd called briefly from Pasadena, simply to say I was in California and would be back the next day, she'd wondered what on earth could have lured me out there. That it was Nina Hardy explained everything. She thought she was a dream subject for me.

"Does she still look like that?" the Fawn asked, standing behind me in the barn one morning. She'd come to tell me she was off to the city. It was one of those blisteringly cold, clear days and she was bundled for the drive, which I knew she'd make with the heat on full blast in the BMW and the sunroof open, and at those breathtaking speeds which made riding with her a constant adventure. I was running a tape of Jeannine's first movie, a black-and-white thriller with a very young Sonny Corral, trying to discover why I was having trouble writing.

"Yes," I said, stopping the tape. "She still looks pretty much like that."

"How extraordinary! How old is she now?"

"Earlier fifties," I said.

"It's impossible. What about her neck, the backs of her hands?"

I remembered Jeannine showing me her hands.

"I didn't look that closely," I said.

"Even so," the Fawn said. "Even if she's been lifted and tucked—they all are, and they're probably careful with the closeups—it's still extraordinary. And she's had children, hasn't she?"

"Just one."

"You know?" the Fawn said. "It's as though she's her own work of art. Her face, her body."

I wondered, in passing, if the idea was original to the Fawn. Lew Rhinelander, I remembered, had called Jeannine a remarkable creation.

"How are you coming?" the Fawn said.

"Slow."

"Oh, you're always that way at the beginning. You and your voice, you have to find it. It'll come. Have you slept with her yet?"

This was an old joke between us, and I gave my stock response: "Never before the contract is signed."

"Well, I'm off, darling," she said. "I'll call you later. I may not be back for dinner. I have to meet Jason at the gallery."

The Fawn had recently discovered, or rediscovered, the old idea of art in things—objects, people—not normally recognized as art. In this she'd been heavily influenced by our friend, the cartoonist Jason, who lived a few farms up the road from us and also kept an apartment on Central Park West. Jason, as he was known professionally, né Jerry Silverman, had made a fortune as a chic magazine cartoonist and illustrator, also as a very shrewd investor of his earnings. Recently, though, he'd become convinced that he was first and foremost an artist, a serious one, even perhaps a significant one. He was soon to have his first full retrospective in a SoHo gallery the Fawn had helped him find.

After the Fawn left, I ejected the Nina Hardy tape and went off for a walk down the woods, puffed and hooded against the big wind that was blowing east, refrigerated by the mountains. Normally, this was something I did for pleasure. No nature buff, I still liked to tramp, liked the squeak of snow, the crunch of frozen leaves, maybe even the echoes of boyhood fantasies of moccasined Indians jumping from tree trunk to tree trunk. But this day, I went in search of some purifying force, something to blast clean a brain full of accumulated sludge so as to make room for Jeannine's soft and penetrating voice.

The problem wasn't that I'd lied to the Fawn, or even that I'd lied so easily. Or even, finally, that we hadn't had sex since I'd returned. If I knew why I wasn't feeling the least desire for my breathtakingly beautiful wife, it was a good deal less obvious than why I kept coming up short at the keyboard.

The sample Jeannine and I had chosen to do was about Jeannine's initial arrival in Hollywood, which she had talked of that last night in Pasadena with seemingly total recall. The first thing she'd done, she'd told me gaily, was buy a car, a General Motors car, a fat Oldsmobile convertible with something called Hydramatic. The second was get a driver's license, which was ridiculously easy in those days. The third was to wreck the car. About the fifth or sixth thing (or maybe it was the seventh or eighth, but no more) was to go to bed with the male lead of her first American film, who was this huge and utterly fabulous creature called Sonny Corral.

Somewhere along the way, she'd had her hair cut into the gamine style she still wore today—and then she'd gone to work.

The work had been different from London. In London, cast and crew made up a sort of club; they'd had lots of fun together, partying all night, and somehow the work still got done. But in America, everything was so organized, so serious, and everybody on the set worried about The Budget to the point of obsession. The reason for this, she'd discovered quickly, was Claude Rhinelander. Already head of production at Olympian Studios though only in his thirties, he'd visited the set at least once a day, usually speaking to no one except the producer but every so often—and it could have been to a hapless stage manager as well as one of his executives—blowing his stack in the most appalling language. He was aware of every detail, every expenditure, and what he didn't know, he found out.

As far as she was concerned, he'd treated her like chattel. Well, she'd said, that was what she was after all; in order to bring her to Hollywood, he'd had to buy out her English contract. For a very long time, he spoke no more than two words to her, but then he'd started calling her, usually at night, sometimes very late at night, always followed by flowers the next day, whole baskets of them. By this time, she was living with someone, had actually married him, a horrible mistake, a young dancer called Tommy Carruthers who did musicals. Then at long last the day came, night actually, when her doorbell rang and there was Claude on her threshold, unannounced and unable to say a word. She finally understood that, at least as far as she was concerned, he was a shy man, very shy indeed.

Or so she had thought.

I had all this and more, and it even had its own natural inner structure, beginning and ending with Claude Rhinelander. And yet I was short, somehow tongue-tied. Furthermore, rewriting didn't help. Nor did watching the movies, neither the early ones nor even *Eva's Story*. Nor did Jeannine herself, by telephone. While she would answer a specific question, her voice was cool, distant, not unfriendly but almost formal, as though the thirty-six hours hadn't happened. She would ask me how the work was coming, and I would say it was coming, and when would it be done, and I would say soon, and then I would hang up and start to rewrite again.

You and your voice, the Fawn had said. Yes, and in the middle of our woods, I suddenly began to wonder what in the hell I was doing. What was it Lew Rhinelander had said: *You don't have to prove yourself to her, do you?* Well, maybe I did. By the end of the afternoon, I'd worked myself into a state of high tension—the kind where even the words on the screen started to look funny—and so, finally, I caved in to temptation.

"I don't understand, Daniel," Jeannine said over the phone. "You say you've finished the chapter but that it's not good? You don't like it?"

"That's right. I'd be embarrassed to show it to you."

She didn't say anything—for long enough that I said, "Jeannine? Are you still there?"

"Yes, Daniel," she answered softly. Then: "But are you really telling me that you don't want to go ahead? That we can't do the book together?"

"No, not at all."

"Then what can we do about it? How can I help you?"

"It may sound strange," I said, "but I'm having trouble with your voice. With what you sound like, how you would say things."

"Well," a small laugh, "we're talking now, aren't we?"

"It's not the same," I said. "I think I need to see you again."

Another pause.

"But why is that so strange?" she said, her voice dropping.

I couldn't answer for a minute. Of course, it wasn't strange. It was even logical, and I knew it the moment her voice dropped. Hearing that suddenly intimate tone, I felt the prickle at my nape, and the strangeness fell away, and the anxiety, and there was only Jeannine's voice and the summons that followed:

"When can you come again, Daniel?"

"Tomorrow," I heard myself say.

"I want you to take the same plane, the same flight. You will be here at five?"

I was.

Chapter Seven

TINKER MCCONNELL THOUGHT the thirty-page chapter the best work I'd ever done.

"I *love* it," Tinker said, and seemingly to prove it, she invited me—unprecedented event—to be in her office the day of the auction.

Tinker said the pages sounded exactly like Nina, even though she'd never met her, and there was good reason for that. Jeannine and I had been over the manuscript, side by side, line by line. Pencil in hand. I'd read aloud to her; she'd read aloud to me. She wore her tortoise-shell glasses and held the pencil, which she handed to me whenever one of us stumbled over my prose.

I learned, in the process, two new things about her, both strange. One concerned the parentage of her daughter. The identity of Christine's father was a secret, and would, she said, remain one.

"I wanted a child," Jeannine said in explanation, "not a husband, I'd already had one of those," making a face, "but I wanted a baby. I thought of it as my gift to myself, something just for me."

"But that was a long time ago," I said. "Why does it still have to be a secret?"

"Because I still feel the same way," she said with a smile.

"But Christine knows, doesn't she?"

"No."

Which left but one logical question.

"Do you?" I asked.

She laughed at that.

"Yes, dear Daniel," she said. "I may have been carefree in those days, but not careless."

"And so it won't be in the book?"

"No, I don't think it will be in the book."

"You won't even tell me?"

"No, I don't think so."

The second thing was how little she recalled of the early films.

"You see, Daniel," she said, "I never watch them anymore. They're too old, too dusty."

"You *never* watch them?"

"Not in years."

"But why? They're still marvelous. They really are."

"I don't know," she said with a shrug. "They don't feel like me anymore. It's all in the past, and I'm here, now."

"But would you watch them with me?"

"Never!" she said, shaking her head. "I don't think I could bear that."

"Is it that you don't want to look at yourself? The way you were then?"

Pause. Eyes averted.

"You've put it cruelly, Daniel," she said quietly. "But yes. I don't think I could bear to watch myself. The way I was."

She turned to me then, her eyes large behind the glasses, and newly wet with tears.

"But Jeannine," I said. "You still look just the same!"

Somehow the glasses, round and framed in tortoise shell, made her look so defended. They seemed her last bulwark, literally since we were lying on her bed, naked and uncovered. Reaching, I took them off, and licked at the salt of her eyes until she shifted, murmured, purred, and reached in turn for me. And I remember thinking fleetingly that what I'd said wasn't true, that of course she didn't look just the same, but what possible difference did that make when she was whispering in my ear, and then calling, crying out my name?

THREE DAYS AFTER I came back from the second trip to California, Tinker sent the manuscript, along with a letter announcing the terms and date of the auction, to six publishers, including the Rhinelander Group. Later that same day, Lew called her. He loved the chapter. It had enormous charm, he said, better than his brother deserved. In fact, he loved it so much that he was ready to preempt the book, meaning that, if we agreed to call off the auction, he would meet any asking price within reason.

Twenty-four hours later, after numerous phone calls to and from Pasadena, we named it: $3.25 million.

Which, among other things, beat the Gloria Farran deal.

And Lew accepted.

A most impressive gesture.

But there was a catch to it. With the Rhinelander Group, Tinker said archly, there always was. Lew's $3.25 million was an advance against world rights, not just the standard United States and Canada. Without going into all the technicalities of publishing deals, this meant practically that any money we made from overseas would go first into Lew's pocket, not ours, and it would be several years before we saw it, if we ever did.

The difference wasn't small change either. Tinker put it at somewhere between five hundred thousand dollars and a million, possibly more. In other words, the real value of the Rhinelander offer was somewhere in the neighborhood of $2.5 million.

Tinker pointed this out to him, but Lew didn't want to hear about it. The offer stood; take it or leave it. Tinker voted to leave it. "Let's take our chances," said Tinker. "The Rhinelanders can bid at the auction."

And then, as Sonny Corral put it when he called me the next day, the shit really hit the fan.

"You'll never guess who I just got off the phone with," he said. "My ole buddy, Claude. It was not the nicest of conversations, Danny Boy. Is he burning! Said it's bad enough Jeannine wants to drag him through the mud after all these years, but now she's sticking it up his kid brother's ass too. He wants to know what's wrong with his brother's money. I told him nothing was wrong with his brother's money except there wasn't enough of it. He said he understood $3.25 million was a record for a Hollywood memoir, what the fuck did Jeannine want? He said that if we didn't take it . . . well, he threatened a lot of things."

"Like what?" I asked.

"Oh, a libel suit for one. He said if we so much as mentioned his name in the book, he'd sue our asses off and we'd never see the end of it. He also said he'd see to it neither Jeannine nor I ever worked in Hollywood again."

"You're kidding."

"I told you it wasn't a very nice conversation. Oh yeah, he also said Jeannine was crazy to give you half. He said his brother said you were a hack, that Jeannine could name any other writer and they'd get him for her for a lot less than half."

"Did he, now?" I started a slow burn of my own.

"That's what the man said."

"And what did you say?"

"I didn't get a chance, Danny Boy. The little runt hung up on me."

"Is it true? Could he get you blacklisted?"

"Jeannine, never. The way things work out here now, he couldn't touch her, and he'd be laughed at if he tried."

"What about you?"

"Probably, yes. There are half a dozen other hungry has-beens around who can play my roles."

Evidently Claude Rhinelander figured that the best way to get at Jeannine was to attack the weak link in her entourage. Or the weak links, counting "the hack."

"What does Jeannine say?" I asked.

"I haven't told her yet. I thought I'd give you the good news first."

"Well, don't you think you'd better tell her?"

"I'm about to."

"And would you tell her I'd like to talk to her, too?"

Less than half an hour later, Jeannine called me.

"Nice people you know," I said.

"Who, Claude? Oh, he's not so terrible. It's just that people who are that short always think they have to shout and threaten."

"Did Tim tell you everything he said?"

"I think so. He also told me you are worried about it."

"*I'm* not worried. But I thought you might be."

"You're very sweet, my dear Daniel, but there's nothing Claude could do to me now that he didn't do years ago. It's the same way for Tim. And as for what he said about you, you should already know that if I can't do the book with you, there will be no book."

"Are you sure of that?"

"Yes, Daniel. Very sure. If you were to say to me: now Jeannine, let's be realistic, we should put our hats in our hands and go back to the Rhinelanders and take their three million or whatever it is, well, I would be very disappointed."

"That's fine with me," I said, elated. "I just needed to hear you say it."

"Good. Then we are all agreed, aren't we? Tim says we should cross the Rubicon together and let's hope we all know how to swim."

We had, in fact, already crossed it. From the moment Tinker McConnell refused Rhinelander's preemptive bid, even before Claude raised the roof, my phone had stopped ringing. Good-by Lew, good-by Jenny Bergler. But the Rhinelanders of this world, it should be said, never stop trying, as I learned the morning of auction day, over coffee. Call it Rubicon II.

I was sitting in the kitchen, trying to make myself concentrate on the sports pages. Normally I'd have been in the barn by that time, but this wasn't a workday, not even a pretend workday. The Fawn was already dressed for the city, eating on the run.

"I suppose you know Lew Rhinelander's furious with you," she said in passing.

"Really? Why?"

"He says you insulted him."

"*I* insulted *him*? How? I didn't call him a hack publisher."

"What does that mean?"

I hadn't told her what had happened, other than that the auction would take place today and that I was going to Tinker's.

"Never mind," I answered. "Why is he furious with me?"

"He says he made you a record offer and that you turned it down. One of these days—maybe even this time—he says you're going to out-greed yourself. Are you being too greedy, Dan?"

I looked up from the paper, focusing in. "That sounds like a threat to me," I said. "But who are you in the picture? Lew's messenger?"

"There's no need for you to get angry."

"I'm not angry," I said. "I didn't know you were still seeing him."

"And why shouldn't I see him? He's a friend of mine. He's also a patron."

"What does that mean?"

"Exactly what it sounds like. He's commissioning me to do a bust of him."

"A *what?*"

"A bust. What's so strange about that?"

Her head was lifted, her chin in a defiant jut, as though she were
waiting for me to laugh at her. But how could I laugh at her? This
wouldn't be her first commission, after all. That had been a head of
Jason, the cartoonist, a second casting of which adorned the mantelpiece in our dining room. And how could I laugh when we had spent
a small fortune converting the old greenhouse, on the far side of the
house from the barn, into a studio for her because she found the light
there so extraordinary? Only to decide, after the fact, that she worked
better in the SoHo loft.

"Nothing's strange," I said. "But you've got to admit it's pretty
original. All anybody who wants to get into your pants has to do is
commission a bust."

Her chin jutted farther, her eyes went wild, her nostrils flared.

"You stupid, jealous son of a bitch."

"Don't flatter yourself," I called to her back as she stalked from the
kitchen. I heard her go upstairs, then, a few minutes later, the whine
of her engine, the high-pitched complaint of her wheels as they whirled
on ice.

It was a hell of a way to start the big day. Bad karma, bad vibes,
followed by rain, wind, and cold on the wet roads into Manhattan.
A message, though, was already waiting for me when I got to Tinker's
midtown office. Good luck from the Fawn, it said. She took it all
back. She loved me, it said. She also reminded me that the opening
of Jason's show was tonight.

When I'd first met Tinker McConnell, several years ago, I'd been
surprised at how young she was, given her reputation. Later I found
out she was about my age. A small woman, small-boned, pleasant-
looking rather than pretty, with light brown hair, and granny glasses
and a still-preppy style of dress, she'd come to the agency fresh out
of college and had built, over the years, probably the strongest single
client list in publishing. What people tended to forget, maybe because
Tinker did her best to hide it, was that the agency she worked for was
a film and television powerhouse, so she herself was only a hired hand,
if presumably a well-paid one.

At Tinker's suggestion, I arrived at lunchtime. The first round of
bidding had just ended. We had two players, one at $1.5 million, one
at $1.7.

I couldn't believe the low numbers.

The other four publishers, including the Rhinelander Group, had already dropped out.

I couldn't believe that either.

"For God's sake!" I said, feeling a rush of heat under my skin. "Didn't they like the chapter?"

"They *loved* the chapter," Tinker answered coolly.

"Then I don't understand. What went wrong? Why don't they want it?"

"It's not that they don't want it. But we scared them off. By now, they all know we turned down Lew's offer."

"But didn't you tell them that was for world rights? That they could buy U.S. for less?"

"Of course."

"I bet Rhinelander himself touted them off it."

Tinker didn't believe it.

"What are you so worried about, anyway?" she said. "It only takes two to make an auction. Now sit down, have a drink, have a sandwich, and I want to hear all about Nina."

After lunch, the $1.5 million bidder came back at $1.8. The $1.7 bidder countered at $1.9. They went up the ladder like that, a hundred grand at a time, but slowly, even laboriously. In between, Tinker took other calls while I bet mentally on the raindrops rolling down her windows. And stared at the photo of me, arm-in-arm with Betty Boylan which hung on Tinker's wall. And talked to Sonny, or listened, because as the day progressed, the more his voice slurred, the more voluble it became. And I wondered, hardly for the first time, what his relationship with Jeannine was all about. I knew Sonny had a place of his own somewhere in Topanga Canyon—hardly a stone's throw from Pasadena—yet he always seemed to be at Jeannine's. "He's my oldest friend," she had said whenever I broached the subject, but the only thing that was clear was that every time something came up that she couldn't handle, or didn't want to handle, she used Sonny to front for her.

Finally, when we reached $2.5 million, Tinker told me to go for a walk. But it was pouring outside, I protested. Then I should go downstairs to the bar; there was one at the corner. Or go buy something, a present for Faith. Anything, in other words, because I was getting on her nerves.

I left. The freezing March rain was slanting east from the Hudson, the traffic in a gridlock of honking horns. Collar up, head down, I headed toward Fifth, down Fifth into a phalanx of umbrellas, around, back. Wind and rain in my face. I think I made the circuit twice, but I doubt I was gone more than twenty minutes, door to door.

The Fawn had called. She was at the loft. I called her back.

"I'm sorry about this morning," she said.

"I am too."

"No, I mean I'm really sorry. I hate it when we leave things like that."

"I do too."

Pause. "Look, Dan. I know this isn't the time—you're in the midst, so am I—but we've got to talk. Soon. There's too much going on, and we're not talking, and I feel it slipping away from us. And frankly I . . . well, I find it a little scary."

I didn't know what to say. She was right—I *was* in the midst, and a lot of things scared me right then. And I didn't particularly want to air my private life in front of Tinker McConnell. I also knew, based on our track record, that the Fawn would say, at the moment of the confessional, that, yes, she'd been "seeing" Rhinelander, or Jason, or somebody entirely other, but that it didn't mean anything. Nothing at all. And I was supposed to say that, yes, I'd been "seeing" Nina Hardy but that didn't mean anything either.

"Don't you?" the Fawn was saying. "Find it a little scary?"

"Yes," I said.

Somehow this admission seemed to be all she was looking for right then.

"Well," she said, the lilt back in her voice. "How's it going? How much money have you made today?"

"I don't know yet. We're at two and a half million now. It's still going on."

"Why are you sounding so glum about it? That's more than you made yesterday. When do you think you'll be done?"

There was no telling. The bidders had dropped their raises from a hundred grand to fifty, and we'd been stuck at $2.5 million since before I went out. Did that mean we were winding down? According to Tinker, it didn't mean anything.

"I have to tell you, Mr. Springer," the Fawn said, "you may be a son of a bitch, but I still love the way you hustle for a buck. You're not going to miss Jason's opening, though, are you? He'd be heartbroken."

I had my doubts about how heartbroken Jason would be; in fact, I'd forgotten about the show. Time was, I realized, when we'd celebrated every new deal I made, just the two of us. A tradition, sort of. In the beginning, it had been nothing more than pizza in bed, later, the Rainbow Room in black tie and evening gown. Once an impromptu flight to St. Martin's in the Caribbean. Now, when the bucks had gotten bigger than I'd ever dreamed of, Jason's opening was the best we could do. But all I told the Fawn was that I'd get there if I could.

A new bid had come in while I was on the phone. $2.55 million. According to Tinker, we were home free, meaning that, by taking her foreign rights estimate into account, we'd beaten the Rhinelander offer.

A little before seven, we reached $2.75 million. A kind of mental fog set in, and the numbers began to lose their meaning for me. Then I heard Tinker say calmly to the underbidder, "It's closing time at the bar. I'm not going to sit here all night while you nickel and dime me to death. Last round. Each of you will be allowed to make one final bid, and that will be it. I'm giving you until seven thirty."

Then she repeated the same message to the other publisher.

In between, I said, "What the hell are you doing that for?"

"Trust me, Dan," she said, unperturbed. "There comes a moment in any auction when it's time to stampede the horses."

"I hope you're right," I replied. And then I told her about our California problem. Although I wasn't sure she'd stick to it at the end of the day, Jeannine had insisted we beat Gloria Farran.

All Tinker did by way of response was tilt her glasses upward and massage her eyes. Then she looked at me, saying she wished I'd told her before. Not that it would have mattered, she said. I said I hadn't wanted to make her nervous. Then the glasses came back down like shutters. Making money, she said, never made her nervous. Besides, she thought we'd still satisfy California.

I didn't see how.

The publisher who'd bid $2.75 million called back first. No new bid. They'd stand pat.

At 7:30 sharp, their competition called. I watched Tinker as she scrawled on the legal pad and, expression unchanging, pushed it across her desk toward me.

$3.05 million. Underlined twice.

With that one change in tactics, I realized, she'd just taken care of the California problem and had made us an extra $300,000. For that matter, in one day's work she'd made Jeannine and me over $1.3 million each, and $305,000 for herself.

I sank back into the couch and reached for the telephone to call Pasadena.

"Not yet," Tinker said. "I've one last call to make myself."

"Who to?"

"Lew Rhinelander, since you ask."

"Lew?" I didn't understand. "How come? You're not going to let him bid now, are you?"

"Why not, if he wants to? His money's as good as anybody's."

"But they passed in the first round, didn't they?"

"For a reason," Tinker said. "I promised Lew I'd give him a last shot."

"You *did?* Why didn't you tell me?"

Her mouth turned up into a smile.

"I didn't want to make you nervous."

It took her three calls to locate him. Normally, I thought in a daze, Tinker McConnell wouldn't make three calls to locate God. And somehow, somewhere, didn't the ethics of what she was doing have to be less than impeccable?

Less than impeccable! Christ, hadn't she told the two bidders: one final bid, winner take all?

No she hadn't, technically. What she'd said was: *One final bid and that will be it.*

Still . . .

Somehow I knew Rhinelander was going to win and that was wrong. It was as though he'd been dealt a secret hand without having had to ante.

While she chased him, I said nothing. Then she was listening, jotting notes, talking to him about the finer points of a publishing deal. Finally I heard her say:

"Congratulations, Lew. Subject to the approval of my clients, I think you've just bought the Nina Hardy."

On her notepad, with the dollar sign in front, underlined three times and circled, was: $3,400,000.

"Now you can call California," Tinker said to me.

I wanted to talk to Jeannine myself, but there was no getting past the keeper at the gate.

"The lady's outside," Sonny said. "Communing with her roses, or whatever she does with them."

"Her roses? I don't give a damn about the roses, Sonny. We've just sold the book."

"I won't tell her you said that, Danny Boy. Roses are a pretty high priority. How much did you get?"

"$3.4 million."

"Three point four? Well, what do you know? Not bad. Not bad at all. Mazel tov. And who's the lucky publisher?"

"Lew Rhinelander, who else?"

"You mean you sold world rights after all?"

"No. Just U.S. and Canada."

Sonny started to laugh.

"You mean we got three point four mil out of the *Rhinelanders?* Holy Mother of God, wait till I tell Jeannine!"

It wasn't until the next day that I talked to my coauthor myself. I couldn't reach the Fawn either. Although I'd had it in mind to go down to SoHo and join in Jason's celebration, or my celebration, or everybody's celebration, when I reached the street, all I could think of was going home.

Who would understand why I came away feeling defeated?

I drove north, alone, along the slick and icy highways. The rain had stopped. When I reached our empty manse (the Irish couple we employed lived in an apartment over the garage), I thought about finding something to eat in the kitchen but settled for a solitary glass of champagne. Then upstairs, for a bath, bed and discovered the Fawn's diaphragm case, sitting on top of her dressing table.

Empty.

And so was the top shelf, left-hand corner, of the medicine cabinet in the bathroom, where she kept the cream.

Empty.

The net, it seemed, had dropped.

Part Two

Chapter Eight

S PRING SAID THE calendar, but the East was a gray and dismal swamp of flooded roads and broken relationships. It was up to its hubcaps in mud and last-minute tax dodges and a stinging, recriminatory rain that never stopped. Even the crocuses had a hard time that March.

I left it all behind. I turned off the computer, put the telephone on answer and my marriage on hold. I knew a place where there were always flowers, and freshly ironed sheets on the bed, and I was there, by request, in time for Oscar night. Also known, in terms of my story, as the night of Nina Hardy's annual boycott.

Or, to put it as Jeannine did, "I let myself be humiliated once, Daniel. It won't happen again."

The humiliation had to do with *Eva's Story*. I'll admit to a certain prejudice, but for my money it was the picture of its year—for which honor it wasn't even nominated, although Jeannine was. It had come out of nowhere, written and directed by Harry Brea, a then-obscure Aussie. Jeannine herself had arranged the financing for it, had fought to get it distributed, had all but stood in front of the theaters selling tickets.

It opened small, in major cities only, but by year's end it was among the top five at the box office. Audiences loved it, went back to see it a second and a third time. Maybe the story itself—about the comeback of a forgotten silent-screen star in the 1950s—owed a little too much to *Sunset Boulevard*, but everyone agreed that Nina Hardy, then in her mid-forties, had pulled off a spectacular tour de force, playing both the ingenue and the adult woman. What few pointed out, though audiences seemed to understand it subconsciously, was that *Eva's Story* was really Nina Hardy's.

I had watched the Academy Awards on television, caught up in the drama of Best Actress. When the nominations were finally read, I remember Hardy's face uplifted in the audience, her eyes alight with expectation, and if you'd seen her on celluloid, you knew that momentarily she would break into the broadest of smiles, or tears of triumph, or—it was virtually her trademark—both at once.

Incredibly, she lost. I couldn't believe it; neither, apparently, could she.

The cameras caught her with her head down, deep into her chest, her face hidden, her hands grasping her hair on either side. Then, discreetly, they left her, but immediately after, it was said, she'd gotten up from her seat in tears and walked out of the Civic Center.

Never to return.

At the time, people said she'd lost because that was how the industry worked. *Eva's Story* wasn't a Hollywood picture. If anything, it was an embarrassment to Hollywood because all the majors had turned it down, Claude Rhinelander included. But Sonny Corral, a decade later, had a different slant on it.

"It was Jeannine's own fault," he told me. "She never paid her dues. She never paid them the first time around either, but she was just a kid then and they could give her her Oscar. They weren't about to do it again."

"What does that mean, though?" I asked him. "Paying her dues?"

"Stick around, Danny Boy," he answered with that ruined grin of his. "Stick around and maybe you'll find out."

Each year, the producers of the Awards invited her back. Each year, even when she was nominated again, she turned them down. She shunned the Governor's Ball too, and all the Oscar Night parties— except one.

"But why are we going?" I asked her. "I mean, if you stay away from the rest of it, what's the point?"

"Because of Claude," she said. "It has nothing to do with the Oscars."

"Why because of Claude? The last I heard, if you went ahead with the book, wasn't he going to have you banned from Hollywood?"

"Because he invited us," she answered coolly, in a tone that ended the conversation.

Us meant Jeannine, myself and Sonny Corral. We left the house around ten, after a full day's work for Jeannine and me. Sonny had spent the afternoon at Santa Anita and, by his own admission, had lost his shirt.

"Poor Tim," Jeannine said lightly, reaching to straighten his black tie in her entrance hall. "Nobody loves you, not even the horses." She stepped back to examine her handiwork, at which Sonny abruptly pulled one end of the tie, undoing it. Teetering a little, he stooped in front of a mirror and retied it.

He'd been drinking since he arrived from the track, but he still had a way to go, I gauged. His eyes were no rheumier than usual, his complexion as ruddy as ever, and the troubles that made him drink, at least according to Jeannine—that people weren't beating down his doors with job offers; that he couldn't hold onto money (she'd cut him in, I'd learned by then, for a piece of her earnings from the book); that, in this particular instance, there was no way he'd go to Claude Rhinelander's sober—were nothing new. As to why he had to go at all, when I was clearly the escort of the moment, Jeannine said, "Because he has to, that's all. His absence would be noticed."

They argued about who should drive. Jeannine wanted me to. Sonny refused that. When the day came that he couldn't handle a car, he said, drunk or sober, well, that would be the day. Jeannine retorted, in the cool voice which bespoke anger, that on one of her rare nights in public, she didn't want to be embarrassed, much less dead. (Did this happen every year, I wondered? With a different escort?) In the end, though, Jeannine and I rode in the back seat of the Mercedes while Sonny piloted us out of the hills and onto the old Pasadena Freeway, driving a little fast maybe but smoothly enough, saying over his shoulder, "One of these days, Jeannie, I'm going to make you give me a chauffeur's cap. I'd look pretty cute in one, what do you think?"

It was a sign, I knew, of how much he'd actually had to drink when Jeannine became Jeannie.

For the last part of the trip, once we swung off the freeways, Jeannine fell silent. Her hand, I noticed, had gone limp in mine, and her head was back, eyes half-closed against the oncoming headlights which, now and then, illuminated her face without seeming to interrupt her reverie. She was, I guessed, preparing herself. "It's the same with any performance or appearance," she'd told me. "If I don't have my quiet period just before, I go all to pieces. It's too frightening otherwise."

The evening was mild, and Sonny had the windows open in the front seat and the sunroof rolled back slightly. He talked to me over his shoulder, and I talked back, but if Jeannine heard us at all, she gave no sign, not even when we rolled through Rhinelander's gates, where there were photographers and camera crews waiting, and up the long driveway, past the darkened lines of black limos parked on the grass. Only when we reached the imposing Tudor entrance, lit by floodlamps sunk into the ground, where gloved and uniformed footmen were helping guests out of their cars and youths, also in uniforms, were waiting to park them, did she come awake. She squeezed my hand and, with a suddenly dazzling smile, kissed me on the cheek, saying, "Well, Daniel, here we are."

Whatever might have frightened her, it couldn't have been that she'd be swallowed up and unnoticed. Almost as soon as she stepped from the car, her hand outstretched, she became the magnet, the focus of all attention. This was partly, I judged, a question of contrast. The style, that season, called for curls, cascading curls, mountains of curls, and it was also marked by the return of the bosom. Star after star appeared that evening in gowns which thrust their breasts showily upward into a glitter of gems and teased hairdos. It was as though the master designer, short on inspiration, had simply rolled the clock back some forty or fifty years—not to what women had actually worn then but to what they'd worn in Hollywood costume dramas of the period. The overall effect was at once electrifying and ersatz, taffeta and paste, pastel and white, and in their midst there was no way you could fail to notice Nina Hardy.

She wore black, a long, sheathlike silk startling in its simplicity. It followed the slim lines of her body up to a low neckline and then, circling her shoulders, ended in a high black collar which enwreathed the back of her head like the opening petals of some giant black flower. Her usual makeup, the dark eyes in sharp contrast to her pale, seemingly untouched skin. Her dark hair short, brushed straight back off the forehead. Her radiant smile. And not a single piece of jewelry. She was already taller than most of the women, and the dress accentuated the impression of a stark, stunning silhouette rising in the midst of their fake and busy finery. The genuine article, in other words, the star of stars, herself the jewel.

Jeannine seemed to know it too. I could feel it in the cool electricity of her touch, the poise of her smile and conversation as, flanked by Sonny and me in our tuxedos, her arms linked in ours, she entered the party. And in the reaction of the people as well, the way they first seemed to yield before us, and then, covering their sudden silence with a kind of audible group gasp, rushed forward to greet her, to be near her, be seen next to her. Flashcubes popped around us, photographs taken not for the press (never, apparently, had a picture from the Rhinelander party found its way into the media) but for selected guests, each of whom would receive a leatherbound mini-album of the event, inscribed by Claude himself.

I stayed with her longer than Corral. He extricated himself almost immediately and lumbered into another room, glass already in hand. Jeannine held onto me, her fingers tightly enlaced in mine, turning now to whisper in my ear, or introduce me, or, words failing in the din, squeezing my hand as the eyes of her admirers flicked briefly at me, in passing curiosity. *Her new one*, they seemed to register. I understood my role; no, I didn't like it; and so, at the first opportunity, I made my escape.

I was no newcomer to Hollywood parties, but this was by far the most lavish I'd attended, from the music, indoor and outdoor, to the cascades of food, featuring fennel-smoked lamb, roasted on open spits under the supervision of a chef flown in from the south of France. And, most of all, the turnout. They really were all there—*le tout Hollywood*. Try as I might to feign nonchalance, it astonished me to behold them all under one roof, the Jimmy Stewarts, Gregory Pecks, Kirk and Michael Douglas, Glenn Close, Loretta Young (still gorgeous, for all her years), and Fonda, Audrey Hepburn, Pacino, Linda Evans, Costner, Eastwood, Reynolds, Goldie Hawn, Don Johnson. How, under your outer cool, to keep from playing the stargazing game? Plus all the power figures—the producers, directors, lawyers, agents, financiers—who had made them stars and been made by them. The men in tuxedos, with all the variants on the theme the California dress code permits; the women, with rare exception, in the showy, bosomy garb of the season. And say what you will about the entertainment business having changed—that the studios are dead, that the creative people and their managers have taken it over—the fact was that the one person who could bring them all together, whose invitation apparently constituted a summons for this one night, was a sawed-off little man with a white crew cut and bad eyesight and gravelly voice: Claude Rhinelander.

My best-selling coauthors were there too, Betty Boylan among them. I saw la Farran holding court before a group of youthful male admirers, none of them familiar to me. Our eyes met as I passed, but there was no recognition in hers. And I saw la Rogers. Or rather, la Rogers saw me.

"Jesus, you look great, you blue-eyed Irish devil!" she shouted, holding me at arm's length after embracing me. "And you never told me, you bastard! I thought I was fixing you up with Sonny Corral, not Nina. A person could shoot herself! How's it going? What's she like?"

In the style of the night, Jilly looked terrific, and I told her so. A naturally big woman, she'd related in our book, with great if rueful comedy, how she'd always had to torture her flesh away for the cameras. Like a jockey in a sweatbox, we'd written. But as a TV hostess, she'd let her body go a bit, and the result was a healthy, ample-bosomed ripeness, with appealing character lines in her face, and her curly hair, once a darker red, now tinted strawberry blonde.

"I heard the whole story, Sweetie," she said. "How she sent Sonny to track you down in New York and how he brought you back. I even used it on the show. But tell Jilly now, what's she like?"

"She's a very remarkable woman," I answered, hoping to let it go at that.

"I'll say! She's what? Past fifty anyway. And she looks thirty-five. But that's not what I mean, for Christ's sake. I want the juicy parts. Everybody knows you've practically moved in with her, and *I* know you don't have to do that to write a book, remember? So let's have it: what's she *really* like?"

Innuendo was not part of Jilly Rogers' style.

"Remarkable," I repeated, grinning at her.

"You bastard," she said cheerfully. "I did a whole book with you and never got you into bed, not once! I must have been too young for you. But I'll tell you this, Dan Springer, and this time you're not getting out of it: You're coming on the show."

She'd asked me several times before, and I'd always ducked. According to Jilly, the guy who wrote the books for the stars was a natural for television.

"It's not me you want," I said. "It's Nina Hardy."

"Not so," she retorted. "Not that I wouldn't kill for a one-on-one with her. She could have my whole hour. Hell, she could have the whole week! But would she ever do it?"

"When the book is done. She says she'll do everything we want to promote it."

"You're kidding!"

"That's what she says."

"You're going to make a fortune, Sweetie." Then, with a nudge, she asked me about the Fawn. They'd met once, Jilly remembered. How come a scamp like me got such a long leash? Was she still that gorgeous? I answered noncommittally. It occurred to me to ask Jilly, in return, why a woman would leave an empty diaphragm case in plain view, on her dressing table, where it was sure to be discovered. But just then I spotted Allen Fryberg's tall figure pushing through the guests, his alert eyes darting all over until, spotting me, he relaxed into a smile of relief.

He seemed ill-at-ease in evening dress, his round face florid and perspiring. His hands fidgeted with his bow tie, and as he reached us, I watched him prepare his words, a now-familiar tic, opening his mouth, then closing it and his tongue licking his lips.

"Hi, Jilly," he said. Then, smiling at me and squeezing my shoulder, "They're looking everywhere for Nina's *escribaño*. That means you, Dan."

"Okay, Allen," I said. "What's an *escribaño?*"

"Oh, you know, the guy with the portable desk in the Mexican village squares? He writes letters for people. The village scribe. I understand there's a lot of money in it. Anyway, I've been dispatched to find and deliver you. Their Royal Highnesses request your presence, meaning Claude wants to meet you. Would you excuse us, Jilly?"

I kissed Jilly good-by, promised to call her, and followed Fryberg off through, as he put it, Claude's castle, half-listening to his rapid-fire commentaries as we went.

We found them in the library, a cavernous room which smelled of oiled leather. Its high mahogany shelves were filled with books and mementos, and though I didn't get close enough to see the titles, Fryberg explained later that many of them were leather-bound copies of the scripts Claude had produced. The furniture was leather-covered too, with brass studs, and there was a fireplace, undoubtedly gas-lit, with a pile of neatly trimmed logs sitting on massive brass andirons. An immense Oriental rug covered most of the wood floor. Some exclusive men's club, you'd have thought, except there was Jeannine, her expression fixed in a cool smile and a full glass of wine in her hand. She was, I noticed with an inner smile of my own, the tallest of the group.

Two of them were attorneys, name partners in the L.A. firm that· represented both Jeannine and Olympian Communications. Another was the Wall Street financier and deal-maker Irving R. Stewart, habitually referred to in the media as an éminence grise, whose company, I knew from my book with Leo Castagni, often served as a bridge between Canadian money and the entertainment industry. I think R. T. "Artie" McAndrew was there too. He'd been chief financial officer of the old Olympian, and Claude kept him around, according to Fryberg, as a combination comic relief and hostage from the past.

Plus our host.

"I'm glad to meet you," Claude Rhinelander said, holding my hand a little longer than I expected. "Is your wife with you?"

"No," I said.

"That's too bad. My kid brother tells me she's one of the most beautiful women in the world. Present company excepted, that is. Well, I hear you took him for a lot of money. Good for you. Good for him, too. But don't worry, he'll make it back. I told Lew: You'd better publish Nina Hardy, she's got one of the great stories. Provided, that is," with a glance in Jeannine's direction, "you get her to spill all the dirt. Are you good at that, Dan?"

Normally, the pointed remark about the Fawn aside, I'd have taken this as idle small-talk, but, given what I knew, his last question carried a veiled menace—toward me and, presumably, Jeannine. I had trouble, I admit, getting a fix on him. I'd been prepared for his small stature, also his ugliness, but not for the deep and gravelly monotone of his voice nor for his steady, unwavering gaze, the pale eyes magnified by thick lenses, one somewhat more than the other, so that even when he said something that sounded humorous, you weren't sure how he meant it. He was measuring me, obviously. He also had his brother's ability to make you feel the sole object of his attention. In Claude's case, though, the attention put you decidedly ill-at-ease.

He was smiling up at me.

"Are you finished with me now, Dan?" he said abruptly.

"I'm sorry," I answered, uncomprehending. "I . . ."

"In the book," he said. "I read your sample chapter, the one that sold Lew." Then, turning to the entourage, "Imagine this. They've got me standing on Nina Hardy's threshold, a bunch of flowers in my hand like some dumb kid, and unable to get two words out. In the middle of the night, mind you. Absolutely speechless." He started to laugh, a deep sound and apparently a signal to the others that he meant to poke fun at himself. "Tell them the truth, Nina, was I really that bad?"

"Yes, you were really that bad," Jeannine answered, smiling at him, which brought on generalized laughter.

"Well," he said, with a self-deprecating shrug, "it was a long time ago. Thirty years, give or take. I guess I was a little short on experience." More laughter, at which Rhinelander turned back to me. "Actually, it's thanks to Nina I'm where I am today. Think about it. Thirty years ago, she was our one big star. If she'd stayed around, Olympian could have *potchkied* along, the Bartons on top, and God knows how long this hired hand would have stuck it out. As it was, I left when she did, the company went into the toilet, and the rest . . . well, the rest is history."

I already knew the story in outline, how the Bartons, Sid and Florence, two of the great, if slightly tarnished, legends of Hollywood moguldom, had brought Claude in to rescue Olympian, and how Rhinelander Films, which had been the independent production company he'd set up after he left, had ended up in control of it.

"But here's something I bet she didn't tell you," Claude went on. "Did you know I once asked her to marry me?"

I glanced at Jeannine, whose eyes were on Rhinelander, the corners of her mouth still creased into a smile.

"That was hardly a proposal, Claude," she said to him.

"What do you mean?" he asked, still looking at me. "What wasn't a proposal about it?"

"Well, you were still married for one thing."

"And what about you? You were about to go off and marry that fake count of yours."

Abruptly, although his voice hadn't changed, I realized that he was no longer bantering. His attention had left me and now seemed to be focused on some place behind me and Jeannine. Or no place at all.

"He wasn't fake," Jeannine said calmly.

"I told you you were making a terrible mistake," Rhinelander said in the same deep monotone. "And I was right, wasn't I? That's how it ended. I mean, how much of a marriage can it be when the husband kills himself?"

Jesus. I remember the moment as if it were happening right now, the rest of us standing like stick figures in some frozen tableau, all, that is, except Allen Fryberg, who was mopping at his forehead with a handkerchief still folded into a small square. As far as Rhinelander was concerned, he simply banished us out of his consciousness. Or maybe he didn't give a damn who heard him. Or maybe, just maybe, he liked the idea of having witnesses.

I was watching Jeannine. Erect, poised, the black collar rising behind her head in a guardian position. I knew enough by then of the count's suicide to guess her reaction, but she didn't so much as wince.

"Well, Claude," she said to his profile, her voice evenly modulated, "in that case you can see what you saved yourself from."

Her wit seemed lost on him.

"Suppose I asked you now," he went on implacably, the panes of his glasses reflecting light. "Would you have changed your mind by now?"

"I think you'd have to ask me first," she replied, "and take your chances."

"And let you rub my nose in it again? So Dan could put it in his book?"

"We all have to take our chances, Claude."

"You're right. And we all have to learn from the chances we've taken."

It bothered me—all right, bothered the hell out of me—that I knew nothing about this. Jeannine had never once mentioned his proposing. If, in fact, he had, all I knew was that they'd kept their relationship clandestine, or so she'd said.

Plus there was the baby, Christine. Had she already had Christine then?

The one thing that was clear to me was that she'd just bested him somehow, and maybe not for the first time. It was as though he'd stormed the walls, but they'd held, yet again, and Jeannine looked down on him from her ramparts, unflustered, her new and much younger lover nearby, leaving Claude nothing to do but take his glasses off and massage the corners of his eyes with thumb and forefinger.

"Did you know I was the one who named her?" he went on, his head swiveling back to me. "When she got over here, she was still Jeannine Hardy. Terrible name. Nobody knew how to pronounce it. It sounded like some godawful imported cheese."

"You wanted to call me Jean," Jeannine said.

"And what was so bad about Jean? Jean Hardy. It had a nice sexy ring to it. The only thing wrong was you didn't like it. Jean Harlow was dead, you said. So we came up with Nina. It cost me too. We had everything ready to go with Jean, but you didn't like it. Did you know I had the right, by contract, to call you anything I damn pleased?"

"Ah," Jeannine said, laughing, "but you were too sweet to do that."

Rhinelander laughed too, and stepped back, as though finally acknowledging that the chorus—the lawyers, the financial guys, Fryberg—did, after all, exist. He seemed to have declared his match with Jeannine a draw, and she to accept it, because when they launched into a game of inventing the worst possible marquee name for a movie star, she joined in.

I didn't.

The way I understood it, whatever had gone on between them years ago was still going on. Unfinished business. Claude could press his claim on her, and she would spurn it, yes, but meanwhile I, the appointed author of her confessions, had been left in the dark.

Which was nothing new. I'd been there before. That didn't mean I had to like it. Or like it when, after their conversation had drifted off to other subjects—Jeannine's next picture, Olympian's prospects, the chances of some new tax bill in Washington—Jeannine said:

"Well, Claude, it's been a lovely party, but I think I'd like Daniel to take me home now."

Tell me I'd been there before too. Tell me I knew full well that film stars, particularly women, think they can treat the rest of us like hired help, and often do, and get away with it. Remind me that Jeannine, from the moment I'd joined them in the library, had hardly looked at me, making it perfectly clear how she wanted the scene played. I was her writer, her escort, marginally her consort. And now her chauffeur.

I was watching her say good-by to them one by one, her arm and hand gracefully extended like a ballerina's, and doing my slow burn, when Fryberg spoke up behind me.

"Gee," he said in my ear, "I didn't know you had that many talents."

I turned on him. "What does that mean?"

"Well, chauffeur and writer, to name two. I wonder what else you're good at?"

"Nothing that would interest you, Allen," I answered tersely.

"Oh, I wouldn't be too sure," he said. Then, when I didn't react, he put a conciliatory hand on my shoulder. "Come on, don't hold it against her. Claude has a way of bringing out the worst in people. He knows it too. It's part of his charm."

Our host himself escorted us out into his front hall, walking between me and Jeannine.

"Any time you want to interview me for Nina's book," he said to me, "just give me a call. Better still, call Allen and tell him to set it up."

He turned then to Jeannine, taking both her hands in his and kissing her European-style, first one cheek, then the other. She stooped a little toward him. I missed what he said to her because other guests were pausing now to say good-by to Claude.

Outside, in the soft, milked night air, a long line of limos waited in Rhinelander's driveway, but Jeannine's Mercedes was already there, double-parked, and one of the uniformed footmen preceded us to open the passenger-side door.

"What about Sonny?" I asked her.

"He's old enough to take care of himself," she replied, entering the car without looking at me.

I turned the ignition key, eased the Mercedes into gear.

"Where to, boss?" I glanced over at Jeannine. She was looking straight ahead, her skin taut over her angular bones, chiseled even in the dim light. Imperious, I thought. Her Royal Highness of the Silver Screen.

"I want to go home," she answered softly, not turning her head.

"Really? On such a beautiful night? I'd have thought you'd want to go out on the town. See and be seen. I'll be glad to take you wherever you want to go, ma'am, it won't cost you any extra."

No answer.

We swung through Rhinelander's gates, where a handful of photographers still clustered together, hoping, I guess, for a last shot of the guests. The brilliant grid of lights stretched briefly beneath us across the flat bed of Los Angeles—an uncommon sight these days except in the prospectuses of promoters. Then it disappeared as we headed down toward the freeways, and I could no longer hold myself in.

"Listen," I said, "maybe it's time you found yourself another scribe. I know Sonny or your friend, Claude, could find you plenty of other candidates. And no hard feelings. Younger ones, too, if that's your pleasure. But the way you treated me back there? *I think I'd like Daniel to take me home?* No thanks, Jeannine. Do you realize you never once looked at me the whole time? Not once! I didn't think that's what we were about, but I've been wrong before. The thing is, I don't give a damn how big a star you are, I've worked too hard, too long, to be treated like just another spear carrier."

It was longer than that. Probably angrier.

Undoubtedly, to use her word, more vulgar. I was pissed, and the more I went on and she just sat there, the more so I became.

"What was all that about anyway, some kind of joke?" I said. "That I had to learn from your friend, Claude, that he'd proposed to you? Do you know what that made me feel like?"

No answer from the passenger side.

"What else is there you haven't told me about him and your count? And Christine, too, where does she fit in? You wouldn't tell me who her father is, but I bet your friend, Claude, knows. Doesn't he?"

Silence.

"Well, why the hell don't you get him to write your book for you? *The Nina Hardy Story as told to Claude Rhinelander*. That's big bucks, lady. That's sure-fire at the box office."

I think it was then that I glanced at her, across the sumptuously padded front seat of the Mercedes, and saw the tears rolling onto her cheeks.

"Christ Almighty," was the best I could manage.

The thwock, thwock, thwock of the seams of the California road under our tires, until: "Let me tell you one thing, Daniel," in that cool voice of hers. "Don't you ever, ever again abandon me the way you did tonight."

"What the hell is that supposed to mean?" I shot back.

"The minute we arrived," she said, "you abandoned me. One minute you were with me, I was holding your hand. And the next you were gone."

"*Abandoned* you?" I repeated, trying to remember what had happened. "But what was I supposed to do? Fight my way through the whole Nina Hardy Fan Club? You were surrounded by people; you seemed to know all of them; I didn't know a soul."

"You abandoned me to all those leering little men," she went on as though she hadn't heard me. "You let them paw at me with their eyes. You have no idea what that feels like. It is as though I have their saliva all over me." I saw, or felt, the shiver rippling her shoulders under the collar. "Don't you ever do that to me again, Daniel."

I stopped the car by the side of the road, and we were sitting in the dark, the headlights on.

"Claude, too?" I said. "Is that what you think of him? Is he one of your leering little men?"

She didn't answer.

I pictured him again in my mind: the ugly little figure in the tuxedo, gleaming white shirt, eyes magnified by the glasses, not looking at her but the implacable monotone of his voice seeking her out.

"Did he really propose to you?"

She seemed to hesitate. I swung around in the driver's seat, my arm across the back of the cushion. I could see the outline of her head but not her expression.

"Well, did he?"

"Yes," she said softly.

"I'm sorry, but I don't see what's so terrible about that. You turned him down, didn't you?"

"Yes."

"Then why couldn't you tell me about it?"

Again, the hesitation.

"It was very painful for me, Daniel. Tonight you saw what he is like, a little. How he keeps after me. He always has. He wanted to buy out his wife—she's dead now—and buy me instead. He . . ." She stopped, or seemed to want to stop. Then, faintly, "He liked to hit me."

Oh shit, I thought.

"You mean he liked to beat you up?"

"Yes."

"And you let him?"

No answer.

"Is that why you left Hollywood? To get away from Claude?"

"In a way."

"And married your count?"

No answer.

And yet she'd come back. Why had she come back?

"Hey," I said. "I didn't like what happened tonight any better than you did. But it was your scene, not mine. Where was there room for me? But there's something else we need to get straight. You say your relationship with Claude was painful. I'm sure it was. The son of a bitch acts like he owns you. But for Christ's sake, do you think you're alone? Everybody hurts somewhere. Believe me, everybody. The thing is: if you don't want something in the book, it doesn't go in. No question. If it's too embarrassing, hurts too much, done, out. But if you can't tell me, if you don't trust me enough, then we're in big trouble."

I realized that I'd made the speech before, and more than once. It was my "trust me" message. Usually, though, it came at the beginning of a collaboration, not in the middle. I realized too that the book, the way we'd approached it, was all wrong—the lighthearted, fairy-tale tone, the nostalgia for a time when, supposedly, movies were still magical, and when a young actress with a taste for adventure could still go off to live in a fairy-tale castle with real peasants working in the vineyards, and a chalet in the Tyrolean Alps, and a villa at Cap Ferrat for when the castle was too cold. True enough, maybe. But where was the heat?

"You're right, Daniel," Jeannine said quietly, in the still shadows of the car. "And you are right about what happened tonight. I *was* angry; I *did* try to punish you. Claude, you see, he always . . . But you are not a chauffeur, and you are much more than a writer to me. Much, much more. But now . . . I think all I want now is for you to hold me."

She shifted in the seat and moved toward me. She wanted to lay her head on my shoulder, but the high collar got in the way until she turned sideways. Then she burrowed into me. We kissed, and I wound my fingers through the short hair at her nape, feeling the prickle; feeling, too, her neediness I drove off that way.

Oscar night, in Chinatown.

It would have been nice to say we ended by making wild and passionate love until the sun peeped over the Pasadena hills, only then to fall asleep, exhausted, in each other's arms, et cetera, et cetera. Instead:

"No," Jeannine said gently in the darkness of our bed. "Not now, my love. We have so much time. All I want now is for you to hold me. Please, Daniel. Please hold me."

This I did—her head on my shoulder, her arm across my chest and one leg lifted across mine—until, by the relaxation of her breathing, I knew she'd fallen asleep. Then I remember the ache coming slowly over me, in me, starting with a poignant pain which I mistook at first for the woes of adolescence but which spread past, in time as well as location, into a deeper and more generalized yearning. It welled in my chest; it seared my lungs, my throat. Is there any ache more powerful for the male, I wonder, any longing more acute, any love more all-consuming, than what we feel, impossibly, recklessly, in advance of our own capacity, when we are small and women beckon, out of reach, lips half-parted?

It came to me again that night, rekindled across the years in all its intensity, all that fevered, wondrously hopeless longing which, when I was seven, eight, nine, had fixed now on this object, now on that— once a heavily perfumed teacher in school, once a dark-haired little girl my own age who wore lipstick and skirts shorter than the rest, but, above all, on one shadowy face with the parted lips which loomed above me, unattainable, in the darkness of the theater.

Unattainable?

My God, I was actually holding her in my arms.

I must only have missed the sunrise by a little. The phone was ringing. I heard it, I think, and fell back to sleep. Moments later, Jeannine was leaning over me, face pale in the dim light, eyes small and puffed and encircled by worry.

"It's Tim," she said. "He's in some hospital in Malibu. He says the police took him there. He says he has no idea how he got to Malibu. Daniel, please wake up, I need for you to go. If I go, it will be all over the media. I have to start calling now, to keep it out. Oh please, Daniel," shaking my shoulder, "for God's sake, wake up."

I woke up, and went.

Chapter Nine

Y OU SHOULD HAVE seen the door," Sonny said, but if he was grinning his lopsided grin, it was hidden by bandages. Apparently he'd fractured two ribs, broken his nose, torn open his scalp, and his eyes were almost closed in a perpetual squint. Both hands were bandaged, as were his forearms above the wrists. It hurt him to talk that first day, and his words came out in throaty wheezes.

"Jesus, Christ," I repeated. "It's a good thing Jeannine isn't here to see this. Are you in a lot of pain?"

"Only when I laugh," he said. "For God's sake, don't make me laugh."

"What the hell happened?"

It came out little by little, none of it altogether convincing. He said he'd passed out at Rhinelander's. When he came to, he hitchhiked a ride with somebody to Santa Monica. Why Santa Monica? I asked. He didn't know. He supposed that was where the people in the car were going. He remembered being in some bar there, maybe more than one. Alone, he said, at first. Later on, he remembered that there'd been some other people, but nobody he knew. Then he'd gone for a walk on the beach. That is, he'd been headed for the beach. He'd had it in mind that a swim would clear his head. But the next thing he knew, they were scraping him off the pavement in Malibu. Who? Some CHPs. Some CHPs had found him, in that little town center after you pass the fancy beachfront houses.

How had he gotten from Santa Monica to Malibu? He had no idea. And what had happened to his shoes, his socks, his jacket? No idea.

When they'd found him, he'd been down to his undershirt and trousers. With suspenders. No cummerbund. No shoes, no socks. No money, keys, wallet.

Maybe he'd left his clothes on the beach in Santa Monica, how the hell was he supposed to know?

But if he'd left his clothes on the beach in Santa Monica, how had he gotten fifteen miles up the coast to Malibu?

He had no idea.

As far as I know, neither the police nor the media got any farther than Sonny's version. Probably somebody checked the bars and night spots up and down the coast, but nobody admitted to having seen him. Thanks to Jeannine, the story got less media attention than might have been expected, and while there must have been a few people who knew what had really happened, I wasn't one of them.

I saw him twice more in the hospital. The first time was to bring him cigarettes, a bottle of Dewar's, the *Daily Racing Form* and a change of clothes. He was on his feet by then, in hospital slippers, his left hand in a cast and some sort of body bandage strapped around his chest, which made him itch. He was still hurting, he said. There were flowers in his room, but as far as I know I was the only one who'd actually visited him, other than his attorney and the Malibu police. Maybe it was that which kept his normal pugnacity down to an occasional jab, because I brought a tape recorder with me and, a little to my surprise, got him talking about Jeannine, and Jeannine and himself.

She was, he thought, the only woman he'd ever truly loved, and that their friendship had lasted so long was probably because, when he himself had asked her to marry him, a long time ago, she'd turned him down. Marriage, he'd decided after three shots at it, was the great wrecker of good relationships.

"The thing I don't get, though," I said, "is that when I'm not here, you always seem to be around, but the minute I show up, you're gone, vanished."

"Well, that's easy, Danny Boy. You're the lover-in-residence, aren't you? It wouldn't be seemly, would it, for me to be hanging around?"

"Yes, but what about when I'm not here?"

"That's Jeannine's doing," he said. "She's one of those people who can't stand being alone for long. But no offense, Danny," with a cracked grin, "I'm hardly what you'd call a rival."

True enough, I thought. At the same time, though, he seemed to be saying that lovers-in-residence came and went, and that there were ways I could never rival him. Longevity, at the least.

"What about Claude Rhinelander?" I asked him.

"What about him? Other than that he's the kind of runt who makes you feel like breaking his glasses?"

"For one thing," I said, trying a shot in the dark, "could he be Christine's father?"

He started to laugh, then caught himself. "Shit, I hope not. At least for Christine's sake. What leads you to that depressing theory?"

"Her relationship with Claude. Jeannine's, I mean." I told him a little about the scene I'd witnessed, and he'd missed, at the Oscar night party. About Claude beating up on her, and her taking it. And why, if it was so painful for her—and surely she must have known what to expect—had she insisted on our going?

"That's complicated stuff," Sonny agreed, but when I pushed him on it, all he said was, "You're the writer, Danny Boy, not me. If you ever figure out the answer, I hope you'll let me know."

I pushed him on the paternity question, but he shrugged in ignorance, saying only that there'd been plenty of candidates at the time.

"Why has she always insisted on keeping it a secret?"

"What does she say?"

"That she wanted a baby, not a husband."

"That's always been the party line."

"But it happened thirty years ago," I said.

"Thirty-two," he corrected. "I think Christine's thirty-two now."

"Okay, thirty-two. How could Jeannine still feel the same way?"

He shrugged again. "I've always figured it was because it embarrassed her. Who the man was."

"If she knows."

"If she knows."

He told me more about Jeannine's daughter than Jeannine had. Or different things. I'd seen little of Christine to that point—she had her own place in Westwood—but according to Sonny, she'd been part of her mother's baggage since she was a baby, and still was. To Christine's misfortune, he thought. It wasn't that she was a bad kid, it was just that she couldn't blow her nose without asking Jeannine's permission first. She'd had a brief run at acting—not untalented, he thought, but it hadn't led anywhere—and she'd had any number of jobs. She was always taking courses somewhere. She'd had a rough trip with drugs at one point. No steady men that he knew of. A couple of times, Jeannine had had to throw her out of the house, but she'd always come back. There'd be a crisis, and the next thing you knew, she'd be back.

"Her biggest problem," Sonny said, "and it's nobody's fault, is that she looks so much like momma. It was worse before she let her hair grow. People would say, 'Isn't it cute, she looks just like Nina,' and I guess it was cute, when she was a teenager. But they still say it, and Christine's smart enough to know that there's only one Jeannine."

The next time I saw him was when I went with Jeannine to pick him up, the morning he was released from the hospital. I was going back to New York later that day, after one last meeting of my own, and Jeannine was to fly to Vancouver for some preproduction work on her new picture. She'd wanted me to come with her. I'd declined. It was a good time, I said, for me to start to put on paper some of the things we'd talked about, and creature of habit, I worked better in my barn. Actually, I needed some time to myself. Since Oscar night an easy intimacy had developed between us, and I found that I liked it, liked it a lot in fact, a realization that spooked the hell out of me.

At the last minute, she tried to duck out of going with me to get Sonny. This time it wasn't the publicity. She admitted finally that she was afraid of seeing him that way. What way? I asked. She didn't know. Maimed, or bloody, or covered in bandages, she couldn't bear it. Actually he was none of the above. A little pale around the gills, maybe, and the cast still on his hand and angry red marks on his forearms where he'd been bandaged before and the hairs had been shaved, but reduced evidence elsewhere of the beating he'd taken. When I brought him out the main entrance of the hospital, where Jeannine was waiting by the car, he hit his familiar lumbering stride.

Jeannine had tears in her eyes when she put her arms around his neck.

"Poor Tim. Does it hurt you terribly?"

"Only when I laugh, honey," he answered, beaming down at her. "Or when I see your pretty eyes again."

I drove them back to Pasadena. Sonny had wanted to go to his Topanga Canyon place, but Jeannine wouldn't hear of it. He'd be better taken care of in Pasadena while she was away. If they had any discussion of what had actually happened to him, it took place after I was gone.

Then it was time for Jeannine and me to say good-by. I'd hired a car and driver to take me first to my appointment, then to the airport.

Why is it that I remember them so vividly—all our good-bys, all our hellos? This time, Jeannine stands in the driveway not far from my waiting car, sunglasses on and wearing a wide-brimmed natural straw hat, in the stark light of a burning midday sun. She has on sandals, white pants that cling tightly to her calves above the ankles, a blousy white shirt with a round neck cutting across her shoulder bones. Her hands are on my shoulders. There is a slight quiver on her lips.

"I can't stand for you to go, Daniel. Every time you leave, I think something terrible is going to happen."

"I'll be back," I said.

"I know you'll be back, but something terrible could happen in between."

"Nothing terrible will happen. You're just jumpy because of Tim. And Vancouver. And because I'm going to see Claude."

My appointment was an interview with Claude Rhinelander, arranged, as he'd suggested, through Allen Fryberg.

"No," she said. "None of those. I'm jumpy because of you."

"There's no need for that."

"No? When you are going off to a beautiful wife? Who is many years younger than I am?"

Her words jolted me. She had taken her sunglasses off, and her eyes, large and intense, fixed mine. This was the first time she'd ever referred directly to her age, the first certainly in comparison with the Fawn.

"Well, go then," she said, her voice uncommonly strained. "I still don't see why you can't go to Claude and then meet me at the airport and we could fly to Vancouver together. But you can't. You can't, you can't."

She started to turn away.

"I want to know everything Claude says," she went on, in profile. "Will you remember to call me after? . . . Oh, my God, but you can't, Daniel! You won't be able to! I won't be here myself!"

This last realization seemed to upset her more than anything. She glanced wildly at me, then away, but I saw that she'd started to cry.

"Never mind," she said, shaking her head when I reached toward her. "You'll call me tonight, in Vancouver."

"I promise I will."

"No matter how late, I don't care."

"I promise."

"Do you have the number?"

"You gave it to me yourself."

"How do I know you still have it?"

"Jeannine, for God's sake . . ."

"Show it to me."

It was crazy that she was that distraught, but she was, and there was nothing for me to do but fish the electronic address book out of my briefcase, which was already in the back seat of the car. I punched in the code I'd used, and a moment later the digits of the phone number flashed on the screen.

"Good," she said. "And you will call me tonight." She kissed me quickly, under her straw hat, her lips barely brushing mine. "Tell me you love me, Daniel. I need to hear it."

Another first.

I pulled her into my arms, kissed her less quickly, her mouth warm against mine, and told her that I loved her. I meant it and, more, realized how much I wanted her to know I meant it. But she struggled free, her eyes wet, and, without another word, went back into the house.

CLAUDE RHINELANDER'S OFFICE was in a bungalow-type building on the studio lot. Apparently Lana Turner had once used it, and Victor Mature, and, last but not least, Nina Hardy. Although most of Claude's executives worked in the Olympian Tower, a glass-and-steel construction which Claude had built a few years ago, he'd stayed on in the bungalow. It gave him a hands-on feeling, he said, a reminder that the business was still about what happened on the lot, not in some corporate boardroom. Besides, he knew where everything was in the bungalow. If he ever let them move him, he wouldn't be able to find a damn thing.

The bungalow, from what I saw of it, also contained a bedroom with bath, a small conference room with kitchenette, Fryberg's office, and a large reception area which also housed the secretaries, all of it furnished in French country antiques, of which Claude's late wife, I was told, had been an avid collector. Except for Claude's own office, the overall effect was of some country cottage, uprooted intact and transplanted, like London Bridge, into southern California. Claude's office had been designed to have the same look, but every available inch of surface was piled high with papers: contracts, scripts, proposals, reports.

The first thing he said to me, when Fryberg ushered me in, was that he'd blocked out the whole afternoon for me, as much time as I wanted. Nina Hardy was his favorite subject, and one of the stacks on his desk turned out to be memorabilia he'd been gathering for me: copies of photos from the 1950s, of her first contract, of newspaper clippings, memos he'd written, even a few notes she'd written him.

Without thinking, I decided to take a different tack. I got my tape recorder from my briefcase and set it up, less for my own edification than because I smelled a set piece: the corporate leader seated calmly at his desk; the stack of memorabilia at his elbow; the secretary serving espresso in fine china demitasse cups; even the sub-honcho (Fryberg) in attendance, to act as . . . what? a witness in case I misquoted him?

It worked, in a way. After all, what titan of industry doesn't wax eloquent when asked to hold forth about his own company? Of course, as he was quick to point out, he didn't own Olympian. He only served at the pleasure of the board of directors, which was voted in by the stockholders. Yes, Rhinelander Films owned a major block of OCI shares, but that was Rhinelander Films? not Claude Rhinelander. But who, then, owned Rhinelander Films? Ah, he said, smiling, that was privileged information. Rhinelander Films was a private company. Of course, since he was among friends, yes, he did own a piece of it. And, yes, I was right, so did his brother. His kid brother, he reminded me. And there were other private investors, friends of his.

The information I had, via Leo Castagni, was that Claude's share was smaller than might be imagined. Allegedly, at the time of the takeover, he'd had to mortgage Rhinelander Films heavily to raise cash. But what he might have held back, in terms of voting rights, buyback options and the like, nobody knew, including, it seemed, the people who worked for him.

"Let me ask you something, Dan," Rhinelander said, "and Allen, you keep quiet." Fryberg, I noticed, hadn't said a word since we'd entered the office. "What business would you say we were in?"

"The movie business," I answered.

He shook his head disparagingly.

"You just failed the test," he said. "Think about it. We're not in the movie business. Or the television business or communications or information or entertainment or any of those fancy words. We're not in the production business or the distribution business or the selling business either."

I didn't get his point, and he seemed to enjoy that.

"I'll tell you what business we're in," he said in his monotone, gazing directly at me so that his eyes were magnified, one more so than the other. "We're in the business of making money." He paused, as though to let the message sink in. "That's what we're here for. That's *all* we're here for. To make money. That's what I keep trying to drum into my executives. Right, Allen?"

"I've heard you say it before, Claude," Fryberg replied in a wry tone.

"But you haven't understood it," Rhinelander retorted without turning his head. "And how do you make money? You make it by buying cheap and selling dear. You make it by exploiting what you already own. You make it by ideas.

"I don't need all these high-priced executives, like Allen Fryberg, to tell me how to make pictures. I already know that. And I don't need three floors of accountants—three floors, mind you—to tell me whether we're making or losing money. You give me the first weekend's receipts on any picture and I'll tell you how much it'll gross, within pennies. You give me the percentages of the pertinent contracts, on a single sheet of paper, and I'll tell you how much we're going to be able to skim off the top. The point is, it doesn't matter whether we're making movies, or books and magazines like my brother. It could be anything. It's about ideas. When's the last time you had a fresh idea, Allen?"

All this in the same deep, scarcely inflected monotone. All this, including the last question, without so much as turning his head.

"Nothing recently, Claude," Fryberg said.

"And how do you think you're going to get them if you spend the afternoon listening to an old fart making speeches you've already heard a thousand times? Don't you have anything better to do?"

One of the small ways Rhinelander wielded his power, I'd already noticed, was by talking to people without looking at them. I saw Fryberg, his round face now florid and perspiring, jump at the remarks. He seemed to swallow some retort that came to mind, then sighed, stood up, asked me to stop by before I left, and walked out of the office.

The performance, I thought, might well have been for my benefit. But once Fryberg was gone, Claude said, "It never hurts to shake up the troops. We all need it. Present company included."

He fixed me again, his eyes magnified, and his short white hair bristling in the light.

"But this isn't what you came for. Let's get into it now. Ask me anything."

Again, he'd somehow caught me up short. I'd prepared some questions on a yellow pad, which I'd taken out of my briefcase, but now I put it aside.

"What's the unfinished business between you and Jeannine all about?" I asked.

"What unfinished business?"

"The other night—at your party, when you were talking about having proposed to her once, I got the impression you had a lot else on your mind. Unfinished business. I—"

"Nothing complicated about it," he interrupted. "And no unfinished business. She should have married me a long time ago, that's all."

"Why?"

The question seemed to take him by surprise. He considered it, his eyes boring straight ahead. The expression, I thought, was one of hostility. At least he had every reason to *be* hostile, being questioned by the lover-in-residence of the woman who'd once turned him down, and would again if he asked. But maybe it was just his normal expression, when he was thinking.

"Nina's a great actress," he said finally. "Or would have been. Should have been. If she hadn't wrecked her career."

"Why do you always call her Nina, by the way?"

"Why? Because that's her name."

"But everybody who knows her calls her Jeannine."

"Everybody? You ask people out there what her name is," with a gesture, "they'll tell you Nina Hardy. That's good enough for me."

There was another reason, I thought: he, himself, had named her—but I said nothing about that.

"How would you say she'd wrecked her career?" I asked.

"By marrying that fake count. By quitting Hollywood when she did."

"You seem to think she had something to do with her husband killing himself."

"Where'd you get that idea?"

"You said it yourself the other night." Here I did refer to my notes. "You said, 'How much of a marriage can it be when the husband kills himself?' "

He shrugged, tight-lipped.

"How do I know what happened? I wasn't there, was I? She once told me neurasthenia ran in the family, that a couple of other male members had committed suicide. Bunch of degenerates, if you ask me. Degenerate royalty, that's what the Austrians are about. What do you expect from a bunch of people who opened their legs wide to the Nazis?"

In an odd way, he'd corroborated what Jeannine had described to me. Her husband—incredibly handsome in a Kurt Jurgens kind of way, at least to judge from photographs—had been distantly related to the English royal family. He'd loved her desperately, she'd said. But there was the history of suicide, and when his moodiness deepened, there was nothing she, or a battery of psychiatrists, could do to stop it.

Rhinelander also corroborated what had happened after the count's death.

"His family treated her like a piece of shit," he said. "They threw her and the baby out. All she got was the Riviera place, and she even had to buy that from them. By the time she came back here some years later, she didn't have a nickel to her name."

This last was news to me.

"What about the movies she made in Italy? I assume she didn't work for nothing."

He laughed harshly. "What do I know? The big-shot producers over there, they pay you in pasta anyway."

In her first years back, I knew she'd had trouble getting work, other than some cameo roles on television. Still, as I pointed out to him, she hadn't been exactly destitute. There was the house in Pasadena, and she'd found the money for *Eva's Story*, hadn't she? Which Rhinelander, in his wisdom, had turned down.

He stared at me for a moment. Again I couldn't read the expression, other than that generalized hostility.

"Is this for the record?" he asked, motioning toward my tape recorder.

"It doesn't have to be. However you want it."

"Off the record," he said. "Nina likes to tell it her way, that's fine with me. But the truth is, if it'd been up to her and Harry Brea, they'd still be out on the street, looking for the money. I got it for them. Some of it was mine. Yes, I thought it was a stupid picture. Who wanted to see a picture about some silent film star? I didn't think it had a snowball's chance in hell, but she was in love with the schmuck. So what do I know? If I knew what the public wanted, I'd be a fucking genius. As it turned out, I made a lot of money on it."

Although Jeannine later claimed she'd never been in love with Brea, yes, she had put her own money in the film. But it hadn't been enough, and, yes, she'd gone, hat in hand, to Claude. She'd hated it, she said, but they'd been desperate. And hearing the way he told it now, hearing his smugness—not in the steady monotone of his voice but in the message he nevertheless conveyed that he was *always* right, *always* on top, *always* the proprietor of Nina Hardy behind the scenes, whether she wanted it or not—I couldn't hold it against her that she'd lied to me.

There was more of this to come.

First, though, I took my shot in the dark.

"Christine?" He frowned, as if puzzled. "You mean her daughter?"

"That's right. Christine Hardy."

"What about her?"

"You know her, don't you?"

"I used to. Not anymore."

"Would you say she'd also wrecked Jeannine's career? I mean, Jeannine's having a baby?"

"It didn't help, but even actresses are women, and nobody's figured out how to stop women from having babies."

"What about Christine's father?" I asked, watching his face for a reaction.

"What about him?" he answered, not so much as blinking an eye. "As far as I know, nobody knows who it was."

"But at the time?" I said. "At the time, you must have been a little curious. You were in love with Jeannine, weren't you?"

At the most, there was a slight tightening at the mouth. Maybe not even that.

"You can't stop women from having babies," he repeated. "She wanted a baby, she had a baby. I called it Nina's Folly."

"There are people who think you were the father," I said.

"What people?"

"Oh, people."

"And they'd be in a position to know, would they?"

"Are they right or wrong?" I asked.

"What did Nina tell you?"

"I think what she told me should remain between us," I said.

"Suit yourself," he answered.

"And that's all you've got to say about it?"

"That's all I've got to say about it. Now," nodding toward my pad, "what other cockamamie questions do you have there?"

I hesitated. In fact, I had a lot, none of them cockamamie, and probably I would kick myself later for having blown the chance, but he'd succeeded by then in blunting my curiosity. Maybe that was a hallmark of his power, too, that he made you want to be anywhere except in his presence, one on one.

"Then here's one for you," he said. "When am I going to see some more of the book?"

I looked at him, disconcerted.

"Well, not till it's finished, I guess. That's what the contract calls for. Even then, I submit it to the publishers first. Of course, if it's all right with them, I'd be—"

"No," he interrupted, shaking his head, "you'll submit it to me first."

I didn't understand. He knew I wouldn't, of course, expected it.

"This is off the record, too," he said, "but I own the book. I put up the money."

It was my turn to be jolted, but I'd be damned if I'd let him see it. I thought quickly about the contract. Signed by the Rhinelander Publishing Group, signed—I couldn't remember, but possibly by Lew himself.

"I didn't know you were in the publishing business," I said.

"Sometimes I find myself in lots of businesses I don't want to be in. Usually where my kid brother is concerned. But in this case, I simply put up the money."

"I don't get it," I said. "I thought you were against Jeannine doing the book in the first place."

"I was."

"Then why . . . ?"

"Lew thought it was too much money. He didn't want it at the price. Now there's an interesting switch for you. Usually I'm in the business of making money, he's in the business of spending it."

"There were a couple of other publishers not far behind in the bidding," I said.

"So I heard. Crazy money, Lew said. Just because they were crazy, it didn't mean he had to be. So I put my own cash on the table."

I couldn't believe it. On the other hand, I couldn't not believe it. My mind raced over what had happened. No wonder Lew had been so nonchalant at that lunch. He hadn't given a damn, one way or the other.

"You mean you put up the cash, even though you didn't want the book to happen?"

"Even though I didn't want the book to happen."

"Why were you against her doing it?"

"What did she tell you?"

"She said you wouldn't want the publicity. You knew you'd be in the book, and you were against publicity of any kind."

"That wasn't it. I don't read what they write about me anyway. But I didn't want her to get herself hurt."

"Why would doing a book hurt her?"

He simply stared at me, as though the answer was too self-evident to need saying.

"So even though you were against it," I said, "you still made Lew buy it, or buy it for you."

"That's right. Once I saw she was going ahead with it, against my advice, do you really think I'd let anybody else publish Nina Hardy's book?"

There was that look I'd seen before, Oscar night, when he'd seemed to focus on some point between and beyond me and Jeannine— dogged, implacable, controlling.

"Does she know this?" I asked him.

"No. Not from me anyway."

"Then why are you telling me?"

"Because I thought you'd like to be the one to pass it on to her."

The son of a bitch pulls all the levers, I thought. And always in the same monotone, boring in on you whether you wanted to hear it or not.

"You really do want to own her, don't you," I said angrily. "Even after all this time."

He laughed. "*Own* her?" he repeated. "I'd have thought you'd have found that out already, a smart and experienced fellow like you. Nobody owns Nina Hardy." There was an unmistakable edge to his voice now, the animus out in the open, and so was the clear message that he'd been there before me and would be after.

He didn't have to say anything else, but I guess he couldn't resist. "Do you know what's going to happen to you? She'll suck you dry. And when she's done, finished? Out with you. So long, Dan, and thanks for the memories. Do you think you're the first ambitious young starfucker to show up on her doorstep?"

"No," I said. "You, for one, were there a long time before me."

No comment. Then: "You're a puppy dog, Dan," he said, "and you can put this on the record if you want. That's what she's into right now, puppy dogs with big cocks. She's getting older, and it's scaring the shit out of her; and who can blame her for that? But the best advice I can give you is: Enjoy it while it lasts."

What was it Fryberg had said—*Claude has a way of bringing out the worst in people, it's part of his charm?*

Amen.

And no further questions.

Stunned, I ran smack into Fryberg outside Claude's office. Maybe he'd been waiting for me. Maybe he'd been listening in, or trying to. In any case, he walked me outside into the heat and sudden sunlight, and around the corner of the building to the shaded parking area where my driver was dozing in the front seat.

"How'd it go?" Fryberg said, chuckling. "You look like you'd just sat through a whole Command Performance with your fly open."

"Pretty much like that," I said, not wanting to go into details.

"And you got him on a good day."

"How come you work for him?"

"Sheer masochism," he said cheerfully. "Nothing that six years on the couch shouldn't fix, except that I'm into the tenth. As whipping boys go, I'm well paid. Apropos, I heard your friend, Timmy Corral, has been at it again."

"At what again?"

Timmy? I thought vaguely.

"What did he run into this time? A brick wall? A door?"

I didn't get it. What did Timmy—Sonny—have to do with anything? Fryberg nudged me.

"You ought to tell him to lay off trade," he said. "He's too old for it. One of these days, he's going to get himself killed."

By this time we'd reached the car, and the driver, up and awake, was holding the rear door open for me.

"I don't know what you're talking about," I said.

But I did know. Incredulous, I glanced back at Fryberg as I got into the car.

"You disappoint me, Danny." Stooping, he grinned in at me. "It's a pretty well kept secret, but I didn't think that well kept. Have a good trip anyhow." At which he closed my door himself, stood back, and still grinning, waved me off.

Chapter Ten

T HE FISH WAS undulating in my stomach as soon as I boarded the plane at LAX, late that afternoon. Old story. I've always had trouble with transitions, even as a kid when my mother shipped me off, summers, to an aunt and uncle who had a small house on the Upper Peninsula. This was presumably a good thing—at least it served her and my stepfather—but I still had to get there, changing trains in Chicago, with my suitcase and lunch in a paper bag, and I had ample time, while the telephone poles flashed by the train windows, to experience the fish.

The same on the plane to New York. I'd just told the woman of my dreams that I loved her, but she was on her way to Vancouver while I was thirty-five thousand feet up in the air, heading east across the continent—to my wife of eight years. And there was Claude Rhinelander, who was out to own us all, and Claude Rhinelander's "kid brother," who'd been nothing but Claude's messenger all along.

Lew had put up $3.4 million—"crazy money"—but if Claude was to be believed, not a penny of it was his. The crazy money was Claude's.

Why? Because he couldn't stand the idea of anyone else owning a piece of Nina Hardy? Yes, undoubtedly. But also because he wanted control.

That was where I came in. True, I'd been Jeannine's choice, but even before they knew that, Lew had been on my trail. After all, hadn't I been burned once before—the Farran "fiasco," he'd called it—and wasn't I the professional, "experienced in dealing with a great actress's natural reticence?" But it wasn't that Jeannine didn't want to talk about certain things. It was *Claude* who was afraid of what she would talk about.

I was to be their insurance.

I wondered if they'd counted on my falling in love with her.

AT THIRTY-FIVE THOUSAND feet, where the air is thin, there are lots of reasons to feel the fish in your stomach. And one of them was waiting for me when I got home.

It was late, the house was in darkness. No Fawn, but a note from her via Mary Murphy, the female half of our Irish couple.

Mrs. Springer called. Decided to spend night in city. She will call tomorrow.

"WHY ARE YOU so angry?" asked the Fawn.

This wasn't the first thing she said. There had been an exchange of niceties:

How was California? Fine.

How's the book coming? It's okay.

How's Nina? She's gone off to do a preproduction on her new film.

Is that why you're home? I have work to do. I work better here.

Who'd you see? Nobody in particular.

Nobody? Well, Eastwood, Fonda, Loretta Young, the Douglases, Goldie Hawn, Peck . . .

At least I still had the ability to make her laugh. "My God!" she said. "Where were you?"

"At a party. Claude Rhinelander's party. Oscar night."

"That's Lew's brother, the one in Hollywood?"

"That's Lew's brother, the one in Hollywood."

"All right," she said, "what the hell's eating you?"

"Nothing's eating me."

"No? You have all the affect of an empty box. Don't you even want to know what I've been doing?"

We were sitting in our living room. This was late the next afternoon. At least I was still sitting at this point, with a Jim Beam on the rocks. I'd called Jeannine in the morning, her time, but she'd already left the hotel. I'd called Tinker, who assured me that as long as Rhinelander Publishing fulfilled the publisher's obligations in the contract, where

Lew had actually gotten the cash was no concern of ours. Still, she must have called him, or maybe Jenny Bergler, because Jenny Bergler called me. Of course they were still very excited about Nina's book. When was I going to show them something? She wanted to see me soonest.

The Fawn had just driven up from the city. Her cheeks were still pink from the April wind. She was wearing jeans tucked into leather boots and an oversized sweatshirt, white with some kind of Japanese calligraphy painted on it. Her hair was pinned up in swirls, and there was an air of exhilaration, triumph even, about her as though she had life at her fingertips.

Not to say clay under her nails.

How we ended up in the living room I have no idea. We seldom used it, maybe that was why. Or maybe because of the wall-to-wall carpeting, pearl-gray with a tight nap. The Fawn enjoyed the feel of the carpet under bare feet. She'd taken her boots off, and I remember her feet as she paced. Even her feet were beautiful, long, narrow, with high arches and long, even toes tripping at the nap.

"It doesn't matter," the Fawn said. "If you don't care, you don't care."

"I didn't say I didn't care. I know what you've been doing."

"Oh yes? Then tell me. What have I been doing?"

"You're into sculpture. I assume you've been doing your sculpture."

"That's right. I've been *doing* my sculpture. But what's your opinion of that? Do you think I'm any good?"

"I'm the wrong person to ask," I said. "I don't know a lot about it."

"Then why don't you learn, for God's sake? You're not stupid, why don't you *learn?*"

Her movements had become restless, and as she paced, she worked her hair with her hands, winding it around her fingers, unpinning, pinning. In a more clinical, dispassionate mood, I'd have enjoyed the spectacle of it, her tawny eyes now narrowed to accompany her tightening lips, now wide and flashing. But all I understood, or half-understood, was that she was determined to get at me; that for some reason—probably because she'd prepared herself—it had to be now, and I figured therefore that sooner or later she'd succeed.

"If it's that important to you," I said, "why don't you teach me?"

This seemed to take her by surprise.

"Teach you?" she said. "Is that what you want me to do? *Teach* you?"

I remember glancing at the mantelpiece. Wrong room, though. Jason's bust was next door. Maybe Lew's would be here, once it was done.

"Listen, Dan," the Fawn said. "I've been saying it so long, I can't stand to hear it again, but we've got to talk. I think we'd better talk now. Right now. This minute. I don't think it can wait any longer."

"That's fine with me," I said. "In fact, I think that's what we're doing. What else do you want to talk about?"

I wasn't trying to bait her, so help me.

"There. Right there, did you hear yourself? 'What else do you want to talk about?' "—doing a pretty fair job of mimicking me. "As though nothing's wrong, everything's fine. Well, I'll tell you what I want to talk about. I want to talk about why you're so *angry*."

"Angry? *I'm* not angry. If anybody's—"

"Don't tell me you're not angry. Just listen to your voice."

"I'm sorry, you're the one who's doing the shouting. This is my voice. It's the only—"

"It's *not* your voice. You sound like you're talking out of a box. Mechanical. A recorded announcement. For God's sake, that's not *you!* Where's the *you?*"

"I'm just going along," I said. "Just doing my work."

"Yes," she said acidly. "And enjoying it, too, from what I hear."

"What does that mean?"

"Just what I said. And it sounds like you're really *into* it too." Sarcasm, however, wasn't her forte, meaning that she couldn't leave the innuendo alone. "It must be great, getting paid a million dollars to sleep in a movie star's bed. Even when she's a dozen years older than you."

"Where'd you hear that?"

"What difference does it make?"

"A lot of difference."

"Are you denying it?"

"Where do you want me to sleep when I'm out there? A Ramada Inn?"

"Are you fucking her?"

"Who told you I was?"

"Never mind! *Are* you?"

"Your friend, Lew," I said. Who else? "He told you."

She laughed at that, a scoffing sound, and tossed her head, but she didn't deny it either.

"And while we're at it," I said, "let's talk about age differences between lovers."

She stopped laughing.

"No," she said. "Not this time, Dan. I'm not going to let you turn this conversation into something else. We're talking about *you*. Now: Why are you so angry?"

"Is that you talking? Or your shrink?"

This was no idle question. She'd been going again—to a Sullivanian, she'd announced. I knew he had his office on East 85th Street and charged her (me) $125 a pop. Forty "Fawn-hours" a week worked out to $5000, and if you figured a forty-four-week year (these guys take long vacations), that meant $220,000 a year gross—not a fortune, maybe, but not bad for asking women why their husbands were so angry.

"While we're on the subject," I said, looking up at her, "why would a woman leave her diaphragm case out—her empty diaphragm case— in plain view? Where her husband was sure to see it? Did you ask your shrink about that?"

She was standing in front of me, a few paces away, arms akimbo. She smiled briefly.

"I'm surprised you even noticed," she said.

Then she shook her head, slowly, side to side.

"It won't work, Dan," she went on. "Not this time. I know you too well. For once, you're going to answer one question of mine directly. Why are you so angry?"

The exhilaration I'd noticed earlier had given way to something else. Defiance, maybe. Her chin jutted, her head was tilted back stiffly. Her eyes, though—always a giveaway where the Fawn was concerned—had a timorous look, as though she was on the verge of losing, and knew it.

"Let's chalk it up to the diaphragm," I said.

She shook her head again. "No. Let's not."

She waited. I reached for a cigarette, lit it.

"Since when are you smoking again?"

"Since just now," I said.

I stood up, glass in hand. I think I had it in mind to get another drink.

"If you're not angry," the Fawn said shrilly behind me, "if you haven't always been angry, then why do you have to beat me up? Why do you always have to find a way to put me on the defensive, and then you beat me up, and that excites you. Is that all that excites you?"

I had no way of answering a question like that. I turned on her, and even as she stood her ground, she seemed to recoil with her head, her shoulders and arms, as though she expected me to hit her.

"Well?" she taunted. "Why *is* that? Why do you only come after rough sex? Do you think that's normal? Is that the basis of a healthy relationship? Come on, Dan, you're the writer, you're supposed to know about these things. If it's not because you're angry, what the hell is it?"

I felt myself starting to lose it.

"That's a self-fulfilling prophecy," I blurted out.

"I don't know what you're talking about. What's a self-fulfilling prophecy?"

"That I'm angry. You're damn right I'm angry now!"

"Well, then, what are you waiting for? Aren't you going to hit me?"

She was facing me awkwardly, some kind of challenge, her fingers balled into stiff fists. I saw her through a hot blur, a sudden jagged veil of dizziness, like the dots that dance on a picture when you look too close.

As far as I knew, our "rough sex" had always been a two-way street. And went way back, to the beginning.

It wasn't in me to hit her.

"Funny," I said, "but I always thought it took two to dance that particular tango."

"Maybe it used to. But it doesn't anymore."

"Nice of you to tell me, now that you've found out."

"I haven't just found out. I've been trying to tell you. You haven't been listening."

"Which is another of your delusions: that I haven't been listening."

"Another one of my *delusions?*"

I'd used the wrong word—or the right one. The trigger word, in any case. She stormed at me then, about exactly who was deluded and what about, ten years' worth of grievances unleashed at once, until I turned in my jumble of dots, the air busy with them like insects. Turned, I guess, to get rid of the dots and, through them, the sight of the tears welling big in her outraged eyes.

And walked away.

"Go on!" she was shouting at me, at my back. "Go hide in your fucking barn. But you can't hide forever!"

IT HAPPENED SO fast.

I did go to the barn, but not to stick around. Instead, I ended up spending that night at my Ivy League club in the city. It was a first for me, and I've no idea why I went there. I used to use the place during the day once in a while, but at night, the all-male smattering of alums, young and old, who clustered at the bar amid the memorabilia, only reminded me how out of it I'd felt, two decades before, at dear old alma mater.

At four in the morning, eastern time, I called Jeannine.

Her voice was groggy from the pills I knew she took, but she said she was still awake.

"I haven't been able to sleep, Daniel," she said. "Not since I got here. I called and called tonight—the two numbers—but all I got was your stupid machine and the other line was busy for hours. I even called the operator. I said it was an emergency. Then there was some woman—was that your wife?—but all she would say was that you were out."

"I'm all right," I said. "I'm in New York."

"I have had this terrible feeling. Something happened to you, I knew it. You promised to call, you didn't call. I was sure there'd been an accident, a car crash. You don't know what it's been like for me."

"Jeannine, I'm all right," I repeated. "I did try to call."

"Once," she said. "There was only one message."

I apologized. I apologized for not having sent flowers too, and she said it would have been lovely to have had flowers but all she really wanted was me. I didn't understand, she said. She missed me terribly. And it was terrible in Vancouver, raining, cold, and she should never have agreed to it, they didn't even need her there, and I was three thousand miles away. Then—she must have looked at a clock (the only watch she wore, sometime, hung from a gold chain around her neck)—she realized what time it was.

"But it's four in the morning for you!" she said. "What are you doing in New York at four in the morning? Are you with someone else?"

"No, I'm alone."

"Then why aren't you home, asleep, with your wife?"

That, presumably, was why I'd called her. I needed someone to tell it to. But suddenly, the words wouldn't come.

"I do this sometimes," I said, "when I have an early appointment."

"And she lets you?"

"Yes."

"I would never let you do that. But if you have an early appointment, what are you doing, awake, at four o'clock in the morning?"

"I'm talking to you," I said. "You're not the only one who can't sleep. We have a lot to talk about."

"Oh, not now, darling. It will be all right. I want you to speak to me as though you were here, Daniel. With your arms around me, and my head on your shoulder, where it belongs. Tell me what it is like where you are, describe what you are wearing. Tell me every little detail. I need your voice talking to me, as though you were next to me."

She found it amusing, the idea of me among the old grads. She asked what the bed was like. I told her it was small, too small for two, monkish. She said her bed was enormous, and perfectly flat, and boring. Hard, new, as though it had just come from a mattress factory. She thought proper hotels should have lumpy beds. She loved sleeping with me in her bed in Pasadena, because I made a depression in it, and it acted like gravity, pulling her into me. She loved waking up, just a little, and feeling me all around her, and going back to sleep. She thought that, if I was with her in Vancouver, there would be some gravity effect, even on such a firm mattress.

I told her about the fish.

She understood. When I'd left, and she'd had to go to Vancouver alone, she'd felt it in her stomach too.

The talking was relaxing her, she said. Her voice, foggy and disembodied in the beginning, was now her instrument once again, soft, melodious, insinuating. She asked me what I was wearing. Nothing at all, I said. She was wearing a nightgown. She always wore a nightgown when she was away from home. Was I lying on the bed, she asked? No, I was sitting on the bed. She wanted me to lie back on the bed, the way she was, with my head on the pillow and the telephone between my shoulder and my ear. My hands free. Then she asked me to imagine entering her hotel room, just then, in Vancouver, and to describe how I would go about taking her nightgown off. She asked me to describe it slowly, in detail.

I did.

"And then what would you do?" Jeannine said drowsily. "Tell me slowly."

I did. For a moment I thought she'd gone to sleep. I could hear her breathing.

I stopped talking.

But then she said, the words heavy, slow, "Keep talking to me, darling. You're . . . exciting me. I'm loving . . . Tell me what you're going to. . . ."

I talked on.

Eventually I fell silent, and I could hear her breathing mingling with mine.

"Jeannine?" I said softly. Then, "Good-night, Jeannine," and I hung up and stared down at my own, still considerable erection until, I guess, the two of us fell asleep.

I WOKE UP with the city—no birds chirping outside my window but trucks in the street below, and horns, cries, voices, and still it was late enough that, gazing down through the dusty panes, I could see people already going to work.

I still needed someone to talk to.

The conversation with Jeannine was like a dream. I wasn't even sure it had happened. The Fawn was more real, in that I knew it had taken place and that I'd fled the combat zone, but it too seemed distant, unconnected, dislocated. The reality was what was there: morning, the street, New York. I belonged to it, and didn't. In a way, it was as though I'd only just arrived.

I made a couple of calls. On some random hunch, I called Falcone, who, the last I'd heard, still lived in the west fifties. He said, "What's up, babe?," as though I'd talked to him just yesterday. I said I didn't want to interrupt him if he was working. Screw that, he said. He'd already been at it for a couple of hours, and he had other business to attend to, including breakfast. Was I in the city? Had I had breakfast yet?

I told him where I was.

For Christ's sake, don't eat there, he said. Places like that routinely poisoned the alums to get the money. Meet him at the Stage Deli in an hour.

You couldn't miss Frank Falcone. He was sitting alone at a table for four, but when he spotted me and waved me over, I had the impression of having to squeeze in. This wasn't just because of his bulk, which had grown steadily along with his success, but the objects strewn across the tabletop. Apparently he'd already eaten, or started eating. In addition, there were opened and separated newspapers (the *Daily Racing Form*, the *News*, the early *Post*), an open briefcase, a hand calculator, a legal-sized pad on which he was writing some abstruse numbers which had to do with his picks for the day.

"Where you been, babe?" he growled at me. Then his head went back down and one hand rose in a stop signal while he jotted some more numbers.

I hadn't seen him in a while. Back when he was a struggling novelist and we both made ends meet writing for Rhinelander's skin magazines, we'd been part of a regular poker game. Falcone was a chronic plunger, and loser, but gambling aside, I'd always known he was going to make it. Numero Uno. He had too big a talent not to. And so he had, but not commercially before his third or fourth novel, the one some critic had dubbed "Godfather III." When he hit the fiction best-seller lists, I'd torn out the page and sent it to him, his name circled in red and some kind of comment, like "Bravo, Franco!" And he, typically, had sent it back, with an arrow drawn up to my nonfiction best seller of the moment—the Boylan, probably—and "It takes one to know one, babe" scrawled across the arrow.

He'd been best man at my wedding—against the Fawn's wishes. She'd thought he was too much of a slob. If so, I'd argued at the time, he was a pretty damn magnificent one.

While the waiter and I cleared a small area for me in the mess, Falcone excused himself and went off, yellow pad in hand, to call his bookie. I'd heard he was deep into his publisher to pay for the habit, also for assorted ex-wives and a couple of kids. As the waiter served my breakfast, Falcone came back and stood behind me a moment—

an old practice, I remembered—massaging my shoulders with his strong hams.

"It's good to see you, babe," he said gruffly. "How're you doing? How's Faith?"

"Funny you should ask," I answered. "Actually, we're pretty rocky right now."

"How come?" he said. He let my shoulders go, sat back down across from me, and, soon enough, was eyeing my untouched bagels, then, with a reach across the newspapers, helping himself.

"I don't know exactly," I said. "It just happened yesterday. She says I'm too angry. I walked out."

He shrugged. "Probably she's the one who's too angry," he said, chewing. "You know, women like that, they're too rich, too beautiful, to make good wives. They get bored, and then they'll drive you fucking bananas. You never had any kids, did you?"

"No."

"Sometimes that shuts them up, sometimes it doesn't. Well, you getting laid on the side?"

"Sometimes."

"Come on, babe, remember who you're talking to," he said. "I always thought, fucking Springer, leave it to Springer not only to make his fame and fortune but look who he gets to spend the night with. You know the one I really envy you? Jilly Rogers. Someday when we're both in Hollywood, Leo Daniels, you will introduce me to that one." Leo Daniels was a pseudonym I'd sometimes used in the old days. "Whose book you writing now?"

"Nina Hardy's," I told him.

He whistled. That was class, he said, a lot of class. It sounded as though he was thinking: maybe that was too much class—for me, for guys like us. Then, on second thought, he said she had to be getting on in years, didn't she? Still . . .

"What's she like?" he wanted to know.

I ducked and dodged, or so I thought, and managed to change the subject by shifting over to the publishing deal we'd gotten. This led us into talking business. Yeah, he was writing a new novel, at least supposed to be. Actually, he had to be—he was on a system where the only way he could squeeze any more bucks out of the fuckers who published him was by delivering a certain number of pages on a schedule. And he was behind schedule. He was thinking of changing publishers, finding someone to give him a new contract with enough down to buy back the old one and still give him some walking-around money. Trouble was, as his agent pointed out, he'd already done that once.

Alternatively, he was thinking of floating a crime series. He'd knock off the first one or two, then get somebody to write the rest under his name.

What was my opinion of that? he wanted to know.

My opinion was it would be cheapening his image, I said.

His agent had told him the same thing. Well, maybe he'd do it under another name. But if he did it under another name, there'd be no bucks in it, would there? Somehow he had to come up with some bucks. He was also working on a screen treatment of one of his earlier books. He was considering changing agents, too. What did I think about Tinker McConnell? About Rhinelander as a publisher?

I told him Tinker was a big-bucks agent, and Lew Rhinelander had a quick checkbook.

Then we got off onto turning forty—which was the cliché of our generation, maybe of all generations, but that didn't keep us from talking about it, about people we'd known and had lost track of, about how it somehow used to be more fun when we had nothing going for us but our wits and our typewriters, and the sense of time speeding up, where had it gone, where was it going? As far as Falcone was concerned, he thought his own midlife crisis had hit when he was fifteen and he'd caught his first winner at Aqueduct, a borrowed two-dollar bet. The gambling had fucked him up ever since. Worse than drugs, he said. He'd tried everything to beat it—the shrinks, hypnosis, Gamblers Anonymous. Only recently he'd decided that he was, in Puzo's words, a degenerate gambler.

Maybe that was the beginning of wisdom, he said with a grin. Or poverty, anyway.

"And what about you, babe?" he asked. "You always seemed so fucking sure of yourself, a front runner, like you were going to make it wire-to-wire. What's gone wrong?"

"Nothing, really," I said.

"No? Then why do you keep looking over your shoulder, like somebody's gaining on you?"

I had no idea that I had been, and told him so.

Falcone laughed, a booming, broad-faced guffaw.

"I don't mean actually," he said. "But there's something furtive around the eyes. There're only two reasons guys get it. Either they owe money, or they're in love. So which is it, babe?"

I don't think I said anything.

"It's not Nina Hardy, is it?" he went on. "When you were talking about her before, you got that look. Furtive, evasive, you know? Like somebody who's holding your marker was about to stiff you? So if you're in love with Nina Hardy, what's wrong with that. Who *hasn't* been in love with Nina Hardy in his dreams? Only you're there, you lucky bastard, you're actually *there!*"

"It's more complicated than that," I said.

"What's complicated? You're not Italian. I mean, an Italian, he's brought up to think he's got to marry every girl he goes to bed with. But you're making how much—1.5 mil?—to do her book, and you get to put your head on her pillow while you do it. Nina Hardy. Jesus Christ, Springer, I've got to hand it to you. And she's what—fifteen years older than you? More? So how can it be complicated? I guess Faith found out, didn't she? Well look, forget about what I said before about her, that was just so much bullshit. If you want her to, she'll come around. Just cool it, babe. She's not the type of woman who's going to jump off, not when you're at the top. Meanwhile, why don't you have it both ways? The dumbest thing I ever did was let the wives throw me out. It was the fucking gambling. Ever since, I've been chasing around after a bunch of twenty-year-olds who want to be able to tell their daughters they once fucked a famous novelist. I've nothing against it, but there's something to be said for a hot meal every night and somebody to keep the bed warm in winter."

While we talked—or he talked—we finished off my breakfast and stood at the cash register, paying up, toothpicks in our mouths, then out on the sidewalk, shaking hands in the dusty April sun. Two successful scribes in their forties. Still good friends, I guess. Falcone had puffs around the gills, and he squinted in the light, and eventually he'd be bald. But none the worse for wear really. There was more of him, was all, and he needed somebody to keep the bed warm in winter.

And me? Well, I guess I had that telltale furtive look.

THE THING WAS: we were both consenting adults, the Fawn and I, and we had been when we met. If our passion had always had a violent

edge to it, well . . . then our passion had always had a violent edge
to it. I didn't start it, but I can't say she taught me either. It had just
happened. Maybe, over time, it—our passion—had come to *require*
the violent edge, and maybe that was trouble, but it didn't make me
a wife-beater or a rapist.

We'd exploded before, and this wasn't the first time one of us had
walked on the other. The scenario, I knew, now called for a coming
together. There would be a huddling, a cuddling, apologies and com-
miserations, tears perhaps, vows, banter, sex certainly, with—just
maybe—a revival of an old tenderness that also went with the lease.
Or had. Because, once upon a time, part of our bargain had been an
acute, shared, even exciting sense of being alone in the world, against
the world—just us—and wanting it that way.

The scenario would play again, I thought. Only this time I was in
no rush.

I hung out in the city and, one way and another, managed to string
the day out till midafternoon. Along the way I dropped in on Tinker
McConnell—unannounced, mind you, but I still got the Very Important Author treatment. Tinker made a show of clearing her desk
for me—"no phone calls," she called out to her secretary—and then,
behind closed doors, she wanted to hear all about the book, about
Nina.

I brought up again what Claude Rhinelander had said to me.

"I still really don't see what practical difference that makes," Tinker
said. "Whatever games Lew wants to play with Claude, our contract
is with Rhinelander Publishing."

"I think it'll make a difference to Jeannine—to Nina."

"Oh?"

"She and Claude Rhinelander go back a long way. He was against
her doing the book in the beginning; now he owns it, or says he does.
I'm not sure she's going to like that."

"You haven't told her yet?"

"No."

"Well, to begin with, let's find out if it's true."

She put in a call to Jenny Bergler, which ended up a three-way
conversation.

"Look, Dan," Jenny said after I'd explained, "what goes on between
those two really doesn't have to concern us. You want complicated
relationships? I give you the Rhinelander brothers."

"But is it true?" Tinker asked. "That it's Claude's money?"

"I don't know," Jenny answered—a painful admission, I judged, because Jenny Bergler, by reputation as status-conscious as they come, wasn't the kind who liked being left in the dark. "But what difference would it make? *I'm* the publisher of this company—not Lew, not Claude. Besides—and I'll be honest with you—if Claude believes enough to put his own money on the line, I think that's great."

"Why?" Tinker said.

"Because he has much better commercial instincts, even when it comes to books. He understands business. Any time there's major money involved, I'd rather have his opinion than Lew's. In fact," her voice loud, as though she wanted the world to hear, "I'll let you both in on a secret. If anything ever happened to Claude—I mean, if somehow he was cut off from the Group, dropped off our board, whatever—I'd be the first one out the door."

Tinker had covered the mouthpiece on her phone to hide her laughter. Later, she told me that in all the years Jenny Bergler had worked at Rhinelander's, she didn't think they'd once had a conversation without Jenny threatening to leave Lew. "Talk about complicated relationships," Tinker said. Meanwhile, recovering, she asked Jenny to pin down Claude's involvement, and Jenny said, somewhat reluctantly, that if it was that important to me and Nina, she would, and I said, yes, it was that important.

By three o'clock, I was back on the street, with no more business, invented or real, and no place to go except home. I drove up the West Side Highway ahead of the rush hour and took the George Washington Bridge, instead of the Thruway and the Tappan Zee, because it was the slower route, and made my way, by the back roads, up our side of the Hudson. I had no reason to believe the Fawn would be home, except I knew she would be, probably working, or pretending to, possibly gardening, in thick gloves and the smock she wore with the multiple pockets, her hair tied back in a bandanna, coming erect, doe-eyed, as I drove up our driveway.

There was still plenty of daylight left when I turned into our dirt road. Spring was happening, all right—buds on many of the trees, banks of forsythia in bright yellow, clusters of bulbs pushing through the earth into air and sun.

But no Fawn.

The house was empty, it seemed. I called out from the entrance hall. No answer. Then I remembered that this was our couple's day off—their weekday off, in addition to Sunday.

And not empty so much as different.

It took me a short while to figure out why, and longer to understand the selective principle involved.

Things were missing.

I didn't quite realize it till I got upstairs to our bedroom, and even there it confused me. Some of her clothes were gone, but far from all. The same with her jewelry. The bathroom, on the contrary, had been cleaned out of all her objects. None of mine, however. Maybe, I thought at first, she'd only taken enough for a short stay away.

Not so.

I toured the house.

Books were gone. Jason's bust in the dining room, gone from the mantelpiece. All the china was still there, though, and the silverware in the long velvet drawer.

The greenhouse—her "country studio," as she called it—had had everything removed that could be. She had to have had a van for that, I realized.

I walked out to the barn.

Everything intact, as far as I could tell. A couple of messages on the answering machine, of no consequence.

No note, no anything.

Back to the house. Same thing in the kitchen. Immaculate, the way the Murphys always left it. Everything in its place, no note.

Eventually I made my way back upstairs, to the bedroom, and saw immediately what I'd missed the first time—missed unaccountably because they were in plain view.

The place of honor, so to speak: her dressing table; the surface empty except for a diary I'd once given her.

And sitting on top of her diary, her wedding band.

The diary was a beautiful book, bound in moiré silk, with a lock and key and, inside, incredible hand-dyed Italian paper. It had cost a small fortune. I'd given it to her for some birthday, or Valentine's, or maybe, I forget, on the sale of one of my books. I know she'd used it, because once she'd lost the key and she'd had to force the lock.

What in hell was she leaving me her diary for? I wondered. Was this the next thing after the diaphragm case?

Suddenly, I understood. I guess the wedding band helped.

It was because I'd given it to her.

And so it was, throughout, without exception. The governing principle was that everything I'd bought for her, with her, had been left behind. Clothes, jewelry, books, the diary, the wedding band. She'd only taken what was *hers*.

I sat down at the dressing table. I held the diary in my hands—for how long, I don't know. After dark, I think. But I sat there, already bleeding, unwilling to open it and unable to resist.

Chapter Eleven

I STARTED WITH the dirty parts, I admit, thumbing through for names, places, dates. Unrewarding. Not that she was lily white and squeaky clean, but if, in the period covered by the diary, she'd gotten it off with anyone other than L (who was, unmistakably, Lew Rhinelander), and possibly W, who was her shrink for most of the period, she hadn't written it down.

L, it seems, had finally worn her down. At least that's how she'd put it.

> Finally with L. *Finalmente*. It happened so naturally I can't believe it took me so long! Broad daylight, his apartment on 55th Street, right after lunch. L very gentle, understanding. I'd forgotten, he has the most expressive *hands*.
>
> My bad luck, the appointment with W was right after. I had to run, even so I was late. W very huffy. Said it wasn't luck at all. Said, "Is it really *luck* that you slept with someone just before coming here?"
>
> He's jealous obviously. I told him so. Of course he had to say, "What makes you think that?"
>
> L thinks that if I was with him all the time, I wouldn't need an analyst.

I read most of it that night in the barn. I also made a lot of phone calls: to the answering machine at the SoHo loft and, the next day, to some of her friends. Her friends weren't very forthcoming, nor was her family. Maybe it sounds strange now that I never tried Lew Rhinelander, but I didn't.

Jeannine called several times, and the Fawn's mother, once.

Jeannine was still in Vancouver, due to go home the next day. She asked how the book was coming in the new version. "The new version" referred to a small argument we'd had before I left, not an argument so much as a "philosophical discussion"—about pain, ironically enough. Why, Jeannine had said, should she dwell on the more painful passages in her life when she was so happy now? Because, I'd told her, life was a mixed bag—and who was going to believe that when Claude Rhinelander, who'd thought he owned her and still did, had beat the shit out of her, she didn't feel a thing?

She'd agreed to try it my way, but I hadn't so much as put a disk into the machine since I'd been back.

"What's wrong, Daniel?" Jeannine asked, maybe ten times in all. "I hear it in your voice. You keep telling me nothing's wrong, but I hear it."

Nothing was wrong, I insisted. Maybe I was a little tired, that was all. Maybe I missed her too much.

When would I be coming out again? If I came the next day, my usual flight, she could arrange to meet me at the airport. We wouldn't even have to go home. We could go down the coast. We could go to Newport Beach, or Laguna, La Jolla. No, she couldn't stand going as far as La Jolla, even though she loved it. She couldn't wait that long. She needed me terribly.

I didn't know when I'd be out exactly. It was complicated. I'd come as soon as I could.

The Fawn's mother wanted to know where her daughter was.

One funny thing about that: Mom was the only person in the family who didn't have an animal name. There was the Fawn and the Badger, and Beaver and the Hawk—who were the brothers—and farther out along the family tree were a Moose, a Squirrel, a Penguin. A regular menagerie. By the logic of such things, Mom should have been the Doe, or whatever they call a female badger. But she wasn't.

Mrs. Graves, to me.

"I think she's left," I said, responding to her question.

"At this hour? Why, it's practically the middle of the night!"

"No. I think she must have left earlier. Sometime this morning."

"But why hasn't she called me?"

"I'm sorry. I don't know anything about that."

"But it's Thursday night!"

There was a line in the diary about how sometimes her mother's voice set the Fawn's teeth on edge. If the Fawn checked in every Thursday night, I didn't know about it.

"*You* say she's left," she said accusingly, as though I was possibly lying. "Where did she go?"

"I don't know."

"How can that be? You're her husband, aren't you?"

I repeated that I thought the Fawn had left. Several times, I think.

"Do you mean she's *left*? Left *you*?"

There was indignation in her tone as well as surprise, and probably pleasure, too, of a well-it's-high-time sort. I ought to have said, Yes, and how does it feel, Mom, that she's left me for a nice Jewish boy twenty years older than I am?

"Yes," I said instead. "That's exactly what I mean."

"Oh," she said.

Long pause. Whatever she was thinking, she said none of it to me. Only, at the end:

"Never mind."

End of conversation.

Mom had her place of honor in the diary. Maybe not as large as mine, but prominent. I skipped a lot of it, but the gist was that the Fawn had learned—"in treatment"—why Mom didn't love her. Never had loved her. The Fawn called this discovery a major breakthrough, and W agreed. *Jealousy* was the operative word—jealous of the Fawn's looks, her flair, her freedom. Not only had Mom married at twenty and been set to breeding almost immediately, but she'd had to endure her daughter's three abortions. "Major resentment," the Fawn wrote, "when probably, if she could let herself think such thoughts, she'd wish she could have aborted me." The resentment went all the way back to when the Fawn was little, and people had made a fuss over her, and her mother had simply not been able to *stand* it.

She couldn't remember ever being hugged, or stroked, or cuddled by Mom.

Gee, what a nasty break.

I'm drifting, I know.

Look, this was my first experience at reading what somebody else had written about me. It shook me. It wasn't that I didn't recognize myself, either. I was right behind the initials—D, DS, once DLS—the guy who paid no attention to her, who acted like he owned her, as though she was a piece of furniture, property, whom she couldn't "get through to." Sometimes he was too busy. Sometimes, she thought, he was sleeping with another woman, or thinking about sleeping with another woman. Mostly he just wasn't "there" for her. It was like talking to a deaf man whose hearing aid was turned off.

There was a lot about her "dark secret," which is what she called the violence of our sex. My violence, that is. I needed it, I learned from the diary, in order to come. For a dark secret, though, she'd sure told enough people about it—her girl friends as well as the shrinks—and everybody she told about it, no exception, said she was crazy to put up with it.

W made a big thing about the Fawn's "masochism" and so did B, the shrink who followed him. B was the so-called Sullivanian. Why she'd left W wasn't clear. Just maybe, I thought, because she'd gone to bed with him. What tipped me off was that, according to the diary, W also had marvelous hands—"long, elegant, expressive fingers."

Hands. Even Jason, the cartoonist, had "good hands."

D's, though, were "peasant hands," broad rather than long. Time was when she must have been into peasant.

Hands also, it seemed, had to do with sensitivity. She loved L for his "sensitivity," the way he stroked things when he listened to her—the air, objects, the Fawn. It was very Oriental, she thought. He was, she wrote, maybe "the most sensitively intelligent man" she'd ever met.

D wasn't. D, apparently, was the one ham-handed slob in a world of, presumably, widespread and sensitive intelligence, the one bad guy all readers of diaries love to hate. Maybe it shocked me—sure it shocked me!—but nothing beats a great villain, particularly one who, in the end, can't defend himself.

The eavesdropping episode got space too, and a lot of outrage. She couldn't even hold a private phone conversation without my listening in over her shoulder and her getting beaten up in the bargain. It became a sign, a symbol, that she had to get out.

"Don't you understand?" she quoted one of the girl friends. "Just because men like him can't keep their hands off women doesn't mean they *like* them. Don't you see? D *hates* women."

The Fawn didn't exactly agree. Yes, I had a lot of anger in me, she thought, and B thought so, too. Probably, according to B, it was a source of strength as well as weakness. A great rage, the Fawn said. "Of everybody I know," she wrote in the diary, "D needs treatment. B agrees. But if I so much as mention it, he bites my head off!"

As to whether all this was "fair" or not (to use one of her favorite words), I'm the wrong person to ask.

But I'll tell you what was unfair, Faith. It wasn't your affair with "L," or with "W" if you shacked up with him, or Jason, which you'd say never happened, or all the ones you didn't write about. I didn't even mind your sharing all that bad stuff about me with anybody you ran into, though it might have helped if you'd laid it on me first, even if I wasn't listening. But what really stuck in my craw was all that shit about kids. That was brand new, right out of left field.

It snuck up on me in the diary. There was mention, a couple of times, of this or that girl friend having a baby. One was pushing forty, I think. Maybe past forty. And discussion of the risks. Somebody the Fawn knew—maybe it was the same girl friend—had pulled a bad test in the fifth month of pregnancy. What would she have done in the same situation? She didn't know. It was so awful, she could hardly think about it. But then, suddenly—another breakthrough, I guess— she was talking to the shrink about having children of her own. It was as though she'd suddenly discovered that she, too, was pushing forty and that the statistics had started to work against her. What was she going to do?

The shrink advised her to talk to me. She said she couldn't. "That would be unfair to D," she wrote. She didn't even know if she could bear a child. Maybe she couldn't. Also, wasn't our marriage built on the premise of no children? How could she load that on me now?

But then came an entry, a long one, maybe the longest of all.

It started out a kind of general meditation on the why of mother-hood. The Fawn imagined that she belonged to a long chain of women who hadn't wanted daughters, of mothers stuck with daughters before they'd had a chance to live themselves, and of daughters hating their mothers' bitterness without understanding it. Maybe, just maybe, if she had a daughter she could break the chain. Because she was older. Because she'd lived. Because she understood.

The entry changed, and she was talking to this daughter directly— this unborn, unconceived child. Pages of it.

I think about you all the time. I dream of you growing in me.
My belly high and round. I can feel you sway. You're not supposed
to sway, I think, but that's how I feel you, deep inside, connected.
As though I'm your hammock.

I sing to you sometimes, cradle songs. Baa Baa Black Sheep,
Have You Any Wool? Hush, I whisper to you. Hushabye, little
girl.

I know you're a girl. In my dream I can't see you, but you are
there, swaying, kicking.

Then there was something about her having burst into tears. And
this line:

But how can a man who likes to beat up on women be father
to my daughter?

I stopped reading.

I DID A lot of crazy things that next day. In order:
I called the girl friends, and Jason.
I told Tinker McConnell I wanted out of the Rhinelander contract.
I called B, the Fawn's shrink.
I went to SoHo.
I told Jeannine I couldn't go forward with the book.
I lit a fire in the fireplace, not for warmth.
I moved into the barn.

As far as the girl friends were concerned, the Great Villain must
really have set their hotline buzzing because I told a couple of them
off, but the best I got out of them was that she must be at the loft in
SoHo. The shrink didn't even venture that much. Of course my wife
was his patient, but I wasn't, and therefore he couldn't discuss her
with me. Nor would he, of course. I think I told him that, of course,
I'd remember our conversation the next time he had a bill to be paid.

I left enough messages on the SoHo answering machine to fill up
her whole tape. None was answered. Maybe she wasn't there. But she
was—as the Great Villain, undaunted, found out for himself.

After dark. I parked across the street from the building.

Funny, I hadn't been there in a while. I used to find the neighbor-hood quaint—pockets of bohemian elegance rising out of the ghettos and sweatshops of yore. Now, at night and deserted, the exteriors of her street seemed only drab, dingy, as though a couple of decades of investment and gentrification hadn't so much as made a dent.

She was there all right. Possibly expecting someone, because when I pushed the buzzer downstairs, she answered quickly over the intercom.

"Yes? Who is it?"

"It's me. Please let me in, Faith."

"I don't think so. I don't want to see you."

"We've got to talk."

"Not now."

"It has to be now."

"It can't be, Dan. Please go away."

"I'm coming up."

There was no way she could keep me out of the building. I had a key to the elevator.

I rode up in the slow and creaking cage. When I'd first moved in, it had opened directly into the Fawn's loft. Since then, she'd had an entrance hall built, with a regular front door and bell chime.

There was a table in the entrance hall, which always used to hold a vase of fresh flowers. In place of the flowers now was her bust of Jason.

I put my door key in the lock, or tried to. No go. That much, it seemed, she'd already attended to.

I rang the bell, waited. No answer.

I rang again, knocked.

"Goddamn it, Faith," I called out, "let me in."

Her voice suddenly sounded very close, as though she was just on the other side of the door. I'd heard no footsteps. Maybe she'd been standing there the whole time.

"You'd better go away, Dan. I'm not going to let you in."

"You didn't have to change the locks."

"No? It's a good thing I did. I'm not going to let you in."

We went back and forth that way, on either side of the door, until she stopped answering. Then I made what must have amounted to a speech. I told her I'd read her diary, that it had shocked me, that a lot of it was stuff I didn't understand but that didn't mean I couldn't, that maybe I was the son of a bitch she'd called me, the Great Villain, but that didn't mean I couldn't change.

I begged, in sum. I pleaded. I also threatened.

I said I was going to bust down the fucking wall if she didn't open the door. It was only sheetrock anyway. Did she think I didn't remember?

She said she was going to call the police if I didn't go away.

I told her to go ahead and call the police. This was New York, I reminded her. Did she really think the New York police would answer a call about some petty domestic squabble, when nobody had been hurt or was going to be hurt?

No answer.

"Why is it so important that I go away?" I asked her. "Are you expecting someone? Is Lew supposed to drop in?"

No answer.

"That stuff about the baby, Faith," I said to her. "That was below the belt. *You* decided you wanted to have a baby—out of the fucking blue—but did you ever think of telling me about it? No. *You* decided I'd be a bad father. For Christ's sake, I may be the heavy in all of this, but who are you, the Great Mother? Who was it who didn't want to be used for breeding? Who was it who had the abortions?"

No answer.

Who, I wondered, had told her not to talk to me?

"I'll tell you what I'm going to do, Faith," I said. "Don't worry about my busting down the wall. I'm going to sit down outside this door. I'm not going to move. I'm going to talk to you. I'll keep on talking. Sooner or later you're going to have to come out, and I'll be here."

No answer.

Then, a little later, small-voiced:

"Go away, Dan."

I was sitting on the floor, back to the white wall, on the wide polished boards like the rest of the loft. I imagined her sitting on just the other side, also on the floor. For some reason, I pictured her with her knees up near her chin, and her arms hugging her shins.

My legs were straight out.

And I talked to her. I talked about a million and one things, and nothing. I said I didn't think of myself as all that angry. Sure I got pissed off at times—who didn't? Didn't she? I may even have talked about those summers on the Upper Peninsula. I didn't need a shrink to tell me I'd been an unwanted child. My mother had always said so, more or less, though she said it had never stopped her from loving me. They'd been too young, she explained, she and my father, and my father couldn't hack it, so he'd taken off. By the time my brother came along, my stepfather was already in place, and things were a little easier. So? I'd never held it against anybody. That's just the way it was.

And us. I talked mostly about us. I reminded her of what she'd looked like, the first time we met. In the rain. In black, her red hair bedraggled. A mess, and pissed off—talk about angry! And snooty. Incredibly snooty.

I loved her so much then. I couldn't believe I'd been so lucky.

I talked about sex in those early days, when the great turn-on had been our catechisms. That had been a two-way street, I reminded her. Sex between us, I'd thought, had always been a two-way street. Was I wrong? How could I be that wrong? I said that if we were breaking up, this was a hell of a way to do it—on opposite sides of a locked door. We ought at least to be able to do it face to face, like adults.

How much of it she actually heard, I've no idea. Maybe all. Maybe nothing.

I called out her name a couple of times.

No response.

Once I heard the elevator go up, come down.

You name it, I experienced it that night: the whole emotional gamut, sitting there under Jason's bust. Regret? Easy. And self-pity, the urge to turn back the clock? By all means. Loneliness too, and, lest we forget, my oh so wounded pride. Even, so help me, a passing horniness.

And anger too. The old reliable infamous Great Villain rage, great stomach-churning spates of it. Angriest of all, needless to say, once it hit me that she wasn't listening and that everything I'd done since she lowered the boom—the diary, the phone calls, the conversations with Tinker and Jeannine, the pleading and the threatening, even sitting right that minute on the polished floor outside her fucking door with the changed lock—was the perfect parody of the jilted husband. Perfect in every way.

Well, we're all entitled to one moment of objective clarity, aren't we? Sooner or later? Like the proverbial chimp who, if he sits long enough at the typewriter, will eventually type the perfect novel?

Sure we are.

And that was what sent me home, at long last. To light the fire in the fireplace.

WHAT WAS IT Jeannine said? Wasn't this what I'd *wanted*?

Tinker McConnell had thought I was crazy.

Tinker had said that, unless she was missing something, there was no reasonable basis for getting me out of the Rhinelander contract. Certainly not to go to another publisher. If I tried that, Jenny and Lew were sure to raise the roof, and frankly she couldn't blame them. They could tie me up in knots forever. Of course, I could always not deliver the manuscript, but that wouldn't come up as an issue for months, and then I'd have to pay back the money. Was I ready to do that?

Was Nina Hardy ready to do that?

And what would it do to my professional reputation? Had I thought of that?

Frankly, Tinker had said, she'd never known me to act so unprofessionally.

I'd thought about telling her exactly what had happened and decided against it. She was, I knew, a congenital gossip who talked to half the industry each day, and the other half the next. Then too, I doubted she'd find the Fawn's leaving me a reasonable basis for getting out of a contract. Out of a marriage maybe, but a sacrosanct publishing agreement?

Jeannine was a different story. She found me late that night, after I got back from SoHo.

She took the news badly. I could hear it in her tone, in the shortness of her breath.

She made me repeat myself.

"I can't go ahead with the book," I said. "Not with the Rhine-landers."

She didn't understand.

"What is this all about, Daniel?" she said. "What does it mean? Is it because Claude put up the money? Look, my friend, you will do what you want to do, but why should that matter so much? Aren't you making a mountain out of something very small?"

I started to say something about *Eva's Story*, that from her point of view Claude always put up the money, but then it occurred to me: how did she already know about Claude's involvement with the book when I hadn't even discussed it with her?

"He told me about it himself," Jeannine said when I asked her.

Nice, I thought. "Oh? And when was that?"

"After he saw you. He called me here, in Vancouver. He said he didn't want me to hear about it secondhand."

"Did he now? He told me he wanted *me* to be the messenger. What else did he say?"

"He said the interview had been very interesting. He hoped he had been helpful."

"Very helpful," I said. "He all but kicked me out of his office, once he'd told me what a genius he was. Oh yes, he also said you were afraid of growing old, which was why you got involved with younger men like me. Puppy dogs, was what he called us. Puppy dogs with big cocks, to be precise."

For a woman who claimed to abhor vulgarity, she could make great exceptions.

"That sounds like him," was all she said. "And yes, Daniel, Claude does want to own me. It's tiresome, I agree, after all these years, but the important thing is that he doesn't own me. You, of all people, ought to know that."

Claude, though, wasn't the point, and I guess she realized it.

"Do I hear you saying, Daniel, that you don't want to see me again? Is that right?"

"No," I answered. "That's not right. It's just that it's complicated."

Then the irritation came, full-fledged.

"Well, *what* is so complicated?" she asked. "I don't understand. Perhaps it's time you told me."

I hesitated. Then I said: "I think my marriage has broken up, that's all."

"Oh?"

"That's right. And guess who my wife has taken up with. With Lew Rhinelander. It's a small world, isn't it?"

"With who? I don't understand."

"I said my wife's taken up with Lew Rhinelander. Your friend Claude's brother."

A long pause, in which neither of us said anything. And what was I supposed to say, that I found myself thrashing in a net of Rhinelanders and that I didn't like it?

"But isn't that what you want?" Jeannine said finally.

Another pause. At my end.

"Well, Daniel," in her coolest voice, "if you find out soon, perhaps you'll be good enough to tell me."

THE FIRE IN the fireplace.

I started with the diary, silk binding down and pages fanned out, over a bed of kindling. Then I made several trips—armloads of clothes and other combustibles from things she'd left behind.

The jewelry was another matter. I didn't know what to do about that.

I was purposeful about it. I was damned if the house—*my* house, whatever the lawyers might say about it—was going to be cluttered by what *she'd* decided she didn't want. I didn't even want it buried, or in the garbage.

Was I *that* angry, while we're on the subject? You're damn right I was *that* angry. I thought: Let me show you what anger's all about, my dear wife till death do us part.

I sat on the living-room floor where the tile mosaic met the edge of the carpet, the firescreen pulled aside, and watched the first twists of smoke curling uncertainly up. Was I drunk? I don't think so. Not enough anyway to keep me from my second moment of clarity that night.

Because why in hell was I burning the diary? We lived in the Age of Greed, mind you, and what were you going to do, Springer, in the Age of Greed, when the Fawn came after you for her piece of the pie?

Oh, not the Fawn herself, mind you. She would never stoop so low. But what of the Fawn's lawyer? Naming Nina Hardy, Gloria Farran, *et alia* in their complaint?

Were you going to say it ain't so?

I fished the diary out. I used, for the purpose, a pair of fireproof gloves the Fawn had given me on some occasion. They worked too.

The book was a little charred, and the scorched silk reeked, but the insides were still readable.

I burned the rest, slowly and not altogether successfully, till the living room stank, but whether that was from silk or taffeta or cotton ramie or linen or rayon or nylon or wool or leather, I couldn't say.

Done and done.

Then I retreated to the barn, with the diary, where, barring a run across the yard to the kitchen every now and then, I was self-sufficient. And which was where I sat, some vague time later, smoking, listening to my old "Jazz at the Philharmonic" tapes and Norman Granz's fight-announcer voice—"On tenor sax, Illinois Jacquet and . . . Flip Phillips!"—when there was a knock at the door and I opened it to the larger-than-life figure of Sonny Corral, also known as Tim, also known (to some) as Timmy.

Part Three

Part Three

Chapter Twelve

I HADN'T KNOWN he was coming. He just showed up, in an olive-colored Burberry that looked as if it had been wadded on some closet shelf, and surveyed the barn from the doorway.

"So this is where the writer works," he said. "When he's working." Then, focusing on me: "The lady thinks it's time you grew up, Danny Boy. I can't say she's wrong either."

In my state of mind at the time, I started to laugh, not so much at the words but at his delivery—straight off the silver screen.

"Come in, Sonny," I said. "Come on in, have a seat and tell me all about growing up."

He walked a little unsteadily—the only visible relic from his Malibu run. He ducked his head till the beams vaulted upward over him, but he stayed on his feet.

"You know," he said, "she's not just some dame you add to your life list and then dump over the telephone."

"Dump? Is that what Jeannine says I did?"

"Not in so many words, but close enough."

"Is that what brings you here?"

"You hurt her. I don't like to see her hurt."

"I've been through a pretty rough time, myself," I said.

"Haven't we all?"

"As a matter of fact, my wife just walked on me."

"So I understand. But I'd have thought that called for congratulations."

"Maybe it does. In any case, I didn't mean to hurt Jeannine. I just

137

needed a little time. Some breathing space. Too much was happening too fast."

He shook his massive head.

"That's my message for you, Danny Boy. There's no time. Like the sign says in the men's room, you either shit or you get off the pot."

"And she sent you all this way to tell me that? Why doesn't she do it herself?"

I had a swivel drafting stool I sometimes used, and he sat on it now, his feet hooking the bottom rung. Under the bedraggled raincoat, I noticed he was dressed more formally than usual: a blazer, white shirt, and a rep tie loose around an unbuttoned collar.

"She didn't send me to do anything," he said. "Believe it or not, I've got some business of my own in New York."

"So you just stopped by to tell me to grow up?"

"I just stopped by to tell you I don't like to see her treated that way. Not when—though the reasons escape my comprehension—you seem to be important to her."

I didn't believe for a minute that he'd come because he had business in New York. Jeannine had sent him.

I wonder, though, what would have happened if she hadn't? Would I still be sitting in the barn, in some kind of weird and timeless hibernation? Maybe I would be. I'd seen no one, talked to no one. All that I'd done, that I remember, was eat sandwiches and watch movies.

All right, they were *her* movies.

But if Sonny hadn't showed . . . ?

Look, she'd caught me at my worst moment. When she'd called, and I'd told her I couldn't go on with the book, all I could think of was what the Fawn had done to me, with a little help from her 55th Street connection. I was down, I was flailing, and maybe it *was* what I wanted, but isn't a man—even The Great Villain—entitled to a period of mourning?

"Well," I said, "what do you suggest I do about it?"

"For starters," he answered with that ruined grin, "you could offer a thirsty man a drink."

The first one was his idea. So were the next dozen or two. We started in the barn that afternoon. Somehow, by the time we were done, we must have hit every saloon along the Hudson between the county lines, and I know we closed the last one because they threw us out. Along the way, we admitted more to each other about our private lives than either of us was probably used to. God only knows what I told him about myself, but I learned among other things that, apropos of his Malibu run, Sonny went on periodic homosexual sprees. He called them "toots," and sometimes they ended, like the one the night of Claude Rhinelander's party, with Sonny being scraped off some California sidewalk.

He made light of the habit—"Smoking's worse for your health," he said—but apparently it drove Jeannine crazy, and he kept reminding me not to let on to her that he'd told me. Jeannine worried about AIDS. Jeannine worried about his career. He didn't give a flying fuck about his career, although people who knew about him in Hollywood were pretty good about keeping it quiet. And if he got AIDS at his age, what the fuck difference did it make? He needed to clear the cobwebs, he said. He had to clear the cobwebs every so often. Every man did. That was what I needed: to clear the cobwebs, that was why I should have another drink.

I remember we talked about Claude. He was one of those things, Sonny said, in and out of Jeannine's life, and you just had to put up with it. And Fryberg: "A prancing fairy," he said disdainfully, "but scared to death about going public with it because it could cost him his job."

At some point, I put the question to him: how come he'd picked me?

"Everybody said you were the best," he answered. "And the most discreet. Shit, you don't even put your name on the books you write."

"That's all?"

"What d'you mean, is that all? You fishing for compliments?"

"Gloria Farran couldn't have said I was the best."

He laughed at that.

"You're a smart kid, Danny Boy," he said, his eyes almost closing between the puffiness above and below. "Actually, Farran didn't bad-mouth you that much. But I thought it wasn't such a bad idea that you'd lost one along the way."

"Sort of like paying my dues?" I asked.

He shook his head, his lower lip protruding.

"You haven't even begun to pay your dues," he said. "The thing is, Jeannie really wants to do this book. She says it's the most important thing in her life. This isn't the first time I've heard her say that, but normally it's a bunch of bullcock. She gets these ideas, people—suddenly it's the most important thing—and then she goes into another picture and it's all forgotten. This one is different, though. You're different. Don't ask me why, but I've been around her long enough to know. You're no one-night stand."

I must have asked him if it was the book, or me, because I remember him saying: "Beats me, Danny Boy. How good are you in bed?"

And more. He rambled on about loyalty. Loyalty for Jeannine—for "Jeannie"—was an unbreakable bond. Major, he said. Very major. For the people close to her—when they were in need, needed her—she was solid as a rock. But she expected in return, and when she felt betrayed . . .

"Look out," Sonny said, more than once. "You better call her, Danny. You better call her and get on a plane. Either way—whether you're in or out. That's what you better do."

When I woke up in the morning, in the barn, in all my clothes, I had no recollection of how I'd gotten home, much less to bed. Sonny's doing, presumably. Ditto my monumental hangover.

But where was he?

I found a note thumbtacked to the barn door.

"Call her for Christ's sake," it said.

But no Sonny, and outside, his car was gone.

A Bloody Mary later, I did what he'd told me to. It was early enough in the East that it must have awakened Jeannine. Though she said not, her voice was still blurry from sleep.

"Sonny was here," I told her. "Tim. Did you send him?"

"No." Then, with a sudden anxiety. "Why are you calling? Did something happen to him?"

"Not that I know of," I said. "He's a little hung over, probably, but none the worse for wear."

"He drinks too much. Why are you calling, Daniel? Are *you* all right?"

"He said I'd hurt you. I didn't mean to, believe me." The words sounded flat to me, hollow. Silence, then. I thought for a moment that she might have hung up, or dropped off to sleep. "Jeannine?" I said. "Are you there?"

"Yes," she answered. Another pause. Then, thoughtfully, "You haven't hurt me, Daniel. I don't think so. What I think is that you are hurting yourself. Whatever has happened—and you still haven't told me everything—it has happened. It is past now, done, and you have your life. I think it is here that you belong now, not there. But it is not for me to choose, you know."

Simply put.

There is, as writers and actors well know, such a thing as timing. Had she sung the same siren's song the day before, two days before, opening her door to me, as it were, I wouldn't have heard it. Wouldn't have been capable of hearing it. Now I did. It was, apparently, all I needed to hear. An hour or so later, I was en route to Kennedy.

Jeannine had insisted on meeting me. It turned out she'd driven the Mercedes to the airport herself—a first, as far as I knew—and she piloted us out, down the freeways to Newport, then along the Pacific Coast Highway south. Another first: in those few times we'd left her house together unofficially, she'd gone in for disguises—sunglasses and no makeup, either a broad-brimmed hat or a bandanna tied around her head. Now there were only the sunglasses. She wore an oversized ocher T-shirt scooped out at the neck, white sailor pants, white sandals which she kicked off for driving.

Her first words to me, at the airport (her head back as she studied me, the faintest touch of a smile around the corners of her eyes), were: "You look awful, Daniel. Just dreadful. How can I be seen in public with you?"

She declared herself in charge of my makeover. We stopped at a shop in Laguna—"the all-white store," she called it, and it turned out to be almost literally true, from the clothes to the fixtures to the cash register. The only exception was the pretty black girl who worked the counters (though she was dressed in white, too) and who addressed Jeannine, discreetly, as Ms. Hardy. I emerged all in white myself, down to a pair of deck shoes without socks, and my old, my "eastern" clothes abandoned at Jeannine's insistence, and a new pair of wrap-around shades from a place down the street.

"Better," Jeannine said, appraising me. "But we still have to get rid of that airplane smell and the eastern pallor."

We did this by the blue waters of the Pacific, somewhere south of Laguna, at the inn she had chosen for our forgetting.

OUR FORGETTING?

Let me explain it this way:

"Here," Jeannine murmured, "let me do what you like."

"How do you know what I like?" I teased. She had already lowered herself so that her short-cropped hair grazed my belly.

"It is part of my witchcraft," she answered, her tongue licking lightly, "to know things like that."

A twilight breeze billowed the curtains of the open windows, and the rhythmic breaking of the surf onto the beach below us blotted out all other noise. A few moments before, we'd been watching the Pacific rolling in from the west, the rollers long under the sun and perfectly spaced, gathering the undertow into them as they approached the beach, then breaking in a steady line from south to north. "It is like a Busby Berkeley musical," Jeannine had said and, when I didn't get it, pointed out the crashing white foam, south to north, that reminded her of a row of white-laced dancers toppling one after the other.

"Come, my Daniel," she'd said then, "I think we have talked enough for now."

Amen to that.

She pushed my thighs apart, still licking with little flicks of her tongue, and reaching with her hands, gathered my balls. She cupped them, licked them underneath, murmured to them. Some electric re-action set loose a delicious tingling all the way to the nape of my neck. Witchcraft. Instinctively, I reached for her, but she brushed me away, laughing softly, her head momentarily lifted so that her dark eyes found mine.

"Lie back now," she commanded. "Listen to the ocean. Let me help you forget."

I obeyed. Her tongue worked, her lips, steady, rhythmic like the breakers, her teeth now joining in small nibbles. And murmuring, purring. This too was new, I thought dimly. As everything was new. Always our lovemaking had been a game of catch Jeannine, matching my performance against her elusiveness. A game, say, of endurance as well as technique. Sometimes I brought her to the edge of coming—always against her will, it seemed—and the sound of her little gasps, followed by the feel of her lithe body arching into mine, and clamping, clamping, invariably brought me off with her. But sometimes I couldn't bring her that far. Sometimes it was as though nothing on earth could.

But I was supposed to be forgetting. I was supposed not to remember what it was like before, nor to think of the Fawn, even fleetingly. Somewhere inside me a resistance began to grow obstinately, and Jeannine must have sensed it in her witchcraft. Her thumbs now dug into my flesh, and I dripped with sweat. Clamping me in her mouth, she swallowed me with her lips, her cheeks, her head falling, rising, falling, rising. I felt the resistance start to give way— like a dam when it can no longer hold back the flood, or the curtains, flapping sails, suddenly breaking before the wind—and I struggled to hold against her, shouting now in anticipation of my inevitable failure. Until, in some sudden and overwhelming escalation, the undertow sucked me powerfully up, and in, and flung me forward, and the rest of me was already floating, weightless, as I came in spasms.

I flopped weakly back, unable to move. Flotsam, washed up, spent, deliciously spent. Somewhere Jeannine's face drifted above me. I glimpsed her smile, her white teeth. This too, new. Somewhere, sometime in my vague history, were other women . . . nothing like this. I had never known one . . .

"What do you remember now, Daniel?" Jeannine was saying.

"Nothing."

"How do you feel now, my darling? Being a kept man?"

Her voice was so warm, close. Her breath warm.

"Wonderful . . . delicious . . ."

At which, I think, I fell asleep.

All new.

THIS WAS HER theme, her answer. If what I was so afraid of was being a younger man to an older woman, a kept man, a darling, a— what was it?—a puppy dog to a woman who was frightened of growing old?—then why didn't I at least experience it once and find out if it really was so terrible?

Later that first day—"The first day," she said, "of our new life"— she sat on the edge of the bed, holding my hand, talking to me. No, making a speech.

"This business of—what did you call it?—my 'track record?' " she said. "All these young men I've used and thrown out with the rubbish? You say you don't want to be used. But I've already used you, Daniel. And you've already used me. You've used me for sex, you've used me for business. And you came with a wife, Daniel, don't forget that.

What was I to think about the wife? Perhaps it is time you found out what I am like without the wife.

"And this, too, Daniel," she said thoughtfully. "Yes, I have thrown young men out with the rubbish. Older men as well. And they have done it to me. There is no way of telling now what will happen to us. Maybe I will throw you out. Maybe you will throw me out. There may even be a chance no one will throw anyone out. But isn't that something for us to find out ourselves? Can't we have our few days forgetting about the wife, the book? Without Claude, too, without my film? Without anyone except ourselves?"

WE WHALE-WATCHED. (We saw none. Probably it was the wrong time of the year.) We swam in the blue pool on a platform above the sandy beach, surrounded by palms. We ate on the wide terrace outside our top-floor suite. We walked, our hands interlocked, our feet leaving imprints in the chilly sand where the surf bubbled. We sunned (Jeannine carefully masked). We bathed each other. We made love. The inn, opened only the previous year, was a discreet and beautifully appointed Shangri-La. Everyone, I'm sure, knew who Jeannine was; no one, guests or staff, made an issue of it. The closest we approached the outside world was the day we ventured to the spot, a few miles down the coast, where Richard Henry Dana had first touched land after his two years before the mast, some century and a half before.

Jeannine was gazing down from our vantage point, her face into the sea wind and a yellow silk scarf blowing behind her. "Imagine the sailing vessel coming into the harbor on a day like this, no bigger than . . . How big would it have been, Daniel?"

"I've no idea," I said, laughing. "A middle-sized yacht, maybe?"

"And no one here. Empty. Who would have been here?"

"Indians selling trinkets," I said. "The missions probably. I think they were here by that time."

"No one," she said, preferring it her own way. "An empty coast, after all those months at sea. And it wasn't so long ago, was it? What is a hundred years? It is nothing. We only missed them by a few days, Daniel."

"What would you have said?" I teased her. "If you'd been standing here when they landed?"

"I'd have said: 'Welcome, Mr. Dana,' " her arms extended. " 'Welcome to California!' "

I confessed that I'd never read *Two Years Before the Mast*, though I'd once seen the movie, probably on some "Late Late Show." Robert Donat, I think.

"You Americans," she said, taking my arm. "You're so unromantic, particularly where your own history is concerned. It's as though history only started the day you were born. But in a way, you're right. They say we Europeans are stuck in history. I think it is so. At the castle they were all there, you know? My husband's ancestors, going back for centuries. They all hung on the walls. Ugly portraits. They cleaned them once a year, on ladders. I used to think they were watching everything we did. Watching him, watching me, Christine. I think they hated us."

She shuddered a little, leaning against me. A moment later I realized that she was crying, but so quietly there was no sound.

I turned her around to face me, her back now to the wind. I asked her why she was crying.

She closed her eyes, shaking her head.

"If I told you," she said, "you'd only laugh at me."

"Why do you assume that? Is it because of him? The count?"

She shook her head.

"Then why?"

"If I tell you, will you promise not to laugh?"

"Of course I won't."

"Promise?"

"I promise."

"It's because I'm an old soul, Daniel," she said. "You don't know what that means, old soul, do you?"

"No, not really."

"It means that I've lived before as other people, that my soul has lived before. Other lives, other places. I know that I have. Please don't laugh, but it's true. I think I've even been to this place before—it's so familiar. But not in this life, I know that."

"Maybe you *were* here when Dana landed," I said, smiling at her.

"Now you're making fun of me," she said, smiling back. "But maybe it is true."

"And if so, was I here, too?"

She shook her head, studying me.

"No," she said. "You are a new soul. A young one. I can always tell. You have just started out on your journey."

"How can you be sure?"

"I can always tell by people's eyes. There is a difference."

"Is that bad?" I asked. "Being a new soul?"

"Bad? It is absolutely *marvelous!* Think of all the adventures you know nothing about yet!"

DID IT WORK, though? The makeover? The forgetting? The old soul and the new one?

Over and over, I told her I loved her. I meant it, meant more, but I couldn't find the words. I was enthralled, spellbound. It was as though all my life I'd been climbing a ladder, and suddenly the ladder wasn't there anymore—maybe I'd kicked it away myself—and instead there was Jeannine. I had my fill of her, and it was never enough, and there was always more.

In the oasis of those few days, certainly it worked. And if somehow we could have frozen time or, better, have teleported ourselves, our small baggage, to some farther place no one ever went to—then yes, maybe it would have worked beyond those few days.

It wasn't as though we erased history. Short as mine was (in this, my first life), Jeannine made me talk about it. It was impossible, she said, for me to know so much about her and she so little about me. Pushed by her questioning, I told her about the Fawn, and what had happened—minus some of the more painful details (like my pining on the floor in SoHo and the fire in the fireplace), but including Lew Rhinelander.

Our publisher.

Under other circumstances, her reaction might have surprised me. She fell silent for a moment, as though meditating what to say. Then, coolly, "I think we will talk about this some other time. For right now, let us have no Rhinelanders with us."

Easier said than done, however.

I was sitting on the terrace in the late afternoon, the headrest of the lounge chair at a three-quarters tilt so I could catch some rays. It had been an unusually warm day. The sun was still hot, the ocean breeze now cool and steady, and Jeannine was asleep inside in the aftermath of our lovemaking. There was no reason under the sun for me to be feeling malaise. True, we were due to leave the next day. But beyond that, there was, somewhere inside me, like the faintest shadow of a cloud drifting across the sun, the hint that not even Jeannine, adept as she was, could freeze time. I'd run west, climbed the ladder to her siren's call, and we'd abandoned our unfinished business, she and I, separately and together. But now the clock was about to start ticking again.

After a while I stood up, stretching, and eyed the vista from the wrought-iron balustrade. Up the coast, out of range of our part of the beach, I could see surfers bobbing, waiting for their cold waves like huddled blackbirds. Closer, a small group of intrepid souls, possibly from the hotel, was trying wind-surfing in wet suits and, to judge, not doing very well at it. Below, where the coast jutted out in a rocky promontory, two horseback riders wended their way slowly along the surf, and on the beach itself a flotsam of sunners still basked on the striped beach lounges provided by the hotel.

Then I saw them.

They were trudging south toward the hotel near the surf line, all in sunglasses, three men in a clump and another one a little behind who, if I hadn't recognized him, might have been thought not to belong to the others. Claude Rhinelander was a bit in the lead, the shortest of the lot, in swim trunks and some sort of short white unbuttoned shirt or jacket, with the collar up. Probably terrycloth. Sandals on his feet. The white bristle of his head glistened in the sun.

Landward to Claude, in white trousers and carrying his shoes in one hand, was Lew. Also hatless. Shirtless. Sunglasses. Dark skin, as though native to the sun. Stooping slightly as he walked, probably in order to listen.

Where was the Fawn? I thought suddenly.

It took me a moment to recognize the stocky figure on the surf side. Shorts, some kind of Hawaiian shirt, a long-billed cap. Black bill, white top. Irving R. Stewart, the money man.

And behind them a few paces—inevitably—Allen Fryberg. Inevitable, too, that he should look somehow out of place, even though he was also wearing swim trunks, and a dark sweatshirt, and sunglasses which hid his darting eyes. Something about his bulk, his pallor. The others, all older, looked in better shape.

Jesus Christ. Was it really just a coincidence that, with all the miles of California coastline, and all the joints and hideaways within driving distance of L.A., this was the one place they'd chosen?

"Small world," Jeannine said, suddenly by my side.

I hadn't even heard her approaching. She'd come across the terrace in bare feet, wrapped in one of those giant terrycloth robes the hotel provided. She was fresh from the shower, hair still wet and slicked back. Some fragrant floral soap scent. Not a smudge of makeup, and you could see the few lines clearly, across her neck, her forehead, crow's feet at the eyes. Still . . .

Together we watched them from the balustrade. "I guess Claude knew you were here," I said, the malaise now loose in me.

"Hardly," she answered. I wasn't altogether sure I believed her. "Who is that with him?"

"Which one? There's Irving Stewart, Allen Fryberg and brother Lew."

"The tall thin one is Lew Rhinelander?" she said.

"That's right. I thought you said you'd met him."

"Yes. A long time ago. He hasn't changed, at least from a distance." *Let's have no Rhinelanders between us,* she'd said. But here they were.

"I wonder if they're staying here," I said aloud.

"I imagine so. People don't come here just to walk on the beach."

"What would you guess they're talking about?"

"Money, darling. What else?"

They stopped at the surf's edge. In profile to us, his head a long and hawklike silhouette, Lew Rhinelander seemed to be haranguing the others. They faced him in a sort of semicircle, Fryberg leaning in from behind, listening over the shorter men. Three against one, you would have said, until Claude suddenly began to argue back, gesturing, his head thrust up and forward in some kind of challenge, while Lew, head down, kicked at sand, the surf. Then Lew stooped, picking up a stone or a shell which he skimmed sidearm into the water—a seemingly irrelevant act but which, for some reason, provoked his brother beyond all measure. I don't think Claude actually hit him, but Lew backed away and Fryberg moved in as if to restrain his boss.

They held that tableau for some minutes, the two brothers menacing each other through, or around, Fryberg, until Claude broke it off, pivoting abruptly toward us. He turned to shout something back at Lew, then marched across the beach in a straight line toward the hotel. Fryberg followed, as did Stewart a few moments later. Lew, however, remained at the surfline, his back to us, his attention seemingly focused on the incoming breakers.

I started to say something but Jeannine, turning, put a hand to my lips.

"I know what you're thinking, darling," she said, her eyes large even without makeup, "but there's not a soul who knew where we were going, not even Christine." She kept her gaze on mine, eyes unwavering. "Now I will tell you what we are going to do. We are going back to bed and pretend nothing has happened. Then, once it is dark, we are going to pack our things and leave. We will steal away in the night."

I started to object, but again she stopped me.

"It is only one day early," she said. "What difference will one day make?"

"Twenty-four little hours," I answered, but despite the attempt at a quip, I knew it was over, the spell broken.

She seemed to feel it, too.

"I said it before," she went on. "No Rhinelanders."

She smiled at me then. Her arms came around my neck and she kissed me. Nuzzling me with her nose, she murmured, "I've never known you to refuse an invitation, Daniel. Come, let us end where we began."

I verified later, by calling the concierge, that the Rhinelanders were in fact registered at the hotel. So we left, and maybe we should have stolen away to Galapagos, Tasmania, Antarctica while we were at it, though chances were, if we had, that one of them—Claude, more probably Lew—would have bubbled up among the penguins in a custom-made wet suit, scuba tank on his back. And maybe, just maybe, the Fawn hanging on to his flippers?

We drove back to Pasadena that night.

"It seems that each of us has a Rhinelander problem," Jeannine said from the passenger side. "Maybe we will find a way of dealing with it together."

And what the hell difference did it make, I told myself, whether it was a coincidence or not? Whether she'd told Claude or hadn't, or her daughter, or Tim, or put an ad in the *L.A. Times*?

Meanwhile, as it turned out, we had another problem waiting for us in Pasadena. Jeannine's problem, that is, though it became mine. And that was Christine.

Chapter Thirteen

S HE'D ALWAYS BEEN around, I guess, though during my first stays in Pasadena I'd hardly been aware of her. I knew she and Jeannine talked on the telephone a couple of times a day, sometimes for a long time, but when Christine did come home, she had her own apartment in a separate wing of the building on the other side from the garage and gatehouse where the servants lived. I'd know she was there from the car in the driveway—a red Porsche—and sometimes I'd see her at the pool, occasionally at meals. To the extent that I thought anything, it must have been of a moody, snotty young woman, still with a silver spoon in her mouth at age thirty-two.

She had the same color hair as Jeannine, but she wore it shoulder-length, sometimes in a pony tail, sometimes loose, and it made her face longer, more vertical, a feature enhanced by the fact that her eyes were customarily downcast, her smile begrudging. She was given to wearing oversized shirts padded at the shoulders, sometimes an un-constructed jacket with the cuffs rolled up, usually over jeans and bare feet, but unlike Jeannine, who invariably made you think that even her most careless, casual clothes had been made precisely with her body in mind and no one else's (as, in fact, they had), Christine reminded you of some drooping flower, still waiting to grow into herself.

What was it Sonny had said? That she couldn't blow her nose without asking her mother's opinion? If so, then the night we came home, she'd apparently caught a massive cold.

Jeannine didn't come to bed till around three in the morning, and when I woke in the morning, she was already gone. I caught up with her having breakfast at the umbrellaed table near the pool and talking on the telephone, apparently to her agent. The coffee pot was almost empty but the food untouched, and I munched on cold toast from one of those silver racks while I waited for her to finish. I remember wondering if she'd slept at all. Not even her sunglasses could hide the pale, drawn look of her face, and there was an insistent, irritable edge to her voice.

Shooting on her new film, I knew, had been due to start the following week. She was now trying to put it off or delay her participation.

"I've *read* the damn script," she kept saying. "There's no reason they can't shoot around me the first week." Then, after listening: "Well, let them redo their schedule. All it is is a piece of paper." Finally: "Please see what you can do," but in a haughty, chilly tone.

She hung up, made a kiss noise across the table at me, then shouted over her shoulder toward the kitchen: "Ma–*ri*–a!" followed by a stream of Spanish when the maid appeared in the doorway, something, I gathered, to do with Señor Daniel's coffee and where was it?

Uncharacteristically demanding and imperious. What was it all about? Christine, she said. How could she go away when Christine was so unsettled? All that morning, talking to me, again to her agent, the director of the film, the producer, the agent again, arguing, cajoling, there was an air of agitation about her, a coffee-drinker's nervousness, haste, the more so when it appeared she'd have to go to Vancouver as scheduled after all. She glanced frequently in the direction of Christine's apartment, as though afraid she would appear, and when she spoke of her, it was in unnecessarily low tones.

The crisis, it seemed, was that Christine had decided to quit law school. Why, was unclear. They'd had a big argument about it the night before. Jeannine had thought Christine should at least finish the first year, which was almost over anyway, and then decide. If she changed her mind back, at least she wouldn't have to do the first year over. Christine had said there was no risk of that. She hated it. It was a waste of her time—"a total waste," Jeannine quoted. Plus she couldn't stand living in Westwood another minute. Jeannine thought, but wasn't sure, she'd convinced Christine to take her final exams. If she'd agree to that, Jeannine said, then she could move back to Pasadena and study for her exams here.

"I'm sorry, Daniel," she apologized to me.

"For what?"

"I didn't want this. Believe me, I don't want anything interfering with our life together. Certainly not when I have to go away."

"Why should it interfere? It's a big house, if I decide to stay here while you're gone."

"You're staying, Daniel," she stated. "Please don't bring that up again at a time like this."

The subject had come up at the beach, but only briefly. At first, Jeannine had wanted me to go to Vancouver with her. I'd refused. I had work to do, I'd said. Also, I'd only be in the way. Then, at the least, she'd wanted me to stay in Pasadena. She had arranged her shooting schedule so that she wouldn't have more than four days in a row, and at least three days off in between. I would stay in Pasadena, and she would buy me everything I needed—the new computer, the printer, everything. Whatever I needed from New York—what was it? My disks?—I could have the next day by Federal Express.

I was used to working in the barn, used to writing at a distance from my subject. So I'd avoided a decision at the beach, but now Jeannine grew adamant.

"You can't be thinking of going back to New York. What on earth for? There's nothing there for you now. It will be dreary, hopelessly depressing. I'll show you where you'll work—a lovely room, and totally quiet. Everything else will be taken care of for you when I'm not here. Please, Daniel, say you'll be here. It's important to me."

There was an imploring, almost rattled tone to her words—a product, no doubt, of her daughter having showed up again. Not that she wanted me there to watchdog Christine—on the contrary—but the idea of my leaving struck her, apparently, as one more threat.

"I'll stay, Jeannine," I said finally. "Don't worry."

This reassured her only briefly. Moments later she was saying that she wasn't going to allow Christine to disrupt her life. She could stay, she would be given maid service, meals, but that was all. And if Christine was the slightest bit antagonistic toward me while she was away, or got in my way, she wanted to know about it immediately.

"You make her out to be some kind of monster," I said, laughing.

"On the contrary, she has many admirable qualities. It has taken her longer than most people to find herself, that's all. By the time I was her age, I'd already had a career and two husbands. But I was as alone as she is now, and I had greater responsibilities. She, at least, has me."

Their argument waxed and waned, but Jeannine, I noticed, took to biting her cuticles whenever she talked about it. Her position was that Christine needed to stand on her own two feet. She needed to make her own money. She needed her own place, she needed a man. She had to be pushed a little, that was all. It was a question of self-confidence. She was smart enough, attractive enough, and God knows she (Jeannine) had always helped her as much as she could, and not just financially. But then, something always went wrong.

By the time Jeannine left for Vancouver, each had seemingly won. That is, Christine had moved back in—"Temporarily," Jeannine said. "We'll see when I come back." —and Christine would take the exams.

I saw little of her. Once or twice she joined us for meals. Sometimes the Porsche was in the driveway, sometimes gone. She was studying, Jeannine said. Or maybe she wasn't studying. But if she wasn't studying, then where was she? It was obvious, even to me, that Jeannine hovered over her as though she were still a teenager, but another way of looking at it didn't so much as enter my mind until Christine herself expressed it later: "It's not such good form, is it, to have your thirty-two-year-old daughter show up when you've just taken up with a forty-year-old man?"

Meanwhile, there was another, equally obvious explanation for Jeannine's jitters. This was the film itself, and it preyed on her to such an extent that she couldn't concentrate on the book.

"I'm sorry, Daniel," she told me. "I know we were going to work together these few days, but I can't. It's impossible. I simply cannot. You know my story, almost all my story. You have to write it your way now. If, anywhere, it doesn't make sense, we'll work on it when I come back. I promise you. But don't make me do it now."

It was the film, she said. She'd always felt the same way, distracted, tense—afraid, she imagined, though she didn't know what of—when she was about to go to work. It was her form of stage fright, except that she'd never gotten it when she was on the stage. Only the camera brought it on, appearing before the camera. When she was younger, she'd compensated for it by acting wild, crazy, anything that came into her head, on camera as well as off. But that was no longer appropriate behavior, was it? She was supposed to be professional. God knows she *was* professional, once the filming started. But unfit for human company ahead of time. Absolutely unfit.

As though to illustrate, we stopped making love the night we came back from Pasadena.

I thought that, at least this time, the film itself might be a loaded deck. If *Eva's Story* had represented a personal tour de force for her, the remake of *Mother & Daughter* was even more obviously one. The original *Mother & Daughter*, a psychological melodrama built around the murder of the mother's lover, had been immensely popular in the 1950s, with Laraine Hayden as the beleaguered woman who sacrificed all and Nina Hardy as her bad-seed daughter. This time Jeannine was to play the mother, and it occurred to me that an actress who couldn't bear to watch her old films would inevitably have trouble with the switch in roles.

Not so, Jeannine said.

"I always *loved* the story. The rewriting is very clever too. They've made me, the mother, much more—how shall I say?—nuanced, and it always was the more interesting part. They've made me really quite wicked this time. They've also given me a fantastic contract."

As well they should, I thought, because the curiosity value of Nina Hardy in the older role almost guaranteed a successful launch at the box office.

Although this time he had nothing to do with either the production or its financing, Claude Rhinelander held a piece of the action. This was because Olympian, which had made the original *Mother & Daughter*, still held the copyright, and would collect a percentage of the gross—a fact of common knowledge but one, given Jeannine's state of mind, I refrained from mentioning.

It was as though we were together and weren't; as though I was there, and wasn't. Jeannine grew more remote from me, and more clutching at the same time. She rushed about the house, gathering little amulets, talismans, good-luck things she always had on the set with her—some crystals she wore on her body, a lava cameo brooch which had belonged to her mother, an antique doll from her collection—and when, temporarily, she couldn't find one or the other, she became hysterical. Then, finally, her last night at home, the flood came.

We were in the bedroom. She was packed. There was nothing more to do except undress and go to bed. Suddenly she was sobbing uncontrollably.

She couldn't help herself, she said. It was too much for her. She couldn't do it. She couldn't stand leaving me.

What would happen if she didn't go? I asked, looking for some way to calm her.

Didn't go? How could she not go? She'd signed a contract! She couldn't afford not to go!

Was that true? I asked. That she couldn't afford it?

Yes. No. It didn't matter.

She was sitting on the edge of the bed, head down, her long fingers splayed in her hair, her shoulders shaking. She was wearing one of those long, faintly see-through caftan affairs, burnt orange, with a deep V-neck. I took her hands away from her face, pulled her to her feet, but she freed herself and stood there rigidly, hands at her sides, face now lifted and tear-stained.

"You're going to leave me," she said, her voice suddenly taut, brittle. "It will happen the minute I'm gone, the minute I turn my back."

"Jeannine, that's crazy."

"You're going to betray me, Daniel. I know it."

"But I'm not going anywhere. I told you, I'm staying here."

"You never say you love me anymore. You never make love to me."

"Whose doing is that? I *do* love you, Jeannine. For Christ's sake, I—"

"Of course you say it *now*, when I ask you. But why should I have to *beg*?"

Maybe I'd had too little experience of women—in this, my first life. I felt like I was being accused before the fact, of what? My own insecurity about her had been turned inside out. Was I leaving? Had I so much as *thought* about another woman since she'd collected me that day at the airport?

I remember the feeling welling inside me, like a rising tide, like some eruption of the land.

"No, for God's sake, you don't have to *beg!*"

At this, I picked her up—so light in weight, even as tall as she was—and then, on the bed, the caftan pulled up, I showed her how much I loved her while she cried out, lubricating her with my love, her arm at last tight around my neck as she mewed and, sobbing again, tore at my shoulders, *more* she kept saying, give me *more*.

"My God, Daniel," she said, and then, in the morning, she was gone, leaving me alone with her daughter.

. . .

I SENT JEANNINE flowers. I signed them: *I do too love you, always have.* (Did I already know then that Claude Rhinelander never let Jeannine's first day of shooting go by without sending flowers?) And though I missed her terribly the first days after she left, suffering my own separation anxiety, I found myself writing almost as fast as I could keyboard the words.

I had discovered an organizing theme, and that was the beckoning lure of Hollywood. Jeannine had once told me that when she'd left America to marry the count, it had been for good. It was as though she was starting real life over—in a new world, the Old World, which was where she'd thought she really belonged. Even after the debacle of that marriage—during those "lost" years, as she now called them, when she and Christine had lived on the Côte d'Azur and there had been the succession of admirers, lovers, suitors, about whom she'd talked freely and wittily—she'd thought Europe was her home, that her years in Hollywood had been like a youthful sowing of wild oats, an aberration in her life, a fling.

But "Hollywood" never stopped beckoning for long. And the reason I put the place name in quotation marks is that, for Jeannine, at least during those lost years, "Hollywood" really meant Claude Rhinelander.

We had set up my workplace in a large corner room on the second floor of the house—an upstairs living room or sitting room which no one ever used—with a view out over the pool at the planted terraces and cypress trees leading to the hilltop. Jeannine had had some of the furniture moved out to make space for the long white parson's table we'd bought as my desk. That was where I went to work every morning, after a swim and coffee by the pool and the first of several phone conversations with Jeannine in Vancouver.

One evening, late because we'd already said good-night by phone, I decided to go back to print out the day's production. I walked down the carpeted, second-floor hall, past our bedroom, to my workroom. And there, sitting at my parson's table, was Christine. Her back was toward me, her head bent forward, reading off my screen.

"What the hell do you think you're doing?" I said angrily.

She jumped at my voice. She stood, blocking my view as I reached behind her and switched off the machine. Then she laughed.

"Aren't you ever going to interview me for your stupid book? She said you would."

In talking to me, Christine never called Jeannine anything other than *she*.

"I've had it in mind to," I said. "But first I'd like to know what you're doing here."

"What it looks like—reading."

"Is that right?" I said. "This is my property, not yours. And I'll thank you to stay out of here."

"I live here too."

"Not in this room, you don't."

She eyed me quizzically, as though to say: Well, what are you going to do about it—call her? call the police?

"What are you so uptight about?" she asked. "It's good, at least what I read. I didn't get to the dirty parts, though." Then, with a sly look, "Well, what about my interview? What's wrong with right now?"

I could think of several things wrong with it. It was late; I was tired, annoyed; I was also unprepared. But she, apparently, was ready. She dropped into my chair, a tall-backed affair on wheels which Jeannine had chosen because she thought I needed a throne, and looked up at me, smiling slightly, as though waiting for my questions.

"I thought you were supposed to be studying," I said.

"Oh, that," she answered. "I'll pass her stupid exams, there's nothing for her to worry about. But I'm not going to be a lawyer anyway."

"What made you think you wanted to be one in the first place?"

She shrugged. "I had to do *something*. It seemed like an okay idea." She looked up at me skeptically, as though to say that she knew, and I knew, I wasn't the least bit interested in her. "Let's get going then. What don't you know about the dirty parts?"

"What do you mean, the dirty parts?"

"You know exactly what I mean. The stuff that makes books like yours sell. Who she went to bed with; who dumped on her and who she dumped on; the pills she took and the shrinks she went to; why a famous actress gets it off screwing younger men. How old *are* you, by the way?"

"Forty-one," I said, already casting about for ways of cutting the interview short. "I think I know most of that stuff already."

"Do you?" she said doubtfully. "But forty-one, that's not so young. She must be slipping."

"What does that mean?"

"You haven't noticed? Every man she's been with, since we moved back here, has been younger than the one before." No, I hadn't noticed. "She never stops trying to turn back the clock. But you've reversed the trend."

"Maybe that's healthy," I said.

"I doubt it," she answered scornfully.

"What makes you so antagonistic toward her?"

"Was I being antagonistic? Well, that's just me, the way I am. Actually, I think she's marvelous. The last of the great courtesans, isn't that what you'd call her? But what I'm really antagonistic about is people like you."

"Oh? Why is that?"

"Because you keep her from growing old gracefully."

Seeing that I wasn't about to get rid of her, short of throwing her out, I sat down on a couch, my arms across the back, while she rolled my chair around, her legs crossing and recrossing. She had put on a man's white dress shirt, the sleeves rolled up, unbuttoned, over a one-piece black bathing suit. Bare feet. Maybe she'd been night-swimming, or was going. The suit looked dry. She complained about how the room reeked of cigarettes—"She'd have a fit," she said—but, having asked if I had any dope (which I didn't), she then started bumming from me, rolling forward for the cigarette and backward to use the ashtray on the parson's table.

"Do you want to marry her?" she asked me.

"I doubt that's any of your business," I answered.

"I figured you didn't," she said. "At least there's that."

"At least there's what?"

"She's like an accident waiting to happen. God, one of these days, out of sheer stupidity, she might just marry one of you."

"What makes you think that will happen?" I asked. "And why would it be so stupid?"

"The closest she ever came," she went on, ignoring my questions, "was Harry Brea. He was the first of the studs, after we came back here. Harry begged her to marry him."

She stopped rolling the chair and was waiting for my reaction.

"I thought it was a joke," she said. "Harry *begging*. Do you know Harry?"

"I know he directed *Eva's Story,*" I said. "And that they were together for a while at the time. Lovers, I mean."

"*Together* is the understatement of the year. She couldn't keep her hands off him." She paused, eyeing me. "Doesn't that bother you?"

"Doesn't what bother me?"

"That you're just the latest in a long line of eligible studs?"

"Not particularly," I said. "Besides, she can't take it back, can she?"

"But you're *writing* about them, all your well-hung predecessors. That's what I don't understand, unless you're some kind of voyeur. Are you?"

"I haven't given it much thought," I answered noncommittally. "Maybe all writers have some voyeur in them."

She rolled forward, leaning a long arm toward the cigarettes, and I shook one out of the pack for her, another for myself, then lit them both with my lighter.

"I suppose you know what happened with Harry," she said.

"They broke up."

"I'll say they broke up. With Harry on bended knee. Has she described it for you?" In fact, Jeannine hadn't, not in any detail. "It was downstairs, in this house. I was there. Did she tell you why?"

"Only that she threw him out. That it was time."

"But not why?"

"No, not really."

"Either she did or she didn't. I guess she didn't. The reason was that Harry had made a pass at me. Well, more than a pass actually."

She was smiling at me, a sly, sideways smile, as she watched again for my reaction. Then, apparently reading it, she started to laugh and covered her mouth with her hand.

"Excuse me for laughing," she said. "I'm really not that horrible, but sometimes I can read people's minds. You're thinking, *Uh-oh, better watch out for this one.*"

She was pretty close. I wondered, at the same time, how coincidental it was that Christine quit law school exactly when I moved in.

"Who seduced whom?" I asked.

"What makes you think anybody seduced anybody? All that mattered was that she thought so."

"You mean you made it up in order to get rid of Brea?"

"No," she said. She paused, smiling. "But I would have if I'd had to."

"And she'd have believed you?"

"Oh, she'd have believed me."

Jesus, I thought.

"So you're the self-appointed guardian of her morals?"

"Not exactly. Usually her young men self-destruct anyway, else she dumps them. I want to keep her from making a fool of herself, that's all."

"Which she would do by getting married again?"

"I didn't say that. It would depend on the person."

Clearly I was the wrong person.

I may have moved as though to get up off the couch. Maybe I said something about it being late, or about wanting to get an early start in the morning.

"Don't you want to know about Claude?" she continued. "Claude Rhinelander?"

"What about him?" I said, sitting back again.

"He wanted to marry her even before I was born. Plus he's rich. She could stop worrying about money."

"Does she worry that much about money?"

"Does she worry that much about money?" Christine repeated sarcastically. "You don't know her very well at all if you can ask a question about that. Try living with her a while."

I'd known Jeannine to allude to money, yes, and during "the lost years" it had been a problem. But ever since *Eva's Story,* I pointed out, she had been making top dollar in Hollywood.

"Yeah, she makes a lot," Christine agreed, "*when* she works. But she spends a ton. Who paid for all this stuff, for instance?" waving her arm at my computer layout. "I bet she did."

"It was a gift to me."

"That's just what I mean," she said, nodding. "Think of all the people on the payroll. All the servants here, and there's still the house in Cap Ferrat. And me. And Tim. Now you."

"I'm not on the payroll."

"Oh no? What do you think it costs to feed you? Who bought the clothes you're wearing?"

I laughed, to cover my irritation. It happened that I was wearing my Laguna makeover.

"So you'd vote for Claude Rhinelander?" I said.

"I didn't say I'd vote for him, are you kidding? That ugly little man? But she could do worse. In fact, she already has."

I didn't much enjoy being baited. But I also knew from experience that there are times when the baiter oversteps, and then, on occasion, you learn something.

"How well do you know him?" I asked.

"Uncle Claude? That's what I used to call him when we lived in the south of France. He used to come visit two or three times a year. He always stayed at the Negresco, in Nice. I thought that was a fabulous hotel, all those mirrors, and the footmen dressed up like chocolate soldiers. He came for the Cannes Film Festival every May, even though he said it was a waste of time for business. Sometimes he also showed up at Christmas, sometimes for her birthday. And always loaded with gifts."

"Santa Claude?" I said, trying to imagine Claude Rhinelander with his arms full of packages.

She smiled.

"Santa Claude," she repeated sardonically. "I like that. But it wasn't for me. All for her, always."

"Whose idea was 'Uncle' Claude?" I asked. "That you call him that?"

She tilted back in the throne, her elbows on the armrests. It had one of those flexible backs which gave a little when you pushed against it. She continued to look at me, smiling slightly and twisting a lock of hair idly through two fingers. Suddenly, thinking the old thought—that her father had to be Claude—I realized I was closing in on what I wanted from her.

Jeannine had said she didn't know.

Christine, though, didn't strike me as the kind who'd take kindly to being left in the dark.

"Well?" I prompted.

"Maybe we'll talk about that some other time."

"Why not now?" But she'd decided that the game was over—at least for the time being. She stood up, her movements suddenly angular.

"Because I'm going swimming now," she said, looking back at me as she headed for the door. "Want to come?"

I shook my head.

"How come?" she said caustically. "Afraid I'll grab your balls?"

I don't remember my retort—she was gone anyway—but later, from our bedroom window, I could make out her shadowy figure gliding up and down the pool below, identical to her mother except for the long hair streaming out behind her.

JEANNINE CAME HOME. A very different Jeannine at first: confident, outgoing, loving. The shooting had gone splendidly, she said, with very few retakes. It was the best organized company she'd worked with in years, and they were already ahead of schedule. Nothing stopped while she was away—they were shooting around her—but she'd been asked if she'd consider a change in her contract. If she'd give up her three-day breaks, they thought they could cut the original ten weeks of filming to eight, possibly seven.

"Of course, that's up to you, darling," she said. "I told them I would let them know, but it *is* up to you. Or us. I can't stand not being with you all that time but the idea that I'm going to have to leave again in just two days is worse."

The truth was that, in the same seven or eight weeks of uninterrupted work, I thought I might be able to finish a first draft of the book. Provided, that is, that I had a couple of days of Jeannine's undivided attention beforehand.

But this was not to be.

How does a thirty-two-year-old daughter throw repeated crises and still get attention for them? Christine managed it. She did it most often, strange as it may sound, by telephone. The phone would ring, day or night, and even though she and Jeannine were physically only fifty yards apart, give or take, it would be Christine. Miserable all over (per Jeannine), hysterical and weeping. I would hear Jeannine's voice getting progressively tighter, higher in pitch, as though the vocal cords themselves were being squeezed. And often as not, day or night, she would end up going down to the apartment at the far end of the house.

The gist of the trouble (per Jeannine) was: What was going to become of her now? It was stupid for her to go on with law school, but what was she supposed to do? She had no one, except Jeannine. She was thirty-two years old, and she was nowhere, had no one, and she was as dependent on Jeannine as when she'd been in diapers.

"She's not wrong," Jeannine said. "It's all true, in a way. What *is* she supposed to do? But then, what am *I* supposed to do about it?"

I stayed out of it as long as I could. It wasn't that hard. When the three of us were together—at meals, mostly—Christine made a point of ignoring me. Suddenly she'd become fascinated about the shooting of *Mother & Daughter,* and it was as though I wasn't there, until Jeannine, quickly aware of what was going on, began directing her answers to me. Christine would then change the subject. On one occasion, encompassing both of us in her sullen gaze, she got up from the dinner table and simply walked away.

"Don't," I said to Jeannine, who started to go after her. "Let her go."

She listened—that time. But my other remedies, logical enough— that Christine should see a shrink, that Jeannine should throw her out of the house—only made her defensive. Christine was already in treatment, she said sharply. She had been for years. She went four times a week (if she went, I thought). And how could she throw her out? Did I mean *bar* her from the premises? Was that what I meant? But how could she do that? No, she could never do that.

"Well," I said, "in the long run, you may have to choose."

Jeannine stared at me, shocked.

"Don't do this to me, Daniel," she said quietly, her eyes fixed on mine. "Please. Not now. Let's simply not discuss it. It doesn't concern you." Then, her tone shifting into anxiety: "What has she done to you? What haven't you told me?"

I told her that I'd found Christine reading the book. I tried to minimize it, but Jeannine was appalled. How *dare* she, she said. She made me agree that, from then on, I would keep my disk in her wall safe, the one in the closet-room that adjoined our bedroom.

Throughout those few days, I had the uneasy suspicion that the same scenes had been played before, that the two female actors already knew their parts by heart. In one sense, Jeannine was right: it didn't concern me. But in another, it clearly did; whatever she wanted to believe, you didn't have to be a shrink to understand that Christine was out to get rid of me. And though Jeannine promised to deal with the situation the minute the film was over, her only solution for the time being was to take her daughter on a shopping spree.

I was summoned when they came gaily back from Beverly Hills in the chauffeured car, laden with bags and boxes, mostly for Christine but including, for me, a nineteenth-century gold pocket watch, with a chime mechanism and chain to match. But the watch, the bags and boxes, were only accessories to the main event. The main event being Christine.

A made-over Christine.

The hair was still shoulder-length, but somehow fuller and pulled back off the face. The eye makeup—I'd never seen Christine with makeup of any kind—was definitely Jeannine-inspired, and so were the clothes, a rust-colored silk pants suit.

For a moment, as I came down the stairs, the resemblance was uncanny, the more so when Christine, seeing me, threw her arms around her mother and hugged her cheek-to-cheek, giggling, as though they were posing in a minute-photo booth. They could have been sisters in that instant, their eyes wide and laughing. But then— it was Jeannine who broke the tableau—they separated, and Jeannine stayed Jeannine and Christine . . . well, Christine, by comparison, became a gawky little girl playing dress-up.

Except that she was no longer a little girl.

"Well?" Jeannine said, amused. "What do you think, Daniel?"

"Yes, Daniel," Christine echoed, eyeing me sardonically, "be our judge."

I thought a lot of things about it, then and later—not the least of which was what on earth did Jeannine think she was doing—but on the spot, I rose to the occasion.

"Well," I said, "I think Christine can take your place in Vancouver now. Which means that you, my good woman, will get to stay here."

The right remark, it turned out. It brought a laugh even from Christine, and suddenly, for what was left of Jeannine's stay, the phone stopped ringing.

As for the book—"my dreary past," as Jeannine had taken to calling it—her solution was that I should give her what I'd done to take along with her and send her more, by courier. She would read it faithfully, carefully. They worked long hours on the film, but they started early, and she couldn't go to sleep at night right away, not without me there, and there was nothing else to do so she would read at night. It would be a little bit like having me with her. She would make marks on my manuscript. Or if I didn't want her to make marks, she would use those little sticky notepads. It would be like talking to me, she said, writing me notes on the sticky papers.

Better still, we would do all that, but I should come up to Vancouver. She would insist on one long break in the middle of the schedule. I would come up and we would go somewhere together. There would be no Christine. It would be like Laguna, except that this time we would work, too, she promised me. And the book would be wonderful, she knew it was going to be wonderful.

Her last night, we made love with an uncommon frenzy, even a ferocity. Astride me, straddling me, pinning my shoulders, chanting, singing, laughing, she refused to come until I came first. In some dimly lit daze of sex, her flushed face leaning above me, her eyes exquisitely narrowed, her mouth half open as she clenched and unclenched on me, I tried to reach for her but couldn't, pinned by her amazingly agile strength. I felt helpless, almost faint when, at long last, she let me go.

And then again, the next morning, just before she left. She was putting on her makeup, part of her ritual from which I continued to be banished, and I was languishing in bed, half-awake, half-asleep, deliciously exhausted. I was aware, vaguely, that she was standing by the bed, in yellow bra and panties, one arm slipped through the sleeve of a yellow silk blouse. Then, wriggling out of the panties, she was kneeling on the bed, the blouse cast off, her arms behind her back to unhook the bra.

"You're too beautiful," she murmured. "I can't leave you like this."

"You'll miss your plane."

"I'll tell the man to drive faster."

I reached for her, suddenly needing her again myself. I smelled her musk, tasted the sweet of her lipstick, her tongue, and I realized with one of those weird clarities that what she was doing, had been doing that night, whether she knew it or not, was claiming me, laying a claim that would last at least for her absence.

I welcomed it, reveled in it. And I claimed her back.

Then she was standing by the bed again, fully dressed this time.

I told her that I loved her, that I would miss her, that I couldn't live without her.

"Write quickly," she said, bending to kiss me good-by.

"Act quickly," I answered.

Chapter Fourteen

JENNY BERGLER CALLED, early morning, all agush. Where did I think she was? At the Bel Air, she answered herself. It was all so impromptu, unexpected, she'd flown in the night before, nobody, but nobody, knew she was here, it was a terrible imposition, she knew, on such short notice, but she couldn't possibly get out to Pasadena, she had no idea it was so far away from everything, but could Nina and I come to lunch—today, at the hotel? She was dying to meet Nina, at long last.

It was impossible, I said, and I explained why.

"Oh." Then: "Well, that's all right. I mean, it's too bad, I really am dying to meet her. Why does she live in Pasadena anyway? I never heard of that."

Because, I was tempted to say, it's so far away from the Bel Air. But I didn't.

I begged off lunch, too, thinking I was letting her off the hook gracefully, but Jenny wouldn't hear of it. It was time we met, she insisted. A couple of phone calls later, while she rearranged her schedule, I found myself reslotted at four o'clock. Around two thirty in the afternoon, therefore, I printed out the curtailed day's work, closed the store, and headed off in Jeannine's Mercedes, wondering what Jenny and I were going to find to talk about.

Two things, as it turned out.

One, although she didn't say it in so many words, was that the Rhinelanders were breaking up.

Two: she tried to make a pass at me.

We were into June, the beginning of the traditional smog season in southern California, but the inversion system had already pushed the air eastward, piling it across the city into the eastern valleys, Pasadena, Riverside, where the San Bernardino range kept it penned. Only those lucky enough (and well-heeled enough) to live up high escaped it, and as I descended toward the freeway from Jeannine's I could see smog spread like a noxious blanket, yellow-tinged, from horizon to horizon. How could people live that way? I thought for the umpteenth time, as I headed west in my air-conditioned cocoon. Of course, those rich enough to escape in their hillside aeries were also those most prone to the other regional disasters—mudslides and forest fires. It occurred to me, as it had frequently before, that California was inherently hostile to civilization, and someday it would simply shrug us all off and be done with us.

Bel Air was a different story. Nestled into the east-west range of hills that separate the city from the San Fernando Valley, and close enough in miles to Beverly Hills, Westwood, Brentwood and the rest of the well-heeled belt of West L.A., it was nevertheless an oasis apart. As green as a rain forest, as though one giant inground sprinkler system misted the whole of it morning, noon and night, it was, in its foliage and its mostly hidden mansions, as close as California comes to the really posh suburbs of the Northeast. And poshest of the posh, though more discreetly so, was the Bel Air Hotel, where I found my publisher sitting in wrought iron on the terrace of the shaded garden, tapping her foot impatiently.

I was late, but my explanation was none of Jenny Bergler's business.

On one of the palm-lined side streets heading up toward Sunset from the freeway, I passed a woman walking on the sidewalk in the same direction I was going in. She was tall, I registered in passing, broad-shouldered, a swing to her stride. All in white except for a broad-brimmed black straw hat and a long thick braid of russet hair down her back.

Unusual for L.A., I thought, glimpsing her again through the side mirror. A stylish, even chic white woman on a residential sidewalk in the middle of the afternoon. And without a dog. What was she doing there?

Then—I was almost at the next intersection, a red light—it hit me right between the eyes.

For Christ's sake, I'd just seen the Fawn!

I looked to park or turn around, but the light turned green and cars were honking behind me. Flustered, I turned right into traffic, some broad, six-lane thoroughfare. The other drivers must have thought I'd gone bananas. I kept slowing down, looking for a place to stop, then speeding up again. A U-turn was impossible. Finally I turned down some other palm-lined street, and right again, and right again, back, I thought, to where I'd spotted her.

Gone.

I couldn't find her.

Maybe it was the same street, maybe it wasn't. I'd registered no landmarks other than the palms, and there are lots of palms in L.A. At some point, though, as I continued to circle the neighborhood, doubling back and looking, I must have gone up the same street. But no Fawn. No woman in white, chic, with the black straw hat and the chestnut braid.

Sure, I know. There must be as many women in California as there are palms, and some of them, at least, must resemble the Fawn.

No sir.

I'd known her to wear her hair in just that braid—at makeover times, usually, when she'd decided she needed a new look.

She loved big straw hats in summer.

Black and white, that was the Fawn in summer.

The walk, striding from the hips, long-legged, almost jaunty.

Jesus. Who else but somebody from the East would find it natural to walk on an L.A. sidewalk in midafternoon?

Where was Lew?

I stopped somewhere. I'd broken into a sweat—sweating, mind you, with the air conditioner on high. And heaving—big drafts of air—as though I'd been holding my breath for the last fifteen minutes.

I guess it didn't matter whether it was the Fawn or not. What mattered was ten years. Ten years out of my life, gone, like that, *whoosh*.

Everything with Jeannine had happened so fast. Suddenly—at least it seemed sudden—I found myself parked on an L.A. side street in midafternoon, late in my forty-first year, in Nina Hardy's air-conditioned Mercedes.

Late in my forty-first year!

"I love the way you hustle for a buck," the Fawn used to say.

That seemed like the day before yesterday.

Jesus Christ Almighty.

JENNY BERGLER WAS dressed in polka dots in the shaded garden, good-sized navy-blue ones on a white silk field. Long-sleeved blouse, matching skirt to below the knees, white and navy matching shoes. Her face was flushed from the heat, and one foot, as I said, was tapping the slate under her table. I've no idea why she chose to cover her whole body in silk, in June in California.

"You're late," she accused, making a point of glancing at her watch.

"I'm sorry, Jenny. The traffic. Is Lew out here with you?"

"No, why should he be?" she answered tartly.

I could think of one good reason: I'd just seen her.

"But you look *wonderful,* Dan!" she exclaimed, her mood changing. "It's absolutely remarkable, you look just like a . . . well, like a Californian! But you haven't been out here that long, have you?"

She was drinking what looked like a club soda with lime. I ordered a gin and tonic. I was tempted to ask for a double gin but thought better of it.

"Now tell me everything about the book," she said. "Tell me about Nina, everything. I'm absolutely *crestfallen* not to be meeting her. I know I should have given you more warning, but I didn't know I'd be coming out myself till the day before yesterday. It's very unofficial. Please tell her how sorry I am."

I did tell her about the book, some. Into it as I was by that time, I welcomed sharing it with someone. But Jenny, oddly, didn't seem all that interested.

"You ought to keep Allen informed," she said.

"Allen Fryberg?"

"He calls me every other day about it," she said. " 'How's it coming? When will there be something to read?' I tell him to ask you. You know each other, don't you?"

"Yes."

Strange, now that she mentioned it, but I'd only talked to Fryberg once or twice since my interview with Claude.

"By the way," she said, "tell me something off the record. How well placed is Allen?"

She said it in an offhand way, but it still struck me as a peculiar question.

"What do you mean by well placed?"

"Well, I know he's a V.P., and Claude's right hand. They're always together, God knows. He's practically Claude's shadow. The joke is that he sleeps at the foot of Claude's bed. Even closer maybe, who knows?"

She giggled a little. The suggestion that Claude Rhinelander might also be gay struck me as beyond preposterous.

"Somehow I have the feeling I can say things to you, Dan," she went on, "that I wouldn't to anyone else. Don't misunderstand, I think Allen's brilliant. Absolutely. He may think he knows more about publishing than he actually does—just because he worked for Lew once—but he's sharp, witty, and if Claude needs him . . . ? But what does he actually *do?* When you talk to people at the studio, nobody seems to know."

Clearly she was leading up to something, but it wasn't immediately forthcoming. Still, why ask me about Fryberg? What was I supposed to know that she didn't? Or was it because of Jeannine—my Jeannine connection, and Jeannine's to Claude?

I made some innocuous comment, whereupon Jenny complained about the heat. It really was too hot, we ought to move inside if I didn't mind. No, not the bar, she hated bars. Maybe the suite, would that be all right? At least we could talk privately there, and she had some things to say to me she didn't want overheard.

She waited until we were ensconced in her sitting room and a new round of drinks had been served—San Pellegrino and lime for her, another gin and tonic for me. Then she made a point of telling me that the Rhinelander Group wasn't footing the bill. She was in California courtesy of Claude.

"Look, Dan," she said, leaning forward with a confidential air, "I hope you won't mind my mentioning it, but I think what's happened to you is absolutely terrible. Terrible and shameless, if the truth be known."

I'd been expecting a different kind of revelation. At first, I didn't even get what she was talking about.

"When I first heard you wanted out of our contract," she went on, "I didn't understand it at all. Not at all. I mean, you'd met Lew, and you knew me—not all that well, granted, but you know I'm good at what I do. And we'd paid top dollar for Nina, more than we should have actually—not, mind you, that I'm anything but thrilled about owning it. So I didn't understand."

She paused, and looked up at me.

"Now I do," she said.

I told her I thought I was missing her point, although by then I wasn't.

"Come on, Dan. Don't forget, I *work* for him." When I didn't respond, she added, vehemently: "It's all over New York, your whole story. *Everybody* knows. It's their own fault, too. The way they're flaunting it, they might as well have taken out ads in the papers. That's what I mean about shameless. Look, Lew's always been that way. He's a hopeless philanderer, and everybody knows about it, and we've always looked the other way. But this time he's gone too far. For God's sake, this time it's the wife of one of our best-selling *authors!*"

Under other circumstances, the distinction she'd made among Lew Rhinelander's lovers, between the permissible ones and the unpermissible, might have amused me. But hearing it from Jenny, and that particular afternoon, the comedy eluded me.

"I've never met Faith," she said. "Is it true? Is she as beautiful as everybody says?"

"Yes," I answered.

She reached over—we were sitting at one end of a polished wood, kidney-shaped coffee table—and put her hand over mine. And left it there.

"Poor Dan," she said in an uncommonly soft voice. Then, withdrawing the hand, "What do you think you'll do? I imagine you'll divorce her, won't you?"

"I don't know," I heard myself say.

Could it be, I wondered in passing, that she didn't know about me and Jeannine?

"Poor Dan," she repeated. "You know, I admire you enormously. I really do. And here you are stuck with a contract you hate—and God knows, you have every right to hate it!—but you're working. You're still working! And working marvelously well—I can tell—when most other men would be practically paralyzed by self-pity. It makes me feel very *proud* of you, Mr. Springer. And it's going to be a great book, Dan, really great. I can tell. We'll take it right to the top of the list, as long as Nina does the promoting."

This pep talk seemed to inflate her. She leaned back, and her ample, polka-dotted bosom sallied forth, and her dark eyes, moist in sympathy just a moment before, now glistened with something else.

"I can trust you, Dan, can't I?" she asked.

"Of course."

"I know I can. Look, I'm speaking a little out of turn, but please don't worry about Lew as far as your contract is concerned. Don't ask me why, either, but it's all going to work out. Meanwhile, just remember you're *my* author, not Lew's."

I had a quick vision of the group on the beach below Laguna, of Lew kicking sand and Claude stomping off in a rage. But I also remembered something Fryberg had once told me, to the effect that when it came to money, the Rhinelanders were as thick as twins.

"What I'm hearing, Jenny," I said, "is that there's trouble between the brothers. Have they had a falling out?"

She hesitated, between the urge to confide and the urge to withhold.

"Oh," she said blithely, "they're always falling out. It's been going on for years."

"And this time?"

"I really can't say."

If it was true, though, and a situation where there could only be one winner, it was clear enough whom Jenny was betting on.

"But that's why you're here, isn't it? Why Claude brought you here?"

"I'm honestly not at liberty to say, Dan. I've already said more than I should have. Believe me, though, it will all work out."

"You mean you can't even tell me why you're in Los Angeles?"

"As far as you're concerned, I'm here to see you."

"Oh, come on, Jenny," I said, laughing, "admit it. Off the record. If you hadn't had a cancellation for lunch today, I'd never have heard from you."

I expected some measure of indignation. Nothing of the sort. Instead, she lowered her head, her eyes, the fingers of one hand idling through her hair.

"That's not true, Dan," she said softly. "You should know that's not true."

Uh-oh.

If this was a sign, it wasn't the only one. There'd been the hand lingering on mine, and when we'd first entered the suite, she asked if I minded if she took off her shoes. And the way she'd been touching various parts of her body, consciously or not, the fingers in her hair, now swinging the pendant which hung between her breasts, now smoothing her skirt when she crossed or uncrossed her legs.

Somewhere I'd read that certain women find jilted men appealing. But did she really not know about Jeannine and me?

Then, abruptly, she launched into a long, feverish and somewhat embarrassing description of her own life, about how she was the model this and the model that—mother, wife, career woman—"your top-of-the-line woman executive, written up in all the magazines"—and how much money she made, and how wonderful and supportive Jim was. (Jim was her husband.) But at the end of the day, what did she have to show for it all? Where was the fun, the drama and—okay—the passion?

"Do you know how many men I've gone to bed with?" she asked me suddenly. By this time, she was standing, eyes gone small in self-absorption, little glitters of black in their white orbs. "In my whole life, mind you? I can count them on the fingers of two hands! And never—not *once*—where it just happened, like that. Always planned in advance, discussed. Even in *college,* can you imagine?"

I said nothing, whereupon she sat back down with a sigh and arched her neck, her head against the back of her chair.

"God," she said. "What on earth I'm telling you all this for, I've no idea. Somehow I must think you'll understand. Is that wrong? Aren't you the kind of man women go to bed with? Nina Hardy, for instance. You're in her bed by now, aren't you?"

She looked across at me then, face a little flushed, one cheek now pressed against the chair back.

"No need for an answer," she said, smiling a little. "I know that's only business, Dan. We all do what we have to do. That's what makes you worth a million and a half, isn't it?"

Apparently, I realized then, she must have come to the conclusion that at a million and a half bucks, she too was entitled to a dividend. I managed to extricate myself with an aggrieved-husband speech, avoiding the subject of Jeannine entirely. Jenny bought it. She even seemed a little relieved when I left. I remember us kissing each other good-by, chastely on the cheek, and my only regret, as I made my escape, was that I was going to have to wait to find out what was really happening between the Rhinelanders.

THAT SAME NIGHT I lay on my solitary bed, unable to sleep, unable to take my mind off the woman in white with the black straw hat and the chestnut braid down her back. What Jenny Bergler had said—that they were "flaunting" it around New York—worked on me. Odd, old-fashioned word, *flaunting,* and what exactly did it mean: to flaunt it? That they were walking down Fifth Avenue, arm in arm? Kissing in public? Fucking in the fountain in front of the Plaza?

For Christ's sake, he was old enough to be her father!

I guess I hadn't believed it, not really. I mean, when I read the diary, it was there, wasn't it? Didn't "L" have those elegant hands? But the more I'd thought about it, the more I'd become convinced that she'd taken up with Lew purely and simply as a way of sticking it to me. It could have been anyone; Lew was available.

Very Fawn, when you stopped to think about it. I could still see her face that last night. *Go hide in your fucking barn!* The sudden outburst, out of nowhere.

Then she'd gone off, to Lew, and I'd gone off, to Jeannine, and until this afternoon, it had seemed like time had simply stopped in the world we'd left behind.

Flaunting it. What that meant to me was rubbing my nose in it.

Somebody was standing in my doorway.

My mind was totally elsewhere—on the Fawn, and how I didn't like having my nose rubbed in it, and somebody was standing in my doorway.

I wasn't asleep either, or dreaming.

My first thought was that it was Jeannine. I may even have said her name. But how could it be Jeannine? She was in Vancouver.

There was a shadow against the darkness of the open doorway, a lighter blur against the dark, and then it moved across the background and disappeared.

When I spotted it again, it was drifting noiselessly across the room in my direction.

All I could hear was my own breathing.

The shadow stopped near the bed.

"You awake, Dan?" Christine said in a near whisper.

"No."

"I can't sleep either. You want company?"

"No."

I got up, blurry, on one elbow. The small digital clock said 3:15.

"I thought we might as well finish the interview." She giggled.

I reached behind me for the light switch. The bed itself was a huge wicker affair, with a massive headboard and a shelf built into it with recessed lighting.

"Move over," Christine said. "Make room for me."

She was wearing a man's white shirt again, maybe the same one, with a couple of buttons undone. As for me, I was stark naked under the sheet.

"Not on your life," I said. "Do you make it a habit to walk into your mother's room whenever you feel like it?"

"Sure. Why not? Anyway, she's not here, is she?"

"Look," I said. I wondered, in passing, if this was where she'd made it with Harry Brea. "I'd be glad to finish the interview, if that's what you want, but you're going to have to let me put some clothes on first."

"I'm not really that interested in the interview."

"Oh?"

"Knowing her, she's probably got you pretty well conditioned by now. She can't live without her stud. Come to think of it, what do you suppose she's doing for it in Vancouver?"

"I doubt she's doing anything."

"Want to bet?"

"Look," I said, "if you want to talk, then get out of here while I put some clothes on."

"And otherwise?" she teased.

"There is no otherwise."

She went then, and I dressed, and when she came back in, I noticed how tired she looked, dark-rimmed around the eyes as though she hadn't slept in a while. Seeing her that way, I was struck again, not by the resemblance between her and Jeannine, but by the terrible irony that, in any comparison between mother and daughter, it was the younger one who came out the faded version. I also noticed that she didn't have anything on under the shirt, and noticing that I'd noticed, she reached down and unbuttoned the remaining buttons.

"Look, Christine . . ." I began.

"I'd rather you called me Chris."

"Chris," I corrected. "The thing is, you may as well button your shirt back up."

"Whatever," she said, tossing her head. "You don't have to make such a deal out of it."

But she didn't rebutton the shirt.

We sat down in a corner that Jeannine had made into a kind of mini-sitting room, with an olive-green wicker couch, two matching armchairs and a glass-topped wicker table. I smoked, and Christine bummed, and she made her usual remark that I'd better get the smoke out of the room before "she" came back.

And then: "Why don't you want to screw me? Are you that much in love with her?"

"Yes." The simple truth.

She nodded, unperturbed. "Most men are," she said. "Anyway, where were we? You were asking me who'd named him Uncle Claude. That's where we left off, remember? You asked whose idea that was, and I said we'd talk about it some other time."

I was surprised by her recall.

"She called him that. It was her way of trying to explain away what he was doing there. I don't know who she thought she was fooling. Of course, in those days, I was shipped out a lot of the time. That was how I knew she was in love again, when she told me I was going somewhere."

She ran through a list of Jeannine's Côte d'Azur lovers, all of whom I already had. But with Uncle Claude, she said, Jeannine always arranged that she be there when he came.

"She used me to protect her from him," Christine said.

"How'd you know that?"

"It didn't take a genius. Besides, that's what she said. She was really very cruel about him. She'd say things like: 'He's so unspeakably ugly. How on earth I ever slept with him, I'll never know.' "

"Who would she say this to?"

Christine shrugged. "Oh, me. And not just me, anybody. Her lovers, for instance."

"I thought you were shipped out when the lovers came."

"Yes, mostly. But you know. Kids overhear things."

"Where would you be shipped out to, those times?"

"Oh, you name it. One year—I was ten, maybe eleven—she tried

sending me to boarding school in England. Later on, it was Switzerland. Good old Lac Léman. That was better, except I think I was
the poorest kid in the school. Some school. Everybody was driving
around in Ferraris, Lamborghinis. It was a good thing I was too young
to drive, else I'd have been altogether miserable."

I was reminded of a weird correspondence. The Fawn had gone to
school in Switzerland, too, when she was older. From Christine's brief
description, it sounded like the same place. Conceivably they'd even
been there at the same time.

"I used to wonder who paid for the schools," Christine said. "She
said it was my grandfather—for England anyway—but I doubt that.
We hardly knew him. I always thought it had to be Claude, but she
said Claude never paid for anything where I was concerned."

"Why did Jeannine need you to protect her from him?" I asked.
"Protect her from what?"

She laughed at that. "You don't understand women very well, do
you? Women use children like that all the time—to fend men off. Men
they don't want to get rid of entirely, that is."

"If what you say is true, why didn't she want to get rid of him
entirely?"

"Are you kidding?" she said scornfully. "It was the money, silly.
She never said no to his money."

According to Christine, they'd always lived hand-to-mouth in those
years. This didn't contradict Jeannine's version exactly, but it gave it
a different spin. Jeannine didn't like talking about money in the first
place, and when you asked her what they'd lived on in France, she'd
say, "Oh, whenever we needed something, I could always go do a
film."

She'd done six during the period, two French, three Italian, one a
multinational, multilingual production. None of them memorable.
Not once, though, had she mentioned taking handouts from Claude
Rhinelander.

It was clear to me too that, having failed to give me the Harry Brea
treatment, Christine had opted for a little character assassination
instead.

"Why do you think we came back here?" she asked, reaching for
another cigarette.

"Why did you?"

It wasn't because of her education, though that's what her mother used to say, nor because of Jeannine's career, though she'd said that too. It was the money again. They'd been flat broke, and desperate, and there'd been nobody to turn to but Claude.

"And Claude came through?" I asked.

Christine nodded, smiling slyly.

"Even though she'd been spurning him all those years? Through all those other lovers?"

"I didn't say she'd *always* spurned him, did I? Anyway, he made it possible. Lucky for us, something else happened at the same time."

"What was that?"

"His wife kicked off," she said.

Jeannine, she said, had always made a point of Claude's being married. I'd heard her say that myself: How could she have taken his proposal seriously when he already had a wife? But when, according to Christine's version anyway, she and Christine had moved to California, that obstacle was gone, and Jeannine had exploited the situation to the hilt.

"I told you she was a great courtesan," Christine said with a wry smile. Then, smoothly: "But why haven't you asked The Big Question?"

"Which is?"

"The one everybody gets around to asking sooner or later. The daddy question. Like, who was your father? Or, sometimes, what's it like, not knowing who your father was?"

I looked at her. She was sitting a few feet away from me, smiling—expectantly or suggestively, it was hard to tell which. Legs crossed, the shirt now wide open. Small breasts, like her mother. Small nipples.

"Oh," I said. "Who was your father, do you know?"

She stared at me for a minute. No change in expression except, maybe, for a touch of scorn in the smile.

"The more interesting question is: why did she make it her Big Dark Secret?"

"All right," I said. "Let's start with that one."

"She always used to tell me: 'I wanted a baby, not a husband.' That was the party line. A gift to herself, she said. Actually, what she'd say was: 'I wanted a *beautiful* baby, not a husband.'" She stared at me a moment, silent. "She'd say: 'And that's what I got, isn't it? A beautiful baby? A beautiful daughter?' Then she'd say: 'You, Christine, are the living, breathing symbol of my independence.'"

Again she stopped talking.

"Some symbol," she said finally. "And then do you know what she'd say? She'd say, 'So you can just put your Uncle Claude out of your mind. How could he be your father? You don't look at all like him, and thank God for that.' "

"But he's still your candidate?"

She nodded. "Always has been. Still is, in spite of everything."

"Have you ever asked him?"

"I used to."

"And what did he say?"

She smiled, the scornful variation.

"Always the same thing. He said I should ask her."

She went on about Claude then, twining her hair through her fingers, running her fingers through it and grabbing on, then letting go. How could a man with an ego like that have taken no for an answer all those years? That was what was interesting, what my book ought to be about. Jeannine had had other suitors, men who were desperate to marry her. She'd turned them all down, and eventually they'd gone away. But not Claude.

"Maybe you've got it wrong," I said. "Sometimes the people with the big egos are the ones who can't take no for an answer. Not ever."

She shook her head, letting go her hair.

"Not when she treated him the way she did. I don't think a week's ever gone by, as long as I can remember, without him calling her. Sometimes she wouldn't take his calls. Sometimes she just laughed at him—mocked him, you know? Believe me, if it had just been her, he'd have quit a long time ago."

"So why didn't he, then?"

"Because of me."

"Because of you?" I tried to keep the incredulity out of my voice. "Because he thought you were his daughter?"

"That's right. Little Chris."

"But why—if that's true—would they have kept it a secret all these years?"

"*He* hasn't. *He* doesn't know. If he knew for sure, don't you think he'd have paid for me, all those years? It would have tied her to him forever. *She's* the one with the Big Dark Secret. She's always held it in front of him like a carrot."

Oh boy, I thought. Two minutes ago, she'd been Jeannine's protection *against* Claude; now she was the carrot to attract him. At the same time, while I held no brief for "Uncle Claude," I couldn't help imagining him as he must have been once, standing on Jeannine's threshold in the middle of the night with a bunch of flowers in his arms. Could Christine have been the result? Whereupon Claude, if it had been Claude, had been banished?

No, not banished.

Used, abused even, but not banished.

"Christ," Christine said with a harsh laugh. "There's no need for *you* to get uptight about it! I'm not anymore. I used to be, but now I don't give a shit. Now it's just my Big Excuse."

"What do you mean?"

"It's my Big Excuse for fucking up. For doing drugs. For still holding onto her skirts. For eating too much, eating too little. For slouching. For sleeping with every man in sight, or not having a man. You name it."

"Is that what your mother says?"

She laughed again. "Are you kidding? As far as she's concerned, I'm still her beautiful daughter, perfect in every way, even while she's paying the shrinks' bills."

And then, abruptly, she switched signals on me.

"Tell me," she asked, sitting straight up, "do you think I'm beautiful?"

The question startled me, and there was no way of dodging it.

"No," I said.

"Of course I'm not," she said, cheerfully enough. "It's absurd. She's the only one in the world who ever thought so. At least now she says I'd be beautiful if I only paid attention to what I looked like. Do you think that's true?"

"I think you look a lot better when you do," I said.

"But why should I bother? Can you imagine what it's like, growing up next to someone who looks like she does?"

I took this for a rhetorical question.

"Come on," she said, flaring. "You were here, you saw. When we came back that day? The day we went to Beverly Hills?" All of a sudden her what-the-hell tone became mean, accusatory. "I bet she told you it was to take me out of my misery, didn't she? 'Poor Christine? I have to do something for poor Christine?' Pul-leaze. It was her mirror-mirror-on-the-wall shit. *Her* salon, *her* couturier. Did you think

for a minute it was about *me*? All it proved was that there's only one
. . . *Jean-nine!*"

She dragged out the name in some scornful, spiteful parody. I started
to protest, but she waved me off.

"I know what you're thinking," she went on. "You're thinking why,
if it's a competition I'm bound to lose, and I hate it, and I hate her
for it . . . why do I hang around all the time? Well, do you think
that's new news? Everybody's asked me that for years! I used to think
it was just my masochism. Then I thought: someday she's finally going
to *look* old no matter what she does, and then it won't matter anymore.
But do you want to know the real truth?"

Another rhetorical question, I assumed.

"Well?" she persisted. "Do you want to know the real truth?"

"Go ahead."

"The real truth is that I need her. How do you like that? I can't get
along without her. I literally can't get through the day. Go ahead and
laugh, but that's the only explanation that makes any sense. Somehow
I just don't function without my Mum."

She started to laugh self-consciously. It was like a joke, she said,
and the fact that it wasn't one only made it all the funnier.

And then she stopped laughing. She didn't say anything, just eyed
me—suggestively, I guess, but I missed it, maybe because it was the
farthest thing from my mind. Then she stood up abruptly, stretching
so that her shirtfront separated again and I could see her dark muff
at eye level. She edged past the glass-topped table toward me.

"Right now I think I want to sit on your lap," she said, smiling. It
happened so fast and unexpectedly that I reacted too late.

"Oh, no you don't!" I tried to stop her, but she was already on top
of me, straddling me, her arms around my neck, forcing me back into
the couch cushions.

"Come on!" she laughed as I struggled with her. "Try me! What
do you have to lose? Are you afraid I'll tell her? I *swear* I won't!"

Then her hair was in my eyes, my nostrils, and she was rubbing her
body into mine. She was all limbs and weight, and the only thing I
could do was to pick us both up.

"Come on, Daniel! I'm better than she is, all her men say so. It'll
be *fun!*"

Out of the room we went, off-balance, toppling furniture, careening
into the darkened hallway. I was amazed at her physical strength. She

beat at me with her fists, cursing, scratching, yanking at my hair while I clutched her, till I managed to get her down the hall, down the stairs and into the front hall. Where I let her go, unceremoniously, onto the tile floor.

"You *bastard!*" she shouted at me, sobbing. "You fucking freeloading gigolo! Do you think I'm not going to tell her anyway that you tried to rape me! You think she won't believe me? You think I can't make her believe me?"

I told her to tell Jeannine what she wanted, that Jeannine would believe what she wanted. But she didn't hear. She was goddamning me from the front hall floor. She was going to fix me, I hadn't seen anything yet.

"I've got your number, you bastard," she called after me. "I made you hard, didn't I?"

I was about halfway back up the stairs.

She was laughing now—a weird, harsh, high-pitched sound.

I didn't answer or turn around. But, for better or worse, she had me there.

Chapter Fifteen

I RAN INTO Christine from time to time in the two weeks, give or take, before I went to Vancouver, but it was as though nothing had happened. She never mentioned that night; neither did I; nor did she make further advances, other than to offer me a joint once, by the pool, which I refused. A couple of times I saw strange cars in the driveway, and one night there were a lot of them—a party in progress, to judge from the decibels at the far end of the building and, later, the shouting and splashing in the pool. But I wasn't invited.

She looked like hell—dark circles around her eyes and a kind of spacy, glazed expression as though she'd been taking drugs. She passed her exams, but when I congratulated her, she shrugged it off. It meant nothing, she said; she wasn't going back anyway.

Maybe, under different circumstances, I'd have mustered sympathy for her. The type to which she belonged—the celebrity child—was well-documented, and it didn't take a genius to recognize that Christine, at thirty-two, was locked into the mold and hurting. But I took her at her word, truce or no truce—that she wasn't through "fixing" me, or trying to—and the time was fast approaching when Jeannine was going to have to find some way of dealing with her other than a shopping spree in Beverly Hills.

I GOT TO Vancouver the last day of shooting before Jeannine's break, carrying a fair share of foreboding with me. I knew I'd be in the way— there's a kind of clubbiness, a weird preoccupation, about people

185

making a movie, even though they seem to spend most of their time standing around, which makes an outsider feel like a Martian—but it wasn't as though I'd never been on a set before. The foreboding came more from all the things I had on hold: the book, the Christine problem, the Fawn (who had started making noises, through our attorneys, about a divorce), even the Rhinelanders.

The one call I'd made about the Rhinelanders—it was after my meeting with Jenny Bergler—had been to Leo Castagni. The stockbroker was on a promotional tour for our book, and I found him in Chicago. He knew nothing about anything going on with the Rhinelander companies. Olympian, he reminded me, was only the tip of the Rhinelander iceberg; the rest was privately held. He promised to make a few discreet inquiries and let me know if he heard anything, but he hadn't called back.

More than anything, though, I had Jeannine on hold. Or vice versa. We had been talking on the phone at least twice a day, but even though we ran the litany religiously—how we couldn't stand the separation, how we missed each other, loved each other—and tried to enliven the dead words with intimate mind games, a tension had begun to sprout in me whenever my phone rang. Undoubtedly Christine contributed to it—the innuendos about her mother—but so did Jeannine's history, more of which unfolded each day on the screen of my computer. The lovers of her European years had been a diverse group, some of them famous—which, we both knew, was part of the appeal of her story—but the trend, ever since she'd come back to the United States, had been younger and younger. Christine was right: in this sense, I was some kind of anomaly.

I knew Jeannine's new director by reputation—up-and-coming, early thirties, something of a ladykiller. "A rising talent," one of the gossip columnists had written wickedly, "in more ways than one." And Sonny Corral was there, at Jeannine's insistence, with a small part in the film—"my chaperon," she'd said teasingly—but hadn't Sonny procured *me*? Each time that she sounded distant, or vague, or evasive over the phone, or when I called and she wasn't there, or when she said, "Daniel darling, I can't talk to you right this minute, let me call you back," I would wrestle with the tension, shaking it between my teeth like a dog with its prey.

They did two scenes the day I arrived, both in the beach house but otherwise disconnected. I met the cast. Jeannine also introduced me to the new Spielberg, who turned out to be an intense young man in a Roger Rabbit sweatshirt, with spiky hair and a habit of blowing his nose frequently. My imagined rival, I discovered to my relief, wore Trotsky glasses and snorted cocaine.

Finally, long after dark, we were alone. And it was all there, intact. Different, but intact.

She loved the book. Of course, she said, it was her own story, often her own words, but in a way it wasn't. She meant that she wouldn't have written it that way herself, even if she could have. She wouldn't have dared. She'd found parts of it so moving, she'd even cried.

"You made me relive so many things, Daniel," she said. "Things we'd talked about, but I'd half-forgotten. And I remembered others that you don't even know about yet. I've put my little sticky papers to remind us, we can go over them as soon as I get home. I'm afraid there's a lot I want to change—quite a lot, actually—but we don't have to do it now, do we? I need you so. I think I'd have died if you hadn't come."

With words like that, and the gestures that accompanied them, her eyes so close to mine, wide, dark, loving, I would start all over again from page one if she wanted me to. I told her so. She loved the idea. If she could only keep me starting over again, from page one, then she'd never lose me, would she? Hearing her say it, expressing and answering my own fears but in her melodious voice, close, almost a whisper, I felt the relaxation wash over me, through me, the letting go, the delicious pliancy which only Jeannine, it seemed, could release in me.

How different, then?

I thought it was because we had the beginnings of a history together. Always before, even in Laguna, we'd been like strangers meeting, and we'd lived the present, and reminders of our separate histories had been like intruders into where we were. Now we had common experience, however small. That meant a past and suggested a future.

To illustrate, weirdly, there was Christine.

Ever since that night, I'd been asking the same question: Why in hell had Jeannine done it? Why, knowing Christine, had she left the two of us alone in the house?

Was it some kind of loyalty test: What would Dan do when "Chris" showed up in an unbuttoned shirt?

Well, I'd passed, and Christine had apparently decided not to tell

Mom. Now, though, when Jeannine herself brought it up—"How is Christine?" she asked. "How have you two been getting along?"—I told her the story.

Somehow I'd expected her to flare, to defend. Instead she simply listened, one hand unconsciously over her mouth, and then, eyes averted, she fell silent.

"You can't be that surprised," I persisted. "Why'd you leave us there in the first place? It wasn't some kind of a test, was it?"

"Poor Daniel," she said at length, sad-eyed. "Yes, I'm surprised. Perhaps I shouldn't be, but she . . . I never thought it would happen."

"Even though it has before? With Harry Brea, for one?"

"Did she tell you about that?"

"Yes."

"But that was a long time ago. I never thought she would try again. You may be right, darling. Maybe I *was* testing, unconsciously—not you, my poor darling, please don't think that. But her." She looked away again, lips pressed tightly together, and when I saw her eyes again, they were like twin moons on a clouded night. "I'm so sorry— terribly, terribly sorry. It won't happen again, I promise you."

I hated to see her like that, stricken, wounded.

"Look," I said, "she didn't get what she wanted. And she said she was going to tell you I tried to rape her, but she didn't do that either. Maybe that's a good sign."

Jeannine shook her head.

"It's not the end of it," she said. The way she said it, sighing, confirmed that Brea and I weren't isolated cases, and it also explained why, when she was growing up, Christine had always been sent away.

"I will have to deal with it," Jeannine said. "This time I will have to deal with it."

"How?"

"Leave that to me, my darling. Meanwhile, let's not have her ruin our few days here."

Later, though, she came back to the subject on her own. She said the film had made her think about it, about how incredibly complicated the relationships between mothers and daughters really were. And this, in turn, took her to her own mother.

"She was so beautiful, Daniel," she said, and she made a small sucking sound, the intake of air. "People always say *I'm* beautiful, but compared with her, I'm nothing. Nothing at all. She was a truly great beauty. And so wonderful, graceful, expressive. She spoke every language you can imagine. We did everything together. We were so close—I can't explain—but it was as though I could think her thoughts before she said them. And she could think mine. We were truly—what is the expression—joined at the hip?

"I was never jealous of her," she said, apparently thinking of Christine. "It would never have occurred to me to be jealous of her. She was . . . well, she was beyond jealousy."

I saw her lower lip begin to quiver, as though she would burst into tears any second. She didn't, though.

"And then she died," she said flatly. "She simply died. There's no way I can describe the effect that had on me. It was terrible, devastating. Suddenly, I was so alone. And do you know? Deep inside me, I've been alone ever since."

I asked her about her father. He was simply of no importance, she answered. Not that it was his fault really, it was the times too, the circumstances, the threat of war, then the war itself. And her mother was Jewish. She used to wonder sometimes if that's why she'd married him—as a way out, a way to safety. Once her mother died, she'd seen him now and then, and he'd paid for her school until she quit, but by that time she was already in charge of herself.

"You know, Daniel," she said, "when Christine was born, I told myself—and I used to say it to her all the time, when she was a baby—'You will never be alone the way I was. No matter what happens to us, you will never be alone.' And it is true, that's the way we have lived. I know it has been terrible for Christine, that in some ways her mother is her worst enemy. But that is why it—all this with Christine—is so . . . so hard for me."

She didn't break down, and there were no tears, but through her words came an emotional power which, if not uncharacteristic of Jeannine, she rarely showed. I tried to comfort her as best I could.

"Do you understand, Daniel?"

"Yes," I answered. "The only thing I guess I don't understand is why you still won't tell her who her father is."

I felt her stiffen.

"Do you really think that's so important to her?" she asked.

"It may be. As far as she's concerned, it's Claude Rhinelander."

"God, does she still think that? After all these years?"

"That's what she said to me."

At that, though, Jeannine withdrew, and having, as Christine had put it, touched on the Big Dark Secret, I pushed no farther.

Our last day, I told Jeannine I thought I'd have to go to New York soon, to deal with the Fawn. In the past, my trips east had invariably panicked her; this time she expressed nothing but sympathy.

"Divorces are so messy," she said. "They always are. How do you feel about it?"

"Mostly all right," I said. "I just don't want to be skinned."

"Do you mean the money?"

"Yes, frankly."

"Well, this is the way I want you to think about the money, Daniel: Whatever it costs you, it will be worth it. The money isn't worth the worry, and you will forget about it once it is over. This is what is most important: that it be over, finished. And then that you come home to Jeannine, who loves you."

FIFTH AVENUE, IN July, was an airless cocoon. Heat oozed off the pavements, the gutters, seeping into my skin to make a sweaty envelope between me and my clothes, and the scorched layer of ozone seemed to hover just at the tops of the buildings. I'd just come from heat, theoretically I was inured to it, but California heat is different somehow. You expect it, grow used to it, adapt to it with a little help from modern technology. New York heat is hostile. Whatever you wear—seersucker, 100 percent cotton—wilts before it. Summer in New York is like the rain forest, except the rain is the sweat of the masses, steaming, and the forest is made of steel and concrete.

I didn't go home. I thought of it—I had some kind of distant hankering to see the barn—but then I thought better of it. Presumably the Murphys were still there. At least I sent them a check every month, and every once in a while we talked on the phone.

I didn't stay at my alumni club either, instead took a room in a small hotel in the east fifties, and, the next day, walked over to my attorney's office on Fifth Avenue.

Vincent Reilly was a heavyweight—an imposing, craggy Irishman, elegantly dressed, ruddy-cheeked, and a specialist in matrimonial law. My regular lawyer, an old college classmate called Busher and a senior partner in the same firm, turned me over to him that morning. All I knew from Busher was that the Fawn was using her cousin, Thorson

Fields, a.k.a. the Squirrel. And that the Squirrel, who was another heavyweight in the field, had started to push.

"My job," Vincent Reilly began, "is to save you as much pain and money as possible in what is at best an unpleasant proceeding. And that means my fees as well as any settlement we agree to."

With that, we got down to business. Some forty-five minutes later, we'd reviewed the vital statistics, meaning my assets (virtually all of which the Fawn had some claim to) and the Fawn's (about which I actually knew little), meaning also Jeannine and Lew Rhinelander. The no-fault alternative, Reilly said, was what most civilized couples chose, but it presupposed a financial agreement.

"The key question is this," Reilly said, leaning back in his tall-backed chair. "She has said she wants out of the marriage. How do you feel about that?"

"I don't know," I answered. "I guess I'm not opposed."

"But in no rush, is that right?"

"Not particularly, no."

"She may be. That's something we have to find out. Do you think she wants to remarry? Or at least cohabit with Rhinelander?"

"I've no idea."

"Well," he said, creaking his chair, "we have a choice to make. We can say, 'Our client has no interest in a divorce right now.' That will smoke them out. Either they'll do nothing—unlikely—or they'll bring charges, at least go through the motions, and that will entail naming your friend, Ms. Hardy, as correspondent, Rhinelander too when we countersue. Major publicity inevitably, major legal expenses on both sides. Alternatively, we can come to them with a no-fault settlement offer."

"What kind of offer?" I asked.

"A very low one," he said, chuckling. "Believe me, whatever we put on the table, they're going to piss all over it. That's how we lawyers make our living."

I asked him what the downside was, the worst case. Half, he said, in a no-fault. Half my tangible assets, including the house; half my earnings as alimony. But that was worst case and unrealistic, he said. These days the courts were less sympathetic to poor, helpless wives, particularly childless ones, than they used to be. Less inclined to strip the husband. And my wife, from my description, sounded neither poor nor helpless.

We talked numbers, and I said I wanted to think about it. The last words of advice Reilly had for me, when he escorted me back to Busher's office and shook my hand, were:

"Whatever you do, don't talk to Faith about this. You're not in touch with her, are you?"

"No."

"Leave it that way. Believe me, right now you both should let the professionals do your talking."

Busher wanted to buy me lunch. I declined. Out on the steaming street at midday, I had no place to go. It was like that other time when I'd filled up the hours with Falcone and Tinker so as to avoid going home, only months had passed, and there were no more clothes for me to burn, and I wanted to talk to neither of the above.

I went into the big Barnes & Noble on Fifth Avenue, as much to escape the heat as anything else. My Castagni book was prominently displayed, selling well apparently. All I could think about when I saw the stacks was that half of my earnings from it would belong to the Fawn.

Begrudging thought, yes. I had a lot of begrudging thoughts. The thing was, meeting Reilly had brought it home finally: *She wants out of the marriage.*

Well, what had I been thinking all this time in Pasadena?

Answer: I hadn't been thinking in Pasadena. It hadn't been real in Pasadena.

In New York, in the heat, it was real.

She wants out of the marriage.

A hell of a way to end it.

Reilly or no Reilly, I dialed the SoHo number from the street on the off-chance, listened to her recorded voice, hung up. Maybe, for all I knew, she was still in California. In white, with a black straw hat and a braid.

I went to a movie. It was air-conditioned, but if my life depended on it, I couldn't tell you what was playing. I walked out after a while.

And rode downtown, to SoHo.

And—call it luck, call it karma—ran smack into her.

Not exactly. I was paying the cab in front of her building when she rounded the corner.

She was wearing a baggy one-piece outfit, kelly green, with shoulder straps, loose pants. A bone-colored shoulder bag swinging on one side and some fancy boutique shopping bag in the other hand. Bone-colored high heels, open-toed, straps at the ankles. The same confident stride. Deeply tanned. The Fawn in summer, no sweat.

I almost didn't recognize her.

She'd changed her hair. It was cut short, all curls and feathers, all glinting in the light with red and brown tints. It changed—I don't know—all her dimensions.

"Dan!" she called out to me. "What are you doing here?"

"I could as well say the same thing," I said, grinning back at her. "I thought you were in California."

"California? What on earth for?"

We didn't kiss, didn't shake hands. We simply gawked at each other on the sidewalk. In the heels, she was almost as tall as I was.

"Well?" she said. "How do you like it?"

"What?"

"My hair."

"When did you do it?"

"Oh, about a month ago. No, more. Almost two months."

If true, this shot the hell out of my black-and-white apparition on the L.A. street. For some reason, this threw me more than the hairdo.

"It takes some getting used to," I said. "You look different. It changes . . . well, everything. I guess I liked it better the old way."

"That's what everybody says," she said, smiling. "But I like it this way."

The truth was, it didn't matter. If it changed her dimensions, lending width to her otherwise long and oval face, she was still gorgeous and, with the tan, practically blooming with health.

I told her so.

"You look good, too," she said.

"Except I'm wilting."

"That's New York for you. Plus you're always ten degrees warmer than anyone else."

The reference—intentional or not—was to an old joke between us. Apparently my body was—is—warmer than most people's. This made me, the Fawn used to say, the ideal husband in winter but a disaster in summer.

She asked me how long I'd been back. Since yesterday, I said. Was I still living in California? Yes, for the time being.

Then nothing. An awkward moment, which we tried to fill simultaneously.

"Look," she was saying, "I'd like to ask you up but I can't."

And I, at the same time: "I thought I could buy you a drink."

We both laughed.

"I don't drink anymore," she said. "It's part of my makeover. I'm on another one of my health kicks."

A periodic event, I remembered, with bran for breakfast, cottage cheese and fruit for lunch.

"An ice-cream soda, then," I suggested.

To my surprise, she accepted. She had half an hour, she said, if that was okay. I couldn't remember the last time I'd had an ice-cream soda. We went to one of those coffee houses that proliferate in that part of town. They had a few tables squeezed onto the sidewalk, but we went inside, where there were high ceilings and revolving ceiling fans.

Black-and-white sodas. Straws and long-handled spoons.

"Actually," I said, "I came back to see my lawyer."

"Oh?"

"The Squirrel's been calling Busher."

"I know. I asked him to. I didn't want to pressure you, though."

"That's okay. But is a divorce what you really want?"

"Yes."

"Why?"

The question irritated her.

"Oh, come on, Dan," she said. She looked away, and when she didn't say more, I said:

"Don't you think you at least owe me an explanation?"

As soon as I said it, it rang wrong. She didn't *owe* me anything.

"If you really need an explanation," she said levelly, "then you're a lot less intelligent than I've always given you credit for."

"Maybe I am," I said. "Maybe that's true."

She shook her head. "You may be a lot of things, but you're not stupid. You just weren't listening. You never listened. You were too . . ." She broke into herself then, faltering that one and only time. It was as though she had a lot of things to say, but suddenly couldn't. To my surprise, I saw tears welling up in her eyes, and I felt a rush of conflicting emotions I couldn't have begun to sort out.

"Look," she said, gaining control again, "can't we just end it decently? Consenting adults? That's all I want."

"Just like that?" I said bitterly, and then the words came in a rush. "Because you say I wasn't listening? What do you think I was doing all those years, when I supposedly wasn't listening? What did you want that you didn't get from me?"

Suddenly, in a split-second, I remembered something the Badger had said a long time ago, at our wedding in fact, to the effect that she was someone who wanted things desperately and then, when she had them, wanted something else. I'd rejected it at the time. Now I heard it again.

"Don't tell me *love*, for God's sake," I went on. "I loved the pants off of you! Does *Lew Rhinelander* love you more than I did? Answer me that: Does *Lew Rhinelander* love you more than I did?"

She didn't answer, of course. And I had it wrong again, an emotional mishmash, too much in, too much left out, but I couldn't help myself.

"Tell me one thing, just one thing. Which came first: your turning off on me, or Lew?"

She let the question float there a moment, like a soap bubble when there's no breeze, and I knew then, without question, that I couldn't win.

"Maybe someday, Dan," she said finally, "you'll ask yourself why that should be so important to you. Meanwhile, though, the answer is you. You came first."

I hated her for that. Not the answer so much as her poise, her calm superiority. It was as though she had it all wired, her mind made up, whisk-whisk with her hands and good-by Springer.

"So we're to end it decently?" I said. "That's what you want. And I guess I'm to pay you decently for it, too?"

"I don't know what that means," she said tersely.

"Oh, no? Well, the Squirrel sure does. The Squirrel's waiting to hear our settlement offer."

"What are you talking about?"

"Just that, in plain English. He's waiting to hear our settlement offer."

"Then he acted on his own. I never told him to."

For a second, I didn't believe her. On the other hand, it would have been typical Fawn to let someone else do her dirty work. She stared back at me.

"You're still not listening, are you," she said. "Let's get one thing straight, without the lawyers. All I want is to end it. A simple divorce, the quickest and easiest way. I don't want a cent of yours, Dan. Nothing. I thought I'd made that clear when I left all that stuff behind at the house. In case you didn't understand it then, let me spell it out for you now: What's yours is yours. All yours."

She said it without contempt, but the words conveyed it anyway. For some reason, I took them like a slap in the face—a final statement, I guess, that, after years, she had no further use for me.

Done is done.

I stood up and—in a gesture I'd long admired in the movies—threw some wadded bills onto the table. I walked out into the July sun, aware, in some wobbly way, that while I'd hardly touched my soda, she'd finished hers to the last slurp.

BACK TO PASADENA. Better put: Home to Pasadena, where, not long after, Jeannine joined me. And, my manuscript in her lap, made the following statement:

"I think the moment has come to be done with this *gamine* business, Daniel. I never was so much of one, even then, and I was younger, much younger! I think it's time now for us to roll up our sleeves and get ourselves dirty."

It snuck up on me, the way she said it, her voice gay and lilting, and she was looking at me cunningly over the tops of her reading glasses. The shock didn't register till later, and then only progressively, like mini-quakes in an escalating series.

All I ventured at the time was: "What are you talking about? Do you mean you haven't told me everything?"

To which she replied: "In some respects, my silly darling, I haven't told you anything."

Part Four

Chapter Sixteen

It CAME AT dinner, over coffee, without warning, the day after Jeannine arrived home.

We were in the spacious dining room, she, Christine and I, at the long, polished mahogany refectory table from some abbey in Catalonia, set with lace mats, white china and silver gleaming under the overhanging chandelier. Jeannine wore a dress of yellow linen, I a long-sleeved dress shirt and summer jacket, Christine—inevitably—an oversized T-shirt over jeans lopped off at the knees.

Jeannine was pouring coffee from a long-spouted silver pot.

"I want to discuss what you're going to do now," she said, turning to Christine and passing her her cup.

Christine started to laugh. "Oh, God," she said, "how boring can you get," or some such, but Jeannine, pouring my cup now, continued undeterred.

"It's very simple, my dear. Daniel and I need to be alone. Since you're not going back to school, and you don't have a job, I think you should go away, on a trip. It might even do you some good."

"You're not being serious, are you? A *trip?* For God's sakes, where?"

"You're going to Europe. It's too long since you've been. In fact, you're leaving tomorrow, everything's been arranged."

"To *Europe? Tomorrow?* But that's crazy!"

I saw her expression go from surprise to bewilderment, and then she glanced at me, as though looking for some kind of confirmation.

"No, it's not crazy," Jeannine went on coolly, "not crazy at all."

"But I *live* here. I—"

199

"No, you don't. I agreed that you should come back for your exams. Now you've passed them. That's over."

I'd never seen Christine cornered before. Her whole body seemed to stiffen. She looked at her mother, open-mouthed, then glared at me with open hostility.

"Mother, I don't want to discuss this now," her eyes still on me. "Not in front of him. I—"

"There's nothing more to discuss. It's been decided."

At that, Christine burst into outrage.

"I see," she began. "Oh yes, I see. *It's* all been decided. The same old story. Well, what did he tell you about me? That's it, isn't it? Daniel must have blabbed. But did he tell you the truth? The whole truth? That he tried to rape me? That he tried to pull my pants off? Here, in your own goddamn house? That—"

"That's quite enough," Jeannine interrupted sharply. "Daniel has nothing to do with this. It's my decision."

But Christine wasn't to be stopped. With an abrupt and violent gesture, she stood, knocking over her coffee cup.

"*Your* decision! *He* has nothing to do with this!" Her face suddenly a twisted grimace and focused down on her mother, her voice acid with rage. "Well, let me tell you something, you bitch, with your paid-for studs. You've been pulling this shit on me all my life. 'Christine, darling,'" mimicking in some wild approximation, "'you've got to go away now, the great Nina Hardy needs to fuck in peace and quiet, why don't you go to Timbuktu?' Well let me tell—"

What happened next came so fast I didn't even see Jeannine stand up. With a sharp crack, she slapped her daughter hard across the cheek. Christine's head jolted back and her mouth gaped.

For just a second, everything stopped—time, sound, expression. The two of them stood frozen in confrontation, eyes wide. Then Christine gave way. I heard her gasp. Her hands went to her face and she started to cry, shrieking sobs, then turned on her heels and stormed off.

Followed, immediately, by Jeannine.

This time, I stayed up for her. I expected her to need me—"to put my pieces back together," she'd once said—and to want to talk it through, but when she came into the bedroom, very late, her eyes tired, her expression was nonetheless still firm with resolve.

"That was the first time I ever struck her," she said quietly. "I'm sorry you had to witness it."

"It's okay," I answered. "Remember, I live here too now."

She shook her head, as though trying to banish the scene.

"It was too ugly," was all she said.

The next day, Christine was gone. Her tickets, I gathered, had already been paid for, her reservations made. Something of the same, minus the violence, happened with Sonny Corral and other friends of Jeannine's. As for Sonny, I hadn't seen him since Vancouver. When I asked Jeannine about him, she said offhandedly that he was busy, but when I pressed her, she admitted she'd told him to be busy.

"My dear Daniel," she said lightly, by way of explanation. "It is nothing more than simple survival. After all," narrowing her eyes slyly, "I've someone new worth surviving for, don't I?"

NOT, I SHOULD say, that we were alone, late in July and into August. In addition to the staff, a trainer now came to the house every morning, plus an "aesthetic counselor" (hairdresser and cosmetician), and there were assorted business visitors, principally a fast-talking young M.B.A. called Peter Singer.

Singer, it seemed, had happened in Vancouver, and Jeannine sprung him on me when she got back. "There's someone I want you to meet," she said, "who has some very interesting ideas for me."

Singer was an agent, of sorts, who specialized in what he called "personal packaging and cross-merchandising," and by the time I met him, in the library room one morning, Jeannine, I gathered, had already been sold. He was good-looking, too, in a blue-eyed, blue-blazered, Gucci way, and, a little to my surprise, I found him smart, direct, also amazingly well-connected in the worlds of television, advertising and retail merchandising.

When he first started talking, I thought all he was after was to get Jeannine to front for a fashion line. In a way, that was true, but he had much more in mind—the *Jeannine* Collection, he called it, and he thought we could be ready to launch it the fall of the following year. It would begin with fashion but range quickly into ancillary products, and Jeannine would be involved, to the extent she wanted to be, in every last detail of its development.

Singer put major importance on Jeannine's book.

"It's a question of credibility, Dan," he said, apparently assuming that part of his job was to sell me. "Since you're a writer, you may not realize it, but for the rest of us out here, a book gives credibility like nothing else. And Jeannine has an unusual opportunity, in that the book and her new film will be coming out the same year. Both are going to showcase her in a new light—high-style, a little outrageous, the woman taking control."

"Taking control of what?" I asked him.

"Good question," he answered glibly. "In fact, the key question. To simplify, taking control of everything—her looks, her body, her environment, her whole life."

The way Singer explained it, the timing and the demographics couldn't be better. All the baby-boomer women were entering their forties. Sure, they were anxious about growing old and losing their sex appeal, but even more anxious, according to any number of studies and focus groups, about the sense of having lost control of their own lives. They wanted to be free again, a little daring, up-market, gorgeous, but above all they wanted to regain control of their own destinies. To make things happen, instead of having things happen to them. They had a lot of money to spend, among the highest discretionary incomes in the statistics. But where was their model?

"Jeannine," Singer said, answering himself. "Personally, I like the name a lot. In my humble opinion, that's what I think you should call the book: *Jeannine,* the autobiography of Nina Hardy. Every fashion collection, every product we put into development, will carry the label *Jeannine,* by Nina Hardy. And when we get to fragrances, cosmetics—which is where the real money is—what could be more perfect?"

Jeannine, I gathered, had heard much of this before, but Singer had taken it farther since they'd talked in Vancouver. He had facts and figures now, projections—downside and upside—of what she could hope to earn in the first two years, and by the time his presentation was done, it was hard not to believe, at least in commercial terms. Jeannine clearly did. What's more, so did the manufacturers and retailers with whom he'd already had preliminary conversations.

"Don't you see, darling?" Jeannine said, returning to me after escorting him out. "I told you it was interesting. Don't you think it's bound to work?"

Her face was flushed, and there was a sparkle of pleasure in her eyes.

"Yes, I can see it. I think you'd make a fortune. I've just one problem with it."

"What problem?"

"I thought you were an actress," I said, smiling up at her. "A great actress. I guess I've a little trouble picturing you carrying a sandwich board."

She laughed at that.

"Leave it to cynical you to put the worst face on things," she said gaily. "But maybe it's time I explained some things to you about how this lovely business of being an actress really works."

Still standing, she struck a pose in front of me, her arms folded, her eyes now serious and gazing down at me. "Look at me now, Daniel," she said. "No, I mean: really look. And tell me what you see."

"A very beautiful woman. And an extraordinarily talented one."

"Come, come, my darling, you're so sweet, but let me do it for you, please. I'm fifty-four years old. That may not be so old today, and I may be very skilled at disguising it, but by Hollywood standards, it is *ancient*. Perhaps the question you should think about is how many roles there are, in films, for fifty-four-year-old actresses. Do you think it an accident that Jane Fonda, Shirley MacLaine, even your Farran woman, have found other ways to make money? They are famous actresses, too, aren't they, and able to work? But the films for them, Daniel, are few and far between."

And she'd been lucky, she judged, compared with some. She'd had *Eva's Story,* but that had been almost a decade ago. And now she had *Mother & Daughter.* The most interesting thing about the remake—although she thought it was also a good film—was that she played the mother's role. Would that be enough at the box office? People thought so, maybe they were right. But even if they were right, would she have to wait another decade—till she was sixty-four—for the next great role to come along?

"You know, Daniel," she said, sitting down next to me in the library, "so much of it really is about image. Always this question of image. It isn't as though I haven't worked in between—I've had other films, and there is always television—but what is my image? Aloof, above it all. I don't do all the publicity, I don't go to the parties, I'm supposed to be very picky about scripts, directors I'll work with, and so forth. Some of that was Claude's doing, too. When I came back here, he said that, if I was going to rebuild my career, I would have to pick and choose carefully. Maybe he was right in the beginning, but the truth? The truth, my dear Daniel," with her same, dazzling smile, "is that it's time we packed the old image away in the closet."

Starting, she said, with the book.

"But I don't see what trashing Claude Rhinelander has to do with it."

"Trashing's a little strong, isn't it? I'm just going to be free of him, Daniel. Once and for all."

IT WASN'T AS though everything she had to tell about Claude was new. Some of it had even been published before. But the spin Jeannine now gave it was new, and the cumulative portrait that came out on paper was at once damning and authentic.

There was, for instance, chapter and verse of Claude's breakup with Olympian—how, once Jeannine had left Hollywood, he'd set out to pillage the company even while he was still working there; how the Bartons had thrown him out; how, after he'd started Rhinelander Films and the Bartons, on the brink of bankruptcy, had gone to all their competitors hat in hand, he'd cajoled and bullied the Hollywood powers into keeping hands off.

"The people who really ran Hollywood," Jeannine said, "always made such a show of how much they hated each other, dog-eat-dog, and of course it wasn't true. The same people played golf together on Saturday afternoons, went to each other's parties, sent their children to the same schools. It was the Bartons who didn't belong, not Claude. Claude knew everyone. For years, he'd cultivated them, learning their strengths and weaknesses. Now, when it really mattered, he bought their acquiescence, and that left him a clear field."

Even then, Jeannine told me, there had been a moment when the deal almost didn't happen. "Essentially Claude's offer called for taking over Olympian's debt. The Bartons held out for cash; Claude dug in his heels. What happened next was that several key people under contract to Olympian—directors and actors—simply walked off the set, charging breach of contract. The Bartons, faced with lawsuits on top of losses in revenue, panicked, and Claude emerged with what, in Hollywood annals, has come to be called the steal of the century.

"Of course he'd orchestrated it," Jeannine said, "and it was illegal, a most flagrant tampering. If they'd fought, the Bartons might have destroyed him. But he judged that they wouldn't, and he was right, and the next year, he saw to it that they were given a special award for service to the industry."

Maybe what was most surprising wasn't that Jeannine knew these things, and in detail, but that her source was Claude himself.

"You see, Daniel," she said, "during all those lost years in France—when he knew he couldn't have me as his mistress, and I told him I would never marry him—I became, instead, his confidante. I used to think it was because I was safe for him—thousands of miles from the business and yet I understood it—and he needed someone to talk to. To brag to, sometimes. The phone would ring at some ungodly hour, six or seven in the morning—what did that mean it was in Hollywood, midnight?—and it would be Claude. But there was something else, too, of course."

"You mean, why he confided in you?"

"Yes. And why the calls so often came at that hour. He was still trying, you see. It was his way, even then, of trying to own me, or at least pretending to himself that he did. And, of course, he also wanted to find out if I was sleeping with anyone."

It was in this way, she said, that she'd found out about Claude's underworld connections, and how it had come about that the two brothers, Claude and Lew, who, by mutual and public admission, hated each other's guts, had ended up so bound together. Both, Jeannine said, had been their father's doing. The popular version—that when Claude left the family business, he'd gone to Hollywood without a nickel—was untrue. Investments had been made—heavy ones when he founded Rhinelander Films. Some of it was Nat Rhinelander's money, some was Nat's "friends," silent partners Claude had never identified by name, except that it was Irving R. Stewart, all those years ago, who'd been sent in to watchdog the silent partners' interests. In this way, Nat Rhinelander had maintained control over his sons, even after his death, because through a trust arrangement in Nat's will, neither brother could sell the trust's holdings in his business without the other's approval.

"It drove Claude crazy," Jeannine said, "especially after his father died. He railed about his brother, but he cursed his father. The dumbest thing he'd ever done in his life was to take the money. Blood money, he called it, and his own father had tied him up in knots. 'Well, Claude,' I'd say, 'you did do it, and if there's no way for you to take it back, maybe you have to learn to live with this brother of yours.' Then he'd turn on me. 'And what the hell do *you* know about it? You don't have to live with the son of a bitch!' "

When she came back to California, the relationship changed again. She continued to talk to Claude, to see him on occasion, but the confidences stopped.

"Maybe he was afraid I knew too much," she said. "After all, here I was, part of the industry again."

"Or maybe," I said, looking for another answer, "the terms of ownership had changed."

"What do you mean by that?"

"Just that you'd taken money from him."

She looked at me, wide-eyed.

"How do you know that?"

"I don't, for sure. It's something Christine said."

"My darling daughter—" she began, but then caught herself, as though, now that the subject had been raised, there was no way she was going to try to fudge it. "Yes, it's true," she said firmly. "He'd always tried to give me money—cash—but I never accepted it. I thought that was stooping too low. When we came back here, though, I was desperate. I had no choice."

"And his wife had died, meanwhile?"

"Yes." I saw her shudder slightly—an admission, of sorts—and then she bit at her lower lip. "And there was *Eva's Story*," she said. "You know, people always thought I did that for Harry—and it was true, I've told you I was in love with him at the time, or so I thought— but I really did it for me. I *had* to play that part. The film *had* to be made. Though I've never been able to prove it, I've always thought it was Claude who set it up so that I'd have to come to him. Yes, the project was a gamble—Harry was unknown here, and I'd been gone all those years—but people here make worse gambles every day. They all turned us down, including Rhinelander Films, and that left me with nothing to do but go begging.

"Beg I did," she concluded. "Claude got us the money. Done is done."

Except that, in a way, it still wasn't done.

. . .

One evening in August, I was working late on the book when she came into my room and, presumably reading the screen along with me, started massaging my shoulders. (Once upon a time, before the professionals took over, I was the one who massaged her tired feet, kneading my knuckles into their soles, and her shoulders, her back, often as a prelude to sex.) Her hands felt strong, her thumbs working deep between my shoulder blades, and it was only when she relaxed her grip that I realized she was shaking.

I swiveled around.

I was still startled by her new look. Part of it was makeup—the flush to her cheeks, the deep violet tinge to her eyes, a more pungent perfume. And she had taken to wearing jewelry, even at home. That night she had on tight-fitting black silk pants, which tapered to clasp her calves just above the ankles, and a silk shirt of the same deep violet tone as her eye shadow, scooped low in the front, lower in the back, and pinched at the waist by a black sash. A large antique topaz pendant on a gold chain, matching earrings, a parade of bracelets on her left arm, ivory interchanged with gold.

"You won't believe this," she said. "Do you know what he wants to do now?"

"Who?"

"Claude, who else?"

I stood up, took her by the arms. She pulled free. "I didn't take it seriously at first. Now I do. He's going to sell the house."

"What house?"

"*This* house," she said. "*My* house." Her lips trembled as she turned her head away.

I didn't understand. I'd always assumed she owned the place.

"My God, what will Christine say?" Jeannine went on, her voice rising. "Christine will *die* when she finds out!"

I didn't see what Christine had to do with it, and said so, which set Jeannine off. The tears came, hot and angry; the imprecations— against Claude, against herself for having been so blind, so stupid. Meanwhile she dismissed my attempts to calm her.

Finally she subsided on her own, wiped her eyes and the smeared mascara with my handkerchief. I brought her a glass of water from the pitcher I kept on my work table, the ice long since melted but the water still cold. Then she excused herself and went down the hall to our bathroom for repairs. By the time she came back, she was wholly composed, and she sat down on the couch, taking my hand in hers, and told me the story.

When she'd come back from France, practically broke, the house had been Claude's gift to her. He'd bought it as an investment from the estate of the woman it had been built for, the former mistress of a California land baron who, having outlived her benefactor by several decades, had died heavily in debt.

At first, Jeannine hadn't wanted to be in Pasadena. She didn't know anyone there, and she hated driving, hated the freeways. But she'd fallen in love with the place the first time she saw it.

"It was a ruin," she said, "an absolute wreck. Dark and dingy and cluttered. Even cobwebs. Mice. And it reeked of mold."

But she'd seen the possibilities in it, and in that sense it became *her* house. She'd spent a fortune on it over the years—her own money. She'd had the roof redone, the pool rebuilt, practically all the interiors renovated. But it wasn't just the money. Everything in it was hers— the plantings, the furnishings, the wallpapers, every last detail. All hers.

"I've always wanted to buy it. I told Claude that. I spent so much on it, it should be mine legally. But he always laughed at me. Said it already was mine, that I could live here as long as I wanted so why did I have to buy it? I should save my money, he said. My God, that I should have to live with my own stupidity!"

"There's nothing on paper?" I asked.

"Not a word."

"Why does he want to sell it now?"

She shook her head. "I don't know. He says the market's stronger than it's been in years. Pasadena has been depressed, that's true. He says he won't throw me out today or tomorrow, but that he has someone ready to pay three and a half million dollars for it."

"Then why don't *we* buy it?" I said on impulse.

"That's hardly the point, don't you see? If we offered him three and a half million, it suddenly wouldn't be enough. If we offered him four million, it wouldn't be enough. Or five, six. He won't sell to me, would *never* sell to us. It's not the money. He doesn't need the money. It's just his way of punishing me."

"Punishing you for what?" I said. "There's no way he can know anything about the book, is there?"

"No," she answered. Then she lowered her eyelids halfway, and her voice softened. "I imagine it's because I told him I loved you, darling. And because I told him I wanted to marry you."

Chapter Seventeen

A LONG TIME ago I sat in darkness, in a creaky movie theater, watching a lithe young actress with impossibly big eyes and dark, close-cropped hair work her magic on a lumbering hoodlum. I remember how her eyes, though half-shut, devoured him in the closeups, how her lips seemed suddenly to occupy the screen.

Sonny Corral played the hoodlum.

At the time, I'd thought Corral was the luckiest guy in the world, even though, in the story, she was doing him in.

Claude Rhinelander had been the executive producer.

A third of a century later, give or take, the same actress was talking about our marriage.

Apparently she'd broken the news to Claude from Vancouver, while I was in New York. I thought she might have broken it to me, too, before now.

"Oh, darling," she said, laughing, "how could I have done that to you? A man fresh from the ordeal of his soon-to-be-ex-wife? You would have been *much* too rattled! But was it really so terrible, what I said?"

"No."

"And would it really be such a terrible thing, if we were to get married?"

"No."

"Then why do you look as though a black cloud is sitting over your head?"

I didn't know that's what I looked like. I guess I found it a little

strange that she'd seen fit to proclaim the news first to someone who'd
been wanting to marry her for over thirty years.

I said something along those lines.

"Oh, Daniel, don't be so *tedious!* I've been a caterpillar for so long,
a grungy, aging caterpillar feeling sorry for myself. I may only be in
the chrysalis stage now, but when I come out of my dead skin, I'm
going to be a gorgeous butterfly. A gorgeous butterfly, all for my
Daniel!"

Her arms went up as she whirled, and the silk sleeves of her blouse,
which connected in continuous fabric from her wrists to her waist,
billowed out like butterfly wings. Then, flinging her arms around my
neck, she kissed me excitedly, passionately. So it was that a night
which had started in tears ended up in bed.

I could never say no.

CLAUDE'S THREAT TO sell the house made her all the more intractable
about the book. It became a battleground for her. The old Jeannine,
as I had written her, had been softened by tinges of sadness, nostalgia
for who she had been. The new Jeannine wanted all sentimentality
out. She'd always lived with her eyes open, she said, knowing full well
what she was doing and why. The rest was pose. If she'd paid a price—
Claude's price much of the time—she'd gotten things in exchange. In
any case, done was done, and now everything was changing.

Yet who can say which was the old Jeannine and which the new?
The old Jeannine had always refused to watch the young Nina Hardy,
lest the films depress her. The new began to watch them with me, at
times poking holes in her performances, marveling and laughing at
other moments, above all remembering—remembering just the kinds
of details I'd never been able to get out of her before and some of
which I now incorporated in the manuscript.

"It's going to be a great book, Daniel," she would say one day. But
the next, worrying over this or that detail: "I think it's just awful. The
whole thing is awful. It's a total embarrassment. It's not me at all.
What are we going to do?"

I had known people like that before, who underwent drastic swings
over their work-in-progress, from depression to elation and back again,
but usually they were themselves the writers. In Jeannine's case, not

only was the book a battleground, it had become in her mind the cornerstone of her future.

"But it's *our* future, Daniel," she'd say when I tried to calm her. "Everything starts with the book."

As for me, I had redone certain parts often enough that I'd lost all perspective. Logically, I told Jeannine, we ought to show it, or some of it, to a fresh reader.

"How could you even *think* such a thing?" she exclaimed. "My God, *he* would get his hands on it!"

"How?" I said. "I'm not talking about giving it to the publisher. And even if he did, he's going to read it soon enough."

"Not until we're ready. Not until we're absolutely ready. And *I* will decide when that is."

At the same time, she overrode my misgivings about the turn the book had taken. Aside from legal questions, like libel and invasion of privacy, how, I asked, could the Rhinelander Group conceivably publish it the way it was? And what, Claude being Claude, might he do to Jeannine's career as an actress if it was published elsewhere?

Nothing, she said. He no longer had the power. Besides, with or without Claude, her career as an actress was winding down, as she'd already told me a thousand times.

As far as the Rhinelander Group was concerned, Leo Castagni had finally gotten back to me. The rumors were various. There was talk that Claude was going to take Olympian private, also that he was planning a takeover from Lew. If that were true, Jeannine thought, then wouldn't Claude look better publishing our book himself, whatever it said about him, than being doubly embarrassed if someone else did?

Maybe so, I said. Unless he tried to stop us altogether.

"But how could he?" Jeannine asked.

"By getting an injunction against us."

She shook her head, dismissing the idea.

"How can you be so sure of that?" I persisted.

"Because I know him, Daniel," she said calmly. "Because he'd let it be published rather than let people know he cared."

I hoped she was right. I'd already been to Chinatown, and no matter how often I told myself that the circumstances were entirely different, my last exchange with Gloria Farran kept coming back into my head.

"Go write somebody else's book, lover boy," she'd said that morning after, as I stood in her boudoir doorway.

IN SEPTEMBER, THE engraved announcements arrived: *Mr. Claude Rhinelander and Mr. Lewis P. Rhinelander ask you to reserve the evening of the seventh of November to celebrate the Fiftieth Anniversary of the Rhinelander Publishing Group, the Rainbow Room, New York, details to follow.* With, in my case, a handwritten note from Allen Fryberg and, in Jeannine's, one from Claude.

Claude *and* Lew—and very Californian in style, I noticed, with a preinvitation preceding the real one.

I called Fryberg to thank him.

"What's going on?" I asked him.

"It's going to be quite a party, Dan. The hottest ticket in town, and I hear people who've been left off the list are already committing *suppuku.*"

"That's not what I had in mind. What's going on between Claude and Lew?"

"Well, they're still talking to each other, if that's what you mean."

"Come on, Allen. Is it true Claude's taking over?"

"Where did you hear that?"

"A good source."

He started to say something. Then I heard him sigh over the phone, then chuckle.

"You know, Claude's going to have a fit. He still believes something can be kept secret in this town, just because he says so. In fact, what you've heard is true: Claude's buying all the family's publishing interests. The only reason it hasn't been announced yet is because they're still arguing over who's going to say what."

"It's been that bloody?"

"You don't know the half of it! Everybody will deny it, myself included, but there was a moment when Lew thought he was buying Claude out!"

I thought of the scene on the beach at Laguna.

"It's better this way," Fryberg said. "Everybody knows that. You and I may not like it, but publishing's become a big business and you can't run it like a corner candy store."

Which, I remembered, was exactly how he'd once described the way Claude ran Rhinelander Films and Olympian.

"It's all going to change now," he said.

"How?"

"All in due course," he answered mysteriously. "All in due course." And then Christine came home.

SHE ARRIVED, TANNED and healthy-looking, with Charles Jourdan on her feet, Dorothée Bis on her back, and her hair swept off her face and held in place by jeweled barrettes. And she'd done it all, she pointed out, without a word of advice from Jeannine.

To a degree, I'd been prepared for the change. Hardly a day had gone by during her absence in which she and Jeannine hadn't talked on the phone, and then there was the letter, the long, *mea culpa* letter. Jeannine had taken to carrying it around like a talisman. She'd read me parts of it—"I'm to blame, not you, dear Mama. It's all been my fault." In the letter, Christine announced that she'd be going back to law school in the fall. Her attitude in the spring had been stupid, a temporary crisis of confidence. The time had come for her to take charge of her own life. "I love you, Mama," she'd ended it, "I always will."

Jeannine still hadn't said anything to her about the house, and I knew she was apprehensive about it. Now, over dinner, the night after Christine's return, Jeannine began to catch her up on her own plans: Peter Singer, the meetings they'd had, the book, using Singer's language, I noticed, whenever she talked about money—the projections for Year I, Year II, upside, downside, the possibilities for the "out" years. But the more she went on, the more I could feel the tension building in her until, apparently out of nerves, she knocked over her wineglass.

She gasped and jumped back from the table. For just a second, she stared at the red splotch spreading on the tablecloth in front of her. Then there was a terrific commotion, Jeannine calling for Maria, and Maria rushing forward, away, and back with a fresh napkin which, with accomplished gestures, she spread across the splotch. Christine, too, was on her feet by then, saying, "For God's sakes, Mother, what's wrong?" Because Jeannine was suddenly, inexplicably, in tears.

And then she told her. Claude was selling the house. Claude was going to kick them out.

Christine questioned her about it, and Jeannine described what had happened.

"But why?" Christine asked. "Why now, all of a sudden?"

"I don't know," Jeannine answered. "You know him when it comes to money. Or maybe he's just being Claude."

Her omission, needless to say, didn't escape me.

Christine said something to the effect that he couldn't just throw them out on the spot. Think of the publicity, she said: *Rhinelander Evicts Nina Hardy!* But then she fell silent—intentionally, perhaps, because if I could feel Jeannine's anxiety mounting again across the table, Christine certainly could, too.

"Well," she said finally, authoritatively, "if you want my honest opinion, I think it's the best thing that's happened to you in years. I really do. I know how you love it here. It's your home, your place. But it isn't really, is it? It's *his*. I think it's time for you to move on. It all fits. It's all part and parcel of the new you."

There was Christine on her feet, comforting Jeannine. There was Christine, staring at me triumphantly over her mother's shoulder, saying, "Tell her it's all right, Dan."

In an odd way, this show of approval and support made Jeannine crazy. Or, if not crazy, at least irritable, jumpy. Somehow the fact that her daughter wasn't the obstacle she thought she would be, the hurdle she had to get past, threw her off stride. It was as though she needed Christine to say no in order to find her own balance, and the absence of struggle made her rely more on her own judgment than she could handle.

And Christine, of course, played her game to the hilt.

I CAME BACK to my room after lunch one day—Jeannine was gone and I'd taken a solitary break by the pool—to find Christine once again in my chair. Evidently she'd been reading, because the page on the screen wasn't where I'd left off.

Jeannine, meanwhile, had become obsessed with secrecy. After each day's work, she made me lock up my disk in her wall safe, and there was, at her insistence, only one hard copy of the manuscript. Whenever we made changes on it, which was virtually every day, the old pages were torn up and thrown away. I had no record of what had been done before, other than the old tapes I'd made of her in the early years.

I knew she didn't want anyone, including Christine, reading it until we were ready.

"Don't do that," Christine protested, standing as I reached past her and turned off the machine. "I was just getting into it! It's good, you know."

"It seems to me we've been here before," I said. "But thanks for the compliment."

"Why won't you let me read it?"

"You'll have to ask your mother. It's her decision."

"I already have. She says when it's all finished. Now I'm asking you."

I shook my head.

"Not even the parts about me?"

"No."

"How do I know you haven't slandered me?"

"I guess you'll just have to take it on faith."

She laughed at that. We both remained standing, Christine with her back to the parson's table and her palms propped on the edge. She was eyeing me with her habitual sly smile, as though measuring me, and I was reminded—again—of how Jeannine's features had somehow gone awry in the repetition, not in the physical details but in the expression Christine gave them.

"It's all so much bullshit, isn't it?" she said, still watching me. "I guess you know that by now. You of all people."

"What's all bullshit?" I asked.

"Everything. Her makeover. Her new career. The house. You. Everything."

"I'm afraid I don't know what you're talking about."

"Really? After writing her whole life story? Unless that's bullshit too."

I said nothing, which seemed to irritate her.

"Do you *really* think she's going to go through with all of it?" she said. And when I didn't answer: "If you do, then you don't know the first thing about her."

"You mean the book?" I asked.

"No, I don't mean your silly book," she said. "You're almost finished anyway, aren't you? But the house, for instance. Do you really think we'll move?"

"If Claude sells it . . ."

"Oh, he's not going to sell it. He's just bluffing. He's bringing her to heel."

"About what?"

"About all this stuff. 'The new Jeannine.' About you, maybe. Do you think it's an accident that she's never remarried, all these years?"

I understood what she was up to then: divide and conquer, and if she'd decided, in her wisdom, that it was no time for a direct attack on Mom, that didn't keep her from working the flanks. No matter that she was also giving voice to my own fears, I'd be damned if I'd let her see it.

"Don't forget," she said, "I've been here before. The same thing's been going on all my life. She's never been able to stand up to him for long. And then it's good-by, Tom, Dick, or Harry, all back to normal, everything as it was. Until the next time."

"You really don't think very much of her, do you?" I said.

"You've asked me that before. I told you, I admire her enormously. I just don't like to see her let herself be taken advantage of stupidly."

"By me?"

"By you, or men like you. Or this Singer she thinks is so wonderful. Or Claude Rhinelander, for that matter."

"Why do you leave yourself out?" I asked.

I could see that I got to her there. She flared—the same reflex Jeannine had, the nostrils widening and narrowing—and started to retort. But then, apparently, she thought better of it.

"It so happens I think you're wrong," I said. "I think this time she's going to make it."

She glared at me. At least with her there was never any doubt about where the lines were drawn.

"I hope you're right," she said.

"Come on," I said, "you don't hope I'm right. You hope she falls on her face."

"You really are a bastard, aren't you? How in God's name could you say a thing like that?"

"Easy. If she succeeds—if she gets what she wants—then what will become of poor little Chris?"

Maybe it was a cruel thing to say, but I couldn't help myself. I had my own insecurity to deal with, and I knew that Christine, having tried once to push me out of Jeannine's life and failed, wasn't about to give up.

"Let me ask you one thing," I said. "Has there ever been a man in her life—*any* man—whom you would have found acceptable?"

She seemed to think about this a minute, then, with her usual shrug, and a short, harsh laugh:

"We'll see who's still around to pick up the pieces, buster. When it's all over."

Chapter Eighteen

I'D KNOWN IT to happen before: sometimes, even though nobody's read a book, even though it's still unfinished, rumors and hype start to circulate. I began to get calls, and not just from Jenny Bergler, Tinker, Fryberg, although coincident with the announcement of Claude's takeover, all of them began pressing me for the manuscript. But when I heard it from Jilly Rogers, I knew that someone, somewhere, was talking out of turn.

"I hear you're writing something very steamy, sweetie," she said, "and that there are certain people out here who aren't going to like it, not one bit."

My first thought was Christine. I'd watched her egg on Jeannine— "Claude's got it coming to him," she'd say—and I wouldn't have put it past her to fan the flames any way she could. But there was no way, as far as I knew, that Jilly had access to her.

I grilled Jilly about what she'd heard and where she'd heard it. I pleaded friendship. I reminded her that she, after all, was responsible for my doing the book in the first place. I couldn't budge her, though— her sources were sacrosanct, she said, and her stock-in-trade was coming up with rumor and gossip before her competitors. It was only when I promised to deliver Jeannine to her show, bound and trussed if need be, that I got it out of her.

The leak was Peter Singer.

After a brief debate with myself, I told Jeannine. At first she didn't believe me. Jilly Rogers was my friend, not Peter's. But I hadn't seen Jilly since Oscar night, I said, and if I'd talked to her since, never in

221

a million years would I have told her anything substantive about the book.

Singer had no choice other than to admit what he'd done.

"Of course, I've dropped a hint here and there," he said, innocently enough, the morning I laid the story on him, Jeannine standing with me. "But I had to. The book's a big part of my selling job. In fact it's the key."

"I may have told you more about it than I should have," Jeannine said coolly, "but it was always in the strictest confidence. I thought I had made that clear."

"You're right," Singer said, starting to squirm. He'd been around her long enough to recognize the veiled menace in her tone. "You did, you made it very clear. But at the same time you've got to trust my discretion. I can't be muzzled altogether. When I mention the book to people, they're naturally curious. I have to be able to tease them with it. If I can't . . . I mean, if I can't talk about it, well . . . I can't really function, can I?"

"In that case," Jeannine replied, "perhaps you can't function at all."

Singer looked incredulous. He glanced quickly at me, as if for help, then back at her.

"Am I hearing what I think I'm hearing? Does that mean you're *firing* me?"

"No," she said. "It means you've fired yourself."

He couldn't believe it. Neither could I.

Even after he'd left, having pleaded his case until Jeannine cut him off, I expected that she'd rehire him before the day was over. She didn't.

When she refused to take his phone calls, he started calling me instead. Surely I understood. How could we let her wreck the whole edifice, and over something so essentially petty? He'd done it all, hadn't he? He'd built the whole concept, and he'd done it with mirrors, too, with nothing to go on but his own hype. Without him, where would she be? Back at square one.

Jeannine had a different slant on it.

"You know, darling," she said to me, "we really don't need Peter anymore. He did invaluable work, and he'll be compensated for it. But his greatest contribution was his contacts, and they're mine now. I don't think any of them will go away just because Peter's left."

She would hear no arguments. It was unthinkable, she said, that she have someone working for her whom she didn't trust. Besides, weren't we ourselves smart enough to manage what he had begun? And if, once the book was done, we needed someone to coordinate and follow up on all the projects, then we would hire someone. But not Peter Singer.

Singer threatened to sue. From what I knew of agent-client relationships, he wouldn't get far. Beyond his commissions on the deals made to that point, he wasn't entitled to anything, and he'd likely cause more damage to himself than to Jeannine. I told him so.

"Thanks for the advice," he said bitterly. His parting shot struck home: "Good luck to you, Dan. I think you're going to need it."

Maybe that seems a strange thing to say—that his parting shot struck home—when Jeannine and I were sharing the same bed and when our passion, our mutual need, was, if anything, at a peak. The truth was that, at least some of the time, I admired what she was doing. Once I'd gotten over the shock that the young actress I'd fallen in love with all those years ago was no more, I'd fallen in love with the new. So it wasn't our feelings for each other that unnerved me.

Maybe it was the book itself. All her worrying, her second-guessing, the rewriting I'd done and the re-rewriting, coupled with her obsession for secrecy, had worn me down. Increasingly, I had become the medium, in my second-floor room, through which her thoughts met her self-doubt. I had never worked so hard on a book or, so much of the time those last months, with the sense of someone looking over my shoulder. I no longer knew if it was any good or not. All I cared about was whether it was publishable—what *would* happen when Claude Rhinelander saw it?—and getting it done.

Jeannine said something that stuck in my mind. "You have done many books, dear Daniel. I have only this one. It is my book, the only one I will ever write. This is why I want it to be perfect."

My book, the only one I will ever write.

I'd experienced something of the same with every book I'd ghost-written except Jilly Rogers'. There comes a point, usually late in the day, when the book is finished or almost, when a process of severance takes place. The ghostwriter becomes the forgotten man, an impediment, even an embarrassment, because the star takes over. *My book.* Ask any one of them, "Who wrote your book for you?" and nine times out of ten you'll hear, "Why I did, of course," even though everybody—at least the professionals—knows full well how it came into being.

But this was Jeannine, wasn't it? The woman I loved? The woman who wanted to marry me?

It couldn't happen again, could it? How could it? No way. To think that it could was not only paranoid, it was stupid. Jeannine's investment in the book was both complicated and real. Wasn't it the cornerstone of her future? Of *our* future?

That's what I kept telling myself.

But we weren't working in a vacuum either. What *would* a publisher think of it? What would a publisher's lawyer think of it? What would Claude Rhinelander think of it?

FRYBERG CALLED.

"I'm confused, Dan," he said. "When somebody's under contract to write a book, isn't his first obligation to deliver it to the publisher? Before he shows it to anyone else?"

His tone was unmistakably belligerent, even nasty.

"I don't know that it's an obligation, Allen," I answered.

"But it's the custom, isn't it?"

"Usually. Yes, I guess so. Why do you ask?"

"We're hearing some very peculiar things. Ugly things."

"About what?"

"About your book. *Jeannine*. That's your title, isn't it? *Jeannine?*"

I saw no need to conceal the title. "Yes, that's what we're calling it."

"Claude's not going to like that. Didn't it occur to you that the publisher might have something to say about the title before you give it out?"

"It's our working title, Allen," I said defensively. "It's not carved in stone."

"That's not all. It's not possible, is it—and I want a straight answer, Dan—that the manuscript's already out, in circulation?"

"No, it's not possible," I said. "There's only one copy in existence. The only people who've read it are Jeannine and myself."

"Are you sure of that?"

"Yes, I'm sure of that."

"Well, we're hearing that the book has some very derogatory things to say about someone we both know. I hope—for everybody's sake—that it's not true."

He said it as a half-question, but I didn't answer. I wondered if someone else might be listening in—someone we both knew—because Fryberg's voice had gone tight, his tone aggressive.

"Well," he persisted. "Is it or isn't it?"

"I don't think that's for me to say one way or the other, Allen. I'd rather let people form their own opinions, once the manuscript's done and delivered."

"That's not much of an answer," he said sharply. "Just between us, I think I deserve better than that."

"Just between us, Allen," I replied, "I deserved a better question."

That was the end of it, in substance, although Fryberg added something to the effect that I'd never struck him as the type who'd bite the hand that fed me. He also said that certain people were going to read the manuscript carefully—"scrutinize" was the word he used—and that they didn't like surprises, especially unpleasant ones.

I reported the conversation to Jeannine, in Christine's presence.

"Let them worry," Christine said. "It's good for them."

Jeannine was sure Claude had been listening in. She looked at me thoughtfully.

"In any case," she said, "it makes up my mind about one thing."

We were going to New York for the party, she said, by which time the book would be done. Then she was going, alone, to a spa up near Napa. She'd reserved for a week—it would be the final stage of her makeover. And then she, and she alone, was going to take the manuscript to Claude.

"That's not how it's done," I argued. "Tinker McConnell represents the book. Properly the manuscript should go to her first, and then she'll deliver it to Jenny Bergler."

Jeannine dismissed the idea.

"You and I both know, Daniel, that they don't count. Any decisions about the book will be Claude's. I don't want other people reading it before he does. And I want to take it to him in person."

"Why? What will you say?"

She smiled, in a way that suggested she already had it planned.

"I will say, 'Here is my book, Claude. Here is my life. I hope you like it. I hope you will publish it.'"

"And what will you do when he dumps all over it?"

"I don't think he will dump all over it," she answered. "But if he does, then at least we will know where we stand. And we will find another publisher."

I didn't like it, not at all. Jenny Bergler, I pointed out, would see dollar signs when she read the manuscript, whereas Claude would see only his own name. But I lost, not for the first time, and this time it was two on one. Christine stood behind Jeannine's chair and, putting her arms around her mother's neck—a touching display—and looking straight at me over Jeannine's shoulder, said, "Don't listen to him, Mother. It's your book, your life. You do it your way."

THE DAY FINALLY came—in a daze of rewriting, discarding, re-rewriting—when we were finished. It was a week or two before the Rhinelander party in New York. I carried the box downstairs—six hundred and two manuscript pages, saying, "Here it is, Jeannine. Your book. I couldn't find a ribbon to tie around it, but it's done."

She shook her head, not unkindly but with the firmness that had become part of her new style. And smiled slightly.

"Not done, dear Daniel," she said. "Not yet. What I want now is for you to go away and allow me to read it alone, without interruption. Then, and only then, will it be done."

I freaked. I know that's a damn poor way of describing it, but how else to say what it's like when the woman you love and have sweated for—your *partner*, for God's sake!—suddenly starts treating you like the . . . well, Fryberg's Spanish word.

No, Daniel, your job's not done till I check your penmanship!

"Why is this so unreasonable?" Jeannine asked. "Look, you've been saying you have to go to New York anyway. Wouldn't it make sense for you to go early, before the party? I'll stay here and read, then I'll meet you in New York."

The New York part was true—I did have to go at some point. Among other things, I needed to put the house on the market. But I'd never said it had to be right then.

"Yes, it's unreasonable!" I said. "For God's sake, I've worked my ass off on this book! I know it's *your* book, *your* life, but it's mine too!"

"Of course it is, darling. I didn't mean—"

"Then what are you reading it alone for? Are you going to sit in judgment? Is that what you're going to do? Thumbs up, thumbs down?"

"Daniel, please stop shouting, I—"

"I'm *not* shouting!" although I was. "I'm just fed up with being pushed into a corner!"

She looked at me, surprised, pained, vertical creases between her eyebrows.

"Could you explain this, please?" she said. "Pushed into a corner? I don't understand."

I tried, but the more I talked, the more I sounded like some peasant come to the castle with his list of grievances. In the end, I just stood there, glaring at her.

"Oh, Daniel," she said, her face tilted toward me, her arms lifted. "Please sit down. Please come next to me now."

I did sit, but in a chair across from her.

"My poor Daniel," she said, gazing at me with sad, dark eyes. "I have treated you abominably, haven't I? But the things you say—you mustn't think such awful things. The book is wonderful, we both know that. I think we have been working too hard, too long, and I've been busy with too many other things. There's been so much tension— do you think I don't feel it too?—and no room for us. No time for us to love each other. But do you really not understand what I'm asking? All I want is to be able to sit down quietly, by myself, and read the book the way I would any other, from page one, and without anyone looking over my shoulder. You of all people should understand that. You've always hated my reading over your shoulder." She smiled across at me, and her tone lightened. "Is this really so strange?"

We needed time off, she went on. We were both very private people, and we needed time off from each other to begin with, then time off together, from the rest of the world. We had both been under a strain. After New York and the spa, we could go away together somewhere. She would even cancel the spa, but she'd moved heaven and earth to get them to take her then, how could she not go? But after the spa, we would go off together, a long way away, far from everyone else.

After the spa was Claude, I reminded her.

No matter, she said. That was only a few days.

While she talked, she'd gotten up and had come over to lean on the arm of my chair. She ran her fingers idly through my hair, and I smelled the new perfume. "How can I reassure you, my darling Daniel? I can't stand it when you're like this. Please let me reassure you."

She knew of only one way, she said softly, taking my hand and smiling as she leaned forward to kiss me.

She did her best, I'll give her that.

And I? I went and did something unbelievably stupid.

I "SENT" A copy of the disk, by telephone, to my machine in the barn.

I'd done this once before, when I'd been working away from home for an extended period of time, and I'd been amazed, on returning, to find all the work intact and waiting for me.

Why did I do that? Put it that I wanted something to read myself, while Jeannine was reading.

I flew to New York where, all along the Hudson, the grounds were awash in fallen leaves. The Murphys were still in residence, and when I told them I was putting the place on the market but that they were free to stay, at my expense, until the actual sale, Mrs. Murphy wept. Even so, I felt antsy there, an intruder of sorts, and after a day of interviewing real estate agents, I moved into a hotel in the city.

Before I left the barn, I printed out a copy of *Jeannine*. It wasn't for my own reading, although I did page through it that night. It was for delivery the next day to Tinker McConnell, someone I could trust and who swore to read it quickly, in utter and total confidence.

Jeannine, meanwhile, loved the book. She told me so every night. She was reading it very slowly, she said, the way she always loves to read really good books. It engrossed her. She was astonished by how good it was. I was really a very, very skillful writer. It had bite, wit, scandal, and still a touch of elegance.

There was one thing she wanted to add, though. She'd written it herself. No, she couldn't read it over the phone, she wasn't quite done. Didn't I have one of those machines?

"A Fax machine?" I asked.

Yes, a Fax machine.

The hotel had one, and the next day it came, with a note scrawled across the top that we would add it to the disk later, unless I didn't like it.

She'd given it the title "Epilogue."
It read:

> I have told my story as though it were over. It isn't. In many
> ways, it has only begun.
>
> I owe both, the story you have just read and the one which has
> just begun, to someone whose name, in keeping with convention,
> never appears in these pages, but without whom both stories—
> quite literally—would have remained locked, expressionless, in
> my mind and heart. He has made the difference. Not only did he
> give shape to the events, people, places, which have made up my
> life, but in doing so he has opened my eyes to who I am, and to
> new possibilities, new adventures, in a life I had thought all but
> over.
>
> I owe him everything, this nameless one, this alter ego. This—
> and I imagine it shows!—is the only portion of the book that I
> have written without him.
>
> There is another reason, though, other than convention, that
> I am tempted not to name him now. That is because I think I
> love him too much to share. But it strikes me this would be an
> unjust, even an unseemly, way to end a book which has tried, if
> nothing else, to be frank.
>
> And so I do name him now, with gratitude: Daniel Springer.

She had one thing wrong: By the current convention in ghostwritten
books, my name, too, would have appeared on the jacket and the
spine, as well as the title page. Even ghosts, nowadays, want their
share of the limelight, and with most of them the size of the type, the
billing, the precise formula—by Nina Hardy *as told to* Dan Springer,
or *with* Dan Springer, or *written by* Dan Springer—would have been
the subject of endless negotiations between the agents and the lawyers.

To me, that's always been so much bullshit, and I've never allowed
it. The public is buying the star, not Springer. A ghost is a ghost is
a ghost.

Still, it touched me. And I told her so.

I still have the Fax copy.

Chapter Nineteen

I DELIVERED THE copy of *Jeannine* to Tinker McConnell on a Wednesday afternoon, at 3:30. The Rhinelander party was the following Tuesday night. I handed it to her alone, in her office, the only copy of the manuscript extant except for Jeannine's. Of course Tinker would read it herself—what else did I think she'd been waiting for?—but she couldn't promise to get to it until the weekend, maybe not even then. She was terribly backed up. All her authors, it seemed, had decided to deliver at once. Some of them were already clamoring for her head. And—of course—she would read it confidentially, I didn't even have to explain.

I did explain, in detail.

I called her Friday. She'd only had time to sample the beginning. She *loved* it.

I called her Monday, twice. I couldn't get through to her. She had an auction, couldn't talk to anybody—even though the day of my auction, I remembered, she'd still managed to talk to everybody and his brother. Her assistant said she'd make sure Tinker got back to me before she left the office. Tinker didn't, and when I tried her at home that night, all I got was an answering machine, to which I blew my stack.

You want paranoia? I'll give you paranoia.

I did speak to her Tuesday, the day of the Rhinelander party. How could I be irritated? she wanted to know. Hadn't she told me she was backed up, that she mightn't get to it? Yes, of course she'd read more, she thought it was great—but she couldn't talk, she had people in her office. Maybe we could find a quiet corner at the party to discuss it?

Jeannine, meanwhile, had come in on Monday, along with Sonny—a reinstated Sonny, apparently. He, too, had been invited to the party. I met them at the airport. Jeannine's big eyes were sparkling with excitement, and she flung herself into my arms. She'd insisted on separate rooms at the hotel—not, she said, for decorum's sake, but she didn't want me in the way when she dressed the next day. Her designer would be coming. I spent that night with her, though, and all night long, she kept saying she couldn't get enough of me. Then it was morning; she was already wide awake and on her way—a whirlwind shopping spree, lunch with some corporate executive from Neiman Marcus, and I was to pick her up at seven.

THE RAINBOW ROOM. They'd redone it since the Fawn and I used to go there to celebrate my small triumphs. The place had been closed for a year, more, while they redecorated, and maybe it was better after, I don't know. The magic, for me, had always been that it was high up—when I sat at the old bar, I got the feeling I was swimming in the air, like some great-winged bird sipping a martini above the skyscrapers—and that it was Rockefeller Center. For most people, I imagine, the power center of the city still isn't Wall Street, certainly not World Trade or the Empire State or Donald Trump's Tower, not even the money alleys of Park Avenue and Madison. It's the group of great old buildings, all that steel and marble rising around the sunken skating rink, and nothing they've put up around it—east, west, north, south—comes close to rivaling it for opulence, New York-style.

Whatever they'd done to it, the Rainbow Room was still high up, still Rockefeller Center, and that particular night, it was *suppuku* time if you weren't on the invitation list.

I could describe it several ways: by those who came in limos and those who didn't, by those who wore evening clothes and those (few) unfortunate or bold enough to appear in Sunday best, by those with tans and those who were pale, or those adorned in paste and those in real gems, the face-lifted and the un-, the old and the young, California and New York, the already rich and the yet-to-be-rich, or simply by those you recognized at a glance and those you needed the name for. Actors, directors, producers from the West, writers, editors, publishers from the East, agents and media mafia from both coasts, and lawyers, executives, money men. The Rhinelanders—less for the anniversary, I imagine, than the handing over of power—had brought them all out.

As for me, though, there was first and only Jeannine.

A deep, deep chartreuse. It started, irregular, near her ankles, chased, it seemed, by matching silk shoes with high heels, and climbed her legs in twining drapes of silk to her waist, where a chartreuse sash held it. Then it rose again, clinging to her torso, to end dramatically draped over a single shoulder. There was something of the ancient Greek about it, more of the climbing plant or vine, and while the dominant tone was that dark lime, there were half-hidden tints of yellow and gold in the fabric, even blue, which made it lustrous under light, deep and mysterious in shadow. For jewelry, she wore a large antique diamond brooch on the clothed shoulder, diamond teardrop earrings. Long, bare arms. Over the ensemble, a long black velvet hooded cape, lined with the same fabric of her gown.

She was taller than usual in the heels, and the backward sweep of her hair, which she'd been growing longer, and the new makeup, the rising, deepening violet tones so perfectly applied, also somehow seemed to lift her upward. She resembled one of those rare ballerinas so tall and statuesque you think it's impossible for them to dance— until they begin to move.

She fairly took my breath away. When I told her so, though, she only smiled faintly, as though to smile more would somehow mar the fragility of her perfection. She insisted on walking the short blocks to the party; she needed the air. We hardly spoke—an echo, I thought on the spot, of that other party of Claude's, when she'd gone into the same interiorized, almost trancelike state of preparation. Only when we entered the building and walked through the shadowy marbled halls to the waiting throng at the elevators, did she take my arm.

Upstairs there was a receiving line. Claude Rhinelander, it seemed shorter than ever, his hair a white stubble, his glasses gleaming in the light. He reached out his arms to Jeannine. She extended hers and, stooping a little, kissed him. He held on to her an extra moment, saying something I couldn't hear, and in the push of people from behind, I was propelled past them. To Lew, resplendent in a shawl-collared tuxedo, with boutonniere and diamond studs.

"Hello," Lew said, inclining his head toward me. "So glad you could come, Dan."

We shook hands briefly. He said something else, or maybe I did, before he turned to greet the next person in line. That would have been Jeannine. But I didn't hear. Because there, equally resplendent, was the Fawn.

She was dressed in black, a new evening color for her, a long black tunic, beaded, which came almost to her knees, over black silk pants, and a massive worked-gold collar around her neck. I'd never seen it before. Gold on her wrists. Her chestnut hair about the same, still short, a little spikier, as though it might have been punked. Her wide eyes. New makeup, I thought at first, but it wasn't that.

Even as she turned toward me, the profile becoming full face, even before she recognized me, I saw.

Resplendent? I thought. Good God Almighty!

I think my mouth fell ajar, stayed ajar. I stopped breathing.

I'm no judge, but she looked a good five months pregnant, maybe more. And her face was broader, rounder, the cheeks a tawny-rosy hue.

I couldn't say a word. Couldn't get a word out.

"Oh, Dan," was all she said. She smiled, a little sadly. Sad Fawn eyes.

Then Jeannine came up behind me. The Fawn noticed her. How could you not notice Jeannine?

"Ah, Ms. Hardy," I heard the Fawn say. "I'm so honored, so thrilled, to meet you. I'm Faith Graves."

I saw them exchange words, smiles, even those pecking women's kisses on the cheek. First one cheek, then the other.

The oncoming line pushed us forward. Jeannine said something to me to the effect that she really was very beautiful. And very pregnant. Had I known? I said that I hadn't.

I drank too much. Probably I danced too much. I thought it was the Fawn, the shock of seeing her, but I was also the forgotten man all over again, and in more ways than I could begin to understand. People crowded Jeannine as usual, clustered around her like groupies, and she, in her stunning, eye-of-the-storm style, held court, but I was used to that. What I wasn't used to were the others—people I knew from publishing, my alleged friends, some of them—who gave me the feeling I was terminally ill. I wanted to say: I've seen the Fawn, it's okay; even if it's not okay, I'll get through it; meanwhile, here's Jeannine.

We ran into Jenny Bergler before people sat down. She was sure pissed about something. Her eyes were lowered in a permanent scowl. Maybe it was her gown, a swirling, gauzy affair, and she was evidently having trouble with it. She hardly managed hello, even to Jeannine (whom she'd always been dying to meet), and introduced us quickly to her husband before disappearing.

I spotted Allen Fryberg from the rear as we made our way among the drinkers. I tapped him on the shoulder, and he turned, whirled would be more like it. Seeing me, his face stiffened. Spotting Jeannine, he forced it to relax. He was sweating, mopping at his brow, and he started talking rapid-fire, quipping, something about "Ah, so California comes to New York, isn't it horrible?" Then, touching me on the shoulder but looking at Jeannine, he excused himself, saying he had to help play host, and rushed off.

It didn't matter to Jeannine. There were always others pushing through to say hello to her, introduce themselves to her, touch her, be touched by her. It didn't matter to me either. My best friend that evening was a waiter, one of dozens who patrolled the floor, trays in hand, but this one was mine, mine alone, and since I'd started with a double bourbon, he was always there, double bourbon at my elbow.

I didn't see Tinker McConnell. I looked. She must have been there. I did see Falcone, but only later. I saw Sonny from afar, then close up. He, too, was holding court, his great ruined head above the multitude. Later, between dinner courses, he came to the table and took Jeannine off for a whirl around the floor. Surprisingly nimble, I thought, for an old boozehound who walked like an arthritic bear.

I shook hands with Irving R. Stewart, too. According to something Jeannine had heard, we had the sawed-off financier to thank for the party. Apparently he was the one who'd brought the brothers together, persuading Claude to pay something more than he wanted to for Rhinelander Publishing and Lew to sit still for it. How exactly Irving R. got his piece of the deal nobody knew, but he presided over the dais table like a smiling marriage broker, even though he wasn't introduced.

Lew served as emcee—a generous gesture on a night of winners and losers. He spoke wittily, warmly, into a microphone about Dad, old Nat, the Founder, and what it had been like the first summer he (Lew) had gone to work—in the warehouse, counting magazine covers, $15 a week less deductions. He followed with a great gob of company history, but what made it so quintessential Lew Rhinelander was that, while deprecating his own contribution, he made sure we knew that he was talking about the House that Lew built.

Then his decision to step down.

"You all know," said Lew, "that this evening wouldn't be taking place if my brother and I hadn't decided to bury the hatchet. And we both know that you wouldn't have showed up if you hadn't expected us to bury it in each other's backs." Great generalized laughter, in which Lew joined in. "A fair enough expectation, I should add. Claude and I could have made a career entertaining you with our rivalry. You know: Claude's the brother who makes money, Lew's the brother who spends it, and so forth and so on. But in all seriousness, if, at the end of the day, the buyer of Rhinelander Publishing had been anybody other than Claude Rhinelander—and, God knows, people have tried—there'd be no party this evening. Because I wouldn't have sold."

There was a standing ovation, first for Lew, then, as they shook hands over our heads, smiling in fraternal congratulation, for Lew and Claude.

Lew sat down, kissed by the Fawn. Claude's turn.

"I've a reputation as an outstandingly boring speaker," he began, after thanking his brother. "I'll do my best to disappoint you in that regard, but don't count on it." Scattered laughter. "Lew has told you about the past of our family's business. I'm going to tell you something about our future."

He read from cards, and he rocked back and forth on his heels a little as he glanced from the audience to the cards and back again. I developed, along the way, an urgent need for another drink. The waiters, though, had disappeared for the speeches, and it would have been unseemly, wouldn't it, to get up while Claude was still talking? Well, I got up. I found a bar, ordered two doubles, one for each hand, and got back in plenty of time for his peroration.

"With change," Claude was saying, "inevitably comes reorganization. In the spirit of the evening, I should say this is the good news and the bad news: We know we can never replace Lew!" Generalized laughter, including Claude's. "But try we must. This has been a particularly hard decision for me, for it carries with it a great loss for Rhinelander Films, but I am most happy to announce the following appointments. The new chairman of the board of Rhinelander Publishing will be my good friend and colleague, Mr. Allen Fryberg."

At Claude's insistence, Fryberg stood up and bowed, pale and sweating, and stayed standing while Claude reviewed his curriculum vitae. Then Claude went on:

"Allen has asked me to make the following two announcements on his behalf. In recognition of her great and consistent contribution to the company's book division, Genevieve Bergler has been named president of that division. Jenny Bergler, please stand up."

I had been watching her, her head down, during the Fryberg announcement. Now she hesitated, then half-stood, half-smiled, while people applauded, then sat before they were done. Well, Jenny, I thought, lifting an empty glass, you win some, you lose some, and welcome to your new boss, while Claude went on to present the new president of the magazine division.

"Finally," Claude said in his monotone, lifting his head and focusing on our table, "with us tonight and seated right below me, when I wish she'd join us up here, is a very great lady, a film star but much more than a film star. It is a great privilege to introduce her and to ask you to join me in welcoming my old and very dear friend, Ms. Nina Hardy."

And everybody did join him. To a man, to a woman, we stood, applauding—the biggest ovation of all. While Jeannine simply sat, face raised, the dazzling smile for all to behold.

No mention of me, to be sure.

No mention—more significant—of the book.

Did I notice this significant omission?

Oh yes. It set me looking for my friendly waiter.

Nowhere to be seen.

Somehow Lew had the microphone again, and people quieted. Handsome Lew, that most distinguished sexagenarian with the slicked silver hair and diamond studs, saying:

"Let me close our formalities on a personal note. Many of you have asked me what I'm going to do with myself, now that Claude has made me both rich and jobless. First and foremost among my projects, the law courts permitting, is to get married again, and I'd like to introduce you to another great lady, the object of my love and devotion, my future bride, Faith Graves." The applause started, but Lew stayed it with upraised arms. "And as some of you have pointed out to me, to judge from her present condition, we'd better hurry!"

Cascades of laughter, pleasure, surprise, amusement, good feeling, applause, standing, the Fawn gazing up at Lew, I think she was blushing, and he, roaring with laughter, head back, then forward, leaning over her, and . . .

I fled.

SOMETIME LATER, JEANNINE found me at the bar.

"I want you to take me back to the hotel, Daniel."

"Oh, come on, not this once. This night's made for music. Besides, aren't they playing our song?"

Some song, anyway. I did a little two-step around my beaker of Wild Turkey, first with Jeannine, then alone.

"You're embarrassing me, Daniel." Furious, my chartreuse statue. "If you won't take me, I'll get Tim."

"Oh, is Tim sober enough?"

"That's quite enough. Are you coming or not?"

Tall, straight, immobilized, lips carved in red ice. My royal highness with the glacial voice, surrounded by penguins in evening dress, eyes wide, beaks agape.

Emperor penguins, a whole orchestra.

I burst into applause.

"How *dare* you, Daniel!"

"I don't have the foggiest what I did to deserve that. Don't mind me, ducks. You get a head start. I'll be along in a little while."

Gone.

Somebody must have come back for the coat check. I found out when I went to get my own coat.

No tickee, no washee. Major pushing and shoving.

I looked all over for Jeannine. No Jeannine.

"Jesus, babe, what happened? I just heard—"

That was Falcone, the illustrious novelist, big-faced, blurry, in the crush of the elevators.

"Hey—"

A sudden, milling surge. Falcone was *in* the elevator, I was *out*. Something about what they were doing to me. What were they doing to me?

"Call me if you need me!" Falcone, shouting through the closing doors.

I came to in Central Park. I was watching the stars, flat on my back.

I mean, *real* stars, and each one had from four to six dancing points, and there were far too many to count. Maybe I'd lost my overcoat and something had happened also to my tie, but what an experience, lying on the cold ground on a very clear November night, when the sky is like a vast, black, shimmering, upside-down lake!

Oh, God.

Segue to morning.

I woke up late, in my own hotel room. The telephone message light was blinking.

I thought it was from Jeannine, calling for my apology.

It wasn't.

It was from Mrs. Murphy, to tell me the barn was burning.

Part Five

Chapter Twenty

A T FIRST GLANCE, you'd have said: What a great old barn, all it needs is some TLC. Until you went inside. I did, in boots.

I couldn't stand to look, and I didn't for very long. It appeared as though everything I'd had built in—the main room within the space, the dropped ceiling under the old hayloft, plus all my equipment, books, tapes, supplies, shelving—had imploded into a lake of black water and sludge. It looked like that wrenching scene in *Planet of the Apes* where they find what's left of New York buried underground, only in my case what was left was floating.

The structure itself was pretty much intact.

I saw my Fax machine sticking out of the water.

A cop on the scene advised me not to touch anything.

It was like some kind of test, I thought. You know, we say it to each other all the time: The only thing that counts in life *is* life—love, family, health—the rest is garbage. All the possessions, the material goods. I guess so. But I still couldn't stand to look.

The cop wore plain clothes, but he had some kind of identification badge on his lapel.

"Funny thing," he said. "People like to talk arson, but people watch a lot of television, too. Sure, we'll take a look, and the insurance boys'll take a look. But for every hundred cases you hear arson, there are maybe two you find hard evidence. Even then, only if they were amateurs. Question you've got to ask yourself is: Why anybody would want to burn you out?"

I didn't answer. I don't know if he was expecting me to. But I was

243

thinking that they went to a lot of trouble to get rid of one lousy disk. They should have been able to find it if they'd known what to look for. I'd hidden it, but not very well. Or maybe they'd found the disk, and the rest was just a gesture.

Nice gesture, Claude.

I walked away from the cop and the firemen and what was left of the barn. Back to the house.

I'd tried calling Jeannine's room before I left the hotel. She'd already checked out. No, there was no message for me. That didn't surprise me, given what had happened at the party, and she was scheduled to fly to San Francisco that afternoon. Now I called Pasadena (got Maria, the maid; no, she hadn't heard from la Señora); the spa in northern California (no Jeannine, but this was because they wouldn't say whether she was registered or not, it was their policy not to say); Pasadena again (Maria again; no, Christine wasn't there either, she didn't know where Christine was or when she would be back); the Rhinelander offices in New York and L.A. for 1) Claude Rhinelander, 2) Lew Rhinelander, 3) Allen Fryberg, 4) Genevieve Bergler (no, no, no, and no); Tinker McConnell (unavailable, she'd call me back); and probably some others I've forgotten.

I walked around kind of aimlessly. I walked in the woods; and from down the hill, through the trees, the barn looked pretty good. But I didn't go in it again.

I also called the real estate agent, the one I'd chosen for the sale. She wasn't there either.

I realized by now that Tinker McConnell was ducking me. But I had her unlisted home number. I started calling that night, and intermittently into the morning hours but either she was out or not answering, because all I got was her machine.

I think I've told about Tinker McConnell's setup before, that on the one hand she was a star literary agent and a powerful figure in the small world of publishing. This was the visible part, what people knew about, talked about. On the other hand, she was only hired help, employed by a West Coast agency, which, if it wasn't as big or as old as ICM or William Morris, was catching up in a hurry.

In other words, Tinker McConnell had a boss. His name was Bernie Siegle, and he flew coast to coast in his own Lear jet (sometimes taking the controls himself, he liked people to know), and the money he made packaging this star with that director with that producer, taking his cut not only as agent but as packager, made Tinker McConnell's very considerable commissions look like just so much walking-around money.

People in publishing knew this and somehow forgot about it. They didn't know from Hollywood, and Tinker was Tinker. More important, *I* knew it and had somehow forgotten about it.

I'd even spotted Siegle at the Rhinelander party.

I caught up with Tinker the next day. In her office. In person.

I barged in. The receptionist told me, after checking, that Tinker wasn't there. The secretary inside, and one of the two assistants from the cubicles that flanked the big office, repeated the message.

Gee. Behind her closed door, behind her desk, on the telephone, pencil in hand, I'd have sworn that was Tinker.

The assistant followed me inside, and the secretary lurked just outside the doorway.

"I'll have to call you back later," Tinker said into the phone, and then she hung up. "Dan, what are you doing here?"

"I've come about the manuscript," I said. "In person, since you no longer answer phone calls. Have you finished reading it?"

She didn't say anything for a minute, just eyed me, expressionless, through her granny glasses. Even before she spoke I had her made, recognized who she'd been and still was.

"I don't think that's something we can talk about, Dan. Not now anyway, under the circumstances."

"Which are?"

"Just what I said. It's not something I care to discuss."

"Care to discuss?"

She glanced momentarily at the assistant behind me, then back, but saying nothing. The cool, placid façade.

"Tinker!" I said. "You *are* Tinker McConnell, aren't you? My agent? And am I *not* under contract to deliver a book to Rhinelander? *Jeannine,* by Nina Hardy? And did I *not* give you a copy of the manuscript to read a week ago? Confidentially, as a favor to me?"

A week ago, I'd have worried about her staff knowing. But a week ago was out the window.

"You don't have to shout, Dan," she said evenly. "As I told you, I can't discuss it."

"First you don't care to discuss it, now you can't discuss it! For Christ's sake, you didn't *give* it to someone, did you? Who'd you give it to? Goddamn it, Tinker, you've fucking *betrayed* me!"

I was really shouting by now. I was beyond livid. It all became clear in a hurry. She'd read enough to get scared, knew she was in over her head, and she'd gone to somebody with it. Who? Siegle? Jenny Bergler? Claude Rhinelander?

"For God's sake, Tinker, I'm your *client!* You *represent* me! Your first responsibility is to me!"

"I'm sorry, Dan," she said, "but I don't represent you anymore."

"Oh? Since when is that?"

"As of this morning, officially. In fact, the letter may already have gone out. Joanie?" calling behind me. "Has that letter to Dan Springer gone out already?"

It was the only time she raised her voice—to talk to her secretary.

Yes, the answer came back from beyond the doorway. It had gone, registered mail, in the ten o'clock pickup.

"What are you going to do, Tinker, when you're hauled into court to testify that you read the manuscript and what you did with it? Are you going to say you never read it? That I never gave it to you? That it never existed? Are you going to say there never was a book contract with Rhinelander, with you named as agent in behalf of me and Nina Hardy? That I made the whole thing up? What are you going to say, Tinker?"

I had her made all right. She was the one in the front row in school, with the crew-necked Shetland and the round white collar and the granny glasses, who took notes in neat perfect script and answered her tests in the same script, and got A's straight through, which you could never figure out because she wasn't that smart.

The last glimpse I had of her, she was already on the phone again.

I never even saw them coming. There were two of them—two black-haired, nose-tackle types, in navy blazers that bulged at the chest and biceps, who picked me up under each armpit. Something told me they didn't exactly belong in publishing. They lifted me clean out of Tinker's office, without a word, and out through the agency, where some people watched and some pretended not to, down the elevator, one on either side, and out the lobby, through the revolving doors, to the sidewalk.

I walked away under my own power. I didn't look back until I got to the corner, and they were still standing in front of the building, side by side in their blazers, arms crossed over their chests.

I needed a drink. I also needed a lawyer. I also needed Jeannine.

Jeannine seemed the most urgent. What I thought had happened, crazy as it may sound, was that Tinker had passed the manuscript on and that it had gotten, through one or more intermediaries, to Claude. And that Claude had reacted by trying to put me out of business any way he could think of—from barn-burning to having my agent fire me, complete with hired muscle to prove a point.

But I was only half his problem. I was only the *escribaño,* the hack-for-hire. Jeannine also had the disk, the manuscript.

I called the spa from the street, and several times more. The lady at the spa refused to put me through to anyone, at first. Their policy, she repeated—it was part of their service—was not to accept any communications with their guests from the outside, except in extreme emergencies. This was an extreme emergency, I said. Could I describe it for her? No, I couldn't, it was too complicated, but was Ms. Hardy at least there? Surely she could tell me that much. No, she couldn't, she said.

I finally got through to the director's office, though not to the director himself. I asked for the assistant director and was told, a-cerbically, that I was talking to her. And got no farther. Their "policy of seclusion," she said, like the secrecy of their guest list, had come about because so many people tried to pry, reporters for one thing, and people who said they were friends of guests and turned out not to be, not at all. She alluded to some bad past experiences. The director, she said, was inflexible about it, quite inflexible. The best she could do, she said, was take a message from me, and if Ms. Hardy was there, she'd make sure it was delivered.

But what about outgoing calls?

Their guests were discouraged from making outgoing calls.

I left a message—the first of many.

None was answered.

The house in Pasadena had not burned down. I found that out when I talked, several times, to Maria.

Christine had come back, and gone away again. Yes, Maria had given her my messages.

I talked to Busher, my lawyer. I didn't even have a copy of my contract with Rhinelander to show him—that too had gone up in smoke. It didn't really matter, he said. If Jeannine and I were listed as coauthors (we were) and if there was no other agreement between us (there wasn't), then we were both responsible for delivery of the manuscript to the publisher.

"What happens if we don't deliver?" I asked him, although I already knew.

"I can't tell you without seeing the document, but I imagined the publisher could at least come after you for whatever he paid you."

"Even if I can prove that my part of the work was done, that the manuscript existed?"

"If you can prove that," he answered, "then you may have a claim against Ms. Hardy."

For the moment, all I had was Jeannine's Epilogue. I had to find out whether she had any inkling of what had happened.

If she didn't, why hadn't she called me?

The other times we'd been separated, we'd talked several times a day, never less than once. Now silence, the more ominous as time passed. Yes, she had a right to be pissed at me—not only for the way I'd acted the night of the party. I'd given Tinker the manuscript, and all hell had broken loose. Without my explanation, Jeannine was sure to take that as a betrayal. But for God's sake, how much difference did it make, at the end of the day, if all hell broke loose at the party or a week later, or whenever it was she was going to have her shootout with Claude Rhinelander? Sooner or later, he was going to read the manuscript!

It wasn't like Jeannine to close the door.

Not on me, no matter what.

Then I thought of Harry Brea on his knees, and that got me thinking of all the others, way back to young Claude Rhinelander with his armfuls of flowers. I saw them on their knees in a single line, all of them, all Jeannine's rejects.

But not me.

Peter Singer. *It means you've fired yourself.* Jesus, I could still see the shocked look on his face.

But not me, goddamn it. For Christ's sake, Jeannine, I can explain, please let me explain.

Any hour, I thought, any minute, the phone was going to ring and it would be her voice: "Oh, Daniel, my poor darling, I only just this minute got your messages, I . . ."

But the phone didn't ring.

I thought of doing several things. I could get on a plane for San Francisco myself, go to the spa. But if they were that way about phone calls—incoming, outgoing—how would they react to a visitor who showed up unannounced?

I could also go to Pasadena and . . . do what? Wasn't the disk of the book still in the wall safe in Jeannine's closet? Presumably it was. But if I had the disk, what was I going to do with it, without Jeannine? Run off copies and sell them door-to-door?

All of which made me realize how dependent I was on her. And—okay—how helpless without her.

Then the phone rang while I was out, and later, on the house answering machine, I caught the familiar voice of the messenger.

"I'm going to be in New York day after tomorrow, Danny Boy. That's Wednesday. Meet me in the bar at the Pierre, three o'clock."

Hang-up.

I sat there by the phone with my heart in my mouth. Sonny Corral was her messenger—dear old Tim—always had been, always, I guessed, would be. And I'd just been through almost a week of not hearing from Jeannine, not once. But if she was going to dump me—me, the man she loved too much to share, and didn't I have the paper to prove she'd said it? the Fax copy?—would she do it by *messenger*?

I got to the Pierre early.

Sonny was earlier.

He was drinking Perrier and lime. I'd seen him just a week before, at the party, but it hadn't registered then how tanned he was or that he'd dropped some pounds. But still that liddy, sleepy expression.

"You're looking good, Danny Boy," he said in his slow drawl. "How's the world treatin' you?"

"The world's not treating me," I replied, sitting down. "But you're looking good, too. Tell me, is it surgical or self-inflicted?"

He laughed at that.

"Self-inflicted?" he said. "I like that. Actually, I've been working out a little. I've always been a little squeamish about the guys in the green smocks."

Actually, there wasn't much a plastic surgeon could have done with Sonny's face that wouldn't have taken the ruin out of it, and the ruined look had been his trademark since the beginning.

I was two gulps into my gin-and-tonic when I said:

"Enough sparring, Sonny. I think we know each other well enough by now. Just give me the message."

He looked at me straight on, that world-weary expression that didn't mean a lot, one way or the other.

"Relax, Dan," he said. "You're tight as a drum." I didn't relax, though, so we just stared at each other until, with a shrug, he said, "The message is that there'll be no book. It doesn't exist. It never will. It won't be published."

I looked back at him, not feeling anything at first.

"You mean that's Jeannine's message?" I said. "That there'll be no book?"

"That's *the* message, Dan."

The little switch, from Danny Boy to Dan, did it. I looked away, unable to think of anything to say.

"I think you've got some explaining to do," I managed finally. "I don't get it."

"There's nothing to get," he said. "It's over, that's all."

The way it came out—without intonation or emphasis, just his normal silver-screen drawl reading the lines—did it, too, and I clamped down, clenched.

It's over, that's all.

What was over?

"If you want my advice," Sonny went on, "you'll take what they offer you."

"What offer?" I said.

"They're going to let you keep what you got. That's something like 850 grand, isn't it?"

He paused.

Was that it? The End? That I got to keep what I'd gotten?

No. There was more to it. Sonny was only working his timing, letting the camera do its stuff before he gave me the good news.

"If you'll be a nice boy," he said, "there's more in it for you. They'll negotiate. I know they're ready to give you half now—half of the balance. That's another 425 grand. Not a bad day's wages."

The good news.

"You mean if I keep my mouth shut—I assume that's what being a nice boy entails—I can get half of what's due me? Whereas if I squawk, I get zero?"

He nodded.

I couldn't tell if he thought it was a fair deal, or I was getting screwed, or neither. I couldn't tell if he remembered that this had happened to me before, only Farran had had the decency—yeah, a strange word, *decency,* but these things are comparative—the decency to kiss me off in person.

"Shit," he said. His lips protruded, pressed together. "You want my advice—though I'll deny I ever said it—hold out for all of it. The whole 850. They'll pay it, to get rid of it. You sign a release and you'll get your 850."

"What about my barn?" I asked.

He looked puzzled. "What about it?"

"They burned my fucking barn. Just to get the lousy disk."

"I don't know anything about the disk and the barn," he said. "So: take their 850 and forget about anything else."

"Who's they, Sonny?"

"You don't need me to tell you that."

"Oh yes I do."

I guess the tendency is always to blame the messenger. In the good old days they used to cut their fucking heads off and send them back in a bucket.

Maybe that's why messengers are pretty well paid.

"Who's they, Sonny?" I repeated.

"Claude Rhinelander. Who else?"

"That's what I want to know. Who else?"

By way of answer, he flagged down our waiter. "Get this shit out of here," he ordered with an abrupt wave at the Perrier. "Bring me a Scotch. What kind of Scotch you got?"

The waiter, shook up and obsequious at once, recited the brands.

"Glenfiddich," Sonny said. "Neat, water on the side. Make it a double. And bring my friend here a double gin."

He said no more till we were served, then downed about half the Scotch, exhaled, and, glancing at the water glass, chuckled briefly. Then he finished the Scotch and called for another, which, however, he let sit for a while.

"It's a raw deal, Danny Boy," he said. "Mind you, I never liked you any better than the others. The point is that she did. At least I thought she did. That's what she said."

Yeah. I was the one she loved too much to share.

"Raw deal," he repeated. Then: "You ask her, she says you betrayed her. You ask me, I say it was a pretty dumb thing to do."

"What was a pretty dumb thing to do?"

"You leaked the book, Danny Boy. That's what she says. Why the hell did you have to do that? Were you self-destructing?"

I still failed to see how much difference it made if Claude read the book a week ahead of schedule, but I didn't say that. Right then what I said was, "I'm glad to know she's been talking to someone. I've been calling her for a week at that goddamned spa. I never once got through. She never once called me back. You know, I'm the guy she loved too much to share. At least that's what she was saying a week ago."

I felt the anger coming, anger at Jeannine for setting it up so that I was baring my goddamned soul to the messenger.

Then it hit me that we were talking past tense, that what was over wasn't just the book but Jeannine, me. And $850,000 was my payoff if I kept my mouth shut. I felt myself going hot, not only in my cheeks but everywhere, all just under the surface of the skin.

Sonny put the finishing touches to it.

"You talking about that place up at Napa?" he said. "No wonder you couldn't get her. She never went."

"What do you mean, she never went? She was there all week!"

He shook his head.

"For Christ's sake!" I shouted. "Where *was* she?"

He was holding his hands up, as though to calm me down. "Hey," he said, "wait a minute. The way you did it, you put her at one hell of a disadvantage. She had it set up to do her own way, and then suddenly—she had no idea what had happened—Claude had the book, and he hit her like a fucking avalanche."

"What do you mean?"

"Said he'd never publish it himself, and no one else would touch it. He'd see to that personally. Said he had his lawyers all lined up. That he could bend a few arms himself in publishing, and those he couldn't bend, he'd break. Those he couldn't break, he'd buy."

Starting, I thought in passing, with Tinker McConnell.

"But he'd never sue," I said lamely. "All along, Jeannine kept saying he'd never sue."

"Well, maybe Jeannine was wrong."

"But I still don't get it! What the hell difference did it make if Claude read the book a week earlier or a week later?"

And then, all of a sudden, I got it.

Sonny said something to the effect that I was probably right, it wouldn't have mattered—not, that is, to anyone except Jeannine. But I had a different scenario working, a Chinatown scenario, according to which Jeannine had known all along exactly how Claude was going to react, and what he was going to do! In that case . . .

Where *was* she all week? Where the fuck was she?"

"She went away."

"Alone?"

He shook his head. "Jeannine never goes alone."

"Who with?"

"Who else?" he answered. "With Claude Rhinelander."

We head now into blurry times. Gin-filled, Scotch-filled. I know where it began, and how it ended, and I know that in some weird repeat of the last time I'd been alone with him, Sonny Corral kept trying to be reasonable, logical, explaining the ways of the kings and the queens to us mere mortals. I was by turns ranting and raging and feeling sorry for myself—in public. And I kept not believing what I was hearing.

Once he had his hands on the book, Claude had taken her by storm. It had started the night of the party. The next morning, Claude showed up at the hotel with the offer she couldn't refuse, already written into a contract. He virtually kidnapped her. They went back to California, in Bernie Siegle's plane, and spent the week rewriting the contract. The money, Sonny said, was huge—far more than people like him and me ever even thought about—but in and of itself that was nothing new. Claude had always been ready to pay big bucks for Jeannine. What was new—and this was the kicker—was Christine. Claude had agreed to recognize Christine—publicly, legally—as his own heir and daughter.

"Even if she isn't?" I asked.

"That's the point," Sonny said. "All these years he'd never cough up a nickel for Christine. Said he'd be damned in hell before he'd pay for somebody else's bastard. But it's what Jeannine wants. Maybe it's not all she ever wanted, but it's what she wants now."

Bang, bang, bang, like nails into wood.

"And what does she have to do in exchange?" I asked.

"Give up the book. Give you up. And this new career business. Claude doesn't like that. I myself always thought it was a phony. Oh yeah," grinning, "and she's agreed to marry him."

"Marry Claude?"

"You got it," Sonny said. "Mrs. Claude Rhinelander. Because that's all *he* ever wanted."

A blur, and inside the blur was this weird kind of mind swing, like one minute it was other people we were talking about, not me it was happening to, or had happened to, but somebody entirely other we both knew about, and it was like Gee, what's she going to do now? and Oh yeah, she's agreed to marry Claude Rhinelander, you don't say? Yeah, that's all he ever wanted and the money's humongous and it solves the Christine problem. And then the next minute, the swing back, and I'd get this stab of white pain behind the eyes, like a flash of lightning except that it hurt and made them water, Jesus Christ, she was going to *marry* him, I couldn't believe it, and then it would be me all right, drinking in the bar of the Pierre, the man she loved too much to share, and what there was to make me feel better was 850 grand more than I had yesterday and forget about the barn.

"At least it's good to know she'll be well taken care of," Sonny said.

"Who?" I asked.

"Christine. She's my daughter, too, you know."

Just like that, no blinking, nothing. *She's my daughter, too.*

"Are you sure about that?"

"Sure I'm sure."

"How long have you known?"

"Since it happened, Danny Boy," he said. "The lady wanted a baby, not a husband, and I was handy."

"And you never told Christine?"

"Never told anybody. That's how Jeannine wanted it."

"Jesus Christ." And: "Why in the hell are you telling me?"

"You're not the only one being bought off," he answered with that ruined grin. "A pension for me is part of her deal."

It ended soon after, still in the bar of the Pierre, crowded now and dusk outside. I wanted to know where she was.

"Home," Sonny said. "In Pasadena. I think only for today. She's closing the place down. It's on the market, and it's up to her to decide what she wants to keep, what to sell. But don't get any funny ideas,

Dan. It's over. There's nothing you can change. This is how she wants it: you get the 850 grand and it's done. She claims she had to fight Claude to get it for you. She says it was Claude's idea to cut it in half."

I didn't need to hear that from him, or have him call me Dan again. Or:

"It was bound to happen. If not you, then to the next guy. Actually I thought you were going to make it for a while. But sooner or later, she was going to marry Rhinelander. You only helped her put him in a corner he couldn't get out of without giving her what she wants."

Or:

"You shouldn't take it personally, Danny Boy. There was nothing personal about it. You just got caught up in somebody else's power play."

This was the one, I remember, that got to me. Maybe the mind swing hit just right—the white knife on its downward path—"no, don't take it personally." Or that mouth shrug of his, lower lip out, corners down. Or Jeannine "fighting" to get me my $850,000. Oh, I bet they had a terrible row over it. Then how much was *she* getting?

Kill-the-messenger time.

What I did was aim the table right at his chest, lifting as I shoved forward into his staying palms. And down he went, amazed, crashing into the drinkers behind him, the table coming down over him, and me behind the table, wanting somebody, I guess, anybody to be paid back for telling me not to take it personally.

A bunch of guys pulled me off him. White jackets, blazers, business suits. It was a mess.

Sonny was a mess.

He was holding his head and grinning at me at the same time.

"Hey, Danny Boy!" he shouted at me as I was being led out. "You're only just starting to pay your dues!"

Chapter Twenty-one

SEVEN HOURS LATER I was driving out of Los Angeles Airport. I had the rental car windows down, and cold air came rushing in. The ridges on the freeway went thwock-thwock-thwock across the flat sleeping valley, past the great glass towers of the city and on out the other end where the ribbons of freeway light twined and coiled into the hills. It was a night of amazing clarity for southern California, moonless, chilly, a night fit for shooting stars and meteors, and the words came tumbling out of my mind to make sentences, paragraphs, spoken, shouted. I was going to make the speech of my life, and there had never been an argument to convince like mine, never a rage so luminous, never a passion so irresistible. I would make it on my knees, pleading like a bleating lamb; I would bellow it, I would thunder like a storm.

I could have walked a straight line, mind you. I could have done it backward or even, I imagine, standing on my hands. Somehow, on the plane, I'd passed through sobriety into some other state. I have no name for it. Senses sharp, alertness high, spells of sheer light-headedness, even euphoria.

I first saw the house in silhouette, blacker than the hills rising behind it, blacker than the black sky itself, when I slowed to park outside the grounds. I went in on foot. There were unfamiliar cars in the driveway, plus the Porsche. Christine's. One of the unfamiliar ones was a light-colored sedan, American, and I could make out the top of a head in the driver's seat. Security, I thought. Slumped down, possibly asleep. If he had a partner, though, the partner wasn't in the car.

I circled past the darkened garage and the gatehouse where the servants slept, around to the pool side where the waters lay still, unlit, like a heart-shaped sheet of black mirror. Far down, at the apartment side, a light was on, and there were lights up on the second floor.

All quiet.

When I paused inside the French doors from the pool terrace, waiting for my eyes to adjust to the interior darkness, all I could make out were odd shapes, unrecognizable forms, ghostly lumps and humps like sleeping animals. I stood still, temporarily disoriented, until I realized what the humps were: white sheets covered all the major pieces of furniture.

What was it Sonny had said? Something about her going home just to close the place down?

But if the place was already closed down, what was the security guy doing outside?

She was there. She had to be. I wanted it to be. I made my way silently into the entrance hall, the cool tiled floors, where, so long ago it seemed, I'd watched Sonny retie his tie in the mirror, and where I'd dumped Christine, kicking and screaming, that night when Jeannine was in Vancouver. From somewhere upstairs, there came a small blur of light. The hall lights, I thought.

Yes.

The pointy bulbs in their Spanish mahogany sconces.

She was waiting for me up there, expecting me.

Had Sonny called from New York? He could have, even though he'd had no idea where I was going. But a smart guess . . .

I went up the dark wood steps, always polished, always gleaming, to the carpeted landing. Time was, when the house was very quiet and I was working in my room at the far end with the door open, I could make out footsteps on the stairs. Then nothing, silence, when they reached the top. Then someone—she—in the doorway right behind me.

The buzz at the nape of my neck, accompanying her first words.

This too seemed such a long time ago.

It wasn't.

A dim shaft of light into the hall from the master bedroom.

The bedroom, empty.

The bed was unmade, the sheets pulled back in a tangle. I touched them, brought them to my face.

I thought I could still smell her. Maybe that was my imagination.

On the shelf built into the headboard, a bed light was on. Sometimes, when she was alone, she slept with the bed light on.

The bathroom. I flicked the wall switch on, off. At a glance, everything in its place.

The closet room. As big in area as the bedroom itself, and when I'd first seen it, I'd been reminded of some designer boutique, all arranged, all perfect down to the last coordinated colors. Now it was an unholy mess. A jewelry box spilled open on the floor. Armoires open, the drawers pulled out. Hangers dangling from the poles, strewn on the floor, clothes in heaps.

Same, at a glance, with her shoes. Were the ones left behind rejects?

Wall safe open. Emptied out.

I thought, for the first time: maybe it is over, maybe all that's left is garbage.

Maybe she wasn't there. Been and gone.

Where? Bel Air? Is that where I should go next, to deliver my speech to her and Claude Rhinelander?

I found myself back in the hall, and I sensed it then, even though I heard nothing, saw nothing other than the wall sconces, the art hung between them. It was there anyway—some other presence, watchful, like a cat's bristle, a candle flickering, a disorienting vibration.

I felt myself start to sweat, warm prickles on my forearms. I think it was in me to quit then, back down the stairs, the front door, the car, the airport, New York, done, over, good-by.

I didn't.

There were rooms off that upstairs hall I'd never so much as entered. Guest rooms. And one, at the end, that was all too familiar. Once upon a time, I'd written a book there. It was called *Jeannine*.

I opened the door. It was dark inside. There were two switches on the inner wall. One worked the hanging light over my table and the computer. I touched that one first. I saw the keyboard, the screen. The screen was dark. Then I flicked the other switch and saw Jeannine.

My first thought—fast, like a beam of light—was that she was asleep.

She'd always taken pills when she was alone. I thought: she went to bed, couldn't sleep, got up, took pills (was the bottle on the headboard shelf? in the bathroom?), wandered into my room, passed out on the couch.

I even thought, so help me: maybe she came to say her last good-by?

She looked right, too, in that split-second. Her head was lolling back against the cushions, in profile, and her complexion was very pale. The last thing she always did after the lights were out—at least they were always out when I was with her—was take off her makeup. Her evening makeup. She had something else she put on for sleep.

Why couldn't she have put the night cream on and then gotten up again, taken pills, wandered into my room—possibly to read the book—and passed out on the couch?

Because she hadn't.

There was something in the posture.

My God Almighty.

Maybe I shouted it: *"My God Almighty!"*

Maybe I murmured it.

Maybe I only thought it.

A bookcase had been pulled free of a wall, as though someone had reached to it for support and books had toppled all over the floor. And blood. My God, it was everywhere. She was wearing one of those light-colored smocks on nightshirts that look like a man's shirt, and it came down near her knees. It was like a blotter, soaked in blood. Blood on the sheet that still covered most of the couch. Blood on the carpet. It was like watching a picture that suddenly changed from black-and-white to color, where what you hadn't noticed because it was in blacks and whites and gradations of gray suddenly transformed, and you saw: vivid red.

It was like something when you're small that you can't stand to look at. So ghastly, grisly, that you hold your breath and cover your eyes with your fingers.

Only then you peek.

I lifted her gently.

There was a terrible bloody wound on the other side of her head, the cheek against the couch.

Kneeling by the couch, I held her, lifeless, in my arms. I kissed her, kissed her wound. I talked to her. I think I delivered parts of my speech—how I loved her, would always love her.

I thought at some point: This isn't happening. This is Nina Hardy, a great actress, playing her finest role. In a moment she will wake up, and none of this will have happened. It will only have been a test. In a moment I will have passed this test. She is going to be kissing me, slathering me with her kisses and her salty tears.

She didn't wake up.

I did.

I couldn't stand to look down at her anymore. She seemed so old, white, drained, battered.

There was the wound. From her cheekbone out to her ear, it was as though her head had been staved in. Once I had her back on the couch, the bloody sheet, it took all my will to turn her head so that no one could see the wound.

My lips had gone numb, like from novocaine. And then I sensed that someone was standing in the doorway, literally filling it with his bulk, watching my back even as I turned around.

HE WAS HUGE—that was all I saw. His body had gone to beefiness the way the steroid types do, but he was strong enough to handle me like a pretzel.

"You fuckers!" I cried out at him. "Why the fuck did you have to *kill* her?"

But that was all I got out. I made the mistake of trying to struggle with him, and he put a choke hold on me and, with his free hand, bent my arm into the middle of my back. Then an excruciating jolt of pain, dizziness. I think I blacked out. We must have gone downstairs that way. The next thing I knew, limp, unresisting, we were coming into the pantry.

Wood and glass cabinets all around the walls, wood cupboards underneath, chintz curtains on the windows, and in the middle the big round oak table. Maria used to hold court there in her off hours, drinking coffee with her sidekicks and chattering in Spanish.

Now, though, there was only Claude Rhinelander.

He sat at the far rim of the table, hands folded on the top as if he were presiding at some meeting. He had on a beige-colored, V-neck sweater, probably cashmere, with the white points of a shirt collar sticking out. He was unshaved. Otherwise he looked like he'd just gotten up for a day of lounging around the house, or riding to the hounds, or whatever the Claude Rhinelanders do on their days off.

Only the woman I loved was lying dead above our heads.

I almost lost it then. It came at me in violent, dizzying waves of nausea, how, at the last minute, she must have turned him down, forever, and knowing it was over, he'd goddamn clubbed her to death. The whole business with Sonny had been his last desperate attempt to buy me off—for $850,000. He'd paid Sonny to do it. He must have told her he'd bought me off. Only it hadn't worked, *nothing* could have worked. And she must have known it, must have known I was coming no matter what he said, must have fled to my room . . . to escape him . . . looking for *me*.

My God Almighty.

Didn't Sonny say Claude had kidnapped her? Maybe that whole week she'd been waiting for me, waiting for me to save her.

Only I had come too late.

And Claude Rhinelander was waiting for me in a cashmere sweater.

"Sit down," he said in his deep, gravelly monotone.

My escort dumped me in a chair and stood behind me, hands on my shoulders. He asked something about whether Claude wanted me restrained. Rhinelander shook his head, then, with a glance, dismissed him.

We were alone.

He stared at me for what seemed like a long time. I had it wrong, I thought. No blood on *his* hands. He'd have had someone else do his dirty work for him. Claude only came in for the cleanup.

Then he spoke.

"Let me tell you what you're going to do now. In a few minutes, you're going to leave here, alone. You will drive to the airport and get on the first plane out. You've never been here tonight, you never left New York. When you're asked, you know nothing about what happened here tonight."

I couldn't grasp what he was saying.

He repeated it.

"But where am I, if not here?"

"You've been on a binge with Corral," he answered, eyeing me with that unwavering stare I'd always taken for condescension. "You were too drunk to remember where you went, but that's what you did. You woke up in his hotel room in New York. The Plaza."

"After the fight I had with him? That was public."

"Yes, you had a fight. And then you went out and you got drunk together."

"But how the hell do you know that? That I even saw him tonight?"

I don't know if he answered. My mind raced on without him. What I couldn't get through my head was how in a million years—if he'd murdered her, or had her murdered—he could let me walk out the door. It wasn't the story he'd invented for me. Maybe that would stick—that I'd never left New York that night—if nobody looked too closely and Sonny cooperated. Sonny, I thought wildly, would always cooperate. But if Claude *hadn't* done it, why did he want me out of there? What was he covering up?

"Don't worry," he said, "it's all being taken care of."

"*What's* being taken care of? *I* didn't kill her! Christ, man, she's the woman you wanted to marry! Now she's lying up there, covered in blood, and what the fuck are you taking care of?"

Maybe it began to dawn on me anyway. It was like coming out from under, when the anesthesia still hasn't worn off and the nausea comes and goes in waves. My mind kept running lists of candidates— if not Claude, then who? Brea? Peter Singer? the long line of jilted lovers? None of them made sense, and then it was as though it hadn't happened, couldn't have, except in some delusional nightmare. Except that there was Claude Rhinelander, sitting across from me, and upstairs was her battered body. I'd held her in my own hands. And there was the welling pain in my throat whenever I saw her again in my mind.

Only a long time later could I appreciate, grudgingly, the spot he was in, the mess it was left to him to manage. Or maybe it was that, once the anesthesia wore off, my first reflex was to deny what must have happened, while his was to manage it.

That smacks of sympathy for him. I felt none.

Uncle Claude.

Christine was the only explanation. Jesus Christ Almighty. Even so, I don't think I'd have believed it if I hadn't seen her with my own eyes.

She came bursting in on us through the kitchen door, at Claude's back. Alone—it took another minute for her caretakers to catch up with her—and when Claude turned, half-standing, and she focused on him, then us, she started to giggle. She was wearing some kind of white shift but not as white as her skin. She looked as if the blood had been sucked out of her. Her eyes were rimmed in charcoal shadows, and her hair frizzed in a way I'd never seen before. A doctor was on his way, I learned later, but he hadn't arrived, and meanwhile Christine was in a dimension all her own.

"A meeting of murderers," she said, still giggling, her narrow eyes flicking back and forth between us. "The murderers meet. Well, how does it feel, guys, blood on your hands? And no one to fuck? Who's gonna marry her now? You bring the cards, Daddy? We've got three for bridge: Daddy and Danny and Chris. *She* can be the dummy, *winner* takes the body!"

This last came out in a singsong—"she can be the dummy, winner takes the body"—like the refrain in some television commercial, and she ran it through again in a mock-sweet voice, hands up, palms flat together, body arched, lips out in some exaggerated parody.

"*She* can be the dummy, *winner* takes—"

Claude made the mistake of fully standing. Now he raised one hand. I thought he meant to stay the men who'd rushed in behind her, but she misunderstood the gesture.

She lunged at him, laughing and screaming as she came.

"You *revolting* little bastard! Did you think I'd actually let her marry *you*? Daddy? Daddy? Leave *me* for *you*?"

She lunged at him in a clawing blur, must have struck him through his upraised arms because the glasses flew from his nose. Two of his men rushed her from behind, pinning her arms while she struggled, kicked. They yanked her back into the doorway, but she clung to the jamb, fighting them off. She was screaming curses, her eyes crazed, and from somewhere in her skinny body came a terrific residue of strength.

Then she focused on me.

"*Help* me, Dan! For God's sake! She was going to marry him, lock us out! I *told* her never to hit me! She *came* at me! I had no choice! I *slammed* her, I *slammed* her, I *slammed* . . ."

She was back into it then, I thought, the bloody scene, staring at me but not seeing, something about blood, she was crying out about the blood. "Mine," I think she said, "all mine." But as quickly, I saw her go limp. It was as though she herself had been clubbed, or a needle had hit home. The two men fell backward with her into the kitchen, followed by Rhinelander. I thought she must have passed out . . . until I heard the laughter again, and the screaming, echoing wildly through the house.

I realized that I was standing, holding my breath, that my knuckles were white from clenching.

My arms were trembling involuntarily. I sat again.

When Jeannine told her she was going to marry Rhinelander, Christine must have detonated. It must have started in the bedroom. Then all hell broke loose. Jeannine must have fled down the hall. . . .

To *me?* Her last refuge?

I couldn't take it past that. Every time I tried, I saw her lying there—so drained, battered—and then the ache would blur and blind my comprehension.

Rhinelander came back. He sat down, his glasses back on.

"You better change your clothes before you leave," he said to me. The same monotone, as though nothing had happened. "You can't go out of here looking like that. You still have clothes here, don't you?"

I glanced down. My shirt front was stained, and there were flecks of her blood on my pants.

"What happens if I don't?" I said.

"Don't what?"

"Don't cooperate. What happens if I go to the police instead and tell them everything I've seen tonight?"

He stared back at me implacably.

"You're not that stupid," came his judgment.

All of a sudden I felt the bile rising, the need to shake the goddamn monotone out of his voice, the steadiness from his cockeyed gaze.

"What do I have to lose?" I said. "*You* may want to protect Christine, but *I* don't. For Christ's sake, she's crazy, dangerous! *Somebody* had better lock her up and throw away the key!"

Again the stare, but one of his eyes, I noticed, had begun to twitch.

"Do you really need me to spell it out for you?" he asked.

"You're damn right I do!"

He shook his head, as though trying to eliminate the twitch, then removed his glasses and rubbed at the corners of his eyes.

Glasses back on. The twitch still there.

"The police are going to be under tremendous pressure to solve this crime," he said. "By the time we're done here, they're going to think robbery, but it would be just as easy to make them look in another direction. You're here, you have Nina's blood on you. They'll find traces of you all over that room. You also had the motive."

"To murder Jeannine? You've got to be crazy! I *loved* her, for God's sake!"

I tried to stop myself even as I said it. For just a second, while we stared at each other, I thought he was going to smile, and if he had, it was in me to throttle him before anyone could intervene.

"She ruined you," he said instead. "She ruined you professionally, and if what you just said is true, she ruined you emotionally, too. There are many people to testify to that."

"Who?"

He shrugged. "I could, for one. And Corral, to name another. I don't know what you've told yourself, but she didn't love you. That too can be proved. You may have been useful to her for a while, but she was going to marry me."

I took a deep breath. At least part of it, I realized with a jolt, was true. All Sonny would have to do was tell the truth about that night. I *had* had murder on my mind when I left him. And there were others who could speak to my emotional state that past week—Tinker McConnell included.

Claude could buy them all. Already had.

He didn't have to say more, but he did. I guess he couldn't resist. Sure there were holes in his scenario and even I could see them; like I'd been on a plane; the time of its landing was a matter of record; so was the renting of the car. And Jeannine was already dead by the time I arrived, wasn't she? But how well these would stand up as alibis would depend on how tightly the time of death could be pinpointed.

Supposing it couldn't?

And what, I thought, of Christine's alibi?

That too he'd taken care of. Like his own. Like everyone's, but mine.

I got the feeling then—not fear precisely, but a coldness. His coldness, like a long shadow, communicated across the table. Sitting in that pantry, I was back in Chinatown, only much worse than any Chinatown I'd ever imagined. The woman I loved—and who'd loved me no matter what he said—was lost to me for good. And Claude Rhinelander was asking me to help cover up her murder.

No, not asking. Claude Rhinelanders don't ask.

"You better go now," he said. "Everything will be taken care of. But we're wasting time."

I looked at him across the table, ugly old man in a cashmere sweater. He had the twitch back under control and, for just a second before the light bounced off his glasses again, the two eyes looked the same size.

"Not before you tell me what really happened," I said.

He hesitated, unwilling, I guess, to give me even that much. Then, in the monotone, he went over it for me. Jeannine, he said, was spending a last night in the house. The staff had already been dismissed. She called him, late. Christine was there, and Jeannine had told her everything. She'd started acting strange. Jeannine was afraid something bad might happen. She wanted him to come get her. She thought he should bring help, for Christine.

By the time he arrived, he found Jeannine dead and Christine wandering the grounds, stark naked, refusing to speak. The first words she spoke were when she burst in on us.

"But why in hell are you doing this?" I asked him. "This whole fucking rigmarole? Why do you want to save Christine? For God's sake, she killed her own mother!"

"I'm only doing what Nina would have wanted."

Maybe it was so. Suddenly it was beyond me to say.

"But why?" I repeated, feeling the terrible ache again. "For God's sake, she killed her own mother! I don't understand. Why would she do that?"

"I don't know." A last shrug. "I wasn't here."

I GLIMPSED SEVERAL other men when I was taken back through the house. The sheets were gone, stuff had been knocked over. The robbery, it seemed, was already in progress. I've no idea who they were. Maybe he kept an army around for crises like murder, or maybe they were people he could trust from the studio. Special effects people, for all I know. But I didn't ask and no one was telling.

Two of them took me off, saw to it that I changed clothes, then escorted me to my car. I drove, as directed, to LAX. Doing what I was supposed to do. On a normal day, in the East, I'd have been up, had coffee, already be working in the barn. But there were no normal days anymore. I was wide awake, and I'd never been to sleep.

I caught the first flight out. The sun, bouncing off the metal of the wings, blinded me, and it continued to blind me even when I pulled the shade over the porthole, even when I got home in the afternoon, with all the pain of the raging hangover which, according to my instructions, was the logical conclusion to the night before.

Chapter Twenty-two

I CRACKED. FINALLY I broke and ran.

It started the minute I got to my burned-out barn, when I realized I'd been had. The woman I loved was dead, three thousand miles away, and by then they'd have discovered her body, the place would be swarming, and if what Claude Rhinelander really wanted was my help in covering up a murder, why had he sent me away?

That much was easy, I thought. On the scene, I was too much of a gamble. Suppose I decided to tell the truth? Why should I want to protect Christine Hardy?

But away from the scene, with a cover story that he could control— or, if he had to, *de*control—hadn't he turned me into an insurance policy? Because suppose, for whatever reason, his robbery scenario *didn't* play. Suppose the police started digging. They'd find me, sure enough, and I'd have my alibi, like everyone else, but what about the charges to my credit card—the airplane tickets, the Hertz rental?

But there'd be no reason for them to dig that deep, would there?

No, none at all.

Unless somebody pointed them in that direction.

Somebody who could also, if he had to, create the impression that I'd fled the scene of the crime.

Not that Claude Rhinelander actually intended to do any of these things. But he had me, if he needed me.

Insurance.

The check came the next morning, by Express Mail, $850,000 drawn on the account of Rhinelander Publishing. According to the stub, it was payable on completion of the untitled memoirs of Nina Hardy, as per contract, and my cashing it signified a full and entire discharge of any further obligations on the part of Rhinelander Publishing.

$850,000. My hands started to shake as I handled it. *It's all being taken care of.* That's what the man had said, and it included me. I put the check in a safe and secret place, along with the Hertz receipt and the chits from my flights to and from L.A.

It got worse. The story had taken over the news by then, and I couldn't stop watching. All of Hollywood, the newscasters kept saying, was in a state of shock. There were interviews with stars who'd worked with Nina Hardy, and a permanent camera setup outside the cordoned-off mansion in Pasadena. The investigation pointed to robbery. I even caught the images of Christine Hardy arriving at the sanatorium up the coast beyond Santa Barbara, the limo turning into the entrance, Christine gazing out the window through dark glasses and (per the journalist with the mike) her "father," Claude Rhinelander, beside her. There must have been something similar about the landscape—a high bluff of land and wind off the Pacific, bending the trees—because it made me think of Dana Point, of old souls and new souls, and her turning to me in the wind, the kerchief she wore, sunglasses, kissing me, Daniel. . . .

Okay, my vision blurred over that one, and my lips went numb.

As far as I know, Christine's still up there.

THEY SHOWED UP—was it that day or the next?—all the way from California. I'd been in some kind of time warp. I just sort of hung out, watching television, smoking, working my way through the liquor supply.

It was freaky warm for the East—California warm, you could say— and though the leaves were all down, it was mild enough to go around in a sweatshirt and jacket. I'd known they were coming. My local constabulary had called to make sure, first, that I was Daniel Springer and, second, that I would be available for questioning. I waited for them near the barn, sitting on a broad stone outcropping, a sort of slab just where the ground dipped away toward the woods. There was no sun, just low-hanging gray clouds milling around, and I was nursing a Bloody Mary, with a view past the corner of the house, when their car came up the driveway.

"They" were two detectives, although the media found me around the same time. All I told the media was to get the fuck off my property; the police was a longer conversation.

I took them into the living room. I told them to take their jackets off, which they did later, and smoke if they wanted to, which they didn't, and offered them a drink, which they refused. One of them—a Detective Willey, tall, rawboned, blond crewcut, with a weak chin and a prominent Adam's apple—did most of the talking, while his partner took most of the notes.

I did fine, just fine. The more so since, as they made clear at the beginning, all they really wanted me for was background. Willey had sat in on Sonny Corral's deposition the night before, in California, and after what he'd told them, they'd been assigned to come east and talk to me.

"Quite a guy, Corral, isn't he," Willey said conversationally, once we got past the preliminaries. "All broke up inside—you could see that—stands to reason, one of her oldest friends, wasn't he? But he sat with us a couple of hours, under all that stress. You don't understand, Dan, this case is a zoo, you've no idea. Anyway, let's get it started."

We began with where I'd been that night. I remembered the hotel bar—the Pierre Hotel, I told them—and not, I admitted under questioning, a hell of a lot else. I knew we'd hit some saloons along the way, but I'd be hard put to say which ones. There were a lot of saloons in New York. The way I felt the next day, when I woke up in Sonny's hotel room, maybe we'd been in all of them.

It came out so damn smoothly.

"No problem," Willey said. "Sonny gave us some names, addresses. We'll be checking them out. But from what he said, you had every reason to tie one on, didn't you?"

"I'm not sure what you mean by that."

"Well, she gave you a pretty raw deal, didn't she? The deceased. Nina Hardy."

Sonny's words, I thought.

"Yes, I guess so."

"And you were pretty pissed off about it, weren't you?"

"Yes."

"Well, I think you better tell us about it."

He led me backward then, from the last time I'd seen Jeannine to the first, and then forward, focusing, I was aware, on our "intimate relationship." I'd lived with her, hadn't I? Yes. From when to when? And how would I characterize our relationship? Was it business or pleasure, or both? Was it intimate? Very intimate? Well, on a scale of one to ten, how intimate?

Even cops, I guess, have their prurient interests.

Little by little, he shifted me to other people in Jeannine's life—Christine among them, "Mr. Rhinelander," her household staff. Since I'd written her life story, I probably knew more about her than just about anybody, didn't I? Anything I could tell them, any leads I could give them, would be extremely valuable. And confidential, not to worry on that score.

But were they all suspects? I asked him. At this stage in the investigation, he answered, everybody was a suspect. Even I would be a suspect—a prime one—if I had wings.

"Maybe so," I said. "But I'm not much of a murderer."

"Nobody's much of a murderer," he said. "But the first thing you learn in homicide is that every corpse has one. A perpetrator, I mean. In fact, of all the people we know of so far, you're the one with the most motive for having done her in."

I managed not to answer.

"Is the book going to get published?" Willey asked. "I mean, now that she's dead? I don't know how these things work."

"I don't either. It's up to the publisher."

"But you get paid for it, don't you?"

"Yes, I've already been paid."

"Well, at least there's that."

Yes, at least there was that.

Under their prompting, I told them what I knew about Jeannine's people, her friends, staff, Christine, Claude Rhinelander. I learned, in passing, that Christine had been at the Rhinelander home in Bel Air the night in question. According to Willey, she'd had some kind of breakdown when she'd heard the news. No one had been able to talk to her yet. It was an amazing story, he said. All these years she'd been Rhinelander's daughter, but she'd never known it. Did I know the story? Yes, I knew the story. Weird, he said. When he'd heard it, it had blown his mind. Imagine living all those years and not knowing who your father was.

"Look, Dan," Willey said finally, scratching at the blond stubble of his hair, "don't get me wrong, but there are things we've got to find out. Who else was there?"

"I don't understand."

"I mean men. During the time you were with her. Don't get me wrong, but a woman like that, she had to have had a list of lovers to fill a telephone book."

"As far as I know," I answered, "I was the only one."

"Really?" he said. "But you weren't with her every minute of every day, were you? No offense, but there could have been others, couldn't there?"

I started to say something but caught myself.

"Not to my knowledge," I said.

"Okay."

He seemed skeptical, though. He took his partner's notebook, a stenographer's pad, and thumbed through some pages.

"A guy called Peter Singer," he said. "Did you know him?"

"Yes."

I told them, under questioning, what I knew about Singer, his relationship to Jeannine, also that she'd fired him. Willey said they were getting a deposition from Singer in California, probably even as we talked.

I wanted a drink in the worst way. By the time they were done stirring up the muck in her life, I realized they were going to trash her. Trash us, too. A love affair that had lasted eight months was about to become a one-night stand.

"I thought you thought it was robbery," I said to Willey.

"I didn't say that," he replied.

"Then I heard it on TV, I don't know."

"That's what we're letting out. That's what it looks like. But killers— smart ones, cold-blooded ones—have been known to make it look like that before. Right now, at this stage, we're talking to everybody, and the door is open."

They left soon after. Willey said they might need me again. I could even, he supposed, be subpoenaed—it would depend on what direc-

tion the investigation took. But when I walked them out to the driveway, where the media were waiting for us, that was the last I saw of
them.

THE CASE—"THE Unsolved Murder of Nina Hardy"—became a cir-
cus, and I guess the police out west were far too busy for a suspect
who had no wings. For a long time, I paid a clipping service to send
me everything that ran on the subject, and their envelopes followed
me around, once I hit the road, and some months my bill was stag-
gering because they charged by the piece. The robbery theory was
displaced in time by a crime of passion and a "Mr. X," some secret
lover (not me), possibly well-known, who'd been intimately involved
with the victim. There was even, for a while, an alleged drug connection and, hand-in-hand, a mistaken-identity theory—"THEY
KILLED THE WRONG WOMAN!" (I saw that one in a supermarket)—
based half on Christine Hardy's striking resemblance to her mother
and half on her own history with drugs.

The cover-up issue ebbed and flowed throughout. The police knew
and weren't telling, it went; they were protecting the Hollywood
establishment. The police protested. They had thrown every resource
into the investigation, which was ongoing. Claude Rhinelander was
rarely mentioned by name. True to form, he refused to grant a single
interview on the subject, and I wondered if anyone in the media, or
even on the police, guessed how deep a shadow he cast.

The public shadow: As far as I know, the police, to this day, have
never succeeded in interviewing Christine Hardy. They have her alibi
for that night. Beyond that, she is under psychiatric care. I imagine
she will be for as long as it takes, and whoever she's told about what
she did, and why, is sealed by confidentiality.

The private shadow: No credit card charges ever came through on
my bill for the airline tickets or the rented car. Somehow, he'd wiped
my record clean.

It's all being taken care of. His payroll must be enormous. The most
amazing part is that no one ever talked. I guess if you give away
enough turkeys at Thanksgiving and bonuses at Christmas, you can
insure even that.

Not that he won in every respect. In fact, maybe he didn't win
anything. *Mother & Daughter,* rushed into release for obvious reasons,

was a big hit, but the push to make it award-winning, and to give Nina Hardy a posthumous Oscar, failed totally. Maybe people in Hollywood were too embarrassed or too squeamish; or maybe they were settling old scores with Claude Rhinelander, once it came out that he was the prime mover behind the push. Every effort to enshrine Jeannine—and I imagine he was behind each one—met a similar result. In some weird and unforeseeable way, she *had* been trashed by her death, and the image people retained wasn't of Eva or any of her other roles, but the police photo of the body flung back into the couch, in my room, which leaked into the media. When you mentioned the name, people thought, not The Great Actress, but victim of an unsolved crime.

As FOR ME, I cashed out. I sold the house, the property, contents included, for the first offer that came along. Everything I owned fit into my car. And off the deep end I went, down and down, like that old Dmytryk movie, *Murder, My Sweet*. Remember? The one where they shoot Dick Powell full of narcotics and his body goes tumbling into whiteness, blackness, pinwheeling away in endless gyrations? That was me. I walked through doors, trying to get away, but there were doors behind the doors, and finally I was on my knees, and when I couldn't crawl any more I ended up on a drying-out farm, up in Rhode Island, for jilted lovers, drunken executives and assorted other self-destructive types.

I'm way ahead of myself, I know, and that's bad. The doctors at the farm drummed that into us: we were to take life one day at a time, and every day an hour at a time. Stepping stones. Each day without a drink was another step forward.

To where?

That they never made clear.

If you really want to know where I went, look at a map of New England. I drank my way north, on a zigzag, Hartford, Worcester, Mass., on into New Hampshire, Maine. Some places—where I found a congenial saloon—I stayed a few days; others I checked out of as soon as I could get my hands to stop shaking in the morning. I had it in mind that I'd end up in Canada, but the farthest I got was Bar Harbor, Maine. There was a blizzard while I was in Bar Harbor that shut down all the main roads for a couple of days. It didn't matter to me. Most of the town was closed for the season, but I holed up in a Victorian hostelry with enough booze to ride out the storm, and when it was over, I headed south.

I've no idea why. Bad dreams chased me wherever I went. It was an accident that I ended up in Rhode Island. A car accident, to be precise, a bad skid on an icy bridge outside Newport, plus drunk and disorderly, plus drunk driving, and though nobody was hurt, they were going to throw away the key on me until I agreed to check myself into the farm.

It actually was a working farm, and farming formed part of the therapy. Maybe that worked for some; for me it only made me want to get out quicker. But if winter was almost over when I got there, the frozen fields turning to mud, before I left I'd done some planting and helped in the first tomato harvest.

One of their big things on the farm, aside from the stepping stones, was to get you to look yourself in the mirror. I did a lot of that. At first I didn't recognize myself; then I could and wished I couldn't. As one of my group members put it, the hardest losers are those who refuse to acknowledge they've lost. That was me, despite the evidence in the mirror, and I had Jeannine to help me. Maybe I could banish her in the furrows with the sun burning the back of my neck, but not at night when, finally asleep, I'd begin to hear her murmuring voice. "Why did you leave me?" I asked her over and over. "But I haven't left you, Daniel. I'm here, am I not?" Until Christine's harsh, high-pitched whinny brought me violently awake, in darkness.

There was even a time—I had myself convinced I owed it to Jeannine—when I decided to try to undo the cover-up. I still had Detective Willey's card. I put in a call to him, long distance, only to learn that he'd left the force. Transferred? No, he'd moved away, was there somebody else who could help me? No, I said, it was personal, and I hung up.

In other words, the drunk part got fixed in time, but the haunting was up to me.

When I got out, that August, I decided to stick around in the smallest state. I found a furnished apartment, actually the second floor of a good-sized house, in a small town not far from the metropolis of Westerly, R.I. Nobody knew me, my contacts with the past were minimal. But though I had enough money to live on for a long time, I needed something to occupy my days—reformed drunks do—and so I also found a job. It's not much, and I get paid by what they use, but I'm covering local sports for a regional paper. It happens I'm even into it, particularly at hoop time. I root for the Rams in college—that's the University of Rhode Island Rams—and the Red Sox come in on cable, as well as the Bruins and the Celtics.

I also have a girl friend. It's a fairly recent thing. I don't know what will come of it, if anything. Still in the promising stage, you could say. She's a college teacher, a very classy, no-nonsense lady, also a lot smarter than I am, with a Ph.D. in history. Doesn't drink, doesn't smoke; my smoking drives her nuts.

That's not our problem, though, nor is our sex life. It's stuff like: Why are we always in my bed, and then you leave in the morning? Why won't you ever show me where you live, are you that embarrassed? Yes, I answer (though not for the reasons she thinks), but that leads to conversations about commitments, the future, and allied subjects I've trouble dealing with.

MY CONTACTS WITH the past, as I said, are minimal. One happened very recently. It was a call from my old buddy, the eminent novelist Frank Falcone. He'd had a hell of a time tracking me down. I pushed him on how he'd found me, but all he'd say was that he'd had help. He wanted to see me—for old time's sake really, but he also needed me for something. What the hell was I doing in Rhode Island? Didn't I ever come down to New York? It was only a few hours, wasn't it?

When he told me what he wanted, I almost hung up, but I didn't—for old time's sake, say—and a couple of days later, I met him at the Westerly train station. He was decked out in a full-length leather coat, matching cap, tasseled Guccis, and he gave me a Falcone bear hug, then held me at arm's length, looking me over.

Apparently there was more of him, less of me.

"Jesus, babe," he said, "what the hell's happened to you? You look . . . well, you've lost a ton, haven't you? I hope to hell you're not into anything, are you?"

I said something about working out a lot, and he said something about all of us getting older.

For part of the day, I took him to a local diner, which he pronounced "vintage Americana," and there he explained.

"Look, babe," he said, "they made me the offer I couldn't refuse.

You know how it is, you take your assignments where you find them."

"Yeah, but I thought you were a novelist."

"Of course I'm a novelist, but what the hell? I gotta eat, too, and I got a lot of mouths to feed."

What we were talking about, and what he'd told me over the phone, was that Rhinelander Publishing had commissioned him to write the "definitive" biography of Nina Hardy. It had been Allen Fryberg's idea—actually, the biography idea was Claude Rhinelander's, but Fryberg had come up with Falcone for the author—and Falcone had thought it was crazy at first, but the more he thought about it, and once they got into the money, the less crazy it seemed.

"But nonfiction, babe!" he said. "Truth is, I haven't written a word of nonfiction since my magazine days. Shit, *our* magazine days. *Research*? Christ, I wouldn't even know where to start."

It turned out he already knew a great deal about his subject. He kept the pose going, though, and little by little got me talking, answering his questions, and I found myself—to my surprise—talking freely for the most part, without feeling too much of anything. Once or twice, maybe, when he pushed too hard about me and Jeannine, what it had been like between us, I clammed up, but when, later, we drove over to the coast beyond Route 1 and walked on the deserted beach, it was in some ways as if we were walking up Sixth Avenue or Broadway, comparing notes the way we used to.

In some ways, I said. But not all.

After dark, I drove him to the train station. I was worried about him missing the train, because only a few on the Boston–New York line made the stop. If he missed it, I was going to have to either drive him to New York or put him up for the night, which I wasn't about to do.

He said, "The one thing I still don't get is what went sour between you and Nina. How did you come unstuck?"

"I'm not sure we did."

"Really? It wasn't the daughter, was it? I once had a theory—knowing you," with a short laugh, "that you'd gotten into the daughter along the way. And that she—Nina—had found out. But I guess I was full of shit, wasn't I?"

"I guess so."

"Still, she dumped you. Used you and dumped you. What was it, then? It couldn't have been her book, could it?"

There was no good way for me to answer.

"There was trouble over the book," I said.

"But how come? You'd finished it, hadn't you? And hadn't she been reading it right along? I mean, you were *living* together all that time."

"You could ask Claude Rhinelander. He didn't like it."

"Surprise, surprise, of course he didn't. Who wants it known that he used Mafia money? But wasn't that an easy fix? Couldn't you have just cut it?"

I didn't answer. It wasn't that I didn't understand what I'd just heard either. You could explain a lot of things that way. Like where Claude got the muscle to burn barns and wipe records clean, and how he'd managed to lock Christine away without anybody asking questions. Even, for all I knew, how Falcone had found me.

"I may as well tell you," he said from the shadows, "though if you ever let on I did, I'd be in deep shit." He hesitated a minute. Then, "I've read it, babe."

"Read what?"

"Your book, what else? *Jeannine,* by Nina Hardy."

I didn't believe him.

"How could that be?" I asked. "I thought every copy had been destroyed."

"Uh uh. Claude has one. Allen put me on to it. Actually, he persuaded Claude to let me see it. They made me go to California. I read it in Claude's conference room, no notes and the door locked, but I read it."

Time was, I might have wrecked the car, hearing that. Time was, I'd have stopped the car and wrecked Falcone.

I didn't say anything.

"You know what?" he said finally. "I thought it was great. Absolute dynamite. I still don't understand . . ." Then, when I stayed silent, he added, "Well, she was quite a woman, wasn't she? She really was."

End of conversation.

We got to the station ahead of time and stood under the dim platform lights, staring up the tracks toward Boston. Then Falcone turned to me, and he put his big hands on my shoulders, as though to make me look at him.

"You know, Dan, there's something I've been feeling in you all day. At first, I couldn't put my finger on it. It was furtive, like some secret you didn't want out. But—tell me if I'm wrong—you're still in love with her, aren't you?"

I didn't answer.

"You poor bastard," he said. "Christ, how long's she been dead? A year and a half. And she dumped you, messed up your life. But, inside, you still got it bad, don't you?"

I was looking away from him—up the tracks again—and maybe it was the wind that brought tears into my eyes.

"Yes and no," I heard myself say. "But I think it's over now."

I WENT BACK to my place after he left and started tearing the stuff off the walls: her pictures, stills from the old movies, some memorabilia I'd picked up here and there, newspaper and magazine clippings. I'd made the place into a small shrine. I'd known it was crazy, self-destructive anyway, and I'd been meaning to do something about it, except I hadn't.

I dumped all the stuff into a couple of black garbage sacks, along with file folders containing more of the same, and then I started on my VCR tapes. Most I'd bought, a few I'd recorded from TV. I had them all except for two of her European films. Once, on the anniversary of the day we'd met, I'd run the whole cycle consecutively, straight through.

I handled them, looking each one over. It occurred to me that I ought to play just one—*Eva's Story,* maybe, or the first one, the one with Sonny—just for Auld Lang Syne, but I knew that once started, I'd go on to another, the night through, and I didn't think I could manage that without finding some booze somewhere.

In the end, I stripped the tapes from the cartridges and dropped them into the bags.

I slept pretty well that night. In the morning, I added a few items, including the chits from that last flight to L.A., the Rhinelander Publishing check for $850,000, and the old Fax copy of her Epilogue.

I wondered if I'd get another letter, this year, from Rhinelander Accounting, asking if I'd lost the check in question or had never received it.

I admit to reading the Epilogue one last time, before crumpling it into the bag.

I love him too much to share.

I drove back over to the coast, near where I'd walked with Falcone the previous day. It was still early, no more than 8:30 A.M., and a strong spring wind blew seaward over the dunes. There wasn't another soul in sight. Well, I don't suppose many people go to the beach to burn their garbage at that time of year. I hunkered down over a hollowed-out place somebody could have used for a barbecue the summer before, tore open the sides of the sacks partway, and then, with some lighter fluid and considerable difficulty, set fire to the contents.

I stayed there all morning. I thought about my schoolteacher friend and how I could have her over now, if I wanted to. I thought about oceans, birds, fish in the seas, and how a fish if he was single-minded enough, could swim all the way around to that other coast, and birds could do the same in the air, and planes like the ones that used to ferry me back and forth across the vast land. It seemed so long ago; I used to take it so for granted.

I didn't miss it, I thought. It belonged to some past life. But I stayed there on the beach, tending my dwindling pyre under the gray and lowering sky, not agitated exactly, but slightly tense as if waiting for something, God knows what—until I started to make a different journey in my mind, back across time, drifting through Jeannine to the Fawn, and from the Fawn to college, and back across time and country to my middle west beginnings, all the awkwardness and the misery of youth, the loneliness, the tedium.

And then, with my eyes closed, my head bent forward under the same wind that had blown at me across the fields and plains all those years before, I had it, what I was looking for. I was sitting in a darkened theater called the Fairmount, almost on my back so that my feet could prop against the seat in front, and up on the great screen before me, in black and white, her lips parted, her eyes almost closed, she began to speak softly, almost a murmur, so that her voice stroked the back of my neck.

Something between a buzz and a prickle.

Oh no, Lord, they can't take that away from me.